CHAPTER 1

The noise from the slamming door had zero effect on me. My brain couldn't process anything, let alone noise. Images of treacherous things passed through my mind as the interrogator took a seat across from me: exploded heads, blood-soaked bodies, and lost friends. I remembered the smells that had come with them, and nausea soon followed. I remembered the pains and agonies of the previous week like they were still happening, but for the first time in what seemed like years, I felt safe from the outside world. Even though I felt as if I could relax, the things I saw when I closed my eyes made me keep them open. The fluorescent lighting burned my eyes, but when they adjusted to the light, the man across from me came into focus.

He was an older gentleman, burly and balding, and he wore a nice white, button-down shirt with a jet-black tie that fell neatly down his chest. He stared at me like my soul was a piece of transparent artwork. His eyes were as piercing as a needle, and his overall demeanor would have frightened the most hardened criminals. I, however, had no fear left after the events I had gone through over the last week. To me, this burly balding man seemed as gentle and emotionally soothing as a cupcake.

In no mindset to start the conversation, I awaited his questions. Exhaustion had overtaken me long before I stepped foot inside the station. The man continued to stare at me, surely trying to read me in the context of the crimes in my statement. The interrogator tossed the statement in front of me, and I could tell by his overall demeanor and attitude he thought the story was a bunch of bullshit.

The room was quiet for another five minutes as we sat across from each other, hardly blinking. I could tell he was doing this to intimidate me, but I didn't blink for the simple fact it took energy for me to reopen my eyes. If my eyes shut again, I would surely pass out without regard to anyone in my presence.

Finally, the man licked his lips and began to speak.

"Well, this is quite a statement here... Mr. See-Muss, is it?"

It took me a few seconds to muster up the mental capacity to speak.

"It's Seamus. Pronounced Shay-*Muss*, and yes, it is quite ridiculous."

"Well, my first question to you, sir, is have you been drinking or doing any other mind-altering substances?"

"Although I look as if I've been sleeping in an alleyway, shooting meth for weeks, I assure you I have not. I am of sound state and mind."

"What you have written here is one of the craziest things I have ever read, and my first impression was that it was conceived of by a person on an untold amount of drugs."

"Look, I have serious rage issues. I will completely lose my mind over the smallest things. I've had this for years and was trying to work through it in therapy until this shit fell in my lap. You are starting to piss me off, so get past the appearance, buddy. I don't want to waste both of our time, so why don't you cut the shit."

"You're being mighty bold! This is a place where disrespect is not tolerated. You will speak to me in a manner you would speak to a respected adult."

"I don't need to sit here and listen to your senseless jargon. I got better shit to do with my time. If you want to listen to my story, then shut up and listen."

The man's face spoke a thousand words. I could tell right away he was not accustomed to being spoken to in that manner. He squinted, and his teeth were showing as if he were growling at me. His lip curled, and his hands balled into fists so tight his knuckles turned white. The fires in the pits of hell could be seen in his stare. Minutes went by before the interrogator finally spoke again.

"Alright. I'll listen to this story of yours. You better hope it's not some made-up piece of shit that has zero relevance to my department or me."

"Buddy, I've had a real long week, and I am sick of your coworkers sending me all over this building to talk to different idiots. I was asked to make a statement as to why I was found entering a country without proper documentation and seeking asylum with the police instead of the immigration department. This statement you so kindly tossed in front of me is what I was asked to do. If it has nothing to do with your department, that's not my fault, and you'd better talk to your coworkers before you go jumping down my throat."

With that, the interrogator uncapped the black pen he had brought in with his little notepad. He looked up at me from the pad, permitting me to speak with his gaze.

"Everything started when my girlfriend and I were headed home to Watertown, New York for a summer vacation. On top of the vacation, my stepfather Doug had called me months before to inform me about one of his rental properties. Apparently, a man had broken up with his girlfriend, went out and smoked crack, and went to her house to work on their relationship. Unfortunately, when the man reached their apartment, he discovered another man sleeping in the kitchen while his ex was in her bedroom. The drugged-out ex-boyfriend grabbed his shotgun from his truck, then came back and shot the man in the kitchen twice in the head before going to the bedroom and shooting his ex in the throat. Then he left the bedroom and turned the shotgun on himself and said goodnight. That was the official report from the investigating officers.

"The crime scene had been cleared and vacated by the police, and now Doug was taking pictures in hopes the insurance company would cover the cost of a crime scene cleanup crew. I was informed Doug needed to re-carpet the entire apartment, replace windows, redo the ceiling and tiles, and other things he wanted my help with. He told me to swing by the apartment when I arrived because he had months of work ahead of him. We weren't very close, so after we hung up that day I didn't bother calling him back to check in. I knew as soon as he asked me to do manual labor on my vacation,I should have stayed home. On the days before we left North Carolina, Megan and I discussed our arrival into Watertown. She planned on dropping me off at Doug's so I could help the first day I was in town. What a shitty way to start a vacation. Anyway..."

'�� '�� '�� '

The two of us returned to Watertown every year since we moved from there to Angier, North Carolina in 1996. We had been making the trip for the last three years and very much looked forward to it. We had both grown up there and still had family and friends we enjoyed spending time with. The ten-hour drive starting at 11p.m. caused Megan to pass out before we got out of North Carolina, and as she slept, I grabbed the bottle of Jägermeister,I'd bought earlier that day. I sipped the bottle over the next several hours as I drove. My level of intoxication caused me to become insanely lost, and I stayed on Highway 95 for an extra hundred miles. I usually took Interstate 81 into Watertown, but my detour brought me in through Lowville.

I remember seeing all sorts of random shit you don't usually see: cars left on the side of the road, trash all over, and no other people driving. Even with me being drunk, I felt things weren't right. I tried chalking the appearance of the place up to the fact it was rural New York, but it still didn't sit right. As I was observing the road and focusing on how hard it was to see out of both eyes, Megan woke up and glanced around.

"Where are we?"

"I ended up getting horribly lost, so now we're on Route 12 heading into Watertown this way," I slurred.

"Are you fucking drunk?" she yelled.

"I couldn't help it. I was excited to go on vacation. Besides, I needed to take the edge off. I don't want to do contracting work sober," I retorted.

She instantly demanded I pull over to let her drive. Drunk and utterly exhausted, I didn't care, so I stopped in the middle of the abandoned highway, and we switched. The farther down the road we went, the stranger our surroundings became. I was struggling to stay awake as I looked at the area.

"Are you seeing this shit?" I asked.

Sadly, she returned with: "Fuck you, your drinking is out of control!" then turned her iPod on and began to zone out listening to music. I watched as she brushed her curly red hair behind her ear and put her vibrant green eyes back on the road. I tried staying awake, but the tunes put me out within minutes. When I woke up, we were at the front door of Doug's house on Franklin Street.

"Just a heads up, babe...I saw some weird shit on the way here. There were cars lining the roads, but no drivers in them. I saw some people off in the distance, but everything seemed strange. I'm not sure what the hell is going on, but I really don't like it. Come to Grandma's when you get done here. I have no interest in seeing what's waiting for you in that apartment," she said.

"Alright, sweetie, I'll head over as soon as I'm done here."

I got out of the car, blew her a kiss, and headed for door to the upstairs apartment.

As I opened the door, a perfume of absolute disgust blasted me in the face with a cloud of hot air. I used my fingers and plugged my nose as I stepped inside.

"Are you here? What is that god-awful smell? Hello?" I shouted.

Soon after entering the apartment, I discovered Doug wasn't there. I was alone. I figured he was out getting supplies, so I went to the medicine cabinet in the bathroom and looked for some Vicks VapoRub to stuff into my nostrils. Luckily, I found a bottle of a knock-off brand that worked well.

What is this awful smell?

I walked into the front room where the girl had been shot and discovered splatters of blood and clumps of skin, tissue, and cartilage covering the wall behind the bed.

Why hasn't this shit been cleaned up? Where the hell is Doug? Why the fuck hasn't any of this been cleaned up? It seems likes it has been like this for months. If nothing has been done since it happened, where the fuck is Doug? If he didn't plan on doing anything, why didn't he call and tell me?

The whole scene made me sick to my stomach, as I had never seen death so close before. I started backing out of the room when I stepped on a misshapen object. I moved my foot and found a piece of jawbone on the floor.

I glanced up to see the ceiling was covered in bloody chunks of flesh and brain. While I admired the fresh coat of red, I observed one of the drop panels was missing. I looked to my right into the small bedroom and saw the ceiling panel lying on the floor. I knelt to pick it up, and as soon as the panel moved, the smell shot through the Vicks knockoff and made me gag. I realized instantly someone had placed the ceiling panel on top of a large portion of someone's brain, which at this point was being feasted on by dozens of maggots. I quickly dropped the panel and bolted for the back door.

My stomach was churning, and I was on the verge of throwing up. I missed the turn that led to the exit, so I ended up in the kitchen where the first guy had gotten shot. The brains all over the window screen behind the chair didn't bother me, and the two slug holes in the screen didn't faze me, but when I peered behind the chair to discover the guy's hat full of skull fragments in a half-dried pool of blood and brains, I lost it and spewed all over the kitchen.

When my stomach was done emptying itself onto the floor, I rested my hands on the sink and turned the water on. Only a slow trickle came out, so I cupped my hands and filled them. I sipped water into my mouth and rinsed the awful taste of Jäger and vomit away. After a few seconds of regaining myself I turned around and headed out of the kitchen and to the apartment's exit. I felt weak in the knees, so I sat at the top of the steps long enough to smoke a cigarette.

As I smoked, I noticed the cigarette trembling in my hand. I had never seen anything like this before, and I was disgusted by it.

With Doug apparently not doing a damn thing to clean this apartment up for months, on top of the things Megan had said to me before she dropped me off, I decided I should find someone to get some information from. I flicked the cigarette down the steps and left the apartment. While walking, I figured I could head toward Megan's grandmother's house and see if she had any information.

Trash was strewn in the front yards of the houses nearby, and the streets were empty. There were no people anywhere, no cars being driven, no people out walking-- nothing. When I realized a stillness in the air I had never experienced before, I began getting nervous. I glanced around, but still didn't see anyone or anything, not even a dog or a cat.

With this weirdness in the air, I decided to take a pitstop on my way to Megan's grandmother's place. I had a good idea who I could talk to, so I turned off Franklin and headed for State Street. As I headed right, I saw someone a couple blocks up the street digging through a trash can that had tipped over. I considered questioning him for a moment before deciding I didn't want to talk to a stranger, much less someone so far out of my way. I wasn't in the mood to talk to someone who would try to bum money or smokes off me anyway, so I continued toward my intended destination.

As I walked, I began thinking about a phone call I'd had with Burto, one of my old buddies from Watertown, a few months before my trip. The call was about the very person I was about to ask for information.

"Yeah, Seamus, I let Marston move in with me after you beat his ass, and he ran away from North Carolina," Burto had said.

"Why the fuck would you do that? That guy's scum."

"Because the fucking loser had nowhere else to go, and I felt bad."

"The same apartment I visited last year?"

"Yeah, that's the one. That son of a bitch fucked me right out of it too. He turned the place into a drug-fueled flop house, and I had to leave. I was sick of finding crack and meth heads strung out in my house. I asked him several times, but he refused to stop. I ended up moving into the building on Factory Street that houses all the parolees. It was the only place I could afford. I did want to get out of that apartment because it was a shithole, but not like that."

"You should have beaten his ass like I did."

"Oh shit, did you hear what you did to him?"

"No, I didn't. What was it?"

"He ended up in the hospital with internal bleeding."

"Serves the fucker right for what he did. That lowlife took Megan's entire music collection and pawned it for drug money. Oh, and not to mention he got my brother, Scott, a couple of felonies because he refused to take credit for his drugs the cops found in Scott's car."

That was the last I remembered of the phone call, and along with my surroundings, this was enough to get under my skin. I knew Marston could probably explain everything, and I knew he would still be held up at the old apartment. I cringed at the thought of rekindling any relationship with him but knew he would be a good lead. I knew the apartment he was in was closer to me than anyone else I knew in town. If anyone else in the world had been closer, I would have gone to them instead. I was sure this reunion wasn't going to be good; I still had a lot of hatred in my heart for the man. I hoped I could get over the past, but unfortunately, I wasn't sure if I would ever get over it.

The walk from Franklin Street to the second-story apartment on State Street took roughly five minutes. The street I walked down was quiet and didn't seem out of place. There were cars lining the curbs, but they could have been parked.

I reached the front door of the apartment and walked through the door. I was surprised at how clean the building was. There was no trash or strange smells in the stairwell I took to the second floor. When I reached the second-floor level I turned right and walked down the hallway to the apartment door. I knocked for nearly a minute, but just when I was about to give up, I heard a low voice.

"Who is it?"

"It's Seamus. Is that you, Marston?"

Instantly upon hearing my voice, I heard him fumbling with the deadbolts on the other side of the door. He yanked the door open, grabbed my arm, and pulled me into the apartment, turning around to lock the door again behind me. Then he turned and we stared at each other momentarily. I hadn't seen this lowlife in a while and now standing before me was a filthy-looking hippy with dirty blond dreadlocks, a septum piercing, and a big bushy blondish beard. I couldn't tell if his facial hair was dirty or just naturally blondish. He wore a mangy tie-dye T-shirt and cut brown corduroy shorts. Before I could speak, he reached out and grabbed me embracing me in a hug.

"I'm so glad to see you, Seamus. Holy shit am I glad to see you!" Marston said, squeezing me tightly.

As he gripped me I glanced over his shoulder to see the hallway we were in had a good amount of trash lying around. Mainly empty pasta boxes and a few twelve packs of Budweiser. The smell Marston was emitting was enough to make me gag. It seemed like he was even filthier than the last time I saw him.

"Dude, are you out of your fucking mind? Let me go!" I said, pushing him off me. "What the hell is going on around here? I went by my stepfather's house and there are still remnants of the crime that happened in there months ago. The streets are empty and there's trash all over the fucking place!"

"Look, man... things are bad, and this town is fucked up. A lot of strange things have been happening, and a lot of our friends have disappeared. My girlfriend vanished, and I sit here at night watching these strange people staggering through the streets. I'm scared to the point I don't leave the apartment."

"Marston, what are you talking about? I didn't see anyone when I came over. Wait... I did see someone digging through a trash can about two blocks up the street."

"Alright, Seamus... this is going to sound crazy, but I am sure you of all people will believe me. I think zombies are roaming the streets of Watertown. At first, the bastards only showed up at night, but since I've been in this apartment, I noticed more lurching around in the afternoons. There haven't been many, but there have been enough."

"Are you high or something? What the fuck are you talking about? Zombies?"

"I told you it was crazy. These things walking around town are like zombies you see in movies. Brainless, emotionless, they stink, and they don't seem to be walking anywhere. They just walk up and down the streets over and over."

"What...? Get the fuck outta here with that bullshit!" I said, already feeling angered.

"I know it's hard to swallow, but I'm not kidding. I noticed it about a few months ago."

"What did you notice?"

"At first I thought they were meth-addled drug addicts roaming the streets both day and night. They were always tripping over curbs, garbage cans, and even stumbling into parked cars. Now they kill and eat other people. When all this started, they didn't seem to bother anyone. It's as if they evolved. In the beginning, when I started noticing things becoming strange around town, my friends called me paranoid. In the very early stages I would tell friends to watch out because something was happening. None listened, including my girlfriend. I begged and pleaded with them, but nobody would hear any of it."

This guy is out of his goddamn mind. Is he telling me this so I don't beat his ass again? I gotta get the hell out of here.

"Let's finish this in the kitchen," I suggested.

We both walked from the door into the messy kitchen of the rundown apartment. There was trash all over and the kitchen table was covered with used paper plates, plastic cups, and food packaging. We took a seat at the trashed table and I started talking again.

"So you tried warning people, but were shunned?"

"Yes, basically. I stopped trying to convince people and went on about my business, but things were becoming too strange not to try to at least prepare some. I mean, there weren't a lot of them at first, but the numbers I was seeing went up daily. I had heard about some attacks from people at stores or whatnot, but never saw any in person. After a week or so I *really* started noticing things weren't right. The Pour House bar had opened up by the park a few months before this whole thing, and I was hearing stories about that place from the start. Nothing too crazy at first, but the stories went from mild altercations to people bashing each other's heads in with barstools. That shit was on the news and one guy is in jail right now for the incident. When the violence began erupting at the bar, they implemented this weird bracelet policy."

"What the fuck do you mean bracelet policy?"

"This bar will let you drink for free, but only if you buy and wear some weird bracelet. It's bizarre looking. It's clear rubber jelly and filled with a strange substance. The thing about this bracelet is an hour or so after putting it on, it falls off, and it's completely *empty*. Nothing ever happens to your wrist: not red, not wet, no marks, no nothing."

"I'm not catching your drift here," I said, rolling my eyes.

"Dickhead, listen real close. There's a bracelet. You put it on, it drains fluid somewhere, and then it falls off. By then you're probably on your third or fourth drink, so you aren't paying attention. Ten minutes after the bracelet falls off, you are completely drunk. I'm talking seeing double and staggering all over the place kind of drunk."

"Dude, we used to get like that every time we drank. Hell, I pounded a fifth of Jaeger on the way here."

"Yeah, you're right; we did get that hammered when we drank, but never once can I remember either one of us wandering off and never being seen again. Soon after the policy began, the disappearances started. My...I guess *ex*-girlfriend at this point wanted to go there, and I pleaded with her not to, but she said I was paranoid. I followed her there, but she straight out refused to listen. That was about nine on a Tuesday. On my way back to the apartment I decided something was definitely going on and decided to stock up some supplies. I got all sorts of provisions, along with a couple bottles of cheap whiskey and a few cartons of smokes."

"So you're telling me you started noticing things long before they happened and didn't try telling your friends and family, or even try to contact the authorities?"

"Man, this dump doesn't have a land line, and the closest payphone is at the Great American. After the shit I had seen I wasn't taking any risks leaving the apartment. I had enough supplies to last, well, basically until you showed up. I'm down to my last few cups of rice."

"Come on, asshole! What kind of shit had you seen?" I shouted.

"Well man, it was subtle at first. When things really got bad, I knew it was too late. The night I stocked up I went to sleep like a normal night, but when I woke the next day, there was uproar in the streets. I peered out the front window of the apartment and saw droves of cars driving toward the square. People were mainly driving, but some were walking with suitcases and backpacks. This went on all day. I assumed they were being evacuated because what else could it have been? I mean there were thousands of cars the first day, and those numbers stayed the same for days after. I wanted to ask someone what the hell was going on, but felt I shouldn't because someone might try breaking in. I don't have a TV or a clock radio, so I was totally in the dark. I sat in here day and night watching the streets. The numbers of people traveling them started slowing, and then eventually stopped altogether. Strangely enough, I did start seeing more of those *drug-addled* things walking around. I remember the first person I saw being eaten. That was terrifying, and I couldn't believe it. I still have nightmares about it."

"I know if there was an evacuation, something huge is happening! They're probably planning on taking drastic measures to stop the spread of these zombies of yours. I'd put my money on it they're going to blow this place to hell."

"Do you think they could get away with that?" Marston asked.

"Watertown isn't even on the map. There has never been anything in or even around this city. Well, except Fort Drum, maybe they are behind it," I stated.

Marston kept talking, but all I could think about was Megan dropping me off. I also found it strange I hadn't seen anyone on the way over to the apartment where Marston was staying. It wasn't that early--it was Monday, but there was no traffic. Marston must have realized I wasn't paying attention because he stopped talking and stared at me.

"Dude, if what you're talking about has any truth, we should check into it," I suggested.

"Fuck you, man. I haven't left this apartment in two months. I have seen too much shit on those streets for me to run the risk of leaving."

"You gotta be kidding me! Your friends have disappeared and you're not going to do shit to find them?" I said.

"Hey, man, I'm no fucking hero. I don't give a shit about this town, and I sure as hell don't plan on figuring anything out."

"You're something else, man... Are your balls still connected to your body or did your girlfriend take them when she left? I came here for a vacation, and if I can't have one, then I'm going to at least try finding out what is happening. This is what I'm going to do this afternoon. I, unlike you, am going to find my girlfriend, ask anyone I see some questions, and try piecing together a story that maybe I can tell a reporter. How's that sound to you?"

"I can't promise anything, Seamus. Like I said, I've been locked inside for months."

"I don't want to hear any of your excuses. I'll be back to pick you up. One more thing: if I come back and by some chance you don't open the door, I will saw the fucking thing off the hinges, drag you out by your pubic hair, and throw you through the fucking porch window. Do you understand me?"

"Dude, I'm not promising anything! Something is going on down in those streets, and I want no part of it."

By now I was sick of looking over garbage to see Marston as he spoke, so I backhanded the trash off the table.

"Jesus Christ Seamus, keep it down!"

Agitated, I continued.

"So you're saying you'd rather sit up here waiting to die rather than try to escape?"

"I've been doing just fine up until now. With you mentioning someone blowing this place to hell, I'd like to get out of town before that happens. Who cares what actually happened? All I know is whatever is going on outside this apartment is horrible."

"Whatever works, but remember what I said... I wasn't kidding. If you want to help, you can, and if not, I don't care, but either way I'll be back in a bit, so you better be ready to open the door."

I stood up from the table and walked back to the only door. I heard Marston exhale through his nose, and I knew he was shaking his head in disgust. As I unlocked the door, I looked back at him, giving him a deathly stern look. Then I stepped out, closing the door behind me. Only a second later, I heard the deadbolts snapping back into place. I quickly descended the steps, heading for the street.

Back on the street, I started feeling nervous. Hearing what Marston had said about zombies in the streets, combined with me being alone and unarmed, made me extremely wary. I brushed these emotions aside, telling myself Marston was more than likely wrong about the whole situation. *There was no way he could be right; he must have dropped too much acid or smoked too much weed. He's clearly delusional.* I thought to myself. At the moment, I had no idea if Megan had made it to her Grandmother's, or if she was hung up somewhere. I began walking in the direction of Megan's grandmother's house as these thoughts pressed my mind.

CHAPTER 2

I headed down State Street toward the town square, paying close attention to the fact there still wasn't a single person to be seen. I walked past stores and shops that appeared abandoned and run down, like I was walking through a ghost town. Old newspapers, fast food bags, and other random pieces of garbage blew all over the deserted streets and parking lots. The fact I was alone and things were rapidly becoming creepier began setting in. I wasn't about to give Marston credit for being right but figured I should find some sort of protection just in case. I knew Marston liked to over exaggerate things, and while face to face I hadn't bought his bullshit, but now that I was out in the uninhabited streets, I decided to arm myself with whatever weapon I could find.

A trash pile was nearby, so I walked over and began rummaging through it, hoping to find any useful item. After moving several bags, I was about to give up, but noticed something buried under more garbage. I moved as much random garbage as I could and uncovered a wood kitchen table. I knew I could use its legs as weapons, so I twisted and yanked on one until it cracked off. It swung pretty easy and wasn't too heavy.

While taking a few practice swings, two sorry-looking bastards came running at me, screaming and pointing guns.

"Hey, hey what the hell are you two doing?" I yelled as I got my table leg ready.

"Who in the fuck are you?" asked one of the men.

"Relax, guys. My name is Seamus. I needed something to defend myself with. Who the hell are you two?"

They appeared like they hadn't eaten anything in a while. They were remarkably skinny, and their clothes were pretty dirty. They themselves looked filthy too, and clearly hadn't washed themselves in a while.

Through deep gulps of air one of the men began talking.

"Oh, we're sorry, bro. We don't see many people these days and think the worst. I'm Gus, and this is Tom. We saw you digging through the trash, and as we approached, we assumed you were one of those creatures, but then we saw you swing the club."

"Those fucking things eat people! They chase them down in packs and eat them alive!" Tom added, with panic in his voice.

"So the two of you are telling me there are actually zombies running around eating people?"

"Yeah, that's the gist of it," Gus said, panting, with a nod and eye roll.

"If that's the case, then what the fuck are we doing standing around? We better try to find a place to hunker down," I said.

Gus kept a watchful eye down the road while Tom and I chatted.

"We've been held up in the old diner down Union Street over there," Tom said, pointing.

"You both look pretty terrible. Both your clothes look pretty ragged, your hair is greasy, and you both look like you had a fight with a cat. What's up with those scratches on your faces?"

"We got into a pissing match about what we should do the other day. I think we need to leave, but Gus thinks we should wait for a rescue."

"How long have you been there?"

"Jesus, man, I've lost track of the days. We just had to start scavenging the area looking for food. The power went out in the beginning for whatever reason, so the diner provided for a while, but what we couldn't eat ended up rotting in the freezers. Dude, it's pretty secure over there. It's a brick building, and we boarded the windows. If you want, you can come over there."

"I would, but I need to find my girlfriend. If what I'm hearing is true, I want to get the fuck out of here!"

At this point my nerves were becoming frazzled. I was anxiously looking around for one of these creatures I had been hearing about.

"If you think you're going to walk the streets hunting for your girl, you belong in a nut house. You won't last twenty minutes on your own!" Tom argued.

"You may be right, but I need to find my old lady. I appreciate your offer but finding her is the only thing that matters. If I need your help, I'll come find you two at the diner."

"Alright, but before you go, I want you to know we tried to help our friends. But like you, they refused to listen. They said we'd seen too many movies, and now they're all dead."

As Tom finished his rant, Gus yelled, "Shit, I think that's one of them!" He pointed down the street. I glanced over my shoulder and saw someone--some*thing*--a block or so down the road. The thing was lumbering up the street toward us, and the hair on my arm began standing on end. This moment put fear into my soul.

"That thing could bring a lot more friends. Given you're the only living person we've seen in a while, I'm not sticking around to find out!" Tom said.

"I'm going to head out to do what I need to do. I know we are all in deep shit and need to get the hell out of here. I'm going to try getting my hands on a vehicle and find my lady. If this place is as bad as you say it is, I don't want to try finding her on foot. I have to get my friend who's squatting in the crack house three blocks up, and after, I'll swing by and pick you guys up, and we can all hit the road."

"Bro, you're crazy. Some of our friends tried the same thing. They wanted to run home and save their families and their pets, and now they're dead. We've wasted enough breath trying to talk people out of doing dumb shit that *will* get them killed. At least take this..."Tom held out his shotgun and continued. "You'll never make it through those things swinging a club. This 12-gauge will blow a hole in anything that gets in your way. It's loaded with six of the seven rounds. I'm sorry I can't give you more ammo. Make sure to use the rounds sensibly."

I took the weapon and began checking it over. I had fired shotguns in the past, so I knew my way around this gun.

"Are you sure you can spare a shotgun at a time like this?" I asked as I checked the weapon over.

"We got pretty lucky and found a stash of weapons the other day. We have three more of these and some handguns back at the diner. Please be careful, and when you get your shit done, come find us. We only come out of the hideout for about an hour each day to search for supplies, so we will be there when you show up, and if we're not, just go in and wait for us," Tom said.

"Why haven't you guys tried escaping?" I said, holding the gun in my left hand by my waist.

"Dude, everything has been crazy as hell. When the evacuation was going on, we felt it would be better to stay hidden. We saw military types corralling people onto buses, and it seemed they were doing it with hostile intent. We thought it would be better to hide out until shit blew over. Then the zombies started roaming around and we figured the military would clean the place up. That never happened, and we've been too scared to try leaving."

"Well, Tom, I'm going to try getting us all out of here," I finished.

I grabbed the gun, and Gus piped up. "It's time to move. That thing is coming toward us. We've got to go! Seamus, let's hope you come around."

Tom and Gus darted off toward Union Street for their safe house, and I began looking around the area. A Wendy's and a Burger King were side by side on the other side of the street, and I figured I'd look in their parking lots for a car I could use. I would have used anything: a truck, a car, a bike, a lawnmower, or anything with wheels. Now I was thinking Marston wasn't entirely full of shit. The two men who had willingly given me a gun made me realize I was in a real nightmare. The creature down the street was stumbling in my direction, and I didn't have much time.

I saw two cars in the Burger King parking lot. I ran up to the first car to find the door locked. Instead of looking through the window for the keys, I panicked and smashed the window with a flat-footed kick. I leaned in and looked in the cup holders and through the busted glass but found no keys.

As I was leaned through the window of the first car, I peered toward the second car and noticed the windows were covered with some type of goo. I pulled myself out of the window and started making my way to the other vehicle. As I got closer, I stopped when I was able to make out the gunk on the windows.

Blood and bone fragments covered the windows from the inside. I knew right away the person had been killed inside the vehicle. I had no idea how they had died, but I assumed it was a gunshot to the head. I thought about the poor bastard in the car, and then it dawned on me. If the driver had been killed inside their car, the keys might still be in the ignition.

I decided I would need to clean the splattered mess off the windows before driving anywhere, so I ran back to the first car, hoping to find something to wipe the windows down with. Next to the car seat in the back, I found a baby blanket. It wasn't much, but it would have to work.

As I backed out of the car, I felt something suddenly grab my shirt. Fear and panic shot up my spine and made the hair on the back of my neck stand up. Momentarily unable to turn around, I quickly threw my ass into my attacker with enough force to knock them down. When I twisted around to see who or what had grabbed me, I saw it was the creature the others had run from. The thing moaned and made gurgling sounds as it struggled to climb to its feet.

I stood there--jaw dropped. Then I reached for the 12-gauge I had set on top of the car, not taking my eyes off the monster.

A sudden breeze blew a whiff of the creature into my face. The smell was atrocious and reminded me of a porta-potty in the hot sun during a football game. At this point the thing in front of me didn't resemble a human anymore. The creature's skin was falling from its face in clumps, leaving part of its cheekbones exposed. Its clothing was tattered and torn, and its skin was black, rotten, and pulling away from its bones. I was even close enough to notice how brownish diarrhea-looking goo was oozing out of its gum line and into its mouth. I stood in awe, wondering what the creature might have been before its tragic transformation. Its ruined clothes were just shorts and a T-shirt, so there was no telling. Being it was the first zombie I had ever seen, I was taken aback for a moment, but then realized I needed to get moving, so I took aim, and pulled the trigger.

After getting a hole blown in its face, it lay motionless as I stood there in a state of bewilderment. I'd never killed anyone or anything before, so I felt inclined to take a moment to analyze what had just happened. I stood there looking at what remained of this monstrosity of a human. My heart beat loud enough to join a drum circle; my mind was in frenzy, and my body started shaking.

When I finally calmed enough to move, I ejected the shell and loaded another round into the chamber. Then I picked up the blanket and headed for the bloody car.

I yanked the door open and was hit with hot air carrying the foul smell of death from inside the car. I turned away and immediately threw up. I pulled the bottom of my shirt up and wiped my mouth, then set the gun and blanket on the roof of the car. This person had clearly blown their head off with the sawed-off double-barrel that rested between the driver and passenger seats. Both rounds had been fired, and the car was a fucking mess. There was nothing left of the person above the neck. The whole scene was appalling and caused my stomach to churn even more than the smell. Letting out a loud sigh I reached inside, grabbed the dead driver's shoulders, and yanked him out of the vehicle.

The driver's window had dried blood, bits of skull, and teeth splattered all over it. The driver's seat had been soaked with blood and other remnants of the person's head, and the windshield was unusable because it was crusted with brains, bones, and dried blood. Gray matter had hardened like glue on the dashboard. As I was looking at the destruction inside the car, I noticed sunlight shining through the two slug holes in the roof of the car. I could tell the blood had been baking for a long time and this poor bastard met his maker long before I arrived in town. I was shocked, but when I saw the keys dangling in the ignition, joy momentarily overtook me.

I wanted to leave the parking lot before anything else graced me with its presence, so I laid the blanket on the driver's seat, sat down, and promptly began kicking out the windshield. It took a few kicks, but the job was done, and the seat of my pants was now soggy from the liquefied remains of the corpse that had already seeped through the blanket. I jumped out and headed back to the other car, hoping to find something else to put over the seat. I ended up finding a sweater and a T-shirt, but I figured they would only last at most a few minutes before they soaked up the remaining putrefied remains of organ and muscle tissue in the seat. I didn't have anything to change into, so I didn't want my only pair of pants completely destroyed. With this notion in mind, I decided to go inside the Burger King to find some plastic bags. I sighed, rolled my eyes, grabbed the shotgun, and headed into the dark restaurant.

I entered through the side door, walked around the counter, and went into the kitchen. It was dark, but the midday sun shining through the take-out window gave me enough light to spot the trash bags on the counter.

When I turned to leave, I stepped on something round and soft. The thing moved under my foot, causing me to lose my balance. I stumbled into the cash register, dropping the trash bags and the gun. I dropped to my knees, grabbed the gun, and twisted around to find another one of the creatures crawling right for me. This time I didn't observe it; I pointed my gun and pulled the trigger. The reality of my situation had set in at this point. I was visible shaken, but I knew I couldn't allow myself to panic. That's how mistakes were made, and people died.

The sound from the blast caused a ringing in my ears. The creature's head exploded, and coagulated blood and chunks of skin and bone flew everywhere. Now my pants, shirt, and face were covered in someone else's bodily fluids. The anger overrode my fear momentarily. I had come into this place to avoid bodily fluids on my clothes, and now I was completely covered in them. Now at my wit's end, I scooped up the bags, turned and headed for the side door again.

As I went through the kitchen doors, I was confronted with a frightening sight. Outside the building, in front of the restaurant, five more of the creatures stood in front of the windows. I figured they'd heard the gunshot, but I didn't think they could see me because the sun glaring off the front windows of the building made them practically mirror-like.

My ears still rang so loudly I couldn't hear the creatures clawing and scratching the windows as they tried to rip through them. The door I had entered through was to my right and clear of danger, so I ran through it back into the parking lot. I knew the zombies were slow, but I still ran to the car, placed the bags on the seat, jumped in, and shut the door. I glanced left but was unable to see through the horrid gunk still caked on the window.

I was relieved, and surprised, when the car started up. Being an older Ford Taurus and not in the best-looking car, it spat and sputtered for a couple seconds. I locked the doors, put the car in reverse, and backed up. When I glanced into the rearview mirror, I saw the zombies rounding the corner of the building. I put the car in drive and punched the gas, at least partly because I wanted some fresh air flowing through the car before I vomited again. Luckily, the windows were power, and they went down fairly smoothly. The driver's side was slower than the others, as it went down dried blood and dehydrated flesh and brain crumbled off and fell to the floor. I was relieved when it eventually went down.

When I left the parking lot, I turned right, heading in the direction of Megan's grandmother's house. As I drove down the road, I began to chuckle, thinking about how silly this idea was. I was already on this side of town, so why not pick Marston up and then head to Megan's?

Instead of doing a U-turn and driving back up State Street, I decided to take the scenic route. I had already driven into the roundabout that was the public square, so I took a sharp right turn onto Factory Street, which ran parallel to State Street. Having grown up in Watertown, I was familiar with the ins and outs and all the nooks and crannies of the city.

As I finished the turn, I felt something grab my hair from behind. In a panic, I slammed the brakes and jumped out of the car. A legless zombie had crawled over the seat and was now making its way out of the driver's door, dragging my makeshift seat covers with it. I stood wondering how this thing survived in the car for so long. The body I had pulled out wasn't eaten, so I wasn't sure what this thing had been feeding on.

The fact it had no legs also made me question how the thing had gotten there. I about kicked myself in the ass for not checking the back seat before getting into the car. I had been so distracted with all the madness in the parking lot I had completely forgotten. My gun was out of reach, and after the last blast, I wasn't looking forward to using it now that my ears had finally stopped ringing, and I was low on shells.

When its face was over the metal doorjamb, I stomped its skull, crushing it like a tomato. I kept stomping until fluids from the inside of its head started leaking out its nostrils and ears. It was disgusting, but I wanted to be sure it was dead before I stopped beating it.

I could tell the thing was finished when it stopped twitching. As I pondered what to do next, I noticed the monster's left wrist was swollen and had puncture holes. The only reason this stood out to me was the size of its wrist. It was three times bigger than its other wrist and was pulsating like its heart was beating just under its rotten skin. I was intrigued, but before I got the chance to look closer, a dragging sound snatched my attention. I glanced up to see about twelve of the creatures stumbling right for me. I grabbed the torso, and after yanking it completely out of the car and into the street, I jumped back in and started rolling the windows up. I had seen two hordes in the span of ten minutes, and I started wondering how many of these things could be around. They were seemingly everywhere, and I was beginning to fear for my life.

The windows had barely shut before the creatures started touching the car. I slammed the gas pedal to the floor, but the engine screamed, and the car didn't move. Quickly noticing my mistake, I put the car into drive, and the car shot forward. I glanced into the rearview and saw the zombies stumbling after me, but they were clearly too slow to catch me,

Still, my nerves were on edge as I drove, dodging downed power lines, trash, abandoned cars, and what looked like severed body parts.

How are all these power lines ripped down? Did a tornado come through here?

About a mile down the road I found the path I needed, and it looked terrible. At this point I thought I might punch myself for not turning around and driving back up State Street. I honestly hadn't thought the place would be as destroyed as it was. I stared at the devastation and tried making a plan to navigate through the debris. There were cars abandoned in both lanes, fallen power lines, busted glass, and even furniture blocking the path. As I drove I began thinking during the madness of the evacuation maybe cars and trucks had crashed through the phone poles causing them to collapse. If there were downed power lines all over the city that would certainly explain the power outage. I glanced in the mirrors and turned my head to check for anything creeping up on me. I didn't see anything outside of the tragic mess to my right, so I decided to sit and collect myself before tackling the hell that was the next road I needed.

I pulled my smokes out of my soggy pants pocket, and to my surprise, the cigarettes were still okay, so I lit one up. I took a few puffs and started thinking about what Marston had said about the bar using bracelets as admission. The zombie whose head I'd crushed had holes in its wrist, but I hadn't had a chance to examine it. After seeing everything I had seen already, I knew it was time to get out of there.

Feeling the sense of urgency to escape growing in my mind, I figured if I could somehow manage to get the car through the chaos in front of me, I could pick Marston up and then drive to Megan's grandma's house.

I sat in the running car long enough to have half a smoke, and then decided the day was wearing on, and I didn't want this to take any longer than I needed. I flicked the smoke out the windshield and put the car back into drive. My hangover had all but disappeared at this point; I guess being surrounded by the walking dead had that effect.

I was stopped at the beginning of a street that looked like a tornado had blown through. I briefly thought about Doug's house on Franklin Street. That was a few blocks behind Marston's apartment. That area was clear of destruction. The only thing that stood out was the lack of people. Now being a few blocks in front of Marston's apartment, I felt like I was in a third world country. Phone poles were snapped in half and hanging by threads of wire twenty feet off the ground, and the ones that weren't suspended in the air littered the street. Busted glass was everywhere, and a few cars blocked the road. Power lines were everywhere, and I wasn't sure if they were live or not. Marston lived a few blocks up on the corner; it would typically take forty-five seconds to drive from my location to his, but with all the rubbish littering the street, I could see it was going to take a lot longer. At this point I wasn't even sure the car could drive through this mess, so the idea of turning around and heading back the way I came popped back into my mind.

I was about to turn around when I glanced into my mirror again and saw a horde in the distance that was very clearly coming right at me. There was no reason to turn around now, so I had to take my chances with the destruction ahead.

I stomped the accelerator and pushed a car out of my way. After I got past the car, I saw piles of clothes and a few shopping carts all over the street. It seemed to me a few homeless people had pushed their carts through and abandoned them. There was so much trash everywhere I didn't see the downed phone pole blocking the way. I backed up a few feet and hammered the gas. I slammed the carts out of the way but hit the beam so hard the front end of the car lifted off the ground and the center of the vehicle crashed down on the timber. I figured I had to have busted the oil pan, transmission housing, or some other vital part of the car.

The tires spun and started to smoke as I tried to rock the car back and forth off the pole. As the car rocked, the front tires would hit the pavement and move the vehicle a couple inches at a time. It took several tries before the front tires were able to pull the vehicle off with a loud thud, only for the rear bumper to catch on the beam and rip off. I had some room for a running start before hitting another abandoned car, so I gassed it.

As I made it past this obstacle, I heard a shrieking sound. I first thought the sound was a wet belt in the engine, but I quickly realized it was coming from a person. I glanced to my right to see a man running out of an alley with six zombies in hot pursuit. Time slowed to almost a crawl as I heard the man screaming at me.

"Help me! Stop the fucking car! I'm not one of them! Please stop!"

I stopped fast, and then yelled back.

"Hurry up, dude! Let's go."

The man yanked the door open, panting hard.

"Man, I'm not one of those things, please drive the fuck--holy shit, Seamus? What in the fuck are you doing here?"

"Jump in; we can talk later. We have to get the fuck out of here!" I yelled.

Climbing into a car as someone hits the gas pedal and scrapes by another vehicle is a challenge. Sadly for Burto, his right calf didn't make it completely into the car before the door slammed against the bumper of a busted-down Geo Tracker. Burto's leg was caught between the frame and the door as our car scrapped along the tracker. His leg must have been horribly crushed because he started screaming.

"Motherfucker, that hurts... oh, Jesus fuck!"

"Damn, dude, I'm sorry. Hold on!"

This happened so fast I didn't realize what was happening until after we had passed the tracker. I peeked over to see Burto pull his bleeding leg into the car. Because I was temporarily distracted by Burto bleeding all over the floor, I crashed into another car's back end. I quickly backed up and maneuvered around it, picking up speed, but soon realized the front tires must have been deflating because it was getting harder to steer. At the pace we were moving, I got nervous and glanced into the rearview mirror again. I saw more dead coming out of the alley and joining the horde already chasing us. I looked over at Burto, who was clutching his leg.

"Damn, Burto, are you alright?"

He glanced up at me; his face had lost all color. He was visibly trembling as he muttered, "Dude... I think I'm bleeding to death."

I heard a screeching sound as smoke started rising from the passenger-side front tire. When the car started pulling hard to the right, I checked my mirror one more time to see the zombies were closing in fast.

The car was pulling so hard I couldn't keep it straight, and within seconds we smashed into another vehicle. Smoke billowed out so thick we couldn't see in front of the car. In a panic, I grabbed my shotgun, and got out. I was at the front checking the tires to see a downed power line attached to a suspended pole had gotten wrapped around the wheel. As I was about to tell Burto we had to make a run for it, the wire pulled the pole down, crushing the trunk and smashing the back window, scaring the shit out of me.

"Time to run, Burto. Burto, hey, man, snap out of it! If we don't leave now, we're going to be eaten. Let's go!" I yelled from the front of the car through the missing windshield.

Burto was reluctant about moving, but he seemed to realize if he didn't, he would be eaten long before he bled to death. I was already out with my shotgun in my hand, waiting for Burto to crawl out.

There weren't many shells left in the gun, so if I had to use it, I would have to make every one of my shots count. Burto was moving slower than whale shit, so I grabbed his arm and yanked him out. He was clearly pissed and mumbling under his breath, but I didn't bother to listen. The only thing on my mind was getting back to Marston's. I desperately wanted to find Megan, but with the number of zombies I had encountered since leaving the apartment, that was a pipe dream. I needed to regroup in safety before I could even fathom a rescue attempt.

Burto began to hobble and limp up the street as I found myself staring at the creatures that were almost on top of us. They were ten feet away when I turned and headed for Burto. When I started to run, I tripped over a wire and crashed to the ground with a *thud*. The gun flew out of my hands directly at the incoming horde, and my palms slammed hard into a pile of broken glass. I quickly got back to my feet and looked at my hands to see large shards of glass sticking out of both of my palms. Blood oozed from the fresh wounds, and I watched for a second as the warm red fluid ran down my fingers and dripped to the pavement. I picked the biggest pieces of glass out but realized I would have to get the rest out later.

My fall felt like it had taken hours, and I hadn't been paying attention. Now the zombies were only five feet away. The creatures were walking over my weapon, so I had to abandon it right there. Frustrated, I began running to catch up to Burto. The sorry bastard had collapsed twenty feet up the road, and when I got to him, I knelt down and scooped him up in the cradle hold and began jogging. He had passed out, so I knew I would have to carry him the rest of the way. Luckily, the adrenaline I had pumping through my veins gave me the strength to carry the weight. I wasn't sure if he was even breathing at this point, but I couldn't leave him to be eaten.

We were a block away from the apartment, and I was barely moving faster than the zombies because I was so out of shape. The pain in my hands was sharp. My blood covered Burto's shirt and the waistline of his pants, and his leg left a blood trail as we hobbled down the street.

We got to State Street faster than I had expected. I looked at the businesses that were beneath Marston's apartment as we approached. There was a bar directly under the apartment and a pizza shop to the left. In between the two establishments stood the entrance to the stairwell we needed to get back inside. As I lugged Burto across the street, I stared up to the open window in Marston's living room overlooking State Street and yelled, "Marston, we're here. Get ready to open the door!" But Marston didn't respond.

As I looked up toward the window, I accidentally dropped Burto, then hastily picked him up again and ran the rest of the way across the street and through the double doors of Marston's building. I briefly glanced around the entrance for something to temporarily block the doors to buy us some time, but unfortunately, the entrance had nothing of use. After seeing nothing, I headed up the steps as fast as I could. It wasn't easy getting Burto up two flights of stairs to Marston's apartment, but I did. I set him down next to the door and began pounding on it, screaming.

"Marston, open the fucking door! Hurry up, asshole, they're coming!"

Then I heard the doors downstairs begin to open. The fuckers must have followed our blood trail. When I heard them coming up the stairs after us, I pounded harder.

"Dude, you better open the fucking door or I'm going to kick it off its hinges!"

The zombies were now clamoring quickly up the stairs. We didn't have time to be screwing around.

"Marston, where the fuck are you? Open the door! Burto's hurt and those fucking things are after us."

After a few seconds, a reply came from the other side of the door.

"I'm sorry, Seamus... I can't let you in here."

"Open this door right now, you son of a bitch!"

"I've seen the movies, motherfucker, and there's no chance I'm letting him in to turn into one of those zombies. Fuck that."

"Listen, asshole! I slammed his leg in a car door. He wasn't bitten or even touched. Now open the fucking door!"

Weak and faintly, Burto spoke up. "Seamus... hurry up. They're here."

I glanced down the hall to see the zombies reaching the top of the steps.

"Seamus, I think my leg is broken," Burto continued.

I was too busy pounding on the door to respond. Apparently, my yelling and pounding caused Marston to have a change of heart, because he was unlocking the deadbolts. I was so caught up in the moment I didn't realize we were being let inside, so I stepped back and kicked the door as hard as I could. As the door flew open it slammed into Marston's face and sent him flying backward.

I heard crashing noises from inside as the door swung open, but the zombies were closing in, so I didn't stop to look. I grabbed Burto and dragged him inside, leaving him on the floor in the apartment's hallway. I turned to close the door behind us as the monsters lurched and staggered for the open door, but just as I went to close it, I was shoved back out into the hallway.

"What the fuck?"

One of the creatures extended its frail arm and almost grabbed the back of my shirt. Before I was turned into lunch, I threw my body back into the door Marston was trying to close behind me. In the process, Marston was knocked on his ass for a second time. I slammed the door and dead bolted it as fast as I could. After the locks were in place, I turned to deal with Marston.

He had flown back a few feet and was regaining himself when I ran at him and kicked him in his forehead. He flew backward and crashed into the counter behind him.

"Fucking scumbag. You're lucky I don't feed you to those fucking things!" I yelled.

"My nose is bleeding, and my front tooth feels like it's about to fall out! What the fuck is wrong with you?" Marston screamed.

"Me? What's wrong with me?"

I grabbed him and raised my fist but stopped as I heard pounding on the door. I faced him and whispered, "Is there a back door to this shit hole?"

Reluctant and bloody, Marston answered, "There's a dilapidated fire escape in the dining room behind the couch, but it's completely useless. It would fall if any amount of weight was put on it."

"Are you sure it's that bad, or are you exaggerating?"

"Dude, *yes*, it's that fucking bad!"

"So you're telling me this place has one entrance? Who decided that was a good idea?"

"I don't fucking know, man!"

"Well it's good to know the only real way in or out is now surrounded by zombies trying to eat us."

Marston didn't reply, and neither of us moved as we listened to the things outside the door trying to crash through.

"They know we're in here and they're not going to stop until they get us. We need to barricade that door now," I said.

I went quickly into the dining room to look for anything I could use to barricade the door. The only thing that caught my eye was the kitchen table, which appeared like it would fit down the hallway and across the door perfectly. I turned the table upside down, broke the legs off, grabbed the top, and ran with it toward the door.

As I was destroying the kitchen table, Marston had been quickly gathering other supplies to use for the barricade, which thankfully ended up being a small bucket of nails and a hammer.

"Where the hell did you get those?" I asked.

"There's a room full of random shit near the bathroom. The room itself is unusable, but it does have things in there that are useful from time to time."

I glanced at him with raised eyebrows, and then we went about our work. Marston pressed the tabletop against the door and held it as I nailed the table's corners into the door frame. He continued to push the table against the door as I went around the entire thing, sinking nail after nail. With the tabletop nailed in place, we had a few minutes to get some other pieces of wood to use as support. We sat down with our backs against the door while the zombies pounded hard enough we could feel the door moving.

Sitting there panting, I had a look at the palms of my hands. They were both covered in blood from my little tumble earlier. I had picked the bigger shards out after impact, and now that I had a moment to breathe, I started picking out the pieces that were left. Right away I realized all the hammering had driven the glass deeper into my hands, so I sat there and picked at the little slivers still embedded. With some patience and a little pain, I was able to get almost all of the remaining pieces out. The wounds weren't as bad as I had originally thought, and I figured there was a lot of blood because of the drinking I had done. The adrenaline had made the pain disappear completely, but now that I had pulled out the slivers, the pain returned.

"Do you think this door is barricaded enough?" Marston asked.

"I think we should put some more shit across it. I really don't want anything coming through it."

"How the fuck are we going to get out of here if we do that?"

"You mentioned a fire escape, so we'll either take that risk or remove all this shit we put over the door."

"Jesus Christ, Seamus, you sure do seem confident! What the fuck are we going to do about him?" Marston said, pointing at Burto's motionless body.

"We'll take care of him after we finish this door."

"Dude, he looks rough. Are you sure he's even still breathing?"

"Nope, but that will have to wait. We can't risk these things getting inside."

After our chat and getting my hands back to normal as much as I could, I thought about how to further secure the door. I remembered a movie where someone nailed a two-by-four across the floor in front of the door. I stood up, leaving Marston sitting against the door, and stepped over Burto as I walked toward the living room. The kitchen had a walkway into the dining room, and then a walkway from the dining room into the living room. The walkway from the dining room to the living room was good enough. I started smashing the molding of the doorjamb with the hammer until I exposed the two-by-fours that framed the casing in place and upright. It took a few minutes, but I was eventually able to get a two-foot piece out of the wall. I went back into the hallway, told Marston to move, and then knelt and hammered the piece of wood in place. I put ten nails through the board and into the floor.

This door is never going to open again.

The pounding didn't stop the whole time we spent reinforcing the door. It was a good thing the four deadbolts had held, because there was no way Marston could have held the table long enough for me to nail it in place.

After we had the table and two-by-four in place, I dragged Burto out of the hallway and into the kitchen, leaving a trail of blood from his leg. After I set him down, I checked his neck for a pulse. It took a second, but I found one. I wondered how much blood he had lost; his face was white, and I knew enough that this was a bad sign.

Although Burto was in terrible shape, I knew we needed to finish barricading the door. Saving Burto would be pointless if the zombies were able to get in and kill us all.

Now that Burto was out of the way, I asked Marston to help me slide the refrigerator into the hallway.

After some huffing and puffing, we finally pushed it flush against the two by four. The fridge was big and barely squeezed through the hallway, but it was a solid fit. The door was finally safely barricaded, and nothing was getting in or out.

CHAPTER 3

After Marston and I had placed the fridge we again took a seat resting against it. As we sat there the reek of rotting flesh worked its way in from the hallway outside. It was the perfect way to spend a day in upstate New York.

Burto was passed out on the kitchen floor, and the three of us were safe for a while. Barricading the door had taken time, and now Marston and I needed to come up with a plan before we all died.

"Thanks, Seamus, for bringing those bastards up here with you. I appreciate it."

"Don't pull that shit with me. If your dumb ass had let us in to begin with, those things wouldn't have seen where we went," I whispered.

"Alright...I should have let you two in right away, but I was indisposed at the time. A strict diet of ramen noodles and pickle juice does wonders for the digestive tract. Second of all, asshole, you said Burto had been hurt, and I automatically figured he was bitten! And one last thing, dickhead! I want to thank you for hitting me in the face with the door, not once, but twice. What the fuck is your problem?" Marston said loudly.

"What's my problem? You practically tried to feed me to those things! You're lucky I didn't beat you to death." I replied with a demeaning glance at Marston.

"Well, I haven't seen a person for weeks. You two showed up and hit me in the face with my own door. That's what you get."

"Same to you, asshole. Don't ever pull that shit with me again."

The pounding continued from the other side of the door. The creatures knew we were inside, and I knew they wouldn't leave so long as they could hear us bickering back and forth.

"We should probably stop arguing and keep the noise levels down. Maybe those things will go away if they forget we're in here."

He nodded in agreement. That was when I turned and stared at Burto's motionless body.

"Let's pull him into the other room and take a look at his leg. It got slammed pretty badly," I said.

We dragged him by his shoulders into the dining room, and then laid him down as I thought about what to do. Daylight was fading, and I wasn't sure I wanted to turn on the lights. That was if the electricity was even working.

"Marston, can you find some candles?" I asked.

"I got a bunch in the other room. That's what I've been using at night."

He left for the other room, and while he was gone, I checked Burto's chest to make sure he was still breathing. Once I confirmed, I glanced down at his wounded leg and saw it had soaked his whole pant leg in blood.

Marston returned with a couple of candles, then started lighting them and placing them around Burto. Now, with the room illuminated, I saw the worry on Marston's face.

"Find some scissors. I'm going to cut this pant leg off," I said.

He left again, and a second later I heard drawers opening and closing in the kitchen. In a matter of seconds, he came back with heavy-duty scissors. He handed them to me, and I immediately got to work.

It didn't take long for me to expose the red-stained skin of Burto's leg.

"Seamus, look at all the blood... We're going to need some water and wet rags."

Marston left the room once again and started looking for more supplies.

"Christ, Burto, there's so much blood. I can't see where you're cut," I whispered.

"Seamus... I need some drugs, I can't take this pain much more," Burto replied faintly. Then he passed out again. He was shaky, cold to the touch, and white as a ghost, and I was feeling nervous.

Marston returned with a few dish towels and a small bowl of water. With Burto lying on his back, the injury wasn't easy to see, so Marston and I flipped him over onto his stomach. When I began rinsing Burto's leg, I found the wound on the back of his calf. I suddenly realized Burto was in so much pain because some of his muscle was hanging out the back of his leg.

The gash was about four inches long. Blood bubbled out of it, and some white tissue was visible outside the wound.

"Marston, I need to talk to you in the other room."

The two of us walked from the dining room into the kitchen, and I began to whisper.

"Dude, I'm going to need your help with this one. The only way the bleeding is going to stop is if we sew it up. We both know I'm no good with a needle."

"Do you think I am"? Marston replied.

"Come on, I've seen you sew a hole in your pants before. I'm sure you can sew up his leg."

"What the hell do you expect me to use?"

"There's got to be something around here somewhere," I whispered.

"Are you out of your damn mind? I don't know how to stitch up a person for fuck's sake!" Marston nearly screamed.

"Stop yelling; those things will hear you and keep banging on the door. If you don't do this, he's going to bleed to death. We have to find something, so come on and help me," I said in a calming tone.

Marston started mumbling obscenities as he wandered off through the apartment. I grabbed a candle and went into the bathroom to look for a needle and thread, but of course, I didn't find any. I did, however, find a bottle of alcohol and a bottle of peroxide in the medicine cabinet, so I returned to the dining room where Burto was. I set the bottles next to Burto, and as I was looking at the exploded mess that was his leg, I wondered if we could wrap a bandage around it the way it was. I was afraid if we did that, the wound would keep bleeding, and we would eventually have had to toss our friend's lifeless body out the window to the creatures below.

As I checked over the wound, thinking about any other options we might have, I heard Marston speak up from the living room.

"Seamus, I got something."

I went into the living room to see Marston holding up an old fishing rod in the candlelight.

"What do you want to do with that?"

"It's to stitch Burto up. The hook is almost brand new, and the line is an eight-pound test, so it should hold up."

"Alright. Let's do it before he dies on us. We have to disinfect the hook before we use it," I said.

"That's fine. There's a bottle of alcohol and peroxide in the medicine cabinet."

"I already grabbed them. Let's get this done," I said.

As we reentered the dining room Marston got down on his hands and knees and examined the wound.

"Seamus, this is bad. His muscle... it's... just flopping around."

"I know how bad it is! Are you ready to do this or what?"

"Bro, I have to push this muscle back into the leg before we can do anything. Then I have to make sure it stays in there while I sew it up."

"I don't care what you have to do. Just do it," I said.

"Alright. I want you to sit on his back. Even though he passed out, he's going to jump around when I start."

Marston swabbed the hook with alcohol as I mounted Burto's back. Neither of us had any medical skill, and we were about to play a real-life game of doctor. The towel Marston used to clean the hook was crusty, brown, and black, so stained it looked like someone had wiped their ass with it. The cloth was so disgusting I had serious doubts it would disinfect the hook. I kind of thought the cloth might cause infection, but we had to try.

When the hook was as clean as it could get, I pulled out about three feet of fishing line and gave the string to Marston, who tied it off.

"Let's do this," he said.

"Dude, rinse your nasty fingers off with some alcohol first. What we're doing is already bad enough, so let's not cause unnecessary issues."

Marston dumped some of the alcohol into his hands and smeared it around for a moment and then got to work. It didn't take long for him to push Burto's exposed muscle back into his leg. I had to turn away when he did. Underneath me, Burto was already thrashing around, screaming like a kid who had broken his arm. He was so strong I was afraid I might fly off, but it didn't last long. I suspected that might have been the last bit of energy Burto had.

Marston had his index and middle fingers inside Burto's leg for a minute or so, and when he finally pulled them out, he said, "The hard part's over... now all we have to do is stitch him up."

"Hurry up."

Marston submerged the stained towel in the water bowl so it was soaking wet, then wrung it out over Burto's leg. The water washed away most of the blood left around the wound. The towel was absolutely disgusting, and I knew if Burto had seen it, he wouldn't have allowed us to use it.

As we sat there in the candlelight, I remembered Marston said he had been drinking pickle juice, so I asked him, "Where did you get the water?"

"I got it out of the back of the toilet."

I somehow wasn't surprised, so I shut up, sat there, and watched Burto's leg continue to bleed. With his muscle back inside his leg, there wasn't as much blood dripping out of the wound. Marston was moving right along, tightly stitching his leg from top to bottom. Watching the first couple of stitches sink into his flapping skin was nauseating, and every time Marston turned the hook, Burto's body would twitch.

I sat on Burto's back until Marston had put about fifteen stitches into the wound. He tied the thread off by wrapping the hook through already-stitched parts of his leg, then snipped the line.

"All finished...my god, that's a lot of blood. Let's put the bastard on the couch; he needs all the rest he can get," Marston said as he wiped his hands on his blue jeans.

Marston grabbed his legs, and I grabbed his arms. As we picked him up off the throw rug, I saw blood had stained it enough for me to want to remove it from the area. As I followed Marston's lead, I stepped in a puddle of blood.

"How is there so much blood?" I asked Marston.

"Man, I don't know. I'm not a doctor. Honestly, with all the blood he lost it would be a miracle in itself if he survives the night. Hell, and let's not mention the horrible way we stitched him up. If he doesn't have an infection that kills him, I will shit my pants. This dude might be finished."

"Well that's reassuring, buddy."

When we reached the long green couch against the back wall of the dining room, we laid Burto on his back. Marston grabbed a pile of nasty old clothes off the floor and put them under Burto's head.

"No pillow?" I asked.

Just then I remembered my own clothes were soaked and caked with other people's bodily fluids. Clumps of brain and pieces of rotting flesh clung and dangled from them. I found it comical that I was worried about my clothes earlier in the day.

"I need to change out of these clothes... I'm covered in blood, guts, skin, and brain. How much water is in the toilet?" I asked Marston.

"Hell, I don't know. When you get in the bathroom, you should see a heap of old clothes. If you're lucky, you should be able to find some new shit to wear."

He hadn't finished his sentence before I was on my way to the bathroom with a candle in hand. On my way, with my left hand, I grabbed the throw rug Burto had been lying on and dragged it to the room across from the bathroom. As I was throwing the rug into the room, I caught a whiff of myself, and it was horrible. I turned and took a few steps toward the bathroom, removing my shirt as I walked. My shirt was in mid-air before I even got through the bathroom door, and everything else I was wearing was tossed into the corner of the room soon after. I stood there completely naked, wondering how I was going to clean myself. The candlelight flickered and caused shadows to dance on the walls as I searched for a towel.

Balled up in the right-hand corner of the sink near the faucet handle, I saw a washcloth. When I grabbed it, I found it hard as a baseball. I removed the top of the toilet tank and started moving the washcloth around the bottom, getting it wet. It was still stiff, but as I un-wadded it; I saw why it was wadded up in the first place: Marston had wiped his ass with it. I reflexively threw it into the pile of clothes that once graced my body. At this point, I figured I wasn't going to get to clean myself, so I began looking for new clothes to wear.

I turned toward the tub and stared down at the clothes on the ground. After seeing that rat's nest pile, it made me decide I wasn't going to wear anything. If these disgusting clothes were my only option, I figured I was better off without them. This irritated me further, because not only was I still covered in nasty shit, but now I was naked.

As I looked at myself in the mirror, I decided I had to try to clean myself off somehow. I was a filthy mess, and I knew being covered in random fluids wasn't good. As badly as I wanted to be lazy, I couldn't allow myself not to clean up. I grabbed the cleanest T-shirt I could find from the pile and went to the sink, twisting the handle. I was shocked when a slow trickle of water began coming out. Setting the shirt in the sink, I cupped my hands under the trickle, letting water fill my hands up. After splashing water on my face, the water fell back into the sink and saturated the shirt. I splashed my face a few times, and then ran the water over the shirt, getting it as wet as I could. Every time the cloth was soaked enough, I would scrub a part of my body as clean as I could get it.

After I had gotten the majority of the blood, brains, bone, and other debris off my body, I tossed the T-shirt on top of the pile of clothes I had been wearing earlier. I wasn't showered clean, but I was a hell of a lot better off than I had been twenty minutes earlier. I grabbed the candle off the sink and headed out of the bathroom, naked as the day I was born.

Candlelight flickered in the kitchen as I walked into the dining room where Burto slept on the couch. I listened for the zombies pounding the door and moaning on the other side of the barricade. I could tell they were still there, but it sounded like there weren't as many as before. Some must have gotten bored and wandered off.

I walked into the dining room at the same time Marston came in from the kitchen. He took one look at me and started laughing.

"dumbass... I put some clothes out for you. They're on the end of the couch."

I walked over to the couch and looked at the clothes he had pulled out for me. The shirt was a tainted old thing that looked as good as the washcloth had. There were unreadable words on the front. The pants were old joggers with holes throughout. When I looked at them more closely in the candlelight, I guessed they were once black, but now had faded to a dull gray.

I got dressed as Marston walked out of the room. The wood was cold on my bare feet, but for the first time, I was comfortable. I took a seat on the floor and saw a pack of cigarettes with a lighter lying on them, so I snatched one and fired it up.

I heard a noise and opened my eyes to see Marston standing in the doorway holding two big candles and a bottle of rot-gut whiskey.

"I've been saving this for a special occasion. I can't find any other excuse to sit down and drink a bottle of scotch. What do you say?" Marston said with a smile.

"With all the crazy shit that's happening all around me all I can think to say is pour me a fucking drink!"

CHAPTER 4

As minutes turned into hours, the noises outside the door had disappeared along with the booze. The first drink I had out of the bottle tasted lousy, but for the moment I didn't care. The candles had burned down to almost nothing, and now the apartment was dark and dingy. With all the drinking and now the darkness, we were getting tired.

Burto panted like a dog as he slept, and I was worried his life would slip away in the night. He twitched a few times and moaned like he was having nightmares. We checked his leg; the stitches were holding, and very little blood had come out. I looked past him, and the piles of trash and empty bottles scattered around, the barricaded door to my left in the kitchen, wondering if anything was lurking behind the door.

"Should we wrap his leg with a T-shirt or something?" Marston asked.

"I have no idea. I know when I have a cut, I let it air out for a while. Maybe we should wait until he's awake to do anything else," I suggested.

We sat in the dining room staring at Burto. I was getting restless, so I stood up and noticed that in the living room, a window overlooked State Street. The room also had a nice set of locking double doors with clothes scattered all over. I glanced around and realized the apartment was a lot bigger than I had thought. The dining room we were sitting in was in between the kitchen and the living room, and in it was the couch Burto slept on. I scowled at Marston's stupid smirk and looked over his shoulder. Straight in front of where I sat was the unusable bedroom filled with old destroyed tools, piles of waterlogged clothes, and soaking wet garbage, and the bathroom. The whole place was a disaster zone and reminded me of a crack den. There were trash and clothes scattered all over the whole place. The smell of the apartment was a very unpleasant odor, but I knew I would have to adapt to it if I wanted to survive in there.

Marston began to chuckle, and after a moment he was laughing out loud.

"What's so funny?" I whispered.

"I just thought of something you did to me a while ago."

"What was it? The suspense is killing me," I said with a grin.

"Remember when you got the idea to tow the pop-up camper on the side of Duffy House?"

"Yeah, I remember. Hell, it must have been four or five years ago."

"Remember using my '79 Granada and ripping the bumper off the back?"

"Hell yeah, I remember!" I said, laughing to myself.

"Yeah, it was fucking hilarious. And the best part of the whole thing was when I came outside to leave, I found you crouched behind my car, unhooking the chain. I figured you were up to something, but I wasn't aware of what you pulled until I got in and began to pull away. Then I heard a thud. I look into my rearview and you've got a huge smile, and you yelled, 'Shit! What happened?' I knew you had torn the bumper off!" Marston said with a laugh.

"That damn bumper was heavy, and before I could push it back on all the way, you came outside."

"I remember coming back to the house later that day and seeing my bumper propped against the house. I went inside and plopped down next to you, cracked a beer, and we bullshitted for hours. I don't think we've ever even talked about the bumper until now."

"You're right... we never did. I remember Megan complaining about it leaning against the house, so I propped it up in the corner of the garage where it sat for years collecting dust."

"Those were the days. Man, it was never a dull moment with the two of us," Marston said.

"You remember the time Dick whooped the shit out of you in the kitchen?" I asked.

"Yeah, I remember, dipshit. I was so pissed I could have shot the both of you."

"Hey, I didn't have any part in that beating, and if I remember correctly, I tried to stop that crazy fucker. Besides, you had it coming. Do you remember not doing anything to help us pay rent or bills? Instead of finding a job you would steal packs of cigarettes and cheap booze from a run-down store, then come back, sit on the porch, and drink all night. That day, I remember watching you and your woman walking back from the store, and Dick said..."

"Check this out; this is going to be funny."

"Then you took three steps through the door, and the fucker was on you like flies on stink. First, he smashed you to the ground with his giant fists and then kicked you in the back. He grabbed your hair and yanked you to your feet, and then you tried to run for the door, but didn't make it. That was when you tried to hide behind the refrigerator. Then the brute *threw* the fridge out of the way in a fit of rage, grabbed you, and pounded until you were limp on the floor, trembling. I remember thinking he took it over the top when he spit in your face. Man, that was a fucked-up afternoon," I recalled.

"I'm glad your memory serves you so well after all this drinking. I remember you were laughing the whole time I was getting beat down. Did you really think it was funny?"

"Well...you did try to hide behind the refrigerator. I'd never seen anyone do that before; it *was* funny. Not to mention I was highly pissed at the fact you were a shiftless lay-about who didn't contribute to any of the bills or groceries," I said.

We both rearranged ourselves and lit cigarettes. My brain was swimming in alcohol and my movements were slowed and sloppy. I shook my head to wake up as Marston continued.

"Well, I remember Dick beating your ass on numerous occasions. Remember when he tipped the fridge on you while you were passed out in a puddle of vomit? That was pretty funny. I'm just thinking about this now, but he did love to throw that damn fridge around, didn't he?"

"Yeah, you've got a point. At least I didn't try to hide behind the fucking thing. Unlike you, I take my beatings when I got them coming. I don't hide from people who want to kick the shit out of me. Besides, if my memory serves me right, I remember being shit-house drunk on a gallon of cheap whiskey."

"We all thought you were dead until you came crawling back from the porch into the kitchen dry heaving," Marston said.

"Wow, I'm glad you assholes are so compassionate. If I thought one of you fuckheads were dead I wouldn't go looking for you either," I said.

"Dude, you were out of your mind that night, and you could have died. The amount you drank was almost certainly lethal. If it makes you feel any better, I did come in and check on you. You wouldn't remember since you were puking on the floor next to your couch."

I looked at Marston, smiled, and said, "Damn, dude. How have we both made it this long?"

He nodded in agreement and offered his glass up for cheers. The familiar sound of glass clinking followed by a burning sensation in our throats left us with empty glasses.

"I think I'm going to pass out. Do you think we will be safe for the night?" Marston asked.

"Well, I haven't heard anything outside for a while, and Burto's sound asleep, so I don't think we're going to have any problems."

"I'm going to sleep in front of the windows in the living room. It gets hot as hell up here in the mornings, and maybe we'll get a breeze. Anyway, I'll see you in the morning," Marston said.

"Wait a second; I wanna check something out," I said before he got up.

I got off the pillow I was sitting on and stumbled; the booze had taken its toll on my brain.

"Dude, I'm exhausted! What the hell do you want to look at?" Marston asked.

"I wanna know if those things are out lingering around outside."

"Dude, I've been watching them for a couple of weeks now. They're not that interesting."

"I'm going to have a look for myself."

"Just make sure they don't see you," Marston said.

Marston clearly wasn't happy about the idea, but he decided to join me. We tiptoed into the living room toward the open window. When we got close, we were hit with a horrible funk I couldn't describe if I tried. We turned our heads, facing each other, and because the moonlight was bright in this room, I saw his look of complete and utter disgust.

"Marston, do you remember when I shit in that kid's microwave and you turned it on?" I asked.

"Yes, I do. It smelled so bad you puked on the floor. Luckily for me, I got out before the sweet essence got to my face."

"At least this isn't as bad as the cooking shit," I said, almost laughing.

The window we were creeping toward was the same one I had yelled at when I was carrying Burto across the street. Apparently, Marston had been keeping it open even though it didn't have a screen. A few steps closer and we were near enough to hear the sound of the things dragging their feet through the broken glass on the sidewalk. We dropped to our hands and knees and crawled the rest of the way to the window.

Poking our heads up to look down into the street, we were astounded at what we saw: the windows to the bar below the apartment had been smashed, and the creatures were walking around in the broken glass. The light from the full moon made it bright enough to clearly see all the decaying bastards below us.

None of them appeared to have died a sweet, smooth death. One of the zombies had large shards of glass sticking out of his face, neck, and even his forehead. His skin had started to fall off in clumps, and his bones were showing through his forearms. What the glass hadn't removed from his bones, the decay and rot had. A hole in the side of his skull exposed some brains that hung out and bounced around with his movements. By the looks of it, I figured someone had bludgeoned this person to death.

"Marston, look at that thing. Man, it's all sorts of fucked up!" I whispered.

"What are you talking about?"

"What do you think they're doing?" I asked.

"I don't know. They're all just wandering around."

"Where do you think the ones at the door went?" I pressed.

"I have no idea. It's strange, because when you guys were in the hallway, it sounded like a herd of cattle coming up the stairs, and I know it had to have been more than five."

"I figure it was at least fifteen, and now there are only five. I guess the rest of them wandered off for greener pastures."

We observed as the creatures went about their business. They walked around, but never left the vicinity of the bar windows or the doors to the apartment.

"When I carried Burto across State Street, busted glass wasn't on the sidewalk. They must have smashed it out while we were barricading the door," I continued.

"Fuck it! The only thing I care about is our safety, and we are safe for now."

I can't believe what is happening here. Is Megan safe, or has she already met her demise? What the fuck are we going to do? How are Tom and Gus?

"I figure tomorrow we can board up the fire escape and put a few extra boards on the main barricade," Marston suggested, breaking me from my trance.

"Why didn't you remind me when we were drinking?"

"What were we going to do with a busted-ass fire escape while we were drinking? Don't worry about it," Marston whispered. "It's useless, and half the stairs are missing. That fucking thing shakes when the wind blows. Some of the bolts holding it to the wall snapped the last time I used it to climb in here. I almost fell four times and had to hold the wall as best I could. No way a bunch of dead things could climb those stairs, trust me."

As soon as the words left his mouth, the zombies started moaning and groaning like a pack of wild dogs that had found food after not eating for a week.

"Shit, Marston, I think they heard us."

"Don't think so. Look, they're all staggering into the street and heading toward the grocery store," Marston said, pointing.

Then, for the first time since I left the two guys I had met in the street earlier, I heard another human's voice.

"Somebody, help me!" a woman cried.

"That voice sounds familiar," Marston said.

"Marston, you're just used to chicks screaming."

"I'm serious, asshole. I think I know the voice."

"Stay the fuck away from me," screamed the woman.

Marston's eyes widened as he dared another look above the window into the street.

"Holy shit, I knew it was familiar. That's Rachel, your brother's ex-girlfriend. How can you not recognize her voice?"

"How the hell do you know it's Rachel?" I asked in disbelief.

"I could never forget the ear-piercing sound of her voice. I remember drinking with her at parties over the years. She was always the loudest person there, and it annoyed the fuck out of me."

"Get away from me!" she screamed again.

"Yeah, that does sound a lot like her doesn't it? Man, I don't know what my brother ever saw in her. She was annoying and always drunk, stating her opinions as facts. Man, back before I left town just her presence would piss me off. I'm glad Scott ended up with me in North Carolina away from her. Oh, speaking of *Scott*, he hasn't been doing so hot since you got him those felonies. That was a real great thing you did to us back in North Carolina."

"Can we focus on the situation at hand; this is no time to bring up the past."

I could toss this asshole out the window right now.

The two of us watched the sidewalk, waiting for her to come barreling through, and it wasn't long before she came into view. She had taken a few steps into our line of vision when she slipped on the glass under her feet. She crashed hard to the unforgiving pavement, sliding about five feet on her right side with her arm extended above her head. Broken glass shredded her clothes and skin, and she screamed in agonizing pain.

She struggled to stand, only to fall a second time. Shredded flesh and muscle clung to her rib cage. Her right side was torn to pieces, and the pursuing creatures were now about five feet behind her. She was quiet for a moment. Then she let out a horrifying scream as the zombies got to her.

"Shit! Seamus, should we help?" Marston asked.

"There's nothing we can do."

"That's harsh, don't you think?"

"Are you going to go pick her up, carry her up the escape, stitch her up, and wait for her to become a zombie?" I asked.

"I guess you're right..." Marston said sullenly.

I know it's a tragedy, but we cannot jeopardize our safety trying to rescue her. I didn't want to see this, but I'm afraid all we can do is look away.

"Jesus, I hope she stands up and gets the fuck out of there!" Marston said.

"Come on, man, she's finished. She doesn't stand a chance."

Rachel had zero chance of getting away. She had five flesh eaters on her, tearing and slashing her body to pieces. Blood squirted from her wounds and was pooling around her body in the street. She screamed and tried to escape, but the monsters kept pushing her back down into the glass. In all the excitement, Marston and I had lifted ourselves higher to get a better look, and I suddenly realized we would be visible from the street if any of the zombies turned around.

By now the glass had turned her pants into shorts. Parts of her rib cage were exposed and could be seen in the moonlight. The glass lodged in her palms shimmered as she desperately fought back against the zombies. Her blood was now flowing like a fountain from all the wounds she had endured, and then she stopped moving. As I watched I saw one of the zombies wore a Dead Kennedys hoodie. I couldn't tell because the creature's face was badly maimed, but it could have been my old buddy Josh Snoot. There weren't many people in Watertown who even knew who the Dead Kennedy's were, so the chances were pretty good it was him. If it was or not, I looked on as the creature pulled a large clump of hair and scalp off the left side of Rachel's head. Her face was now gone, the majority of it eaten. Her teeth and gums were exposed, her lips torn away, and her neck spewed blood.

We gazed on even after she lay silent in the street below. Both of us were changed after this evening. Even though this woman had been a nuisance in the past, watching her be devoured was very disturbing. Hair stood on end all over my body, and Marston seemed very shaken. We glanced at each other and left our perch by the window.

Marston skulked out of the room, and I went back to the dining room where Burto was and lay down. No matter how hard I tried I couldn't shake the images of bloody, screaming Rachel in the street. I don't know how long it took me to fall asleep.

CHAPTER 5

A faint whiff of an odor other than death brought me back to consciousness. Marston had woken up before me and was brewing coffee. I walked into the kitchen more slowly than I had ever moved in my life; my body was beaten and sore, and I was really feeling it now. Still somewhat intoxicated, I wobbled back and forth, rubbing the sweat from my forehead as I walked.

"Morning, fucker. What time is it?" I asked Marston.

"About 10:30. You want some coffee?"

"No, I'm good. Where the hell did you get water for coffee? You used toilet water to clean Burto, and I could barely wash myself?"

"I have a couple gallons I set aside for it. I need my coffee," Marston said with a laugh.

"You're unbelievable! Do you have a smoke?"

"Yeah, have you seen Burto yet?"

"I slept next to him, but he wasn't there when I woke up. Is he alright?"

"He seemed to be catching a new wind. He was very wobbly and weak but ended up hopping around fairly decent. He's in the living room looking out the window."

I reached into my pocket for a lighter but couldn't find it. Still groggy, I asked Marston for a light. Instead of a lighter, he handed me a book of matches.

"Really man?"

"You said you needed a light."

"Matches have a distinct smell. I have no idea if those things would smell them or not. Call me crazy, but I don't want to take that chance," I said.

"I've been using them for a while now, and besides, we smoked a bunch of cigarettes last night, and nothing happened."

"I'm not running the risk."

Marston shrugged and went back to brewing his coffee. I turned with matches in hand and headed for the dining room. Seeing my lighter on the floor, I picked it up and tossed the matches behind the couch. I lit my smoke and glanced up. Sure enough, Burto was at the living room window, looking into the street.

"Burto, what the hell are you doing? You should be resting. Man, you lost a lot of blood and you have a major laceration on your leg. Not to mention its daylight, and they're going to spot you," I whispered as I walked up behind him.

"I feel pretty lightheaded, but I want to try and power through the feeling. We're in too much danger to by lying around all day. And who is going to spot me? There's no one down there," Burto replied.

"Man, we are barricaded in this place for a while. It's okay to relax, and what do you mean no one down there?"

"Exactly what I said. Have a look."

Scowling at Burto, I joined him at the window and poked my head out. The only thing out of the ordinary was a big pool of dried blood. Other than that, there was nothing--no bodies and weirdly enough, no zombies.

Where the hell is Rachel's body? Why are the streets so quiet? Where the hell is Megan? How long has this been going on? How is Burto even alive after the amount of blood he lost?

I pulled my head back in and rubbed my eyes with the tips of my fingers. When I realized I still held the smoke, I took a drag, and flicked it out the window.

"Are you sure you feel alright?"

"I don't feel tip top, but I think I'm ok. I do feel weak and should probably not stand too much. My fucking leg hurts more than anything I've ever experienced. It burns and throbs every time my heart pumps a beat."

"Just sit down for a while, man. That wound is no joke, and it could possibly become infected, so take it easy."

"Why would it become infected?"

"Have you looked around this place? It's a shithole and probably loaded with disease and filth."*And we stitched you up with highly unsanitary items...* I said, leaving the last part out.

"Yeah, yeah, alright. I don't think I can stand much longer anyway," Burto said.

I went to the kitchen and grabbed two of the chairs while Marston leaned on the counter reading an old Rolling Stone magazine. I returned to the living room and offered Burto a chair. He took a minute to get situated, but soon was sitting with his leg stretched out.

"What the fuck happened here?" I asked.

"Man, this shit has been happening for months. I was holed up in my shitty studio apartment right there on Factory Street when it all went down. I heard gun shots and vehicles screaming through the streets the first night. There were sirens and all sorts of emergency vehicles racing around. I sat up the whole night looking out the window. I eventually got some sleep, and when I checked the streets the next day it seemed like there was an evacuation or something going on. Cars and people lined the streets and headed toward the public square."

"You didn't try talking to anyone?"

"Oh, I did for sure. I tried talking to several people, but the only one who didn't brush me off in a panic was some chick. She told me the army was evacuating the town because of an airborne toxin."

"And you didn't think to leave?"

"Hell no. I didn't believe that bullshit."

"Really? Are you fucking dumb?"

"No, I'm not dumb, I didn't believe there was a real threat. I watched as the army guys slammed and pushed people in line, and I wanted no part of it, besides, I didn't think it would be as bad as this."

"So how did you survive this long?"

"Well, as the evacuations turned into total chaos I stayed in my apartment and observed through the curtains. There was mass hysteria for weeks, and I believe the army was killing unarmed citizens. Those first few weeks were rough. I heard explosions, people screaming, gun fire, and anything else you could imagine from a war zone. I had enough shitty canned food to last through the first week. I ate so many kidney beans I damn near threw them up. After that I snuck out of the apartment late at night and headed for the gas station down the street. I stuck to the shadows and when I got to the place it was completely deserted. The doors were locked, but I threw a brick through the glass of the door I went in and grabbed whatever food I could and darted back to my place."

"Go on."

"The first trip was the easiest for me. I didn't have a single encounter, but after that I began running into trouble. I tried to get enough food to last the week if rationed properly, and I was doing a good job at it. The only problem was as the weeks of being shut inside went on, it got way worse outside. The second week, men with trucks began showing up during the day. I saw them plow paths through the destruction on Factory

Street. I never did see where they went, only what they did in front of my apartment building."

"That's the blue building a block down Factory Street from where I picked you up, right?"

"Yeah, that's the one. Anyway, the third week was when I had to start being stealthy."

"Why the third week?"

As Burto began explaining the horrors he had experienced in the first few weeks of the pandemic I studied him closely. His eyes where jumpy and his body began quivering. I could tell by his body language that what he had gone through was enough to scare anyone. His voice cracked a bit when he began speaking again.

"The second trip to the store I encountered a creature, and I was caught off guard when it stumbled out of a doorway in the building next to where you picked me up. I realized then that I really needed to pay attention to my surroundings on my next trip. By the third week, the men were coming around less and less, so I was happy about that, but there were a hell of a lot more zombies out and about. Thankfully this summer has been fairly dry, so there aren't a lot of clouds at night. I used the moonlight and paid close attention to everything while I was out."

"So if you did this for months why were you out during the middle of the day where I picked you up?"

Burto's body language had calmed, but I could see he was getting restless in his chair as he continued.

"I had to start scavenging during the days because supplies had become so scarce. I needed the daylight to look through the businesses and apartments that run along Factory Street. I had cleaned out the gas station a week before, so I went through the bar, the laundry mat, and a few apartments. Yesterday when you found me, I was running from a horde that was trapped inside an apartment building I opened up. I have no fucking idea how they ended up inside or how I didn't notice them."

"Dude, that's one hell of a story, and I'm sorry I fucked up your leg."

"Yeah, I'm pretty pissed about it, but I'm more pissed that I'm back in this fucking apartment with Marston. That grimy piece of shit basically kicked me out of my own house."

"Oh, I remember our phone conversation a few months back. Trust me I'm not even close to over what that sack a shit did to me down in North Carolina. I just have to bide my time, and I'll make sure he gets what's coming to him. Didn't you say you were filling your backpack with supplies? Where was it when you came out of the alley?"

"When I opened and apartment door I was ambushed by those things, so I took it off and started shoving them back with it. They ended up pushing me out the back door, and as I fell I let it go, and the zombies took it. I got up and got the hell out of there."

"Didn't you have a weapon?"

"I had a hunting knife but forgot to take it out of the bag before I entered the apartment."

"Really, why the fuck did you do that?"

"Man, I don't know. I wasn't thinking clearly. I hadn't eaten much in a few days. Speaking of which, I'm starving; is there anything to eat?"

"I don't know; you'll have to ask the sweet prince out there."

I stood up and offered Burto a hand getting out of the chair. I pulled him to his feet as he winced in pain. He put his arm over my shoulder, and I walked him to the kitchen entrance. I left him there and headed toward the bathroom. My mouth tasted terrible, so I found a small amount of toothpaste in a tube and squeezed it onto my rancid tongue. I turned the slow trickle of water on, sipped some, swished the paste for a few seconds, and spit it out. I stood with my hands on either side of the sink, thinking about what was going on. As I watched my reflection stare back at me, the past twenty-four hours finally hit me.

I decided I wanted to find out what the game plan was. I used the trickling water to fill my hands, and then splashed my face. The feeling was so nice I didn't bother looking for a towel before heading for the kitchen.

"So, what's the plan for today?" I asked.

"Well, let me think... probably the same thing I do every day: sit here and wait for someone to rescue me. I mean us."

"No one is coming for us. If we're going to survive this, we're going to have to save our own asses."

"There's no way out of the apartment, and Burto's smashed up real good, so he couldn't leave if he wanted to!" Marston protested.

"Dude, you acting like a bitch is pissing me off! There's not enough food to last three days. Burto's leg is fucked, and we have no way in or out of here. If we don't attempt something, we'll all die here. If you don't help me, that means Burto and I don't need you, and if we don't need you, I am going to feed you to those fucking things! Then it will be Burto and I up here watching you get eaten like Rachel did last night. You think about that for a second."

I stormed out of the kitchen. As I entered the dining room, I realized I didn't have any smokes, so I went back to the kitchen and grabbed Marston's whole pack from him. I pulled one out as I walked back into the living room to join Burto.

"What happened on the sidewalk?" Burto asked.

Burto pointed to the black pool of blood and shattered glass. Following his finger, I saw the sad twinkling blood angel Rachel had made as she'd thrashed and flailed while Marston and I stared at her being torn apart.

"Last night my brother's ex-girlfriend Rachel came running through, getting chased by zombies. Then she fell and that glass shredded her side pretty bad. They caught her."

"What did you guys do?"

"Not much we could do. One of the creatures had this tattered Dead Kennedys hoodie on. Resembled good ol' Josh Snoot, but we couldn't tell for sure because its face was chewed up. It might have been him."

"Man, that's shitty. He was supposed to go on tour with some lame pop-punk band."

"Well, if it was him, he's not going to be doing much of anything."

"Guess not."

Being an oblivious self-centered son of a bitch, I finally noticed Burto's appearance. He was in his underwear, and his leg from knee to toe was caked with dried blood.

"How's the leg?"

"It throbs, and it's hot to the touch."

"Where are your pants?"

"I took them off because one leg was missing."

"For a guy who had his leg popped like a balloon and then stitched up with some fishing string, you seem to be doing fine."

"Don't judge a book by its cover. If I put the slightest bit of pressure on any part of my foot, it sends splintering pain up my leg and I collapse. I learned that the hard way."

"This morning?"

"Yep. I almost fell on top of you."

"Let me take a look at it."

Burto repositioned himself so I could look at the wound. I moved closer, crouching down. I glanced up at Burto, and then gave the area around the wound a sturdy flick.

"What the hell are you doing? I let you *look*, not smack or flick! What's wrong with you?" Burto screamed.

"I was trying to see if your skin was bruised or dead. Judging by your reaction I would say it's a bruise."

"Yeah, dumbass! That hurt real fucking bad!"

"You wanna keep it down? We don't want those things to hear us. Anyway, it looks like the skin is mainly bruised, so I think that's a good sign. At least now the color seems to be coming back to your face; last night you looked albino. I think we should wrap it with gauze and some Neosporin. We wanted to last night, but figured you needed some rest, so we decided to wait until you were awake."

"That's a wonderful idea, but we don't have either of those things!"

"I'll go look in the bathroom for something useful," I said, walking off.

I started my search around the sink and medicine cabinet but didn't see anything I could use. Putting my hands on the sink I thought about a plan. I knew there was a grocery store a few blocks down the road. I figured it had been ravished, but there had to be some over-the-counter medical supplies left. It was at that moment I decided Marston and I would take a trip to the store. I knew Marston would be a hard sell, but I had to convince him.

I grabbed the cleanest shirt I could find from the pile behind me, and then ripped it so it could be wrapped around Burto's leg.

"Marston, bring some tape," I said as I walked back to Burto.

"Duct tape should work just fine," Marston said as he approached.

Both Marston and I were looking at the leg when Marston said, "I'll make short work of this."

"Are you sure you know what you're doing?" asked Burto.

"Of course I know what I'm doing. How hard can wrapping a wound be?"

"Hurry up and get this shit over with," Burto retorted.

As Marston was working on the wrap job, I thought it would be a good time to at least mention my plan.

"So I've been thinking about taking a trip to the store," was all I said before Marston started acting like an asshole.

"Well that's cool. Yeah, *you* head to the store. Grab me some things while you're there."

"This is a two-man job, buddy."

"Be quiet and let me finish this shit. I need to pay attention, and you blabbing about some store outing is distracting."

Marston's reaction annoyed me, but I stopped talking and saw him scoff at the idea. Burto wiggled and winced as Marston wrapped the leg in a manner that surprised me. He did it like I assumed a doctor would have, or so I thought at the time. The ordeal took five minutes, and when Marston finished, the leg was as good as it was going to get until Burto saw an actual doctor.

Shooting me an angry look, Marston stood up and left the room when he finished.

"In a little while, Marston and I will be at the Great American grocery store getting supplies, and I'll make sure we grab some gauze and Neosporin for that leg."

"How the hell are you going to get there?" Burto asked in disbelief.

"We're going to descend the run-down fire escape, and then we're going to walk the rest of the way."

"You're out of your fucking mind! That fire escape looks like it couldn't hold a cat, how will it stand two grown men?"

"How the hell do you know what it looks like?" I asked.

"When I woke up this morning, I moved the blanket and had a look at it. It took me a minute to move, and I fought through a lot of pain, but I wanted to see what was behind the blanket."

"Do you have any idea how stupid it is for you to be walking on that leg?"

Burto rolled his eyes before speaking.

"Relax I wasn't exactly walking on it. I was hopping on my good leg and using the couch for support."

"I don't like you doing that shit. You could really fuck yourself up, try and take it easy. You're not out of the woods with that wound. Anyway...we're going to have to risk the fire escape. Either that or we stay up here and starve. Besides, your leg needs some help in the healing department."

"I do need ointment and other supplies, but what about those things outside?"

"Well, it looks to me like they've left the area," I replied.

"You're fucking nuts! I know we need things, but risking your life?" Burto asked.

"I'd rather die trying to prolong my life than wait up here to starve to death. Fuck it. What do you have to worry about? It's not like you're going out there."

"You know I would help if I could."

I reached for a smoke before reassuring Burto. After taking a puff I exhaled slowly and continued.

"I know...I'm just busting your balls. Oh, don't you worry, you're going to be helping. I have a few ideas I think will help"

This mention put pep in Burto's step. His eyes shot wide open and he asked," Are they good ideas, or are they ideas that could kill us?"

"Ideas about making this place impenetrable from the outside."

"What do you mean?" Burto asked, wide-eyed.

Marston came back into the room with a fresh cup of coffee. "What are we talking about here?" Marston asked, sipping his coffee.

"Seamus wants to make this place impenetrable. And he also wants to go shopping," Burto explained.

"Correction, Burto, I *am* going shopping."

"Sorry, buddy, you're going to be flying solo on that mission. Like I told you, you're nuts, and I'm not going to leave this apartment," Marston said firmly, taking another sip from his cup.

"No, friend, you'll be the one flying solo when I throw you through the fucking window. Now go get ready; we're leaving in thirty minutes," I fired back.

After my reaction I noticed Marston's shoulders tense up and he became more ridged.

"Shit, why can't you understand this is a terrible idea? We'll likely die trying to save ourselves," Marston cried.

"Look, shithead! I don't care if I die in the streets. I'd rather it happen there than up here in this musty apartment. Besides, you haven't even heard my plan yet."

"What is it, genius?" the others asked together.

I took one last drag off my cigarette and flicked the butt out the open window in the living room before I continued.

"Bear with me, because it might be a tad complicated for your feeble minds. First, we're going to make some weapons, and then we're going to use the busted fire escape to descend to the ground level. After we reach the pavement, we're going to jog over to the store and do a bit of shopping. I'm thinking we grab a wheelchair on our way out if we can find one."

"What the hell do we need a wheelchair for?" Marston asked.

Marston's facial expression was dumbfounded. His dreadlocks were half in his face, and his beard looked like it had crumbs in it. Just looking at him pissed me off.

"Because Burto needs to be able to move around up here. Nonperishable foods like cans of soup and bags of ramen, anything that's not going to rot. We're also grabbing medicine for Mr. Burto, a few cases of beer, and maybe a carton of cigarettes."

"I can understand the beer," said Burto.

"So can I," Marston agreed.

"Alright. After we grab the supplies, we're going to put them into carts, rush them back here, and then run over to Ace Hardware. We need to grab supplies to board up that fire escape. After it's boarded up the only way in or out will be through a window, and we'll use rope to climb in and out. Once we hit the ground Burto can pull it up so nothing can climb in. Now, it's time to make some spiked clubs and get moving. Is there any more coffee? I need a cup."

I didn't even want coffee, but I did want to know what they thought, and I knew they wouldn't speak their minds with me present, so I left. Both of them stared at me as I turned and walked to the kitchen. I stepped just out of their sight and waited to hear what they actually thought about the plan. After a few moments I heard them begin to talk.

"What do you think of his plan?" Burto asked.

"I really don't want to go outside. I watched those things eat someone last night! Who put him in charge?" Marston griped.

"The world's in total disarray, and you're still completely fucking useless! Some things never change. Why don't you stop being a fucking cry baby and try helping? We got here to find you clean and dry, so I'm guessing you've been hiding in here the whole time. Before Seamus picked me up, I was scavenging houses every day trying to stay alive. I had to sneak around those things day and night. Do you know how fucking scary that is? Of course you don't, because you haven't been out there! If I didn't have a gash in my leg I would be doing the same thing he is. Seamus picked me up soaked head to toe in disgusting shit and then saved my life when I couldn't move. Knowing you, I'd say you would have run away like the bitch you are, and that's what puts him in charge. Don't roll your eyes at me you piece of shit!" Burto retorted.

"I've stayed alive in here; that's all that matters to me. I'm not going out halfcocked on some insane mission to die," Marston protested.

"Did you eat lead paint as a kid? Do you not understand we need supplies, or we will die? How is it before the world collapsed you were a lowlife sack of shit, and now, you're still a sack a shit, but a coward to boot? You have some fucking nerve on you. I still can't believe we were ever friends. You fucked Seamus over, and you race right back to Watertown and fuck me over. How has anyone ever put up with you?"

"Shut your mouth before I do," Marston said.

"Go fuck yourself! I'm sick of looking at your worthless face!" Burto yelled.

As Marston turned for the kitchen, I poked around the doorway and saw his head hanging dejectedly. He stared at the ground, and the look of anguish on his face was priceless. As he got closer, I took a seat, waiting for him to enter the room.

Marston came through the door without saying a word or even looking at me. He went right for the pot of coffee and poured the rest into his cup. He went back to the counter with his magazine and began turning pages. I didn't know what he was thinking, but I was contemplating what was waiting for us outside the walls of the apartment.

CHAPTER 6

"Let's get this shit over with," I said.

Marston looked up and rolled his eyes as he shook his head. We walked together into the front room where Burto was now sleeping against the wall underneath the windowsill. I woke him up with a shake of the shoulder to tell him we were about to leave. He was still tired and not much for conversation, so Marston and I left the room.

"Let's pound some nails through those table legs," I told Marston.

The process was harder than we thought. One of us held the table leg in place as the other pounded nails through the end.

"This is a pain in the ass!" Marston cried.

"Hurry up, we only need one more."

Five minutes in, Burto came over to watch. As he watched, he made comments like. "That's going to hurt like a bitch!" and "You're going to take their heads right off!"

Our completed weapons were terrifying to look at. Our clubs had nails sticking out on all sides, and I knew nothing would get past them.

I turned to Marston.

"Well, are you ready?"

"Fuck no. This is a suicide mission!"

"We'll be fine. All we have to do is keep a low profile and not make too much noise. If anything gets too close, whack it upside the head. Whatever else happens, just stay calm," I said with a grin.

"We're going grocery shopping in a town full of dead people! What the hell makes you think I can keep a cool head?" Marston hissed.

"Burto, you're going to hold down the fort while we're out," I continued, ignoring Marston. "Pay attention to the hardware store. Remember, if those things spot us, we're fucked. Do you understand?"

"Sounds good to me. Oh, you should write a list before you go so you won't forget anything."

"Good idea," I said.

"I agree, plus it will keep us up here and safe a little while longer," Marston chimed in.

"Hey, do you have a pen and paper?" I asked Marston.

"There's a junk drawer next to the sink--check in there."

I checked the drawer and found a few scraps of receipt paper and a pen, so I pulled them out and leaned against the counter and started writing.

We started the list with all non-perishable goods: ramen, soups, instant coffee, beer, canned juice, triple antibiotic ointment, bandages, gauze pads, peroxide, rubbing alcohol, mouthwash, toothpaste, toilet paper, chewing gum, and several gallons of water.

"We need a lot of everything on this list. I don't want to make more than one trip," I told Marston.

"Well, I don't want to leave at all, but since I have to, I only want to do it once. What about the hardware list?" Marston asked.

"That's easy. Even though we have that bucket of nails I think we should get some more. We used a lot on the barricade and the clubs. We only need a box or two of nails, some rope, a screw gun, and some screws. I'd say a sheet of plywood for the window, but there is no way we can get that in here. We're going to have to board it up with whatever we can use from inside the apartment."

"Alright. Let's get this over with!" Marston said with sarcastic enthusiasm.

The list didn't take long to finish, and once we were done, I pulled on the arm of the couch, sliding it out of the way so we could access the window.

I moved the shabby blanket covering the window and a musty odor like a thrift shop hit my nose. I opened the window and was met with a mid-summer breeze. The sun was high, and the sky was cloudless; the only strange thing was the lack of birds or any other movement outside the apartment. Looking at the clear blue sky brought me some sense of joy and happiness, but then I peered toward the streets and felt dread thinking about all the death, destruction, and chaos that waited.

Before we went out to the fire escape, I decided to tear my ragged joggers into shorts because it must have been ninety-plus degrees outside. I glanced over to my right to tell Marston to do the same, but he wasn't anywhere to be seen.

"Marston, you might want to change into shorts. I don't want you passing out from heatstroke," I shouted.

Marston came slinking back from the bathroom like a sorry dog.

"Good idea," Marston said as he walked off.

Marston went off to change, and I took a seat as I waited for him to finish. He was taking forever in the room, and I was getting pissed at him for procrastinating, so I leaned against the wall as Burto hobbled in and started talking.

"So, Seamus, how long do you think it will take before I can walk right again?" Burto asked.

I fumbled a pack of smokes out of my pocket grabbed my lighter and fired it up. I inhaled deeply and enjoyed the burning sensation that followed.

"I don't know. If I were you, I wouldn't try it at all. Just wait for the wheelchair, it'll be safer," I said.

"Hey, Seamus...why not grab a car and get the fuck out of here?"

"I thought of that but decided against it."

"Why?"

"Well, we don't know what we're up against. You mentioned the army and guys with trucks. What's to say we get a car and start heading over to find Megan, but those men find and kill us? I think it would be a whole lot safer if we didn't rush this thing."

"Dude, what about Megan?"

"Honestly, man, at this point there's nothing I can do. Should I rush this and get killed trying to find her? I mean she could be dead for all I know. If I can find a payphone at the store, I'll try calling her grandmother's. Hell, I'll call anyone I can."

"Those are some good points, but you won't be calling anyone. I've checked every payphone I have come across and they're all dead. I checked the land lines in the apartments I rummaged through and those were dead too. It seems whoever is running this show cut those lines the first day...what if those things are chasing you when you get back?"

"Well, we keep on running. Let's not worry. We'll deal with it if we have to when the time comes."<i style="font-size:1em;">I'm going to kill this fucking idiot! "I already told you I'm not fucking around! Let's go!" I yelled at Marston, then continued more quietly, "Alright, Burto, make sure you watch the store for us."

"That's no problem. I already put a chair in front of the window."

Once Marston joined me, I pulled the couch out of the way and moved the blanket aside. I pushed the window up until it latched and had a look out. The platform on the other side of the sill was crude looking. As I stared at the junk I was about to climb on, I started to sweat. I told Marston to go first because I was nervous, but also because I didn't trust he would follow me out.

"This is bullshit," he protested, but then stepped out of the window onto the platform. Once his foot touched it, it began to shake like a dead leaf in a fall breeze. When he was all the way out, I turned back to where our clubs were propped against the wall. I grabbed one at a time, making sure to hand them to him very carefully.

Before I exited, I asked, "Do you see anything?"

"No, but you better hurry up... this thing's not going to hold much longer."

I poked my head out and realized the supporting bolts were visibly moving in the brick wall as we spoke. I figured I needed to go right then because if it fell with me still inside, we could kiss the supplies goodbye, because Marston would take off running and would never be seen again. I sat on the sill, put my feet down on the platform, and then slid out. Before I realized what was happening, Marston yelled unintelligible words I couldn't make out. Bolts began snapping, and I realized the platform was even less stable than I'd thought.

The rail Marston held began to tilt toward the ground. Realizing what was happening I tossed my club to the pavement, and Marston did the same. Before either one of us had a chance to throw ourselves back through the window, we were descending toward the warm pavement below, and the two of us screamed together.

"OHHH SHIT!"

The whole staircase was slowly crashing to the ground with the two of us along for the ride as I braced myself for impact.

The sound of the stairwell crashing into the pavement was tremendous. Marston was first to hit the ground, and I crashed on top of him. He broke my fall, and it hurt like a son of a bitch. I snickered at the fact I had crushed him.

Servers the fucker right for some of the shit he's done. "Are you alright?" I asked, not moving.

"God damn, I'm banged up pretty good."

We waited for the dust to settle before either of us tried to move. Marston was panting underneath me, and it wasn't long before he said, "Get the fuck off me!"

I rolled from my side onto my back, groaning while Marston lay there extending and resting his arm across my chest.

"Son of a bitch, my ribs might actually be broken," Marston said.

As I lay there with my eyes closed, a voice startled me from above. Right away I thought I was dead and the angels were taking me up to the heavens. I didn't open my eyes; instead, I lay listening to the voice that seemed miles away. The words were impossible to make out at first, but as the seconds went by, they slowly became clearer.

"Are you guys alright?" Burto yelled from the apartment. "Hey, you guys, can you hear me? Move your arm or something! Give me some sign you're okay."

I suddenly remembered where I was and what was going on.

"Marston, we have to move. Come on, get up."

I grabbed the rail directly above my face and hauled myself up. Marston was still lying there, so I bent over and extended my hand as a helpful gesture. He batted it away with a quick swat.

"I don't need your goddamn help!" he yelped.

He reached up and grabbed part of the rusted rail that was nut level with me and began to pull himself up. As soon as he pulled himself almost upright, the pipe broke, and he crashed down onto his back. I couldn't help laughing.

"Fuck...can you believe that shit? Here, help me up," he groaned, extending his arm.

"Yeah, sure. Get up yourself, asshole! I already tried that, and you were too thick-headed to take it."

He stayed on the ground for a few more moments, seemingly in protest.

Marston finally got to his feet. We stood regaining our composure before looking up at Burto. I shot him a thumbs up to let him know we were alright. Marston in turn shot him the middle finger.

Burto nodded at me and then spat at Marston.

"Let's get the fuck out of here!" Marston said.

We had walked a few feet when I realized we had forgotten the clubs, so I turned around and jogged back to them. I grabbed them and returned to Marston saying, "At least we don't have to board up the fire escape."

As we began walking, I started thinking how lucky we were to have had just the wind knocked out of us. I was winded, and Marston may have had some bruised ribs, but we had survived the fall fine.

We had crashed on the backside of the apartment in a hidden parking area, and when we came to the corner of the building, we cautiously poked our heads around it. We couldn't see anything on either side of the street, and the store was only a few blocks away from us, so we started jogging. We jogged for a block and a half and were sweating profusely, so we decided it would be easier on our bodies if we walked. On our right stood a large three-story house, and suddenly crashing, moaning, and breaking-glass sounds came from inside.

There was a putrid smell engulfing us when Marston asked, "Do you smell that?"

"Yeah... what the hell, it smells like a chicken farm!"

The stink was so bad we were gagging even with our shirts over our faces.

The two of us started jogging again despite the heat, and within seconds were at a full sprint. As soon as we reached the entrance to the Great American, I looked over my shoulder to see a zombie stagger out onto the porch of the three-story house.

"Holy shit, Marston, look. It's going to come after us," I said in a panic.

We watched the monster head toward the porch stairs, and then burst into laughter as it crashed down the stairs face first. But it was back on its feet quickly, and now it was stumbling toward us.

Marston reached for the door and gave it a tug.

"Locked," he said.

"That sumbitch will be on us in no time," I told him.

"Stand back!" Marston said.

Marston gave one of the windows a boot, but his foot bounced back. He kicked the window three more times, and the whole lower pane fell to the ground.

We crawled through and were greeted by the foulness of spoiled milk and rancid meat. There was sunlight shining through the front windows, but the aisles behind the register were pitch black. This foul air was worse than the chicken-shit odor we had just passed through. We looked at each other, shrugged our shoulders, and went about our business.

"We have to be quick. This place reeks, those things could be in here, so be careful," I whispered.

"If that thing knows we're here, I say we wait, and when it gets here, we clobber it. If we do, we won't have to run around like idiots. What do you think?" Marston asked.

"Sounds like a plan... let's hope none of his friends join him in the hunt," I replied.

We decided to take refuge in the checkout lane closest to the door. It turned out this was the lane that had the cigarettes, so I grabbed a carton of Marlboro Reds, and set them at the end of the lane. I figured I'd toss these into the cart when we started shopping. We continued waiting, and due to the heat and smell, it seemed to take longer than a church sermon.

The creature finally got to the door and bumped into it several times. It took a few minutes before the damn thing realized it couldn't just walk into the store. Soon, however, a dog started barking in the distance, and within seconds, the zombie turned away.

We poked our heads out and stared as the zombie lurched away toward the sound of the barking, moaning with every step.

"Marston, come over here."

"What do you want?" Marston said as he came closer. "There's a hardware section somewhere. I say we find that aisle and grab some flashlights."

"That's your best idea thus far."

Using our lighters, we made our way down the first aisle, which was the bread aisle. The stink of rotten fruit, vegetables, and meat stayed strong and revolting until our sense of smell became used to it.

We continued down the aisle toward the back of the store when my lighter went out.

"Don't fuck around, Seamus! Light it back up," Marston said, sounding anxious.

I tried to light it again, but the flint wheel had melted.

"Shit. It's done."

"Where's the goddamn hardware section?" Marston said angrily.

"You've been in this shithole town for a while. How do you not know?"

Marston moved on, the flame of his lighter fighting to stay lit. Seconds later he turned in the light and smiled before making a confession.

"I'm just fucking with you. I know exactly where that section is. You should have seen your face. Man, sorry, I have to enjoy these little moments."

"You stupid cunt," I snarled. "Keep moving!"

He led us past three aisles and then turned left. His lighter was a beast and held its ground as well as a Zippo. We got to the middle of the aisle when Marston stopped. The flashlight packages including the batteries were on the bottom shelf, so those were the ones we went for.

"Next time you decide to fuck with me, make sure we're not in the middle of a goddamn zombie apocalypse," I said.

"I thought it would be funny," Marston replied.

"It wasn't. Now hold your damn light still," I whispered.

He did as commanded. The light was sufficient enough for me to tear open a flimsy flashlight box.

"Dude, this lighter's been melting and burning me since the first aisle, hurry up."

"I almost got it!"

"Could you please just hurry? It hurts pretty fucking bad!"

I loaded the batteries in time for the baby to drop his lighter. My eyes were in a state of shock in the sudden darkness for a few moments. For a second, there was complete silence, and then Marston spoke.

"Turn the light on, asshole; I can't see anything."

"I would, but I think I loaded the batteries backward, and now I can't fix them because you let the light go out! Don't stand around, start looking for the lighter."

He dropped to his knees in a frantic search for the lighter, and in the total darkness, I could hear him patting the floor like a mad man.

"Dude, I can't find it... shit. Try switching them anyway," Marston said anxiously.

"I can't reverse batteries in the dark, you moron. Maybe if I help, we'll find it faster."

"Great, get down here and help."

Instead of bending over to help, I flicked the flashlight on and pointed it at the floor, spotting the lighter quickly.

"I found it," I chuckled.

"You motherfucker, what's wrong with you?" Marston hissed.

Marston stopped complaining long enough to pick up his spiked club again, then turned to face me in the light of my flashlight.

"You do that again and I'll put this thing right into your belly," Marston claimed.

"If you think you're brave enough to threaten someone, maybe you should go threaten helpless Burto. Now, if you're done being tough, grab a fucking light and make sure it's ready."

He turned and looked down at the flashlights on the bottom shelf.

Once he made his pick, it only took a few seconds for him to load the flashlight and turn it on.

Now that we both had sufficient lighting, we headed for the front of the store where the baskets and carts were stored. He grabbed a cart while I went past the hum around scooters and grabbed a wheelchair. I turned the chair around and tossed the smokes into the basket.

"Let's split up; this will go a lot faster," I suggested.

"Goddamn, man! What the fuck is wrong with you?"

"Fuck off and do what I say! It will make this a lot faster if we're not stuck up each other's asses."

He mumbled obscenities and headed the other way.

As I pushed the wheelchair down the center aisle, using my light to read the signs above each one, I figured Marston, the selfish drunk he was, would be in the beer section, already drinking. At this notion, I shook my head, and made mental notes about where the things I needed were located in the store. My first note was the canned goods and soups. As I passed this aisle I noticed most of the products had been knocked onto the floor. I was sure this wasn't the only aisle that was a mess. I figured people would have been in here taking whatever they could.

It wasn't long before I was in the medical aisle, where I grabbed peroxide, rubbing alcohol, hand sanitizer, Neosporin, and self-adhesive bandages.

I turned around to face the shelves behind me to find the oral care section. I was thrilled at this sudden idea, because none of us had even thought about our teeth. I searched for the biggest bottle of Listerine I could find, and on the bottom shelf I found an economy size bottle of orange citrus flavor. I tossed that, along with as many boxes of toothpaste I could grab, into the wheelchair's basket. I decided I had enough medical and dental supplies to last for months, so I began heading to the soup and canned goods aisle taking a small detour along the way. I walked toward the area where the butcher was and realized I should have gone another way. All the fresh meat was packaged and ready for sale in the windows of the butcher. I don't know why, but I decided to walk over and take a look. The sight was sickening; maggots had taken over the meat. It was buried under sheets of larva, so I quickly left the area and went for the canned goods.

In the aisle, I put my arm behind the cans and pulled them into the basket. Then I pushed the wheelchair through all the debris scattered all over the floor. So far, this aisle had been destroyed the most; boxes, cans, bags of coffee, and other junk was scattered throughout.

I was leaving the aisle when I saw Marston's light heading my way from the beer department. As I shoved my way through the last of the garbage lying on the floor, Marston came up, pushing his cart.

"Dude, what did you grab?" Marston asked in a low whisper, looking into the wheelchair basket.

"A lot of soup," I laughed.

"Did you grab any medical supplies?"

"Yeah, I got them. They're just buried underneath the food."

"Alright. Hey, I thought of a few things we should add to the list," Marston continued.

"Really? What might they be?" I asked.

"I think we need some sleeping pills. Sometimes those damn creatures wake me up at night, and I figure we all would benefit from some help in the sleep department."

"That's a good idea. Come on, leave your cart of beer here and let's grab some pills. We still need a lot of water. Is your whole cart full of booze?" I asked.

"Pretty much. I wanted us to have a selection while we're trapped."

"Sorry to be the bearer of bad news, but we'll need room for water," I told him.

"I figured you would say some shit like that," Marston said, disgruntled.

We left our carts where we had met up and headed back toward the aisle with all the pills. I grabbed some Tylenol PM and stuffed them into my pockets. After, we headed for the juice aisle where the water sat on the bottom shelf. We each grabbed a case and lugged them back to the beer trolley. Sadly, we had to remove a case of Labatt Blue and a case of Bud Lite to make room. Both his cart and my basket were now full to the brim with supplies that would last us a while.

We began to wheel our goods toward the front door when a yelp came from outside. I instantly turned my light off, and Marston did the same without even thinking about it. We were behind the fourth register looking out the windows onto State Street. I didn't see anything at first, but then Marston tapped me and pointed toward the left of the store.

Out in the middle of the street, a zombie was taking a significant bite out of the dog that had distracted the creature earlier. The zombie had already won the battle; the dog was lying on its side, panting, and bleeding from its neck where the zombie had bit it. The poor pup was being devoured, and again, all we could do was watch.

The zombie was working on the dog's rib cage and would occasionally lift its head to reveal strings of bloody tissue dripping from its jaws. I peered at the creature, trying to make out any defining features. The thing's face was nothing more than a black and decayed slab of meat with eyes.

"Look at that thing... they'll eat anything they can get their hands on," I said.

"This is disgusting! Its legs are still twitching because its brain is telling it to run," Marston replied.

"Well, like they say...it's a zombie-eat-dog world."

We couldn't do anything until the zombie finished its meal. I was irritated with Marston earlier about the smell the matches put off, but at this point, there was no way they could smell worse than the store, so we sat in the dark and smoked while we waited. After what seemed like a decade, it finally got up and lurched up the street toward the park.

We put our cigarettes out, and then crept toward the front of the store directly behind the windows, trying to see if the zombie was far enough away it wouldn't see us. We waited and stared for ten minutes until it finally turned left off State Street and disappeared behind a building. After it disappeared, we walked back to the supplies.

Suddenly, I heard a faint noise, and we stopped in our tracks looking around. It seemed to be coming from the fruit, vegetable, and beer aisle to the left.

"I think I know what that noise is," I said.

"I have a sneaking suspicion it's one of those creatures," he replied.

"I think if that's a creature we should kill it. That way, it's one less we have to worry about later."

"I don't know Seamus. I've stayed alive by staying away from things that can kill me," Marston said.

"Stop being a bitch and let's go."

With our clubs clutched tightly, we started toward the noise. Our flashlights were off now, but here the sunlight provided enough light for us to advance on the creature. And then we saw it. It wasn't moving, just swaying back and forth in place. The reek the thing was emitting was horrendous. I figured we missed it because the whole place smelled awful, and for whatever reason it hadn't come after us. I began to crouch so it wouldn't see us closing in on it. Before I knew it, I was crawling along on my knees, my club still clutched in my fist.

The whole trip up to this point had lasted about thirty minutes, but it seemed like hours, and this was going to set us back even further. I observed what I could of the creature in the dim light. The top of its scalp had begun peeling like an orange, and bone was visible on the left side of its head. Its skull was not a bright white, but more like a burnt brown. It had been hit in the head hard enough to split its skin, but not fracture the skull. Flesh hung off the side of its face and scalp in clumps, enough to reveal the matted muscle underneath. Its left arm was missing the skin and muscle. The more I stared, the more I noticed most of the damage seemed to be on its left side. If it had once worn clothes, they were now long gone, leaving only tatters of fabric hanging around its neck. What was left of its skin was so decayed it had turned into a leather-like suit of brown.

How long has this shit been going on?

That's when Marston jumped to his feet and lunged at the zombie.

"Die, you bastard!" he screamed.

I remember hearing two thuds: the first when Marston hit it in the side of the head, and the second came from the zombie hitting the ground.

Marston smiled and showed me his club, which still had the zombie's head stuck on it.

"Damn, Marston, talk about knocking his block off."

I gagged as I saw strings of skin, tissue, and veins hanging from the base of its neck. Brownish fluid dripped and plopped from the neck onto the floor, and I realized that brown goop was once the animal's blood. The odor its exposed throat emitted was worse than the meat department.

Marston began shaking his club furiously, trying to dislodge the head. He ended up having to place the head on the ground, step on it, and yank the club free. It worked quickly, and the noise of the head tearing apart reminded me of smashing a pumpkin. Marston raised the club and began spinning it like a wild man, sending fluids and other shit flying off in every direction. When he was done, he began walking toward me. He got close enough so he wouldn't have to yell, and then spoke.

"Do you think anything heard that?"

"I doubt it. I hardly did, and I was right here. I don't think anything outside would have heard a thing," I replied.

Suddenly, I remembered something I had seen the day before.

"When I was out yesterday, I was almost killed by those things right on Factory Street. While they surrounded the car I was in, I noticed holes in some of their left wrists, maybe about the size of a BIC pen. The skin appeared to have been injected with silicone, and it was swollen and bouncy. Their wrists were pulsating and leaking pus every time they moved," I explained.

"Big deal. We're wasting time, let's go," Marston bitched.

"Yeah, in a minute. You remember that bar you told me about?" I continued.

"What about it?"

"I think the zombies have something to do with it," I said.

"Yeah, no shit they have something to do with it, get a grip! We haven't got all day. I'm leaving."

It didn't happen often, but I realized Marston was right, so I caught up to him. I tossed the contents of the wheelchair basket into a cart. I figured it would be easier to get these supplies inside the apartment this way. After clearing the basket, I folded the chair up and slid it underneath on the metal rack where people put dog food. My cart wasn't even half full, so I decided to take a case of water out of his and put it into my cart.

"This should lighten yours up a bit."

"Well, put some of the beer in it too."

"Fuck no. You're the idiot that grabbed all of it."

"Well, you're going to drink it too, so help carry some."

"Jesus Christ, you big whine ass, hand me a couple twelve packs."

Marston handed me three twelve packs, and after that both of our carts had roughly the same amount of shit.

I should clobber this dumb asshole right now.

We pushed our carts through the first set of doors looking through the dusted windows at the sun beating off the pavement. It was so hot outside the ground shimmered. Marston glanced at me as soon as my fingers touched the metal lock on the door. The streets were empty, and nothing moved anywhere we checked. The remains of the dog that had been eaten were all we saw. I twisted the lock on the second set of doors, and then pushed the door open. I was immediately greeted by the humidity and heat, causing me to sweat even more than I already was.

We pushed our carts back toward the apartment without incident. A sense of relief came over me when I didn't see anything roaming the streets between us and the apartment. As we walked, I started thinking about Megan, and I felt the urge to get her right at that moment. I considered it, but I was scared to try without a gun. I tried to think about anything else, but when Megan came into my head, I couldn't get her out. I almost began to panic, but then I saw the apartment, and the feeling of dread went away. Knowing we were close to safety, we started to jog. The carts rattled loudly, especially when they hit bumps in the sidewalk. As we approached the window, we struggled to push them through the broken glass. We shoved and pushed until we finally ended up in front of the apartment window.

"Burto, where are you?" I shouted.

He poked his head out of the window.

"Hey, guys, I'm glad you're back. It's been uneventful so far, but I found a porn stash under a pile of clothes. It was a little saturated, but it did the job."

"So you're telling me instead of watching the door like we asked you to do, you decided to look at moist porn magazines?" I shouted angrily.

"No, I did both! I was beating off by the window and looking at the storefront every few seconds. I couldn't stand up to shoot out the window, so I came all over the front of my pants," Burto said, laughing.

"Really, congratulations, you're a multi-tasker. Now tell me about the front door to the hardware store," I said.

"There was nothing to see."

"Nothing at all, anywhere in the streets? Or just by the shop?" I continued.

"Nothing, nada, zip. I didn't see a bird, let alone a decomposing person."

"Alright...we'll be right back," I shouted up.

"Seamus, do I have to go? I don't want to!" Marston protested.

"Jesus man, you just knocked a zombie's head off with one goddamn swing! Would you prefer standing here in the open, drawing attention to our location? Stop being such a fucking pussy! We only need to get rope and nails. I'm sure another ten minutes isn't going to put you over the edge."

CHAPTER 7

We left the carts in front of the apartment, and then walked across the street toward the store. After we crossed the road, I glanced back to see Burto hanging out of the window, looking down at what we had brought.

The two of us approached the hardware store's doors carefully. I grabbed the door handle and gave a firm tug. These doors were also locked, but that wasn't going to stop us from getting what we had come for. I kicked the bottom window, shattering the pane of glass.

"Well done; let's go before something or someone shows up," Marston said.

I kicked the glass a few more times to make sure it fell out of the frame completely. We kicked as much of the glass away from the door as we could, so we wouldn't have to crawl through it. We got down to our knees and glanced at each other. Marston peered at me as if saying, *you first.*

I poked my head into the store to be greeted by the warm musty smell of stagnant air and sawdust. It smelled as if there hadn't been anything roaming about in the place for weeks. I crawled through the door and stood up, and Marston was right behind me.

He stood up next to me and started covering his nose, but then stopped and said, "Wow, it smells like an average hardware store."

"Good, we won't have to worry about another creature."

I smiled as I turned my flashlight on. At this moment I had this strange feeling I wanted to see if the lights would come on. I turned to face the cash registers and right behind them on the wall were the light switches for the store. I walked over and flipped them to the on position. Surprisingly, the lights flickered to life, and the store was illuminated.

"Hey, Marston, have you tried the lights at the apartment?"

"Of course I have. They haven't worked in months, and I haven't seen any other lights on anywhere."

"Well they're on now."

"Maybe whoever's behind this is turning the grids back on."

"Yeah, I guess. I mean what else could it be?"

"Who cares, you idiot; let's get this shit over with."

"Hey, before you wander off, make sure you only snag the things we need or can use. And if anything happens, just yell, and I'll run out the front door," I laughed.

"Very funny, asshole. You remember who clobbered that zombie back in the grocery store, right?" Marston said as he walked off.

I walked down the first aisle looking for nails, and luckily for me, I found them right away. I was crouching down to pick up a couple boxes of nails when Marston yelled. "Look what I found!"

"Bring it over, I'm in the first aisle," I shouted back.

He came skipping over and held out his hands to show me a rope ladder.

"Well, what a shock! Marston found something useful! I'm impressed; you're not as dumb as I thought. Well, now all we need is rope," I said.

"Getting in and out of the apartment will be so much easier with this," Marston said eagerly.

"You did good, congratulations."

"I spotted some rope next to this ladder; I'll go grab some," Marston said.

"I'm going to go with you. Maybe there's something else of use over there," I replied.

I picked up the nails and walked to the other side of the store where Marston had found the ladder. As we walked by the front counter, we both set our gear on it before continuing.

When we got into the aisle, I saw all sorts of ropes and chains spun around big metal dispensing wheels. I glanced around and saw a machete on the back wall of the aisle, so I walked over and grabbed it.

As I tore the packaging off, I said, "Pull about twenty-five feet of rope off the spool."

Marston grabbed the thickest rope they had, pulled out roughly twenty-five feet, and laid the rope on the floor. He stepped back a few feet, and I swung the machete toward the ground. I swung the blade so hard it cut the rope and smashed onto the tile, causing me to drop it.

"Next time swing softer tough guy," Marston chuckled.

"Yeah, smart ass, I think I will. Now let's get out of here!"

Marston picked up the blade and rope as we headed for the front of the store to grab the rest of our supplies. I grabbed the nails and Marston took the rope and the rope ladder. Before we left the building, I had enough sense in me to turn the light switches off. This place was a gold mine, and the least amount of attention the place attracted the better. We walked over to the front doors and unlocked them. Even though the door windows were dusty, we were able to see through them enough to search our surroundings.

We searched for any zombies that might have been lurking around looking for lunch. To our liking, there were no zombies to worry about.

That's when I looked toward the apartment to see two guys digging through our carts. Above them, Burto was struggling to maneuver a chair out the window to throw at them.

The two were digging through the food cart and ripping bags of ramen open then stuffing the dry noodles into their mouths. While chewing the noodles they began tossing our stuff onto the sidewalk. Marston and I ran through the unlocked doors and headed right for the two thieves. We were nearly sprinting, but when we were almost on top of them, they spun around and pointed guns at us. The threat of being shot stopped us dead in our tracks. Marston dropped the ropes he was carrying and pointed the machete at the men.

"I don't know who the fuck you two are, but you better get away from our shit!" he shouted.

"Hold up, Marston, I know these guys. They helped me yesterday. That's Gus and Tom."

Just as the others lowered their guns and slight smiles of recognition began to cross their faces, Burto heaved a heavy brown wooden living room chair out the window.

From the second floor, it packed a hell of a punch when it hit Tom's head. I stood in awe as Tom fell to the ground, unconscious and twitching.

"Jesus, that was hard," Burto yelled from above.

"What the fuck was that?" yelled Gus.

"Well, my buddy up there thought you two were trying to steal our shit, so he was protecting it," I said.

"Are you fucking kidding me? We help you yesterday and you kill us today?" Gus yelled.

"Technically, I didn't do anything to either of you. We don't have time for this; we need to get these supplies into the apartment before we have some unexpected party guests," I continued.

Marston tossed the rope ladder up toward the window where Burto caught it and yelled, "Hold up a second," as he hobbled out of view. Moments later, Marston and I heard pounding from the apartment. "All set," Burto yelled down as he tossed the ladder to the ground. To all of our likings, the ladder was longer than we needed.

I sent Marston up first because I knew he was excited to get back in the apartment. After he got inside, he turned around and poked his head out the window. I threw the rope up, then stood there contemplating how to tie the beer cart to it. In the meantime, I tossed my boxes of nails into the cart and scratched my head. Then Marston called down to me.

"Hauling the whole cart up is the only option. That ladder's too wobbly to climb up carrying anything."

"What the fuck are you going to do about Tom?" shouted Gus.

"Do you wanna keep it down, buddy? Those fucking things are everywhere, and they *will* kill and eat both of us. Let me figure this out and then we can deal with Tom."

I was figuring out how to cross the rope through the cart to evenly distribute the weight and I could hear Gus in the background trying to comfort Tom.

"Hang in there, buddy. You'll pull through this I know it."

I ran the rope through several holes across the top of the cart, and after it was secure, I gave the others the go-ahead to start lifting. I figured each cart weighed a hundred pounds, and with the weight evenly spread out the two would struggle, but eventually get the supplies inside.

As they worked, I walked over to Tom's body and stared at him. "I don't know what to do," I said.

"Well you better fucking do something. He's in this shape because of your friend!"

"*No*, he's in this shape because he was trying to steal shit, and someone caught him. We can fix this just give me a minute to get these supplies situated."

Gus went back to comforting Tom, and I glanced up and realized the wheelchair was about to fall off the cart.

"Grab that damn chair off the bottom before it falls," I yelled up.

From below I watched Marston grab the wheelchair, disappear from sight, reappear, grab a case of beer, and then disappear again. It wasn't long before Burto yelled at him, and Marston was back unloading the cart's goodies.

The cart was now empty, so I stood back and waited for them to lower it.

"Alright, this cart's coming down, stand back," Burto shouted.

Gus and I each grabbed one of Tom's arms and dragged him off the sidewalk and into the middle of the road. The cart came crashing to the ground a few seconds later, bouncing three times before finally coming to a rest a few feet away from where we were standing.

"What the fuck are you doing throwing that cart down here, you idiots!"

"We thought you were in a hurry," I heard Marston say through laughter.

"Are you ready for the supplies?" I shouted up.

"Yes. Tie it up the same way you tied the beers," Marston replied.

The rope was still attached to the first cart, so I untied it, and then tied off the supply cart. As the two of them began hauling the cart back up toward the window, I turned and grabbed the chair Burto had thrown, moving it out of sight to the side of the building. I finished moving the chair, and with nothing left to do, I turned to Gus.

"What should we do with your buddy?"

"Man, I don't know. Look at him; he's in pretty bad shape."

I looked at Tom, who was lying unconscious in the middle of the street. I had seen people in worse shape, but never had I seen it firsthand. Both his ears were bleeding, and his eyes kept flickering as if he was trying to open them but couldn't. A gash on the back of his head was spewing blood and beginning to puddle underneath his body. I knew he was still alive, because I could see him breathing, but I wondered if he could be paralyzed.

"I think we put him into the cart and haul him in through the window," Gus suggested.

"That sounds like it could be hard," I replied.

"What the hell do you mean it could be hard? Your buddies just hauled a cart full of beer up a two-story fucking wall! If your asshole friend upstairs hadn't done this, Tom would be fucking fine! Are you saying we leave him down here to be fucking eaten?" Gus shouted.

"Relax! I didn't say that, I just said it could be hard."

It was clear Gus wanted to throw a punch.

"Alright, relax, we'll figure it out," I said, hoping to calm him.

I glanced up to see Marston had unloaded the cart and instead of dropping this one he lowered it like a normal person.

The second cart came down a lot smoother than the first one. I grabbed a hold of it and started working the knot. While working on the knot I heard scuffing noises come from inside the bar. This made me nervous and I wanted to get this done as quickly as I could. The sounds weren't as loud as some of the noises I had heard that day, and when I peeked back, I knew Gus hadn't heard them.

This guy is going to be a big fucking problem. What am I supposed to do about this?

I didn't want him or his half-dead buddy anywhere near my hiding place, so I needed to come up with a plan. As I glanced around, I saw Tom had dropped his weapon when struck from above. This gave me an idea, but I wasn't sure it would play out in my favor. As I untied the rope I began talking to Gus, hoping to distract him momentarily.

"Gus, are you ready to load him into a cart?" I asked.

"Yes, I am! Come over here and help me with his feet."

Gus and was so preoccupied he didn't notice me tying the gun Tom had been carrying to our supply rope.

"Are you going to fucking help me or what," Gus shouted.

"Yes, in a second I'm still trying to get the knot out of the rope."

"Don't worry Tom we're going to make this right. Those guys are going to make you comfortable. In a couple of minutes, you'll be inside and safe. How does that sound?"

After the firearm was secured, Marston yanked the weapon up and into the apartment. With the gun now inside, the rope ladder came out the window. I climbed up as fast as I could, and when I crawled through the window Marston pulled the ladder in behind me. This was the best plan I could come up with, and I must admit, it wasn't my finest hour.

Gus was now lifting Tom by the shoulders but dropped him when he turned to see I was already inside the apartment. The sound Tom's head made when it whacked the pavement could be heard from the window, and it gave me a sickening feeling in my stomach. I was focused on the fact I wanted to puke when Gus started yelling.

"Fucking stupid assholes! What's your fucking problem?"

I headed for the kitchen to put supplies away in hopes Gus would leave, but Marston felt the need to antagonize him.

"Sorry, dude, we've got enough supplies for us. Not for us, you, and your wounded buddy. Haven't you ever been taught not to screw around with other people's things? We don't give two fucks about you or your friend! You two shouldn't have acted so fucking slimy!" Marston continued, "Take your buddy back to your hideout, nurse him back to health, grab a cart full of supplies, and then come talk to us,"

"You guys are fucking dickheads! Who the fuck ditches a person in a time like this?" Gus yelled.

Marston walked out to the kitchen, where I was putting things on the counter. We began to talk about the trip and the beheading of the one zombie when Gus started yelling again. I figured the dude would have gotten the hint and hit the road, but no, not this guy, he continued to yell at the three of us. Burto spoke up from the living room while we were putting supplies away.

"If he doesn't shut up, he's going to have those things here in minutes."

Realizing Burto was right and Gus was seriously endangering everybody sent me over the edge of anger. I was too pissed for words, so I grabbed the empty liquor bottle off the dining room floor and vigorously made my way through the apartment to the window.

"Look asshole, if you don't leave right fucking now, I am going to smash this bottle in your face, do you understand?" I shouted.

Instead of doing as told, he yelled, "Go fuck yourself, you greasy-looking sack of shit!"

I chucked the bottle at his head as hard as I could, but my aim was off, and the bottle smashed a couple of feet away from him.

"You pathetic coward, you fucking missed. What a douche bag!"

That's when Marston came up and pushed me out of the way. He pointed the gun at the loudmouth below and fired a shot. Instead of giving the guy a warning, Marston, ended up spraying Tom with birdshot.

"Marston, what the fuck are you doing, you crazy son of a bitch?" I yelled.

"Are you going to leave now, you loud-mouthed fucker?" Marston yelled down.

The words fell on deaf ears, as the only thing down on the street below was a dead guy next to a cart. Gus had run off before the smoke had settled.

"What the hell did you do that for?" Burto asked from his new wheelchair.

"That fucking dude was going to bring hell fire down on us and blow our cover. It had to be done."

"Do you think a fucking gunshot would also bring hell fire on us?" I asked angered.

Marston didn't reply; he just set the gun down between his legs, leaned out the window, and stared at the body lying in the street below.

"I don't think Tom is going to be an issue anymore," Marston said calmly.

I shook my head in disgust. I couldn't believe Marston had done what he did. The barrel of the gun was still smoking as I turned to walk to the kitchen to finish putting the supplies away.

CHAPTER 8

"Dude... you shot the guy," Burto said, panicked.

"Yeah, I know, Burto. Do you think I meant to? I meant to blast off a warning shot, not kill a guy," Marston responded.

"I have no idea what you meant to do!" Burto stated.

From the kitchen, I could hear in Marston's voice he felt horrible for what he had done. But the way I saw it, none of us were doctors or had the slightest idea what to do about a head wound like that, so it was either let him die a slow and painful death or put him down. It sucked it had come to that, but maybe it was a blessing in disguise. I started to feel sympathetic for Gus and Tom, because they had helped me on my journey, but I chalked it up to survival of the fittest. As soon as that notion popped into my head it was followed by another question. *What kind of animal am I becoming?*

With that behind us, I went to the refrigerator to grab some beer. Even though we were using it as part of our barricade, we were able to keep it plugged in and usable. I grabbed a warm can of Budweiser from the fridge and drank its contents almost all at once. The refrigerator was a piece of crap and would probably take a day and a half to chill the beers, and I wasn't willing to wait that long.

The fridge was now full of adult beverages. We had Budweiser, Michelob, Michelob Light, PBR, Miller Genuine Draft, Miller Lite, and one twelve-pack of Michelob Amber Bach bottles. There wasn't a selection for a guy like myself who mainly drank imports and fine spirits, but with the situation at hand, I had to acclimate. I reached into the fridge and grabbed a bottle of Amber Bach. With beer in hand, I walked back to the living room where the idiots were still bickering back and forth.

I hadn't even made it to the doorway of the room before Burto verbally ambushed me.

"Do you think it was right for Marston to shoot that guy?"

"Look, you morons, what's done is done. Drop it and talk about something else! Look, there's plenty of beers in the fridge. Why don't you guys grab some?" I suggested.

The comment sent Burto into a frenzy. He wheeled himself out of the room and to the kitchen faster than an Olympic wheelchair racer. Both he and Marston had been so caught up in unloading the carts, and murder of Tom, they forgot to grab a drink.

"How do you think Burto will take it when you tell him he shouldn't drink because of that wound you caused?" Marston asked.

"I'm not telling him anything," I said.

"If you're not going to tell him, I will," Marston replied.

As Marston was about to leave the room to tell Burto the lousy news, I suddenly heard a dragging noise coming from outside the window.

"Holy shit, Marston... I don't think you killed Tom," I said.

"Seamus, I highly doubt that noise is from the guy sprinkled with birdshot," Marston said.

Burto wheeled back into the room with a can of Bud and asked, "What's the problem in here?"

Instead of answering the question I pointed at Marston and said, "Go on and tell him what you told me."

I wasn't surprised when he failed to mention the beer but went straight to the point.

"We just heard some sort of dragging noise outside the window," Marston said.

"Well, why don't you walk over to take a look?" Burto replied.

The three of us ventured toward the window, but only two of us were able to look out at a time. Marston and I checked first because Burto seemed content with his beer. We watched Tom's body for a while, but he didn't move. Eventually, I decided the noise must have come from somewhere else.

We had only taken one step away from the window when a series of noises came from the bar underneath the apartment. I heard crashing, slamming, shattering glass, and other noises associated with destruction. The three of us stared at each other like schoolboys who had just seen their first boob, and then turned back toward the window to see what was going on. At first, I didn't see anything, but then, all of a sudden, a zombie smashed out the front door of the bar into the street.

It was an outrageous-looking thing. Its clothes were shredded, and its foul odor only took seconds to reach us on the second story. The smell of zombies was one thing I could never get used to. Marston and I stepped back, almost tripping on Burto.

"I can't believe a zombie was in the bar the whole time you were standing in front of it..." Burto said. "Wow, that's luck."

"No, it's not luck Burto. I heard the thing when I was untying the second cart. That was one reason I scampered up the ladder so quick. I knew it was only a matter of time before that thing got out."

Burto's wheelchair was too low to let him get a good luck out the window, and every time he tried to move, he winced from pain. I couldn't help but laugh at the look on his face. Eventually, Marston moved, and Burto pulled himself up to the sill and peered down into the streets.

We watched as the zombie stumbled toward Tom's body. The monster fell to its knees, picked up Tom's arm, and began to gnaw on it. Then, without warning, another zombie flew out of the bar onto the sidewalk.

Amazed, like it was the first zombie he had seen, Burto said, "Damn, guys, look! Two of them! You know, if they weren't so decayed and rotted, they would almost look normal."

"Yeah, you're right, Burto... maybe because they *were* fucking normal at one point," Marston yelled.

I turned around and shoved Marston toward the dining room, grabbed Burto's wheelchair, and pulled him back into the room. I didn't see the face of the newcomer, but I was sure both creatures were now staring at the windows above the bar.

"Man, what the hell is the matter with you?" I said, angered.

"Well, maybe he shouldn't say such stupid shit!" Marston said, staring at Burto.

"Yeah, maybe you're right Marston! I'm getting annoyed with your piss-poor attitude. How about if you make one more cocky remark or you do something that draws attention up here, you and I are going to have words! Do you understand?" Burto asked.

"Man, Burto... I was just saying...you need to relax!" Marston spoke softly.

"Don't tell me to fucking relax! Just try shutting your goddamn mouth when you're about to say something dumb!"

"Fine, forgive me! I won't try to add lighthearted humor to our situation anymore!"

Marston sulked off to the kitchen and headed to the fridge. I went back to the window for a look as Burto again tried getting a better viewpoint by arching his back. As he was trying to look out the window, he kept asking me things like.

"What are they doing? Did more show up?"

"Burto, you saw the second one come out of the bar. How can you not see down now?"

"I wish I would have saved my strength to see this shit. Are they eating the kid or what?"

"Yes, Burto, they're eating the meat right off the bones! Hell, half the kid's arm is meatless already."

Burto kept talking, but I wasn't paying attention. I was too gripped by the two zombies eating Tom's body below. Both of the zombies had large holes in their necks, one of which was larger than the other. One was the size of a tangerine, while the other seemed like it could fit a softball.

The first zombie had a tattered red shirt around its neck and looked noticeably less rotted. The second creature was so decayed I couldn't even tell if it was male or female. The meat on its face barely clung to the bone, and its skin almost looked like chocolate pudding that had been left in the sun.

"I bet those two were friends before they died."

"What makes you say that?" asked Burto.

"Fuck, I don't know if they were friends. It seems to me they might have been. I'm bored, man! I'm just passing time making shit up."

I didn't say anything else and returned to gazing out the window. The monsters seemed to be almost finished with their meal now. The red-shirted zombie sniffed at Tom's neck as the decayed slab of meat pulled Tom's leg up and began eating his calf. After a couple of minutes Red Shirt bored with Tom and began to stagger up State Street toward the park. I watched as the rotten one stayed behind to finish the meal it had started. By the time it had eaten its fill, there was nothing left from the knee to the ankle, and most of the arms had been devoured.

"So, Marston," I started as I turned away from the window again. "Do you think that bar has any liquor left?"

"Holy shit, Seamus! I hadn't thought of that once in all the time I've been trapped in here!"

Does he want to get punched?

"I know we have a ton of beers, and getting them wasn't easy, but I'd like some whiskey. Wouldn't a beer and a shot end this day well? I think getting it would be a hell of a lot easier than the supply run. Think about it: the ladder drops next to the entrance of the bar. If we had some bags, we could be down, loaded up, and back up here within five minutes. What's wrong with that?" I asked.

"Alright, Seamus, let's think about this for a minute. We've been up here for a day or two, and it took those things that long to make a noise. What makes you think more of them aren't in the bar?"

"It's sad, but the truth is, I don't care. I want whiskey, and I'm willing to go after some."

"Don't get me wrong, I would love to ingest some hard spirits myself. How about we wait up here for a while, maybe eat something, and then if we don't hear anything, we make our move?"

"That sounds like a good idea. Besides, I'm starving."

"We have enough food for an army, go get some," Marston said.

"Ya know, I think I will take this trip solo. I appreciate your help, but I know how much you like going outside," I said.

"Man, are you sure? Wow, you are a true friend...would you like me to grab you a beer?"

"Nah, I'm good. I don't want a drink. Warm beer is disgusting, and I need to be sober if I'm rolling out solo."

After our short discussion, we all went different ways in the apartment. Burto went off to the bathroom; Marston went in the kitchen for some warm beer, and I grabbed a box of nails off the floor and walked with them to the barricade. Admiring our handy work from the day before, I realized nothing was getting through the door. I set the nails down and walked over to the counter in the kitchen I grabbed a pack of beef ramen noodles and headed toward the living room. Marston was in the dining room playing solitaire, working on a warm can of beer.

"Bro, take it easy on the drink! I don't want to get back here, and you be trashed!"

"Don't worry about me, buddy!"

I walked to the living room, grabbed a chair, and positioned it in front of the window. I took a seat and opened my bag of noodles, searching for the seasoning pouch inside. Staring out the window, I poured half the seasoning into the bag before crushing the noodles and starting to eat.

This afternoon weather was terrific from the inside. The sun was shining in the cloudless sky, and a midsummer breeze blew gently through the window. The day would have been perfect if I was spending it on a hike in the mountains with Megan. I pictured the two of us lying in the small waves on the ocean shore, letting the warm saltwater roll over our shins. I found myself lost in a world of daydreams; physically I was in a zombie-infested town on the brink of destruction, but mentally I was at the best place in the world. With the amount of alcohol and stress I had endured over the last two days I let my mind run away with the daydream. The bag of ramen fell to the floor as I fell asleep from exhaustion.

I sat in my beach chair under an umbrella, sipping the best whiskey sour I'd ever had. Across the crystal-clear water shimmering in the sunlight, I saw a shrimp boat a few miles past the pier. The waves rushed in and out, causing my chair to sink slightly in the sand.

I turned to find Megan returning to my side with a large, frozen, red drink in her hand. She walked up to me as I leaned my head back over the chair and planted a big kiss on my forehead. She sat in the chair next to mine, and we enjoyed the pearl-white sand beneath our feet. The breeze blew through my hair as I sat, and the sounds of the water made me sleepy. The palm trees danced back and forth in the wind, and as my chair sank farther into the sand, I looked back out over the water and saw a dorsal fin. I wasn't sure if it was a dolphin or a shark, but whatever it was, it was swimming around the reef, probably looking for lunch. Beyond it were three sailboats, and even farther out, a cruise liner sailed by.

All was calm, and then a tropical breeze began to blow. The breeze was relaxing at first, but then it began to change. Suddenly, strong gusts whipped sand into our faces and kicked up massive waves in the sea. The shoreline, that had been calm for the better part of the day, was now alive with chaos. The white caps crashed down onto us so hard it felt like the whole beach was shaking.

We both abandoned our chairs for safer ground, but we couldn't escape the storm. We ran for a nearby cabin, chased by heavy rain and thunder and lightning. I held onto Megan as we ran, but I couldn't help but turn to watch the ocean smash into the shore hard enough to move mountains of sand. The waves had gone from inches high to feet high in a matter of seconds, and the wind was blowing so strongly I was afraid the palm trees were going to be uprooted. I wasn't sure where the storm had come from, but we were both terrified. My soothing summer afternoon had quickly turned to hysteria.

I turned to face Megan to see if she was alright... and watched her start to decompose before my very eyes.

At first, she looked frightened, but then she began aging at an alarming rate. Her drink fell from her hand to the sand below as her face became a mess of wrinkles. Her hair had grown considerably and had changed from a fiery red to a bright white.

I stepped away from her, unable to believe what I was seeing. Her skin began dissolving, revealing the muscle below, which began to liquefy and fade, leaving only bones. I stared at them in horror, but then the bones themselves turned to dust and then, from a strong gust of wind, were blown away to oblivion.

My world felt like it was spinning at a thousand miles an hour. The trees, water, pier, boats, and everything else were in complete disarray. I felt pressure building in my brain, and I thought my head was going to explode. The only thing I could think to do at that very second was to scream. As I screamed, the world stopped, and then everything went black.

"Seamus, wake up! Dude, are you alright? Wake up!"

I heard Marston's voice and felt someone shaking my shoulders.

I opened my eyes. My mind still whirled with what I had just seen, and in an instant, I was throwing up my lunch onto the floor next to the window. I wiped my mouth on the sleeve of my shirt and turned to Marston, who was crouched next to me. Burto had even wheeled himself into the room to see what all the fuss was about.

I regained my composure and moved the rope ladder out of the way so I could lean out the window for some fresh air. As the summer breeze made my sick feeling dissipate, I glanced all over, but still saw only the partially eaten remains of Tom's body in the road below.

As I turned to face the others, they had backed up near the door, staring at me in disbelief. Marston spoke up first.

"Dude, what the hell was *that*?"

"I passed out and had a nightmare about Megan."

"Are you worried about her?" Burto asked.

"Of course I am. I'm actually terrified she's dead, but what can I do? I have one gun with a couple rounds of ammo at most. Here, let's check.

I shucked four rounds out of the gun and turned toward the guys.

"You both have seen how many of those *things* are out there. What am I going to do with four fucking rounds?"

"Megan's tough, and I doubt she's met her end so quickly," Marston claimed.

"I hope you're right. Man, I want some whiskey! I hate this feeling of being trapped and not being able to go after her.

"*You* can," Marston said.

"If I tried to go after her now, I'd be killed."

"You could at least try," Marston said.

"I know exactly what you're doing, you fucking snake, so shut your goddamn mouth! You want me out there and possibly dead so your bitch ass can horde all these supplies and stay up here until you starve to death. I'm not buying your bullshit concern."

"Why do you always have to be so quick to judge? I was only offering a suggestion."

"One more fucking word from you and I'm going to punch you in the face! Now, shut up we have other issues at hand. We're going to have to do something with that body. The damn thing is going to attract attention. I don't want another living person seeing it and looking up here. I'm not so worried about zombies, but I've seen three people, and we don't need any more incidents with anyone else. Besides, if this heat keeps up, that body is going to rot faster than a hobo eats a ham sandwich."

"Where do you think we should put it?" Marston mumbled.

Burto spoke up before either of us could say anything.

"I have an idea. Put the body in the cart, push it to the corner, start running, and let go. The cart will cruise down the street and probably roll pretty far. Hell, the road goes downhill anyway."

I sat there thinking and said, "You know what Burto, that's a good idea. I actually walked that road earlier and it was pretty clear of debris."

Marston chimed in with his two cents.

"The first cart was dropped from a second-story window, but the second cart was lowered, so that might actually work. Good luck, Seamus. I have full faith you can get that done. Hell, I'll even have a whiskey with you when you get back."

"Marston, are you kidding right now? It's kind of your fault we have to move this body."

"Burto killed the guy with a fucking chair!" Marston argued.

"Come on man. I can't move the body by myself I need some help."

"This is the last time I'm lifting a finger to help with some bullshit," Marston protested.

"Half the body has been eaten. At least it won't be as heavy," I said.

I grabbed the clubs and tossed them out the window where they clattered to the ground. I turned grabbed the gun and propped it against the side of the window. Then I thankfully remembered we'd need something to carry our booze in, so I ran to the bedroom. I yanked two stained pillowcases off some pillows and headed back for the living room. I tossed the cases out and motioned for Marston to go first. After he was down, I turned and began climbing out. Before I went below the windowsill, I looked at Burto and said, "Dude, make sure you pull this ladder up as soon as I'm on the ground."

Burto nodded. As soon as I touched the pavement, the ladder flew up the side of the wall and out of sight. When I turned around, Marston was already standing by Tom's mostly devoured body.

"Okay, let's deal with this first," I said.

Marston didn't say anything, and I noticed he didn't look well. He opened his mouth, but instead of speaking, he turned his head and began dry heaving. He did this for a minute but regained himself.

"The dude is still warm to the touch," Marston said.

"No shit, smart guy, its ninety degrees out here. Help me lift him into the cart," I replied.

I pushed the cart that hadn't been dropped next to Tom, and we each grabbed for areas of the body still grabbable. Neither of us spoke as we moved the dead body. I had never experienced a moment like this one. I had smashed some dead thing's head in a car door the day before, but this feeling was completely different. This man had helped me with a weapon and was now dead because of me and my friends. I quickly pushed the thoughts out of my mind and continued with our plan.

It didn't take long for us to push the cart to the corner. We had originally planned to shove him off somewhere down the street away from the apartment, but instead, I stopped.

"Alright, let's harvest the liquor first, and then we can send this guy down the road."

"Why don't we push him now?" Marston asked.

"The cart's wheels will be a lot louder when they're going full speed and might bring zombies snooping. I don't want that right now."

"Don't you think the shotgun blast might have brought those things snooping?"

"I remember two zombies after the blast. That's why our friend here is a bloody mess. Let's get the liquor and then send this fellow down the road."

"Whatever. Let's just get this shit over with. I hate being out of the apartment," Marston said.

I made sure we had our pillowcases and clubs, and then realized I forgot the gun in the apartment. Shaking my head with distaste we slowly headed toward the bar. As I walked toward the entrance I couldn't help notice the disaster that was directly in front of our escape window. The blood from the two bodies stained the road as it baked in the sun. There was busted glass all over the place, and a mangled shopping cart in the street. I didn't want debris lying in the street that could potentially attract attention.

"Hang on I want to get that cart out of sight," I said to Marston

It took a millisecond for me to place the shopping cart on the side of the building where I had put the chair from earlier. I returned to Marston, and before we went inside, we stopped and peered in through the busted window. The sun was lower in the sky now, but still gave us enough light to see the inside was completely trashed.

"Hey, Seamus...do you remember Rachel sliding through here last night?"

"Yeah... where do you think her body went? I bet she turned into a zombie and walked into the bar," I said with a laugh. "Let's go I need a drink!"

CHAPTER 9

Thinking about my gun irritated me, but I knew not having it was for the best. Although the clubs we clutched were barbaric, they were silent killers, and that's exactly what I wanted at the moment.

Broken glass crunched beneath our feet as we walked to the door. I reached out for the handle and gave a tug, and then, finding it unlocked, I held it open like a gentleman and motioned for Marston to go through. He clearly wasn't happy but didn't bitch or moan. I was about three feet behind him when the door swung shut and the bar was cast into darkness. Right away I noticed the smell of stale booze.

"Did you happen to bring a flashlight?" I whispered.

"Yes, I did, actually."

He pulled a little flashlight out of his pocket and turned it on. The first thing he pointed the beam of light at was the shelf behind the bar. I walked noticing the top-shelf liquors were basically untouched, but all of the bottles in the wells had been smashed. I was struggling to walk because broken glass and puddles of booze made the floor sticky under my shoes.

"Those things must have been in here a long time to smash the well bottles like this," Marston said.

"Who cares, those top-shelf bottles are calling my name," I said gleefully.

"Would you shut up! Let's just grab what we came for and leave," Marston replied.

I was walking through broken glass and peering at the shelves when I realized only a few bottles had been removed from the shelf.

I set my pillowcase on the bar and prepared to load it with precious alcohol. I quickly began to load the bottles into my case: Glenlivet, Jack Daniels, Jim Beam, Chivas Regal, Skyy Vodka, Jägermeister Jägermeister, Captain Morgan, Bombay Sapphire, Malibu Rum, and Bacardi 151.

Even though my bag couldn't hold much more, I searched for the one bottle I wanted more than all of the others. My eyes widened when I saw the bottle of Jameson at the end of the bar on the counter. I was amazed it was still there and not destroyed like all of the loose bottles had been. As I put the bottle in my bag I decided I wouldn't be sharing this with the guys.

I was about to heave the pillowcase over my shoulder when Marston yelled from the back of the bar.

"Seamus, come check this out!"

I set the pillowcase down and walked around the corner of the bar into the kitchen. Marston was standing in front of a working cooler full of cold beers.

"Hell yeah! Hand me one of those, I need something to calm my nerves."

"My sack is stuffed," Marston said as he handed me a Guinness.

"Good. Let's get the hell out of here," I said after chugging half the bottle.

"Dude, I just opened this. You dragged me all the way down here, the least you can do, is let me finish my drink," Marston returned.

He lugged his pillowcase out to the bar, set it on top of the counter, grabbed a stool, and had a seat. I didn't hesitate to grab the stool next to him. I reached into my joggers to grab my smokes, and the crusty pockets scratched the top of my hand. Setting my smokes on the bar, I grabbed for my lighter, and Marston grabbed a cigarette before I managed to pull it out.

"Dude, I need some different pants. These pockets just scratched me. How long have these things been laying around up there?" I asked.

"That is a good question I have no answer for; when we're back in the apartment, find something else to wear."

We sat for a few minutes, smoking and drinking.

This is the craziest shit I have ever experienced. I have no idea what is going on two blocks from here let alone the rest of the world. I'm hanging out with a guy I wanted to kill for what he did, but now what he did seems insignificant. What the fuck did I get myself into?

"Alright, let's head back up; it's dark in here and I'm ready to leave," Marston finally said.

I stood up and went to grab my pillowcase. I had to hold the club and the bottom of the case with one hand, and the top of the case with the other. The Santa sack of booze weighed about ten pounds and brought a smile to my face. I walked back around the bar where Marston was waiting for me, and the two of us made our way toward the front door. Marston hunched over as he tried to carry his bag and the club.

"These things aren't even heavy. Do it like this," I said, showing him how I was carrying mine.

As he moved his pillowcase, my nostrils filled with the stink of death.

I glanced at Marston, who didn't seem to have noticed anything. Just as I started to speak, however, he saw my face and knew something wasn't right.

"I've smelled that before; we're about to be in some trouble," I whispered.

"Son of a bitch! We're going to be stuck in here for who knows how long. Let's see how many of them are out there," Marston answered quietly.

We crept to the window to look outside, and the stink was unbearable. Luckily for us, we had the cover of darkness on our side. The sun was disappearing, and we were hidden in the shadows of the bar.

When we poked our heads up to see what was outside, to our horror, we saw what looked like some kind of huge zombie-animal, and I figured it was an overweight rottweiler. It was wandering in the street, and the animal was missing hair randomly throughout its body. In the hairless spots, it was stripped of skin to the muscle. As the creature turned, I saw it had a few massive holes on the side of its body. The holes weren't bloody or dripping, but they appeared to be full of a black substance. I quickly pulled my head back into the bar and crouched on the floor.

"I think it's a bear! Jesus Christ, man, what the fuck is that goddamn thing?" Marston said fearfully.

"Dude, chill out. It's probably a dog that was bitten by one of the zombies. It looks like an overweight rottweiler," I whispered."

I took a chance and decided to look at it again. I wasn't sure what it was, but I was sure I didn't want it anywhere near me. As I watched the thing started walking toward the cart holding Tom's body.

"Seamus, I think we're looking at a werewolf."

"Shut up with that bullshit."

We had to crane our necks, but we were able to watch the creature as it wandered over to the cart. It jumped up and placed its paws on the side as it drooled on Tom's corpse while sniffing at his head.

"Marston, look... it's just a normal dog. It's a dead dog, but definitely a dog."

The dog was now tugging at Tom's hair like it was trying to rip the rest of his head off the body.

Before it could get much further, we heard a shout from upstairs, and I immediately recognized Burto's voice.

"Hey, guys? Are you two down there? Can you hear me? Hello! There's some weird creature out here. If you hear me don't come out yet."

"Why didn't he just keep his mouth shut, and why is he just noticing this thing now? What has he been doing up there this whole time?" I asked.

"Knowing him he's looking at those crusty porno mags again."

We didn't answer; the last thing we needed was unwanted attention. For now, we had to stay in the bar. The ladder would be right outside the door once Burto dropped it, and we could have been back up in seconds.

After sitting for a while longer, Marston suggested we make a break for it, and I agreed. I grabbed my sack of liquid courage and headed for the door.

We exited the bar carefully, and the dog wasn't anywhere in sight. We didn't see where it had gone, but we didn't care, it was gone, and we were happy. Marston set his bag of booze down and headed over to the cart, and I assumed he was getting ready to push.

"Hey, Burto, we're down here. Toss the ladder and the rope down," I called up to the window.

Immediately, the rope and ladder flew out the window almost directly at my face. I had to step back a few feet, tripped, and almost dropped my pillowcase of alcohol.

After regaining myself, I tied the rope around the tightly cinched necks of the sacks. I yanked and pulled, making sure my tie job would hold as the booze went up the wall. I knew Marston and I would have to pull these up because there was no point having Burto do anymore heavy lifting. I ran to Marston, but just as I was about to tell him to hurry, he turned to face me, looking frightened.

"He's starting to twitch; we need to move him *now*."

"Are you sure your mind isn't playing tricks on you?"

"I have no idea, but this is creepy, let's hurry the fuck up."

Without hesitation, we took the cart and started jogging, quickly progressing to a full sprint. Marston let go just as he was about to trip over himself from running too fast, so I let go too. We slowed to a stop and watched as the cart sped down the street.

The cart wobbled so much it was practically bouncing from side to side. Eventually, it bounced back to its right side, running on two wheels for a few seconds, and then crashed on its side far down the street, sending Tom's body flying into the road and smashing into a curb. The cart slid another five feet, and then stopped in the street.

I wanted to spook Marston, so I started running for the ladder. I climbed up as fast as I could, and Marston was right behind me, moving as quickly as I was. As soon as he made it inside, he pulled the ladder up, and then we began pulling the rope and drinks up the wall.

All the alcohol in the bags made hauling them inside a bit troublesome. It took longer to than I expected because we were surprisingly cautious with the fragile bottles. When we finally got the bags inside, I leaned out the window and caught my breath. As soon as I was able to breathe again, I turned from the window to see Burto already making his way through the Malibu Rum. It seemed like he drank half the bottle as I watched, astounded.

"Well, Burto, that's all the liquor you get for today, buddy," I said.

"Fuuckyouuuuuu... whooo, put you in charge any wayyy?" Burto slurred.

"Honestly, I thought you did. I heard you yell that at Marston, so I just assumed I was."

I waited for him to respond, but nothing ever came. As I was looking at him, the bastard closed his eyes and passed out.

I grabbed two candles that were sitting on the floor and lit them. When the room began lighting up, I walked toward Burto to move him farther away from the window, and that's when I realized he'd had way more than Malibu. There were ten cans of PBR and Budweiser behind his chair.

Before I could even make a comment, Marston was yelling.

"Thanks for getting shit-faced while we were out there risking our asses! We weren't doing it so you could sit up here and get drunk! What's your problem?"

I wasn't sure Burto even heard what he'd said, but then he lifted his head and mumbled, "At least you can walk asshole."

Then his chin slumped onto his chest, and he began to snore. I decided to take the nasty shirt off Burto's leg and wrap it with Neosporin, gauze, and an ACE bandage. Burto was passed out dead drunk and didn't twitch a muscle as I worked. The shirt we had used had some crusted blood on it, but nothing fresh. In the candlelight I could see Burto's leg was off-colored.

"This leg is pretty bad, Marston."

"I know. I think I can smell it."

"He needs a doctor."

"Yeah, no shit. If you want to play the hero, be my guest. Go steal and car, lower him out the window, and race him to the hospital."

"With all that shit out there I need to find Megan first. I know it's selfish because I fucked him up, but that's my priority right now."

"You haven't even tried to do that either."

"Yeah, I know. I don't have the protection to do it. I can't go strutting to her grandma's house without several fully loaded weapons."

"Sure, buddy, you keep finding those excuses. I'm not judging."

Marston's comment boiled my blood, but I focused on Burto instead of ripping his throat out. Looking over the wound I saw the stitches were holding, so I put a gob of healing ointment on and smeared it around. I grabbed a few square gauze pads and stuck them to the ointment.

I was unwrapping the ACE bandage when I realized I needed to piss. With Marston standing over me the sounds of him breathing was shooting spikes of hatred up my spine.

"Wrap his fucking leg up. I need to piss."

"Yeah sure, whatever you say."

I went into the bathroom and practiced some deep breathing techniques for about thirty seconds, and when I returned, Marston was done with the leg.

The candle still burned beside Burto. I looked over Marston's work and was impressed. Marston had left the room and grabbed a couple of beers for us. When he returned we popped the tops and started drinking. I could tell by the way he was slamming his beer he didn't have a care in the world. I on the other hand only sipped on mine. The comment he made about me making excuses was really setting in.

CHAPTER 10

After the first couple drinks my noble heart started disappearing, and for the rest of the evening, Marston and I sat around drinking beer and liquor. We talked about the craziness of the world around us as Burto snored in the background. With all the "shopping" we'd done, we now had enough supplies to last a few weeks if we rationed them properly. Eventually we ended up back in the living room where we pulled chairs up to the window and talked about our lives.

Every so often the wind blew the scent of death into our faces. There had to have been hundreds of rotting corpses out there to cause that kind of stink, but luckily, the wind quickly faded, and the stench died off. The two of us caught up in front of the window as Burto snored.

"Yeah, Megan and I have been doing real well. After that shit you pulled, we went out to Vegas for a few shows on the strip."

"Why do you have to bring the past up right now? Couldn't you just tell me about the Vegas trip?"

"You sure do have a set of balls on you. Burto told me about how you moved in and fucked him over after you got back. How the fuck do you sleep at night?"

"That was all the past, brotha. Let's focus on the present."

The fucker sounds like Charles Mason.

"You're lucky this shit is happening, or we *would* be focused on the past."

"Well, since I got back from North Carolina, I haven't done much. I looked for work, but all the places wanted me to cut my hair and clean up my image. I wasn't going to do that so..."

In the middle of Marston's bullshit conversation Burto spoke out of the darkness.

"I could beat your ass for what you pulled on me."

We sat quietly, waiting for another comment, but nothing came.

"Anyway, I wasn't changing my image for no job, man," Marston continued.

"You are a piece of work, buddy," I said, shaking my head.

"You're too negative, Seamus. You have to let go of the past so your heart can heal."

"Fuck this. I'm going to find another candle; this one's almost finished. Where are the flashlights?"

"I think they're in the kitchen."

I went into the kitchen with my lighter in hand, burning my thumb with every step. I hadn't found a candle or a flashlight when Marston whispered loudly from the living room: "Seamus, forget the candle! You've got to see this!"

I turned quickly and stubbed my toe on the bottom corner of the door casing. I hopped back, shouting obscenities.

"Seamus, come look at this shit!" Marston repeated.

I shot Marston a nasty scowl, but he didn't see it because he had blown out the candle and turned back to face the window.

"What the hell do you want me to look at, another zombie?"

Marston hushed me. I was standing in the dark behind Marston when something hit my right leg. I freaked out and jumped toward the wall to my left. Before I had even processed that Burto had woken up, Marston reached around and swatted at him to stop moving. When he had, he'd hit Burto in his injured leg, but to my surprise, Burto didn't yell as loud or as much as I thought he would. Instead, he clenched his jaw and breathed hard through his teeth.

When I finally looked out the window, I saw what held Marston's attention. Coming from the public square about a block away was a massive parade of the undead. From the looks of the group, I guessed at least four hundred were walking toward us. There were so many, and if they knew where we were, they could easily come crashing through our barricade, and tear us to pieces. The hairs on my neck stood on end, and I felt an overwhelming sense of fear shoot through my body. There was nothing we could do but to wait to see if they were coming for us.

Soon, the aroma of hundreds of dead bodies reached my nose, so I left the window and went to the bathroom. There was no window in there, so I took out my lighter and lit it up. I found some Vicks Vapor Rub and slapped a big glob right under my nostrils, then took the container with me when I went back. I dropped to my hands and knees as I approached the window, then handed the Vicks to Marston.

He unscrewed the cap and smeared a bunch under his nostrils, and then gave it to Burto who actually put it up his nose. The whole time they were preparing, the army of the undead got closer.

Then, Burto nudged me. "Hey, do you hear that?"

"Hear what?" I asked.

"Just listen."

I gave it thirty seconds, and was just about to give up, but then I heard a strange noise. The sounds of the marching parade of zombies were incredibly loud, but over the moans and groans, I heard what sounded like a person yelling through a bullhorn.

"Did you catch it that time?" Burto asked.

"Yeah, what the hell was it?" I said.

"I have no idea, but I don't like the sound of it," Burto replied.

As we all sat listening for more strange sounds, the parade was almost on top of us. The moans sent shivers down my spine, and the wretched odor coming through the ointment made me want to puke. I dry heaved a few times, and just when the Jameson was about to come up, I got a hold of myself.

The first few lines of the army started to make their way past the window, and then I definitely heard someone speaking through a bullhorn.

"Move faster, you worthless sacks of shit!"

"What the hell is going on?" Burto asked, sounding nervous.

"How the fuck should we know? We're all up here staring just like you. I gotta take a piss," Marston replied.

Marston turned and began to crawl toward the door as the rest of the army passed by the window. The smell was so bad even with the Vicks, Burto and I still ended up puking all over the floor. Luckily, nothing below seemed to notice us. They were loud enough to cover any sounds we made, and the stench was so unbearable our eyes watered. When my vision cleared, I saw something behind the group.

Three living people were walking behind the parade of rotting bodies, and from what I saw in the darkness, they all had bullhorns in their left hand. Unfortunately, it was too dark to tell who they were or what they were doing following the zombies. The creatures were walking in formation and even seemed to be listening to the bullhorns.

As the tail end of the parade passed underneath our peering eyes, I could make out the three people with the bullhorns snickering back and forth. As they passed, I started asking myself questions.

Are those three somehow controlling the beasts?

"Seamus, who are you talking to?" Burto asked.

"Nobody, I was just thinking out loud."

We waited in front of the window for a few more minutes while the dead army made its way up State Street. When they finally disappeared from sight, Burto and I decided to move. My legs had cramped from sitting on the floor for so long, and when I stood up, the combination of booze and stiffness almost knocked me over. I relit the candle and followed Burto out of the room into the dining room. That's when Marston came out of the kitchen and started talking to us.

"You guys are pretty funny," he slurred.

"What are you talking about?" Burto asked.

"It's like the blind leading the blind with you two morons."

"What the fuck are you talking about?" I asked.

"Do you know why people like you two get taken advantage of? It's because you types are such easy targets," Marston said, drunkenly laughing.

"You'd better simmer down there, tough guy," I said.

"Oh here we go, big bad Seamus threatening me again. You're a fucking joke, man. You act high and mighty, but you're just a pathetic piece a trash. I'm glad I fucked you guys over down there. You fucking deserve it."

At this point I casually handed Burto the candle and moved his chair out of the way. I turned to face Marston who had a smirk on his face and went to speak.

"So you think--"

"Fuck you!"

I saw red and lunged at him. I gave him a right hook to his jaw, and he collapsed to the ground. After that, I was on him and slammed his face into the wood floor. Instead of continuing to beat him I straddled his back and twisted his right arm behind his back like a cop.

"Get the fuck off me!"

"You kind of did this to yourself there, pal."

"Fuck you and the high horse you rode in on."

That was when I slammed his face into the wooden floor one last time, knocking him unconscious.

I stood up and looked at Burto who didn't look surprised at what happened.

"What the fuck is his problem?" I asked.

"He's fucking wasted. He used to do this shit to me before I moved out. He's a verbally abusive drunk, and it looks like he finally got what he had coming."

"I'm going to tie him up. I'm not dealing with this fucking idiot for the rest of the night."

I went into the living room and grabbed the rope we had used to haul up the supplies and returned to the dining room. I tied his hands and ankles together behind his back and dragged him into the room across from the bathroom.

"I think he needs time to sleep," I said.

After Marston had been dealt with, I decided to have a look at Burto's leg. I had Burto hold the flashlight as I un-wrapped the ACE bandage and moved the gauze. A small amount of blood leaked through the gauze and the wrap, but the stitches were still intact. As I was looking at the wound, I saw Burto's leg was still very off color. I figured it was completely bruised from the car door, so I re-wrapped it thinking nothing else about it. After I re-wrapped the wound, Burto and I had a couple of beers while we sat in the living room, looking out the window. The moonlight cast enough light on the street for us to see there was nothing outside.

"Man, Seamus, you slammed his face pretty hard...you think that was necessary?"

"I should go do it a few more times! After all the shit that guy has done to everyone throughout his miserable life! I honestly feel he deserves an ass beating so severe he's in a wheelchair forever. All the shit that lowlife has pulled. He fucked my brother, Megan, me, and even you. That's just to name a very close few off the top of my head. Imagine how many other people he has fucked over. Man, he's lucky I didn't fucking kill him!"

"Yeah, I guess."

We returned our drunken gaze to the dreary city below. We didn't see anything interesting for a while, but then, suddenly, the lights in the retirement home across the street came on. Seeing this caused Burto and me to jump in panic. I had seen some places with electricity, but with all these lights coming on now shocked us both.

Then some streetlights began to flicker to life. Then the stoplight next to the apartment came on and started to flash yellow.

"What's going on out there?" Burto asked, then suddenly continued, "My god, did you hear that?"

"I didn't hear anything," I said distractedly, watching the lights. Then off in the distance, I heard a scream.

"What the hell was that?" I asked.

"I told you I heard something," Burto stated.

"Man, what is going on out there? Look, more lights are coming on. They must be fixing the grids."

That's when I heard the screaming again.

"Shit, Seamus, that sounded a lot closer than before," Burto said.

"Yeah, it did... where, or *what*, do you think it came from?" I asked.

"I can't tell. Its close, though, whatever it is. Do you think they need help?"

"I think if someone is screaming *yes,* they probably need help, Burto."

"Do you think we should try to help?" Burto pressed.

"Well, if we try to signal them, we might attract a mob of monsters. I'm thinking who or whatever it is might be fucked! We should have another drink and put it out of our minds."

Burto wheeled off, mumbling obscenities under his breath. I kept watching the town that had gone from entirely dead to lit up in a matter of minutes.

The screams continued, and then everything was silent. I focused on listening as intently as I could and heard the moans and groans of zombies in the streets outside the apartment. This meant even though the army had passed I was still surrounded by monsters, and this fact scared me.

A lighter flicked behind me, and I turned to see Burto holding a bottle of 151 Bacardi with part of a sheet hanging out of it. Before I could say anything, the son of a bitch lit the fuse and threw the bottle past my face out the window. It landed in the center of the street, and flames shot everywhere creating a massive burst of fire right in front of our apartment.

"Burto, what the fuck are you doing?!"

"Fuck you, Seamus! I'm sick of you being an asshole!"

"Look, fuck-face, we don't have enough food for the entire town! Besides, the person stopped screaming right after you left, so I'm guessing they're no longer with us."

"I don't care; you're still an asshole."

"You're just fucking drunk! Look at that fire, you goddamn idiot! Those things are right down the street, and now, thanks to you, they're going to be coming after us."

"We'll be fine," Burto slurred.

The fire had already burned almost entirely out, but I could already hear the bastards coming. Thankfully the only light from below now came from the streetlights. I was insanely pissed off at this point. If the guys who were marching the creatures before were walking by, or watching, they would have busted us for sure.

"I still can't believe you did that," I said, pissed off.

"Stop being a bitch!"

"You might want to reconsider talking to me like that," I snapped.

Burto turned his wheelchair around and headed in the direction of the bathroom. I watched him momentarily, and then turned to look at the smoldering remains of his signal fire. The moans and groans were getting closer, and the stink was growing fouler by the second. I knew they were close, so I poked my head out the window and looked toward the square.

"Son of a bitch," I said. No fewer than thirty zombies were staggering for the spot Burto had thrown his little firebomb. I sat in the dark, counting as many heads as I could, and got to twenty-three before I lost count. With the streetlights on, I could see the creatures much better than the night before.

Their bodies were mangled, and strips of decayed skin clung in random spots throughout them. Their clothes were all gone, except for the collars of the shirts dangling around most of their necks. There were holes, tears, and bodily fluids all over them, and sometimes pieces or chunks of flesh would fall to the ground as I watched. They moved about with no actual plan, and they were just starting to disperse when I heard Marston's voice from behind me.

"Crazy shit, isn't it? I used to know some of them."

"How the hell did you get out?" I cried, jumping to my feet.

"The drunkard came in and untied me while mumbling about you being a prick. He passed out in his chair and here I am. I ought to beat you for smashing my face the way you did, you cocksucker!"

"Dude, you're lucky I didn't throw you out the fucking window!"

"Look, I'm sorry. I had way too much booze for dinner, and you know I can't handle drinking. I don't know what came over me; again, man, I'm sorry."

"I have always known that... but now it's time to grow up. Look down there. Do you realize what's going on here? Do you want to be turned into one of those fucking things? I need you to keep a cool head. I mean, I have Burto, but he's pretty useless. Let me make this very clear: if you start running your mouth again, you're going to catch another beating, and I can't promise that one won't be a hundred times worse. Do you understand?"

"Dude, that's rough, don't you think?"

"Hell yeah, it's rough, and I mean every fucking word!"

"Alright, calm down. I'll try to keep the drinks to a minimum."

"Good."

Do you want so coffee?" Marston asked.

"Yeah, sure, why not? I'm sick of this smell."

I followed him toward the kitchen, and as we exited the double doors of the living room, a window downstairs smashed. I jumped, but Marston kept walking.

"They must have gotten into the pizza shop."

We entered the kitchen, and Marston pointed to me. "Have a seat, I'm going to warm up some coffee."

CHAPTER 11

As we sat in the kitchen, I felt my irritation levels begin decreasing. I knew Marston had acted a fool, but he was a sloppy drunk. We had been chatting for a while, and I hadn't heard Burto the whole time.

"Hey, man, why don't you go check on Burto?" I said.

Marston eyeballed me for a moment, then wandered off to the other room. I stared into the bottom of my coffee cup and pondered the things that were going to happen over the next few days. I figured we were probably drinking way too much, but hey, we were alcoholics.

My blood pressure had dropped, and I was finally feeling somewhat normal when lights in the living room, dining room, and bathroom came on. From the dining room Marston yelped, "Turn the lights off, Seamus! Our cover will be blown if they spot us in here!"

After his wise words he dropped to the floor and began to commando crawl.

I dropped the coffee cup to the ground, stood up, and jogged off. I went to the bathroom and flipped the switch off and returned to the dining room but had no clue where the switch was for the overhead light.

"Where are the switches?" I yelled to Marston.

"In the normal places where else?... go into the living room and throw the main breaker."

I ran through the double doors of the living room and began looking around for the breaker box. It was on my right, so I yanked the door open and turned the main breaker off. Except for the candlelight in the kitchen, the apartment was back to black.

Relieved, I wiped my forehead with the back of my hand, turned to leave, and tripped. I fell to the ground with a thud and smashed the hell out of my funny bone. Turns out, Marston had commando crawled into the room and was cowered behind me. Shaking my head and lying on my back I asked, "Marston...what the hell are you doing?"

I was getting back to my feet when he spoke up.

"The lights scared me...I stayed near you for safety."

I started to chuckle and then asked, "Where is Burto?"

"He passed out in the room you put me in after you tied me up."

I got to my feet and walked to the window, wondering if anything was outside or coming our way. Marston had no intention of getting off the ground, and as I got closer to the window, a breeze blew up, and an appalling stink entered the room.

A lot more lights were on outside. The bowling alley up the street was lit up, and so was the gas station to the right of the apartment. All the streetlights that hadn't turned on before had now come to life. The street below was crawling with a dozen or so zombies staggering aimlessly. The lights from outside lit the room enough we could be spotted if someone or something looked our way. I crouched down next to the sill and peered down into the streets. Some monsters were looking up toward the window, and I wasn't sure if they could see me, but I didn't move a muscle. I figured if they *had* spotted me, moving would cause them to start gathering outside and eventually enter the building. Marston began to talk, but I hushed him quickly.

"Stay on the ground."

Three of the zombies were now looking in our direction, so I waited them out. They stared up for a minute before they got bored and wandered off. I lowered myself from sight and crawled back to Marston.

"Let's head back to the kitchen," I said.

He nodded, and we both began to crawl over that way. I stood up in the dining room and walked the rest of the way, but Marston crawled the whole way back. When I got into the kitchen, I grabbed a chair and waited for him. He was just about to grab the other chair when we heard a loud *thud* behind the barricade.

We stared at each other, utterly speechless. Something was investigating our door. I looked over to Marston, who looked completely terrified. I put my index finger over my mouth and hushed him. Then another thud came from the door. I bent over, put my lips to his ear and whispered, "Keep quiet and walk toward the living room."

As we turned to walk, I remembered the living room was lit up from the streetlights, so I tapped his shoulder and pointed at the ground. We both got back on our hands and knees and began to crawl again. I was so nervous, and my heart was beating so fast I thought it was going to explode.

We crawled to the living room, hoping the zombies out front would have already left, but to our dismay, we could hear shuffling noises outside as soon as we entered.

"It sounds like it's only one of them near the barricade. If we don't make noise, the thing should go away."

"When we built that barricade, a bunch of them were in the hallway, and it took hours for them to leave, right?" Marston asked.

"I hope the thing gets distracted and wanders off soon. I hate that there's even one out there. It seems strange that one would stumble to the door for no reason, but if that's the case, how has it been so quiet?"

The thumps lasted fifteen minutes, and the noises from outside got quieter, but we stayed where we were. My ass was starting to go numb, and I thought about getting up when we heard a series of thuds and tumbles from the kitchen. This startled me and Marston damn near jumped to the ceiling. Without even moving my head I said, "Guess that zombie fell down the stairs."

"let's fucking hope. I don't think my heart can handle another scare like that."

Listening to the moans downstairs I looked over at Marston and winced. With the streetlights I could see his nose was crooked, and a couple of his front teeth had been chipped and broken. The swelling around his mouth was pretty bad. Blood from his nostrils had run down to his chin, dyeing his once-blond beard red. Seeing the destruction I had caused made me weary of what he might do to me when I slept. I knew he was a coward and cowards always pull shady moves.

Eventually Marston pointed out that we had sat there for a long time and heard nothing. I crawled over to the window and rested my chin on the sill. Doing this gave me enough headroom to look at the street below. Marston joined me, and just as he did, the door at the entrance to the apartment building shot open with a crash. A zombie stumbled out onto the sidewalk, and then fell over the curb and into the street. We both knelt and watched as it wandered down the road toward the square. Aside from the lone zombie, however, nothing else was moving along either side of the street. Suddenly, I had an idea. I turned, sat down, and began speaking.

"Alright, I've been watching, and I've noticed a lot of the zombies seem to come out during the evening. If that's the case, maybe we should venture out in the afternoon."

"What do you mean?" Marston asked.

"Well, first, I think we should hide the hooch from Burto. I don't want him getting blasted and passing out while we're out in the streets. Second, we're going to need an arsenal, not just spiked clubs. There's a gun shop up past the park on Gifford Street, right behind Stewart's ice cream shop. We can take the pillowcases to the gun shop, fill them with guns and ammo, and then come back here. I have an idea, but I haven't figured out all the details."

"Don't think you're going to be pulling that shit with me. It's fine to leave Burto in the dark, but not me, you got it?" Marston stammered.

"I'm not leaving anyone in the dark. If he wasn't passed out, I'd tell him too. Anyway, this idea's not set in stone, just so you know. After we get back to the apartment with the guns, I want to go off on my own to follow a group of zombies. After seeing that army I am really curious about who is behind this and what the fuck is really happening. Once we have an idea what we're up against, other than the zombies, we can plan an escape. I think doing some recon on the surrounding area would be wise. We should have an idea how bad the streets are for the route we take. Well... what do you think?"

"I don't like hearing the word 'we.' Why can't you go get the guns on your own too?"

My blood began to boil, but I bit my tongue and answered calmly.

"Look, we're a team, and each of our roles is important. You've heard the plan and how it's going to go down. At least you don't have to go with me when I try to find out where they go. You should be grateful."

"I am. Believe you me!"

"I'm going to go pass out. I'm exhausted."

I turned to walk away when Marston piped up again.

"Why don't we go up to the mall? After we have the guns, we can go grab new clothes and all sorts of other cool stuff."

"I don't think it's a great idea. People used to flock to the mall, and now that they're dead, there are probably dozens or even hundreds of zombies walking around that place. Plus, it's more than three miles from here. This town almost sucked the life out of me once, and I'm not going to let that happen again."

"Why is it we can't try to do everything on the same day? Like get the guns, find Megan, and get the fuck out of here," Marston asked.

"I don't like drawing more attention than we need. The shit that's happened right in front of this place hasn't brought anyone snooping, and I want to keep it that way. We've gotten lucky with Burto's signal fire, the dead girl, and of course, the guy you shot not drawing much attention. I figure we have enough food for a few weeks, and if we stretch our sneaking out, it won't look as suspicious."

"What do you mean?"

"Well, it seems humans are controlling these things, right? If the humans find out we're trying to escape, we're more than likely going to be killed. If we pace ourselves and stay out of the eyes of anything that moves, we should be alright. I bet nothing outside this apartment knows about us. Well, except for Gus, and who knows if he's even still alive. I heard screams earlier, and that might have been him."

"Dude, what about Megan? You gave me a ration of shit because I didn't help my girl, and you don't even know where yours is," Marston said.

"I know, I know. I have to find her. Depending on how long it takes to get the guns maybe we can go to her grandma's house?"

"You are out of your mind! I don't want to go to her grandma's! That's as far as the mall from here," Marston whined.

"It doesn't matter, we'll figure this shit out tomorrow. I need some fucking sleep!"

"Alright. Where's the aspirin? I think my swelling will go down if I take some before bed."

"In the kitchen on the counter. I'll see you in the morning."

"Goodnight," Marston said as I walked away.

After he left the room I closed and locked the double doors. I went over to the window and looked out: the streets were quiet now, and the humming of the streetlights was the only noise I could hear. The foul odor from outside had faded, and the glow of the streetlights made the room bright. I walked over to a pile of clothes and scooted them into the darkest corner of the room. I lay on them and slid down so my head rested on the pile like a pillow. I wanted to pull something over my eyes to block the light, but the smell of old mildew mixed with vomit wasn't inviting me to do so. I passed out as soon as I closed my eyes.

I dreamed I was putting the finishing touches on the house I was building. Pounding deck nails with a hammer that looked oddly oversized, and when I stood up to admire my handiwork, the pounding sound didn't stop. I searched all over to see if I could locate where the sound was coming from, but I couldn't figure it out.

I awoke in a panic, jumping to my feet. Still basically unconscious, I thought there were zombies slamming on the barricaded door.

I ran to the double doors, unlocked them, and ran through the dining room and into the kitchen. Marston and Burto sat there as I stood in front of them completely naked.

I listened for the door; I soon realized it was my head that was doing the pounding from all the booze the night before. I rubbed my eyes as Marston spoke up.

"What are you doing? Go put some fucking clothes on!"

"I heard pounding and thought those things had found us. I realized the pounding was from my hangover. Three days of heavy drinking and little to no food will do that I guess," I said with a laugh.

"Well, Seamus, the zombies have not found us, so go put some damn clothes on," Burto said.

"And hurry up, I'm going to need some help with Burto's bandages. His wound bled a bit through the night," Marston added.

"Probably from all the drinks he had," I said.

"It was definitely the drinks. I've lost a lot of blood; my head hurts, and I feel weak and woozy. Fuck, I might even puke."

"How did you think you would feel? Did you think consuming a ton of alcohol with a wound like that would make you feel great?" I asked.

"The drinks were the only thing taking the pain away."

"You could have really messed yourself up. Alcohol thins the blood you know."

Burto was annoying me, so I turned and walked back to the living room where my clothes were. I had run out of the room so fast I didn't realize how beautiful it was outside. I figured I had gotten hot when the sun came up and taken my clothes off while I slept. I'd had evenings in the past where I woke up naked the next day without a clue as to why, so it getting hot was probably the issue. It was another gorgeous day in Watertown. There were still no birds chirping or any sounds of actual life, but the weather was perfect for a short hike to our local gun shop.

I grabbed the boxers I had been wearing, turned them inside out, and put them on. I pulled them up and the fabric had crusted enough to scratch my legs, and I started to sweat immediately after I pulled them over my ass. I picked up the short pants I'd been wearing and put them back on. After, I pulled my shoes on without putting my crunchy socks back on. I was looking for my shirt when I happened to spot an old black T-shirt. Picking it up it had a musty odor, but it was better than my other option, so I put it on.

As I was about to leave the room, I saw a pair of black dress socks lying on the floor across the room near the wall. The tops were rolled together, leading me to believe they were clean, so I picked them up, and to my surprise, they were not disgusting. They were soft and didn't emit a foul or unpleasant odor. I sat on top of the clothes, took my shoes off, and put the socks on. Now that I was dressed, I stood up and headed for the kitchen.

As I walked back through the double doors into the dining room, I could see Burto in the kitchen drinking a can of Budweiser, and Marston nearby smoking a cigarette.

"Burto, what the hell is the matter with you? After all that shit you just told me, you're drinking another beer?" I asked.

"I need the hair of the dog with this one. Wow, my head feels like its floating--oh, and my leg hurts too, so I figured a couple a beers would help."

"Do you always drink this goddamn much?"

"Well, no, but I've really went off the deep end these last few days."

"Drink some water and take some aspirin for Christ's sake," I added.

Shaking my head, I walked over to the coffee pot, grabbed a mug, and poured myself a cup. I grabbed a bottle of aspirin off the counter and tossed it at Burto. I felt my stomach rumble and realized I desperately needed some food in my belly. I turned to the counter and grabbed a can of Campbell's chicken noodle soup and a spoon from the nearby sink. I pulled the top off the soup and started eating the contents without heating or diluting the contents of the can with water.

"Dude, you're going to have a fucking stroke eating that shit like that!" Marston said.

I took a seat across from Marston next to Burto. The three of us were sitting spaced apart in the kitchen where the table should have been. I set my coffee near my ankle and sat back up. I tilted the can up and started drinking the soup. After drinking more than half the can I set it on the floor and picked up and sipped my coffee.

"It sure would be nice if we had a table."

"I think it looks better blocking that door," Marston said.

"I'll take this mild inconvenience over a busted-down door any day. So, Burto, let me fill you in on this plan I have," I said, looking at Burto.

It only took me a few seconds to realize there was something off with Burto. I tried writing it off, but he looked too pale and shaky.

"Hey, Burto, are you alright? You look like shit!"

"No man. I feel a bit light-headed; my stomach feels like it is digesting a rock, and I'm pretty tired," Burto said with a raspy voice.

"We better have a look at that leg," Marston said.

I looked up at Marston. He had cleaned the blood off the lower part of his face but still had a good bit of swelling.

Burto closed his eyes and tilted his head back as Marston and I stood up. Marston stood behind the chair holding the handles as I knelt and had a look. I took Burto's leg and began un-wrapping the Ace bandage and gauze pads. I made sure to be as gentle as I could as I was uncovering the mess.

The smell caught me off guard, so I leaned back to breathe fresh air while Marston propped himself on the back of the wheelchair. I got a look at Marston's face when he caught a whiff, and right then I knew Burto was in serious trouble.

I continued to loosen the bandage from the wound until the entire thing was off. With Burto's leg unveiled, I couldn't believe what I was looking at. Marston, the dumb asshole, had wrapped Burto's leg too tightly. Because the leg had very little blood flow, it had started to rot off his body.

"Holy shit, look at my fucking leg!" Burto screamed.

"Burto, we both saw him doing it. The wrap job looked pretty damn good. It could be a very serious infection," I said.

"I thought if I wrapped it tighter, it would heal faster, and the blood wouldn't seep through as much," Marston chimed in.

"Why would it be an infection?" Burto asked.

"Well we haven't exactly cleaned the wound at all, and you've been pounding drinks like you're at a high-school keg party," Marston replied.

"Marston's right, Burto, those drinks are doing you no good. There was one more thing that *might* be causing this infection."

"What the hell is that?" Burto said angered.

"Marston why don't you take this one."

Marston looked at me and rolled his eyes before speaking.

"Burto we might have fucked up your leg, buddy. We don't have any supplies in here for a wound like yours, so we improvised."

"Asshole, what do you mean improvised?"

"We sewed your leg up with a fishing hook and fishing string. The hooked looked newer, and we tried disinfecting it as well."

"Marston, that cloth we used was far from sanitary," I added.

"So, my leg's about to fall off because you two incompetent fucks half-assed my stitch job, and then wrapped it too tight?" Burto shouted.

"We didn't have a lot of options, Burto; it was either that or you could have bled to death," I said.

Burto wheeled his chair backward into Marston's shins, and then tossed his beer over his shoulder onto him. I stood up and got out of the way.

"You are such a piece of shit!" Burto yelled at Marston.

"Hey, Seamus is the one who did that shit in the first place."

"Would you two keep it down? We've got a big day, and we don't need things showing up before we even get out of the apartment."

"What do you mean big day?" Burto asked.

"Well, after you passed out last night I kind of came up with a plan."

"Well let's fucking hear it! I need to get to a doctor before this leg kills me."

For the next few minutes I ran the plan over with Burto. He seemed to calm down as I explained to him we were now going to be planning an actual escape.

"Well, what do you think, Burto?"

"It sounds like it could work. Let's get this thing going. I want this leg looked at by a professional."

"Let me have another look," I said.

I knelt down for a better look. The stitches were still holding, and some of the skin even looked like it was fusing back together, but I could see some pus seeping out. The muscle Marston had pushed back in was a visible bulge behind his sealing skin, and the area was warm to the touch, so I knew he was in serious trouble. At that moment I didn't want to instill more fear into Burto, so I downplayed his situation.

"Bro, you're going to need a cane when this is over. On a lighter note, leave the wound exposed to air and it should heal faster. Your blood needs to start circulating again, and when it does, it should heal. Leave it alone for a few days; the color will return, and the throbbing should go away within a few hours," I explained.

After my little doctor bit, the three of us stood there silently.

"Alright, Burto, this is your only task. There are a lot of beers in the fridge, and you're not to drink any of them. This includes the liquor. We need you to have a sharp eye and wait for our return. If you fuck this up... and this is no joke, I will blow your fucking head off when I see you again. This is very important. Our lives are in your hands."

"I can't believe you think I'd dick you guys over like that. Christ, man, you didn't have to threaten me."

"Not intentionally, but, dude, you've been drinking way too much. I mean we've all been putting 'em back, but you've taking it to a level I'm not comfortable with," I said.

"I will stay sober as long as it takes. Do me a favor and watch each other's backs out there."

Jesus, I hope he stays fucking sober.

Marston had grabbed the spiked clubs and the other table legs without the nails and walked out of the room.

"Where are you going?" I asked shaking my head irritated.

"I've heard this part. I'm going to toss the pillowcases and weapons out the window."

I left Burto in the kitchen and met Marston in the living room.

"Well, you look eager," I said.

"Yeah, I'm as ready as I'll ever be. I want this trip over with."

"Do you think we should bring the shotgun?" I asked.

"Well yeah, but considering those things flock to gunfire, maybe we should leave it here with Burto."

"I really don't think that's a great idea."

"Man, it would be a lot better to do it silently. We haven't got a plan for escaping, and if those men find us, we have nowhere to go. I think the gun will get us killed in some way."

"Alright, if you say so. Let's hit the road."

This is going to be an interesting day.

I looked down to where Marston had tossed the supplies, noting that our clubs had landed near the cases. I turned to look at Marston, who gave me a nod, and then I instructed Burto to get ready.

Marston picked the ladder up and threw it out the window. I still didn't completely trust Marston, so I motioned for him to go first. He climbed down the ladder and immediately picked up one of the spiked clubs. I turned to Burto, shook his hand, and then headed out myself. I had barely stepped one foot on the ground before Burto yanked the ladder up into the window.

I glanced at Marston, who stood near all our gear. I walked to him, and he handed me a case, and then handed me my clubs. I placed my non-spiked club into my case as we walked past the entrance to the apartments, and I stopped in the piles of glass on the sidewalk from the pizza shop windows. I looked inside to see the place trashed, tables tipped over, cash register on the ground, and pizza boxes everywhere. I shook my head and said, "Let's get a move on."

CHAPTER 12

Marston followed my lead and placed the club without nails into his bag.

"Do you think the spiked clubs would be safer in the bag?"

"Hell no. If something runs up on me, I want the puncture power over a dull thud. Besides, the nails will poke through and stab your hip."

We didn't talk much because we were focused on moving fast. Still, when we walked past the building the zombie fell down the stairs, I snickered. Seconds after, we were passing the grocery store at a jogging pace.

Eventually I slowed down so I could catch my breath, and Marston was right on my heels.

"This time we've got a lot farther to go, so be ready for anything. We're going to be walking by the bar you said you were scared of...right?"

"First of all, I didn't say I was afraid of the bar, and second, this heat is too fucking much!"

"Welcome to July, buddy. You said this bar is up near the park, right?"

"Yeah, a half a mile up the road on the left. After we hit the gun shop, we can stop in for a drink and catch up," Marston suggested.

"At least you still got your humor. Just remember, keep a cool head, follow my lead, and if anything happens, we run and hide until everything blows over."

Marston listened, and as we walked by the Jet Gas station, crashing sounds came from inside the store. We started to run, and I wasn't sure if we made it past without whatever was causing the noise seeing us, but now wasn't the time to worry about one zombie.

I looked behind me to watch the front door of the gas station. To my relief, nothing was coming out. We slowed again but kept haste in our step as we walked across the Central and State Street intersection. I looked to my left down Central Street and noticed three zombies stumbling toward a mound in the street. The stink was ungodly even though the monsters were at least two hundred yards away from us. I tapped Marston on the shoulder and pointed. Luckily, the creatures were obsessed with whatever was lying in the street and didn't notice Marston and me.

"I thought I would be used to the smell by now," I said.

"I don't think I'll ever be used to it."

We kept walking up State Street through the intersection until the zombies were out of sight, then slowed some more. We'd had no encounters for a while. And this was just fine by us. We had a long walk ahead of us and the heat was making the journey even harder.

"Did you bring any water?" I asked.

"No, I thought you grabbed some."

"Fuck, this is going to be rough without it."

"We should be fine. The gun shop's only a couple miles."

"I hope you're right," I finished.

The houses all looked normal as we went on; in fact, nothing was out of place. The power lines were still up, and this whole block looked untouched by the devastation that was all around us back at the apartment. We kept going up State Street, our heads constantly moving back and forth, looking for anything out of the ordinary. The sounds of our feet were all we could hear. We were sweating profusely, and I felt like I had already lost a few pounds.

As we started up the hill shortly after the intersection, I heard something I hadn't heard in days: a vehicle's engine.

I stopped moving, and Marston did the same.

"Do you hear that?" I asked.

The noise was constant and getting louder.

"Yeah...I do hear it."

We listened as the noise grew louder and louder. I realized in an instant whatever was coming wasn't good, and we needed to hide. I looked across the street to see a four-foot hedgerow and decided hiding behind them was the only option.

"I'm hiding behind those bushes over there, you can do whatever you want," I said, pointing.

"I might try to flag them down," Marston said jokingly.

I was too worried to realize he was joking at the time.

"You're out of your fucking mind! What is wrong with you? If you do they'll more than likely kill us both, but not before they torture us for information. Think about how stupid that is for a second. Burto told me about the men during the evacuation, and they didn't sound friendly. I highly doubt that sounds like anyone we want to talk to. I'm fucking hiding."

I sprinted across the street, remembering to toss my club before I leaped into the air and dived face-first over the bush. The club fell a few feet in front of me as I slammed into the ground. Through my deafening heartbeats, I could hear the vehicle's engine roar as it got closer. I turned to face the road and crawled virtually into the bush. I made a peephole in the hedge with my hand and began to lookout. Marston was nowhere to be seen, and the noise was pretty much on top of me. Whatever was coming sounded enormous.

Suddenly, Marston came crashing through the top of the bush. Apparently, he hadn't gotten enough speed or height, because he was now stuck in the hedge. I stood up and yanked him by his shoulders through the rest of the vegetation.

His face was scratched and swollen, his cheeks were bleeding, and he had sticks and leaves in his hair and beard. I couldn't help laughing.

"It's not funny, dick, the hedge ripped my shit up!" Marston whimpered.

Before I could respond, the noise suddenly stopped. We were silent, hardly breathing as we waited. After several minutes, the engine started again.

A small dump truck with a plow attached to the front tore past us without even tapping the brakes. I figured the plow was for pushing cars and other random debris out of the roads around town. State Street up to this point had been cleared very well and was a highly used road. Considering the other streets I had seen in the area, this made me ask myself why State Street was so important. As the truck sped down the street I glanced up and noticed the tailgate was gone, and the bed was full of dead bodies. I only caught a glimpse as the truck rushed past, but some of the bodies looked like they hadn't been infected. A truck full of bodies was a big deal and put fear into my soul.

After the truck passed, it went down the hill we were about to walk up and back in the direction we had just come from.

"Did you see that?"

I looked at Marston, who had buried his face in the ground like he was trying to crawl under it. I tapped him and repeated my question.

He picked his face out of the dirt, looked at me, and began brushing the dirt from his face.

"Do you think I saw anything? I figured if I can see them, they can see me, and I didn't like that!"

"Well, I saw them, and they didn't acknowledge my existence, so I think we're safe. Anyway, the point is, that truck was full of fresh dead bodies," I said.

"What are you talking about?"

"Shit loads of bodies were piled on top of each other in the back of the truck. They weren't rotted and were still wearing clean clothes. Imagine if you had tried to flag them down. You very well would have ended up in the back," I said with a chuckle.

Marston brushed off my comment and then asked, "Did you look at the driver?"

"Hell no, the tint was too dark, and they went by so fast I couldn't make anything out."

Just then, the stench hit me, and I puked into the bushes. Marston pulled his shirt up over his face after I started to puke, but it was too late; he began to throw up inside his shirt all over his sweaty stomach. Thanks to the foul smell in the air, the food and coffee we had consumed that morning was all gone. We both stood up, wiping our mouths off.

"Are you going to take that shirt off?" I asked.

"Nah--I don't want to get a sun burn."

"You are one nasty dude. You know, Marston, that truck could have been a good sign."

"How do you figure?"

"I don't know for sure, but since they were coming from the direction we're going, maybe there aren't any zombies over the crest of this hill."

"I hope you're right... I don't want to run into anymore fucking zombies!"

With the sound of the truck gone and the smell blowing away, we started our journey again, walking around the hedge and back onto the sidewalk.

"Seamus, let's cut through the backyards of these houses. It will keep us off the roads and out of view of anymore of those trucks."

"I think that's a bad idea. The road is cleared of cars, and we have no idea what's behind these places. Besides, those trucks are loud as hell, we'll hear them coming."

"I sure hope you're right."

All the houses up to this point looked decent, and their yards semi-clean. This area didn't look as if a zombie outbreak was happening. We walked on for another ten minutes and things increasingly started looking like a hurricane had blown through.

"The bar's just up the road on the left," Marston said.

"I figured, look at this destruction. What the fuck happened here?"

The surrounding devastation had become insane. The houses on both sides of the streets were in shambles; the sight reminded me of extreme storm damage. The porches were smashed, and the furniture that had been on them was strewn all over the front lawns. Windows on both floors of the houses were smashed out, and there was a body impaled on a fence post in the front yard of a home to my right. Some houses even had holes in them, like someone had tossed grenades at them.

Cars lined the curbs on both sides of the street halfway up the hill.

"Does this feel almost like an ambush to you?" I asked quietly.

"Seamus, yes it does. We're probably going to be killed at any moment."

"Keep it together, man! We need to get to the gun shop. Let's check these cars for creatures. I don't want to be taken by surprise because we didn't."

I took the right side of the street and Marston took the left. The first car I came to I saw thousands of flies swarming, and like an idiot, I decided to peek inside.

Lying on the front seat in a neat little pile was a dismembered body. Its legs and arms had been purposefully formed into a box-like shape on the seat, its torso set in the middle and its head placed neck-down on the chest. One eye was half open, the hair disheveled and greasy, and the dead man's tongue dangled through his teeth.

Hundreds more flies were stirred by my presence and began buzzing around my head. The smell wasn't as bad as the dump truck full of bodies, but it was still pretty foul. Marston, who saw I was looking at something, joined me despite the swarm of flies around me.

"What the fuck is that?" Marston shrieked.

"It seems someone had a bad day. Who and why would someone do this?"

"Seamus, there's no telling what were up against. If someone is capable of this, then what else are they capable of?"

"Well, there are zombies being controlled, so let's not rule out whoever's behind this has a few psychopaths in their mist."

We stared at the horrid scene until the flies were landing on our faces and getting into our ears. I started to walk again, and Marston followed. As I walked away, the thought of someone cutting a body into pieces and stacking it in a parked vehicle disturbed me.

The two of us were just cresting the hill when we heard another rumbling noise. This sound was closer than it had been before, so we didn't have much time to hide. I ran around the car on my right and crouched by one of the tires. In seconds, Marston was next to me, cowered down. A few seconds later, another truck came barreling down the street. Whoever or whatever rode inside hadn't seen us, so I poked my head up and had a look. The bed of this truck didn't have as many bodies, but I still saw quite a few.

The truck hadn't quite made it to the Central and State Street intersection before I saw four zombies in the street ahead of it. The truck's brake lights didn't so much as flicker as they closed in on the wanderers. Only after running them down did the truck stop. Two men got out and walked toward the bodies with bats in their hands. We had about two-hundred yards between the truckers and us, but I was able to see they were wearing mechanic suits with shaved heads.

We observed as one of the guys walked up to a twitching body and placed a bat on its chest. As he did, the body went ridged and trembled.

"They're using a taser on the damn thing. Now why would they taser a zombie they just ran over?" I asked.

"I have no idea man. Why would they do anything they've been doing?"

When he stopped with the taser, the other guy grabbed the body's arms while the first man grabbed its legs, picked it up, and heaved it into the back of the truck.

At that moment, I realized we should have been paying better attention to ourselves, because a dragging sound behind us made my neck hair stand up. I looked at Marston, and he had the most significant look of fear on his face I had ever seen. We both knew what was behind us: a zombie staggering toward its lunch.

With my club in hand, I bounced to my feet, twisted around, and stared at the monster.

It was a horrible sight. The dead guy in front of me must have been rotting away for weeks. Its hair was on the longer side, but clumps had somehow been pulled out in a few spots on its head. One of its eyeballs was missing, and its teeth were broken. The skin on its face was peeling off, and there were spots where the brownish bone under its skin and muscle was exposed. Being face to face with death smelled atrocious, and for a split second, I did nothing, but stare.

Marston spun around and dived out of its grasp as I started swinging like a crazy person.

I broke clumps of head and face off, and when the zombie fell to the ground, I continued to bludgeon it. I smashed it until its head was just a stew of brain, bone, hair, and skin. The body stopped moving, but I still whaled on its head.

I stood over the mangled mess below me and observed my work. My club was now soiled with clumps of gore. The gray matter made me a little queasy, but there was nothing left in my stomach, and the feeling soon passed.

I turned to Marston, who was on the ground rocking back and forth.

"You better get off your ass; we have to move now! Those things aren't going to wait around for you to regain yourself, and neither am I. We have to go now!" I yelled.

He seemed sluggish and hesitant, but eventually, he started to move. I grabbed him by his shirt and pulled him the rest of the way.

"Sorry. Seamus, that scared the shit right into my pants. We better move before more of those things come after us."

As I was pulling Marston to his feet I glanced back down the hill toward the truck. It was now gone, and I didn't see any bodies lying in the street. I sighed a sigh of relief they hadn't spotted our encounter with the zombie. For all I knew, if they had, we both would have been in the back of that truck.

We were both back on the road and away from the mangled body in seconds, walking faster as we went. The houses and businesses on either side of the street were smashed, and the contents of the homes were all over the yards and in the streets. The windows were busted out of every house we looked at, and smoke rose from a few of them.

When we finally got over the hill, the bar was a hundred feet away on the left, and piles of bodies were stacked at least six feet high, and seven across, all the way to the front of the building. I counted thirteen piles before I started to dry heave. I looked over to Marston, who once again had placed his shirt over his nose and mouth.

"I would rather smell my own puke than hundreds of bodies decomposing and cooking in the sun," Marston said.

Still walking and regaining myself I looked at the bar. The building was made out of cinder blocks and looked as if it were a bomb shelter. I was shocked to see it looked as big as a motorhome and had no sign. It was gray and had no windows I could see. The sidewalk out front of the place was blocked with trash, and cars, and the door was boarded up. Just past the bar in the direction we were heading, there were a bunch of cars abandoned bumper to bumper scattered in both lanes of the road

"That's the bar with the bracelets?"

"That's the one."

"Look at this place; it's destroyed!"

"Seamus, I'm not comfortable walking through all this. What do you think those trucks will do if they find us now? Hell, we've almost been killed once, and I have vomit all over my shirt. Sorry, but I think I'm going to go back; I'm not trying to die out here looking for guns and ammo," Marston said.

"Look, man, I'm not trying to die either. I want to get the guns, then my girlfriend, and get the fuck out of this town. Like I already said, I would rather die trying to escape than sitting around getting drunk with you and Burto! I plan on hitting the road soon, but if you want to go back and hide, that's fine with me. But just remember, when I leave, I'm going to drive by the apartment, honk my horn, and wave to you as I roll out. What would you like to do now?"

"Well, since you put it that way... I think... I will be joining you on this fabulous afternoon. We should get the hell out of this place before another truck shows up."

I realized the trucks had both left the bar and passed us going down the hill toward the public square. I glared at the stacked barricade and wondered why the road had been blocked.

"Why do you think they blocked the road right there?" I asked.

"I have no goddamn idea! Let's get the fuck out of here!"

We moved through the piles of dead as fast as we could. Some bodies were twitching, and some in the center of the piles were moving their heads, looking at us and groaning.

"Why are there so many bodies?" I asked, but then something in one of the piles of bodies to my right caught my eye. I stopped and walked closer for a better look.

"What are you doing?" Marston asked.

"This is the bar you said gave out the bracelets, right?"

"Yeah, but why does that matter now?" Marston continued.

"I think this is where all of this shit started. Look at the destruction all around *this* area. I think you were right about those bracelets. I'll put money on it those bracelets had super thin needles that injected the clear fluid."

"Yeah, okay, so what? Can we get the hell out of here?"

"Yeah, in a minute. Hear me out. Most of *these* bodies have holes all around their wrists. The holes are all swollen and full of pus. You see that?" I asked.

Marston looked and then nodded.

"Almost every single body in this pile has holes, but the bodies in that pile over there don't have any," I continued.

I walked with Marston over to the other pile of bodies I had mentioned. I pointed out that this pile had more twitching bodies in it and that almost none of them had holes around the wrists. The closer I looked, the more I realized they had bite marks all over. Seeing all these piles of bodies began messing with my mind. I was starting to get blurry vision as I began explaining my ideas to Marston.

"Think about it, Marston... you said the bracelet drained some sort of liquid into the wrist, right? Then the person wearing it disappeared, and nobody saw them again? Well, the piles with the swollen wrists have no bite marks; some are missing their head, but there are no bite marks. I'm getting some ideas about what the truckers are doing."

"Well let's hear it, Sherlock!" Marston said like a wiseass.

"I'm thinking those sons of bitches have created some sort of zombie potion, or maybe a zombie army. Have you noticed there are not as many zombies out in the afternoon? There's a lot at night, but not in the afternoons. The zombie that attacked us back there... I didn't see any holes, did you?"

"You think someone is creating and controlling these things?" Marston asked.

"Remember the other night with the parade of zombies and the guys with the bullhorns?"

"Yeah, they were leading the army. So what you're saying is the zombies with the holes only come out at night, and the other ones we see in the day were bitten by the nighttime zombies?" Marston asked with an intrigued look.

"Yes, that's exactly what I'm saying. Alright, I'm done; let's get over that barricade of cars, and away from this place."

"Yes, let's get the hell out of here!" Marston said promptly.

Being the door was boarded up, and we had no real idea what was inside the place, Marston and I decided to skip stopping at the bar. It seemed insanely stupid to check out a place that could easily get us killed.

We walked around all the piles of bodies and got to where the cars started to block the road. We jumped on top of a car's trunk, walked across the roof, hopped down to the hood, and jumped to the next cars trunk. We kept this up for another ten minutes before we were able to hop down and walk on the street.

"Well, Seamus, those trucks definitely don't go past the bar."

"Yeah... but I'm sure the zombies do."

"Why do you think those trucks were there today, and where the hell could they have come from?" Marston asked.

"I'm pretty sure they were taking bodies from the piles for some reason. If I were to guess I'd say those trucks drove right past our apartment at some point."

"I didn't hear them if they did. Maybe they're using roads we don't know about."

"Either way I'm glad we moved the shit out front of the place. If they had driven by and saw all that, they would have found us for sure."

Being so close to the cars and walking through them made me nervous, but this had to be done, so we continued walking.

CHAPTER 13

Past the bar, the plowed paths were history; all that remained were abandoned cars and other random things scattered in the streets as we walked down the other side of the hill.

"Not far now," I said after the bar was out of sight. "About fifteen minutes but be ready for anything."

I glanced over at Marston, who appeared pale and sickly.

"Are you alright?" I asked.

"Yes, I'm fine...you got a smoke?"

I grabbed the half-empty pack of cigarettes out of my pocket, lit one, and handed it to him. He puffed so hard and fast the thing had a cherry on it as long as his finger.

So many cars were in our way we decided to travel on top of them.

"How in the hell are there so many cars blocking this street?" Marston asked.

"If I had to guess, I'd say people tried evacuating and they were caught up for some reason, so they ditched their vehicles where they had stopped."

"What inconsiderate dicks."

Yeah, Marston, inconsiderate.

We climbed on top of an Oldsmobile and continued our journey across the car tops. As soon as we jumped onto the fifth car, a creature crawled out of an open passenger door and stood up.

Apparently, the sap had been dead quite a while, because its spine was hanging out of its skin. The thing had the remains of a long-sleeved flannel clinging to parts of its arms, and I figured it must have been one of the first to go. The skin that had once been its cheek flapped close to its chin, and its hair and scalp were missing, leaving the top of its skull exposed.

Luckily for us, the thing was trapped between three cars that formed a triangle. The two of us stood watching as the creature tried to grab us from below, opening and closing its mouth like it was chewing on the air.

Marston finished his smoke and flicked the butt at one of the empty eye sockets on the creature's face. The smoke almost went in, but instead bounced off the rim of the socket and fell to the ground.

"Really tough guy," I said.

"It can't hurt me from there, so yeah."

We started descending the windshield, but then I stopped and walked back up to the roof of the car.

"Seamus, what are you doing?" Marston asked, puzzled.

"Just watch and learn."

The zombie scratched at the roof as I stepped closer. I shouldered my club and aimed it at the creature's head, then shouted "FORE!" as I swung. Unlike my last attempt at decapitation, this time the creature's skull caved in and flew right off the top of its body. It went flying up the road and bounced off a car, leaving a brown smudge. Its body slumped to the ground a moment later, and I was on my way again. The end of my club was covered and dripping with blood and gunk, so I shook it off toward the side of the car. The zombie's brain jelly slopped off and to the ground close to its rightful owner.

"Dude, what the hell is wrong with you? You didn't have to do that. It wasn't going anywhere," Marston shouted.

"Yeah, maybe not...but maybe sometime down the line it would figure out how to escape. I don't want anything sneaking up on me again, and I will kill any zombie I can!" I said.

"It doesn't matter, you're still sick. Did you have to yell 'fore'?" Marston asked.

"I wanted to make sure you weren't in the way," I laughed.

Marston gave up and continued to walk, and I followed suit. We were almost at the intersection of State Street and Route 3. The gun shop was behind the Stewart's up ahead, and this sense of achievement brought a smile to my face.

As our journey continued, I kept glancing behind me to take note of anything following or chasing us. We had walked past some zombies stuck inside of closed-up cars, so I wasn't worried about them escaping and catching up.

All the houses and businesses in the area were trashed and had been so for roughly a mile. By now, neither of us paid attention to them.

We were nearing the stoplight for the intersection that turned left onto Route 3. Everything up to this point had been in disarray, but things were starting to clear up in the streets ahead. There was still a lot of shit in the road, but it didn't seem like a junkyard anymore.

From a car roof, I peered at the intersection.

It seems like everyone who lives out in Black River and Felts Mills came through this intersection. What the hell were they thinking?

"Jesus, are you seeing this shit?"

"Umm, yeah dude. I'm right here with you," I replied.

"It seems clearer up ahead. I'm glad we're going straight."

We continued to walk on top of the cars until they were too far apart to do so. We hopped down to the street and gazed around. I focused up toward the shop; the road was even drivable at this point. Cars were still scattered around but maneuvering around them was doable.

"Hey, Marston, I got an idea,"

He stopped walking and turned to face me.

"Let's hear it."

"Well, the roads are fairly clear, and I don't think we have to worry about anyone coming from behind in trucks."

"Yeah, so...what's your point?" Marston asked.

"Well, I say we find a car that runs and drive it the rest of the way to the store. We can then drive it back to the apartment."

"Man, it's right up the road, let's keep walking! It's only five or ten minutes. Come on, man, let's just concentrate on the gun shop. You can stay here, but I'm going to keep walking," Marston bitched.

"Dude, we're going to need a car at some point, and what better place to find one than right here were there are hundreds? We can find one that works and use it to get the hell out of the area a lot quicker."

Marston stared as I wandered up to the first car I hoped had keys: an old Honda Accord. I first pulled my spiked club up, ready to swing, but changed my mind and reached for the door handle instead.

As I was about to pull the door open, someone started speaking behind me.

"Hey, buddy, what the hell are you two doing?"

The sound made me jump, and I reacted in the fight or flight mode. Before I could stop myself, I swung around with my spiked club leading the way. When the club made contact, it sent vibrations shooting through my arms. Whoever was behind me stopped talking right away.

When I opened my eyes, I realized I had just stuck a spiked club into the head of some guy with the name Rob-o on his grease-stained work shirt.

"Holy shit, I'm so fucking sorry! Damn it, don't you know better than to sneak up on people in a situation like this?" I yelled.

Marston came running back and Rob-o was stumbling around with a club piercing the side of his head.

"Damn, Seamus, what did you do?" Marston asked.

Even though Rob-o was wearing glasses, they hadn't stopped the nails from shooting into his eyeball and into his brain.

Rob-o fell to the ground twitching, his eye secreting a white liquid I had never seen before. I watched him flop around as his brain tried telling his body to stand up, blood seeping out of the holes in his face and eye in a slow trickle. Then he began to seize, every muscle in his body tightening up. A half dozen nails stuck in Rob-o's face and I felt awful.

"Ya know, he could still be alive," Marston said.

I was speechless as I watched this person flop around in the street, smashing his teeth out.

The thrashing went on for a few seconds, the club scraping against the pavement until it had almost twisted itself loose. As I looked on in sickened horror, the club fell out with a leaky jetting of blood. Seconds later, Rob-o stopped moving.

The blood that began to pour out of Rob-o's face quickly got my mind on other matters at hand. I knelt down next to him and started saying a prayer.

"Grant to them eternal rest. Let light perpetual shine upon them. May his soul through the mercy of God, rest in peace. Amen."

"Where the hell did you learn that, Seamus?" Marston asked from behind me.

"I've been to a lot of funerals."

"Why didn't you speak up when Tom was killed?"

"The dude was trying to steal our shit."

"Man, you're one coldhearted motherfucker."

"In a situation like this you can't have a bleeding heart for anyone."

"Remind me not to piss you off."

You already have, and you'll get yours too.

Standing up I began wondering where this guy had come from. I looked down at the body and realized he was in pretty great shape considering the situation. This fact was peculiar to me. He wasn't skinny or frail, and his clothes weren't ripped or dirty. I looked all around the area and saw a minivan with the sliding back door open on the side of the road in the cluster of cars we had walked over.

"That must be where he slept. Let's check it out," I suggested.

Marston didn't reply because he was still in a state of bewilderment. I paid him no mind and continued to scout the area near the van. As I got closer, I spotted gallon jugs around the outside. When I was close enough to peek into the back window, I was thrilled to see at least three gallons of water were on the seat.

"Hey, Marston, Rob-o had a lot of water!"

I got no response, but I didn't care. I had realized how thirsty I was, so I grabbed one of the jugs, popped the top, and began to chug. As I gulped, I smelled something that wasn't a decomposing body. I stopped drinking, set the jug down, and walked around back of the vehicle.

I was greeted by several piles of shit baking in the summer sun. I walked around the piles and headed for the passenger door. Blood dripped from the bottom of it, pooling in the street. Then I glanced into the window and was amazed by what I saw.

"Marston, you gotta see this!"

I got no answer, so I glanced over to see Marston still in the same state I had left him in earlier.

"Hey, Marston, come check this out!" I repeated.

The words broke his trance, and he snapped back to life, shook his head, and wandered over toward the vehicle. He reached the van, took a peek through the window, and leaped backward.

"What the fuck is that?" he yelled.

Inside the van, lying across the floorboards of the front seat, was a half-eaten body. From the looks of it, Rob-o had eaten the man's calves and hamstrings. His legs had been devoured to the bone, though his feet were untouched. Seeing more bite marks, I assumed Rob-o had recently started on the fleshy part of the body's right arm. Judging by the dark bruises around his neck, I figured Rob-o had strangled the life from the poor bastard. Marston was already walking away, so he wouldn't have to stare at the horrible scene.

"Seems like ole Rob-o had some hunger pains and decided to strangle his buddy for a source of food," I said.

"I'm getting the hell out of here before anything like that happens to us," Marston said.

"You don't find it strange that this guy was eating someone?" I shouted after Marston.

"Yes, I find it about as fucked up as that dismembered body, but we need to get this show on the road. I think your car idea has some merit; we need to hurry up."

"It's a good thing we didn't decide to drive earlier," I said.

"Why is that?"

"Well we would have been spotted pretty quickly, and there was no way around those cars."

"That's true. Are you done back there, or are you still looking at that mess?"

"I'm coming, I'm coming."

Choosing to dodge the piles of shit, I walked around the front of the van and picked up my club from where it rested in a pool of thick, dark blood. Right then I realized I was indeed a heartless son of a bitch who lacked empathy.

I'm not a bad person; the people who were killed meant nothing to me from the start. They died doing dumb things, and I am not wasting emotions on them.

I stood up and stared at Marston, who was climbing into a mid-nineties Ford F-150, and I suddenly remembered the Accord. I returned to the car, and as I was reaching for the door handle, I glanced in the back seat. I wasn't about to have another thing crawl over and try eating me. I didn't see any creatures, but I did see two duffle bags that appeared to be packed.

"Hey, Marston, I found two duffle bags in the back seat. I bet they were someone's bug-out bags."

"Why the hell would someone leave their bug out bags behind?"

"Something must have scared them to the point of running away without them."

I opened the back door and grabbed the first bag. Both bags were a medium size and for all I knew could be gym bags. I opened the top zipper and looked in to see what goodies awaited. My mind was racing too fast to find anything inside useful. There were boxers, shorts, and T-shirts. I dumped the contents on the ground and pulled the second bag out. As I unzipped the second bag, I heard the sound of an engine fire up.

"Haha! Seamus, it works!"

"That's awesome. I say we take that to the shop right now," I said with a laugh.

Marston revved the truck's engine like he was a NASCAR driver.

"Take it easy on that thing," I said, pawing through the second bag.

"What are you doing over there? Let's go."

"I was thinking we could use these bags for the guns. Those pillowcases are pretty flimsy."

"Great idea, throw them in the back and let's get out of here."

As I found nothing of use in the bag, I dumped that on top of the clothes from the first and jogged over to the truck.

"Marston, do you know what this means? We could fill the entire bed with whatever is in the gun shop! I mean, we'd have to find a different route back to the apartment, but I'm sure we could figure something out."

I tossed the bags into the bed, yanked the passenger door open, and hopped in with my spiked club.

"Hold up; I forgot my pillowcase," I said to Marston.

"Who cares, you don't need that or the spikeless club. We're going to be armed to the teat soon."

The truck was facing in the direction of the apartment, so Marston had to turn it around. I sat quietly as he pulled up to a spot near Rob-o clear enough for him to make a twenty-seven-point turn. He ran Rob-o's lifeless body over a few times and every time more bones snapped under the tires.

"Sorry, Rob-o," Marston yelled every time he crushed more bones.

As soon as Marston got the truck turned around, he punched the gas like an eager sixteen-year-old, making the tires squeal. It was the first smile I had seen out of him in a while.

"Hey, take it easy on this thing. We don't want it to shit the bed on us," I said.

Of course driving made the trip much faster. We had to drive by several residential and commercial properties for the next mile or so, but it was a straight shot. We passed the Carvel ice cream shop, the Perkins restaurant, and then past the Stewart's gas station. The gun shop was in the Stewart's plaza behind all the other useless shops.

When we got to the plaza, Marston decided he didn't want to use the driveway, and plowed over the curb. The truck got a bit of air, and when we crashed down, he had to cut the wheel sharp to the left or we would have driven right through the gas pumps.

"*Christ*, man, take it easy!" I shouted.

He punched the gas again, flying to the end of the plaza and right past the gun shop. He put the truck in reverse and backed the bed up until it bumped into the door of the shop.

One of the shop's windows was full of hunting and fishing pictures the locals had brought in, but the window on the other side had been smashed.

"Looks like someone else had the same idea," I said.

"Only one window is busted. Do you think there are any weapons left?"

"Let's go look."

On that note, we opened the doors, stepped out, held onto our clubs, and made our way to the busted window of the gun shop.

I glanced back at the truck and realized both our windows were down. I didn't want to risk anything climbing in or even stealing the truck while we were inside the store, so I made my way to the cab to put the windows up.

I guess the old world is still stuck in my head. Who cares about windows and doors?

Just as I was about to open the passenger door, I caught a glimpse of Marston, who was staring up the street leading to the gun shop.

"What are you doing?"

"I'm watching for creatures. I'm not going inside until we're together. Fuck this always-going-first shit!"

I opened the passenger door, crawled over the seat, and turned the latch until the driver's-side window went up completely. Then I turned back to the passenger side and put that window up. I stepped out and looked for the latch that released the seat back. I wanted something stronger than my club and thought the truck might have a crowbar behind the seat. After pulling the latch the backrest slid forward, and I was surprised at what I found sitting on the floor.

I found a pump-action twelve-gauge shotgun. I pulled it out and pumped seven slugs out and onto the ground.

Now why in the hell would this be behind a seat at a time like this? Maybe someone stole the truck and didn't know it was back there.

"Seamus, you're mumbling, and you better watch your back."

I glanced up through the driver's-side window toward the junkyard of cars.

"It's behind you, fool," Marston added.

I turned around to see a zombie about ten feet away, stumbling toward me.

"Where the hell did this thing come from?" I yelled at Marston.

"I think it came from around the corner of the building."

I had a little time, so I knelt down and loaded four slugs before I decided I didn't have time for the rest. I stood up, put the gun to my shoulder, took aim, and pulled the trigger. I expected a loud boom, but there was only silence.

I peeked at the safety key and saw black. I pushed the key, exposing the red side of the switch, and repeated the process of putting the gun to my shoulder. I pointed at the creature's head and squeezed the trigger. With a tremendous boom, the monster's head exploded like a balloon, and the recoil blasted me into the passenger seat.

"Dude, let's fucking go and get this over with. Stop messing around," Marston said.

"I killed a creature that would have followed us into the store, so calm down."

"Well then, are you ready, cowboy Bob?"

The gunshot still rang in my ears as I pushed the safety back into place. I turned and took a few steps toward the bed of the truck, where I placed the shotgun on the floor, and then hopped over the side into the back.

Marston walked around the truck and started for the door of the shop where he waited for me. He poked his head in the busted window and looked around.

"It looks all clear. Hurry up," Marston said.

I turned to face the back window of the truck and kicked it out. I didn't have much force behind my first kick, so my foot bounced off, but the second shot was as fierce as a kung fu kick. At this point I was figuring none of the creatures would be in the bed of the truck, and I knew we were going to leave the bags of weapons in the back. Easy access is what I was going for the whole time.

The glass shattered into hundreds of pieces all over the interior of the truck. The glass fell behind the pushed-up seat and wouldn't stab us when we made our getaway. I picked up the gun and used the butt to knock out the rest of the shattered window. I then reached into the cab and pulled the seat back into its proper position. I turned and kicked one of the bags over to Marston, and then picked my bag up.

"Alright, karate kid... I think you should go first. You have the gun, and I have a spiked club. It only seems fair!"

I walked to the back of the bed and watched Marston eagerly step out of the way. I shook my head as I walked by him. I placed my hands against the doorway, leaned over, and peered through the glass door.

From where I was standing, I could see nothing dangerous inside the store. I turned to tell Marston things were safe, but again found him in a trance, looking up the street for more of our flesh-eating friends.

"Dude, are you ready or what? I know I will be a lot happier when I have loaded guns by my side," I said.

I jumped out of the truck toward the busted window of the shop and made my way inside. I was first greeted with stale gun oil, and then I caught a whiff of body odor and old beer. As my eyes adjusted to the store's interior, I realized the sun was actually lighting the place well, and from what I saw, most of the shotguns and rifles were still in their original places on the walls. All the glass cases inside were untouched, and there was an abundance of ammo and handguns inside them. Seeing this made my day a whole lot brighter.

"It doesn't seem that whoever broke the window wanted guns," I said to Marston.

I clicked my gun's safety back off because I wasn't going to be mauled by something I had overlooked. Marston jumped out of the truck and came into the store seconds after I had taken my first steps inside.

"Dude, we're going to have to make this as fast as we can. That gunshot brought them out of hiding, and there are twelve of them coming from Stewart's heading toward us."

"Damn, that many?" I asked.

"I counted three times."

"Alright, we'll make this quick. I'm sure they'll come smashing through that other window and try to eat us, so make sure you stay alert."

Marston walked over to the rifles on the far-right wall. I, on the other hand, went straight for the glass case full of ammunition. There were shotgun slugs, birdshot, 9mm bullets, black powder, 357s, 38s, 44s, 45s, and all sorts of rifle shells. I walked around to the locked doors of the case and busted the glass with the butt of my shotgun.

I carefully reached in and began grabbing boxes of 9mm, 44s, 45s, 357s, and 38s. I knew I didn't have the most room in the bag, so I only grabbed the ammo for the guns I would hopefully be finding.

Next, I moved over to the handguns and quickly broke the top glass of the case. These weapons had the tags on them, so it was easy to grab the weapons I had already gotten the ammo for.

Having enough handguns, I looked up at the wall of rifles. My bag was starting to get heavy, and I felt a dull ache coming from my shoulder. Not wanting to overload my pack I decided I didn't need any rifles and went over to Marston.

He was screwing around at the accessory shelf, so I snuck up behind him. I glanced at his bag and saw he had grabbed two shotguns and a rifle. As I got closer, I walked up behind him, placed my palm on his shoulder, and spoke into his ear.

"Having a hard time, buddy?"

Marston jumped backward and almost fell.

"Are you about done, princess?" I continued. "Stop dicking around and let's get moving!"

"I'm going to grab a couple handguns, and I should be ready."

Marston walked past me to the case I had taken guns out of and asked, "Did you grab ammo for these?"

"Yeah, of course I did. Hurry up!"

"I need some ammo for my shotgun and rifle too."

"Just grab the shit, let's go, man!"

As Marston was grabbing the guns and ammo I began to sweat. The heat and the weight of the bag was starting to get to me. I walked to the front of another case full of hunting knives. I put the butt of my shotgun through the top of the case with a quick jab. I went right into the mess of glass and grabbed a six-by-three blade, its handle guarded by brass knuckles with sharp spikes on each knuckle.

I turned and saw a display of holsters behind me against the wall. I walked over to them and began looking for the holsters that fit the guns I would be carrying. I saw a leather cowboy holster that held a weapon on each side of the waist, so I threw it in the bag. I found a chest holster that held two weapons that also went into the duffle. I grabbed one ankle holster for my .38 and was done.

The bag over my shoulder was roughly twenty pounds and was full enough for me. I turned with shotgun in hand to find Marston at the back of the truck by the front door, staring out the plate-glass window at all the zombies heading our way.

"Hey, Marston, did you get enough shit, or do you need more?" I yelled.

"Yeah, I'm ready."

I walked up alongside Marston and looked at the approaching monsters.

"Why don't you load up one of those shotguns before they break that window and kill us, you fucking idiot!"

Marston didn't even look at his bag when he reached for the gun. While he was loading his weapon, I watched the creatures smear themselves all over the window. The glass looked like it was bending, and it was covered with a shitty brown substance that smeared whenever the zombies touched it.

"Hey, Marston, hand me some shells. I'm going to reload Mr. Goodtime."

He tossed a box of birdshot that fell to the ground. I picked up the shells and began to reload my weapon.

After reloading I decided to toss the bag into the bed of the truck. I stepped outside the busted window on the passenger side and noticed there were a lot more than twelve zombies. It seemed many more had joined the herd since Marston's original headcount. Some of the creatures were starting to stumble around the front of the truck.

"Man, we need to get out of here! Those things are coming around the truck, and if they do, we're going to have to blast our way out of here. I don't have enough guns loaded for that, so let's go!"

The words apparently fell on deaf ears because Marston shouted from inside the store.

"Seamus, we have to get the hell out of here! They're trying to break the fucking glass! If we don't get moving now, we are going to be killed."

Most of their faces were missing skin, and thankfully their scent had not hit me yet. The monsters scratched the windows with the bloody stumps at the ends of their fingers. Some creatures did have fingernails but connected only by cuticles.

I knew in less than thirty seconds, the window would be reduced to a pile of shards, and they would breach the store. The majority of the monsters I could see had gaping holes up and down their arms. I didn't think to look at their wrists because at that moment all I was focused on was escaping the horde.

I stood near the truck's bed, holding my gun, suddenly I heard a *BOOM*.

"We have to go right now!" Marston yelled as he shucked another shell into the chamber.

Marston had fired a shot through the main window the truck was backed against. The shards fell to the ground as the monsters smashed out the window they were pressing against. I watched Marston toss his bag into the bed of the truck and then dive over the tailgate as the creatures pushed their way into the store. Marston then scampered through the truck's bed, through the back window, and into the cab. As all this was happening, I stood near the truck bed watching everything unfold in slow motion. I looked toward the front of the truck, the creatures had made their way there and were about to come right for me.

I glanced back to my left and saw five monsters coming at me from the window, so I aimed and started shooting. The first shot destroyed the face of the closest zombie, and it dropped. I pumped the empty round out, loaded another, aimed, pulled the trigger, and *kaboom* went the flesh from several faces and necks.

There were more of them walking over the bodies before I got the third round into the chamber. Then, from behind me, I heard the groans and moans of monsters coming from the front of the truck. I knew I'd die if I stuck around, so I set my weapon into the bed, and hurled myself over the side.

The truck started right as I hit the floor, and I crawled toward the back window of the cab. The truck was now surrounded by hordes of zombies on either side. Zombies began trying to crawl into the bed, and one of them was to my immediate left.

I snatched my shotgun off the truck's bed, pumped another round into the chamber, extended my arm, and pulled the trigger. The monster's head blasted apart, but the round didn't stop there. With one shot, I blew the head of one zombie apart, and maimed the face of the one behind it.

Marston had been watching over his shoulder, and when he saw the creatures trying to climb into the truck, he put it into drive and took off. The bags of guns slid to the back of the bed, hitting the tailgate. I almost fell over but caught my balance.

Marston wasn't messing around; he had the gas pedal to the floor, but there were still two zombies hanging on. I carefully slid toward the back of the truck, cocked my gun again, placed it directly against one of their foreheads, and pulled the trigger. It slumped to the ground and slid for a few feet behind us. I turned to shoot the other zombie, but Marston cranked the wheel sharply to the right. The creature fell off, and I almost fell over the side with it.

"We need to go to the left," I yelled.

"That path is out of the question."

I gathered myself, and I looked back at the gun shop. To my astonishment, there were about twenty more of the monsters walking around the building, coming from the end of the plaza by the Stewart's entrance.

"Seamus, get in here," Marston yelled from the cab.

Marston slowed the truck a little as I grabbed the handles on the bags and slid them back toward the front of the bed. After putting them against the wall, I climbed into the cab. Marston gave the truck some gas, and we picked up speed, heading up the State Street hill.

"Where the fuck are we going?" I asked.

"From what I saw this is the only way we can go if we want to get this truck back to the apartment. I have no interest in going this way, but unless you have a better idea, this is the way we have to go. I don't know about you, but I'm not trying to carry a hundred pounds of guns while running from zombies with the hopes of finding another running vehicle."

"Goddammit, you're right; we have no choice. If we're going to be taking the long way, let's make sure this thing isn't going to run out of gas."

"The gauge reads a little over a half a tank," Marston replied.

I didn't say anything, still concentrating on the ringing in my ears and the pounding of my heart. The blasts were so loud I was surprised I could hear at all.

A few abandoned cars were scattered along the side of the road, but otherwise the road was clear of debris. It was pushing three in the afternoon, and we were now in a speeding truck heading in the wrong direction.

"Seems like everyone who drove through here got hung up down at the Route 3 intersection," I stated.

"I just want this goddamn day to end," Marston said with a sigh.

CHAPTER 14

"You know, Marston, we have to go through three different towns to get back to Watertown. If those places are overrun, we're completely fucked!"

"I know a shortcut that will bypass one of those places. Besides man, this is rural upstate New York, what do you think is going to be out here? If we're lucky, this should be quick."

"This is going to be the longest trip around the block in history," I claimed.

State Street hill is a massive hill on the outskirts of Watertown, and as we drove up, I twisted in my seat for a view from above the town. From here I could see clusters of cars scattered across town, and massive black clouds of smoke were rising into the clear summer sky. Soon, however, Marston went around a corner and cut off my view.

"Hell yes, we're almost at the top!" Marston exclaimed.

As the road flattened, things briefly seemed normal. A few houses had trash and garbage all over the yards, but that was all. It appeared all the devastation was behind us in the city below.

I glanced toward Marston, who had his eyes fixed on the road. Something on my left shoulder caught my eye. Small bits of blood, brain, and bone had splattered on my shirt, so I picked the goo off and tossed it out the window.

We drove in silence for a while because I was trying to regain myself after the gun shop. When I finally started feeling better, I spoke.

"Marston, I don't see much activity around here."

"I'm sure those things are lurking and watching our every move."

We drove for the next ten minutes at eighty miles an hour. I knew the shortcut Marston had mentioned, but that cutoff was another fifteen minutes ahead. Eventually, Marston eased off the gas.

"If I keep this speed up, we're going to be walking, and I'm not so sure this old truck can handle it."

Everything up here on the top of State Street hill seemed normal, except for the lack of people. As we continued, a silhouette of a person appeared a few hundred yards ahead of us.

"Maybe you should slow down, it could be someone who needs help."

"Like you care," Marston retorted.

The closer we got, the more we were able to make out the features of what was definitely a zombie. The creature was in the oncoming lane, stumbling toward Watertown. Marston started veering into the other lane.

"I've always wanted to do this."

I didn't say anything to him and let him have his disturbing moment.

Its upper body had mostly rotted, and small pieces of muscle and tissue clung to parts of the rib cage. Its head was skinned, its skull exposed, but its eyeballs were still intact. Though it was looking right at us, it didn't try to avoid Marston slamming into it.

Just as he was about to mow the creature over Marston moved the truck to the left and the right-side bumper clipped the monster. Marston planned the hit expertly, and the monster went flying off the road into a nearby drainage ditch. I had always assumed hitting a person with a truck would be bumpier, or even jarring, but at these speeds, it was just another bug on the bumper.

I watched Marston after; he didn't even glance back in the mirror.

"Feeling better, psycho?" I asked.

"One less fucker trying to kill me."

We drove another short while before Marston spoke up again.

"Look at these houses. The cars are still parked in the driveways. Did they try to run?"

I shrugged, not thinking about what he had said. He looked insane, scared, worried, and sick all in one. I started wondering if the things he had seen over the past few days were finally catching up. His face had started turning white, and he was gripping the steering wheel so tight his hands showed little spots of purple. His dreadlocks clung to his face like the sweat pouring from his scalp was glue, his face grimy and still swollen from the beating I'd laid on him the previous day. His baby blue eyes looked damp, and I thought he was about to tear up.

"Hey, man, are you alright?" I asked, placing a hand on his shoulder.

Instead of answering, he lifted his right pointer finger. Up ahead I saw another outline of a person in the road.

"Hey, I have an idea. Pull up along next to it," I said.

He hit the brakes, so the truck was rolling at about five miles an hour. I turned around and leaned through the busted back window to go through the bag I had filled. I rummaged through holsters and ammo until I got down to the cold steel of the guns. I came to a .45 and continued to fish until I found a box of shells. Then I pulled myself back into the cab.

I popped the clip out, loaded it and pushed it back in. Cocking the hammer back, I said, "Pull up alongside of that bastard."

Marston crept up alongside the beast, and then came to a complete stop. The thing just stared at us as I got my window down. As the monster started walking toward us, I took aim and pulled the trigger, shooting the thing between the eyes. The beast hadn't even fallen to the ground before Marston got us rolling again. I glanced over at him to see he was now shaking uncontrollably.

"Marston, stop the truck! You look like hammered shit! I think I'll take over."

I got out and walked around the front as Marston slid across the seat. I got into the cab, and I saw he had already put his head on the window, trying to get some rest. I set the .45 on the seat, put the truck in drive, and continued our mission.

I stared at the gas gauge; we'd need more soon.

The turn off was coming up, and by now, Marston had passed out from what I guessed was mental exhaustion. The thought he had been bitten came to mind, but I knew that was highly unlikely, so I kept driving.

Soon, we would be turning left onto the road that would take us to Felt Mills, New York. This small one-light town is where I had grown up. I knew it well and even considered stopping by my mother's house. I quickly talked myself out of that because I knew she was on vacation in Florida. I had spoken with her a week before my arrival, and she told me she was extending her vacation another two weeks because she was having such a great time. When she had mentioned this, I had blown it off without a second's thought, and now, I was grateful she had done that.

I cruised by one more zombie, watching in the rearview as it stumbled out of a driveway and into the street. Marston didn't stir at all when I made the left turn that would eventually take us home. This road was in the same shape as the others, clean and empty. As I rounded a corner, I saw something up ahead. I smacked Marston, who woke up and immediately rolled the window down for some fresh air.

"Dude...are you sure you're alright?" I asked.

"Yeah, just a little woozy. I'll be fine soon enough."

I looked back through the windshield to see someone was running right toward us. I hit the brakes and brought the truck to a crawl. He was probably in his early twenties and in decent shape from what I could see. As I watched the man close the gap between himself and our truck Marston yelled, "Dude, what the fuck are you doing? Drive, you idiot!"

The guy was just barely ahead of a pack of monsters as I stomped the gas, the tires squealing. He kept running straight at us, screaming, trying to wave us down.

"Help me! Help me! I don't want to die! Please help me! They're going to eat me! Stop the fucking truck!"

I floored it, forcing the man to dive off to the right, and ran down his enemies. I hit every one of them, and some met their demise underneath the tires. I didn't completely stop all of them, but at least I'd given the guy a better chance at survival.

I looked into the rearview to see the dude running to the church we had passed seconds before. Marston and I glanced at each other, and I noticed some color had returned to his face.

"Feel better?" he asked calmly.

"Man, I don't know what the fuck came over me. That guy could have been bitten, tried to kill us, or stole the truck. What was I thinking?" I replied.

Marston shook his head and turned to gaze out the window. For the first time, I noticed the old AM/FM radio in the center console. I turned the knob, and to my surprise it lit up. I went through every channel but heard only static. Discouraged, I turned the thing off as fast as I had turned it on.

We approached a stop sign, and I turned right, heading for Felts Mills. The ride was uneventful until I turned left onto School Street.

"This shit is pretty disturbing," Marston said softly. "Yeah, it's rough," I said, lighting a smoke.

We didn't speak for a while. I drove until we got to Burnup Road. Burnup Road was a few miles long, and when we got to the end of it, we would end up at the Route 3 intersection just outside Black River.

Burnup Road was stranger than the others. It seemed every third or fourth house had a handful of zombies standing in their yards. The majority of these homes were trailers and didn't offer much in the line of security for anyone living in them.

"Hey, Marston... where do you think the survivors are at?"

"I have no idea...I've only seen a couple in the past few weeks, and they were running for their lives."

"I'm sure the highways would have been overflowing with cars after the evacuation," I said.

"Isn't that the way you came into town?" Marston asked.

"No, I came in on Route 12 through Lowville. I remember trash being strewn all over the place, but not much else. I had passed out, and when I woke up, Megan was dropping me off on Franklin Street. She had said things were strange, and before I passed out, I'd thought the same. Because I was drunk and exhausted, I didn't think anything of it when I didn't see anyone driving around. There was trash all over the sidewalks, and I thought it was a little excessive, but I figured there may have been a windstorm. When I walked over to your place, I saw a person staggering near a trash can a few blocks away, but they paid me no attention. I thought the whole scene was strange as hell," I explained as we drove.

Soon, we stopped at the end of Burnup Road.

"What are you doing?" Marston asked.

"Why don't you load up some guns? We're going to need them when we're back in town." I said as we pulled onto Route 3.

Marston reached through the back window and grabbed some of the guns he had put into his bag. He set them on the floor and started digging through the bag I had loaded with ammo, hauling up two boxes of shotgun slugs.

"Check the safety!" I demanded as he started to load the shotguns.

He checked it, set the loaded weapon on the floor, and grabbed the other shotgun.

After the weapons were loaded, he sat back, reached into his pocket, and pulled out his smokes. He started to say something, but I cut him off before he could.

"You better load up some pistols too," I said.

"I'm getting to it. I want to relax for a minute."

"Look, we're about to turn onto Route 342, so that means Lafave road is only a few minutes away, *meaning* we are going to be in Watertown momentarily...so you better hurry."

"Shit, man, take it easy. It'll be done!"

He put the pack of smokes away and turned in his seat again to grab some pistols out of the bag. He brought back five guns and the ammo needed for each one.

Marston picked up the first one, popped the clip, and had the thing loaded in seconds.

"My pops had a lot of .45s, and I shot every one of them," Marston said, setting the gun on the seat.

"What do you got there, Marston?" I asked as he grabbed another gun.

"It's just a nine mill."

The next two were .45s that took no time to load. The last gun he loaded was a 38 special that held five rounds, making it the smallest.

"The safeties are on the right?" I asked.

"Yes, what do you think I'm, an idiot?"

I looked at him with one eyebrow raised and then put my eyes back on the road.

CHAPTER 15

After five minutes of driving we pulled up to the end of Lafave Road and found the intersection had a broken-down Volkswagen Bug in it. But other than the trash all over, everything seemed to look normal. I stopped ten feet behind the busted car, put the truck in park, and shut off the engine.

"What the hell are you doing, man?" Marston asked.

"Well...you can load *your* guns, and I can stretch my legs," I replied.

"I just loaded a bunch of them."

"Yeah I know, but those are the ones *I'm* taking."

"Really man? You need that many?"

"Yeah, I do."

"Alright, whatever."

Both of us got out at the same time, and he walked to the back of the truck. He climbed into the bed, took a seat on the wheel well, and dragged his bag in front of him. Watching Marston made me think I should start gearing up for my upcoming trip across town. I walked to the passenger side and grabbed my bag, lifting it onto the seat.

"Hey, make sure you keep a watch out for monsters," I said.

"Ten-four, little buddy."

"Remember, we don't have much time before the sun starts to set, so move quickly."

"Jesus, man, shut the fuck up, would you?" Marston snapped.

Marston's outburst surprised me, but I wasn't mad. I had been busting his balls pretty badly for a while, so he was due for some hostility toward me. I shook my head, looked back into my bag, and saw the knife with the spiked brass knuckles. I pulled the blade out and set that aside.

I grabbed the double shoulder holster. It took me a second, but I soon figured out I had to put it on like a jacket. Once it was on and tightened up, I turned to Marston.

"How do I look?"

"Isn't that supposed to be under a sport coat or a jacket of some kind?" Marston asked.

"Yeah, but who cares? Those things aren't looking at my sense of fashion."

I grabbed two .45s off the seat and placed them into the holsters. After they were secured, I found the leather cowboy holster that held a gun on each side of the waist. I put that on and crammed the other .45 and the 9mill into the stiff leather. Before latching the belt in place, I slipped the belt loop of the heavy knife's sheath onto the leather. The guns looked absurd in the holsters, but it worked for me.

Next was an ankle holster, into which I put the .38 special. Between the five handguns and the shotgun I would be carrying, I felt a lot of pressure lift from my shoulders. Finally, I loaded my pockets with bullets, and decided everything else could go back to the apartment.

"Alright, Marston, you ready?" I asked.

"Yup. Just finished loading these bitches."

I tossed my bag through the cab's back window and into the bed. Marston set his guns in a pile behind the window for easy access, then took the duffel bags and pushed them against the guns so the pile wouldn't move as easily.

I hopped back into the driver's seat and waited for Marston to get in.

I dropped the transmission into drive, swerved around the abandoned car, and started our drive down outer Pearl Street toward Watertown.

We hadn't even made it to town before the chaos started to appear again. I had to slow the truck from fifty to fifteen within seconds. The road was passable only with careful alternating of the gas and brake pedals. We crawled the last three-hundred yards to where the traffic light was. The New York Air Brake Corporation was on the right, and the fence that once surrounded it was lying on the ground as if someone had driven through it. The closer we got to the traffic light, the more we realized this road was impassable.

"Holy shit, this place looks worse than State Street," Marston observed.

The sun was moving down in the sky, and our current situation wasn't going to make getting home any quicker. The streetlight ahead had fallen, and power lines and phone poles lay on the ground. There was a row of massive, old oak trees that had once lined the median, but they had been burned, and now vast pillars of charred blackness stood in their place.

CHAPTER 16

"How are we supposed to drive through all this shit?" Marston asked.

"I guess we're going to have to proceed with caution and hope for the best."

"I'm sick of this shit. I want to go home!" Marston exclaimed.

While blanketed with trash and paper, the field on our right was free of obstacles. I cranked the wheel hard to the right and gave the truck enough gas to drive up over the curb. When I got onto the sidewalk, I put the truck into reverse and straightened the wheel so I could drive between two of the burned oaks.

By the time I made it to the end of the field, I realized we weren't going to be able to go back the way I had planned. The intersection I wanted to take was trashed, and at least fifty cars blocked our way.

"Well, that route is completely fucked," I sighed.

"What do you mean?"

"Have you lost your vision? This truck won't go through that shit!" I said.

"Well, the only other way to go is through suburbia. How much gas do we have left?" Marston asked.

"Less than a quarter tank, but that's enough for now. Since we have to go that way anyway, we can stop by Cooper Street. Maybe Megan is still at her grandma's."

"Dude, what the fuck? Let's just get back to Burto. He's probably shitfaced and will pass out soon anyway."

"Why wouldn't I want to at least try to swing by there? It's not even that far out of the way."

Marston stared out the window as if pondering the idea. He looked at me, took a long, deep breath, and looked like he was about to speak, but he only nodded.

Abandoned cars were all over the place, but the power lines still hung in their proper places. Some had begun to sag but had not fallen, and the cars were easy enough to maneuver around.

I drove two blocks, took a left, and saw there were fewer and fewer abandoned cars. There was still trash all over the place, but unlike the houses on parts of State Street, these houses looked habitable.

The only sounds in the cab were my heavy breathing and the truck's engine. This area of Watertown had always been more on the upscale side, but now looked just as rundown as everywhere else. We drove through the streets of suburbia until we came to the street I needed to turn left on. I knew Megan's grandmother's house would be the fourth down on the left. As I eased the truck down the street, fear began to overcome me. Trash cans had been tossed everywhere, and this street had more abandoned cars than the roads leading here.

I pulled over to the side of the street across from the house, briefly looked at Marston, then got out and began walking across the street. I didn't see our car in the driveway, and panic shot into my heart.

As I crossed the road, I pulled one of the .45s from my shoulder holster. I clicked the safety off as I walked but kept my index finger away from the trigger. The last thing I wanted was an accidental discharge because I got spooked. Still, I had come a long way, and if anything crossed me now, I would blow it to hell.

I stepped onto the curb and looked back at Marston. He was sitting in the truck with a shotgun across his chest, looking around nervously. I returned my gaze to the front window of the two-story home. This house was older and normally had a lot of wind chimes and birdfeeders, but now they were gone, and the window on the first floor where Megan's grandfather always sat was boarded up. The second-story window was also boarded up, and made me wonder what they were afraid of getting in. The only way to that window would be a ladder, and last I checked, zombies didn't use ladders. I walked as quietly as I could to the front door.

As I climbed the steps to the clean white screen door, I heard something shuffling and moaning behind the six-foot wooden fence. I knew if I decided to kill the thing it was going to take a minute, and more zombies could be lurking, so I paid it no attention.

My nerves were on end, and my heart was thumping hard in my chest. I looked at the front door, instantly noticing a note taped behind the screen. I yanked the door open, grabbed the note, and then turned and headed for the truck. I wasn't sure how this letter would read, so I wanted the safety of my vehicle while I read through it. I jogged, making sure to look both ways as I crossed the street. When I got into the truck, I immediately unfolded the letter.

Babe, if you're reading this, it can only mean one thing...you've survived long enough to try to rescue me. I'm so sorry I've left you in a town crawling with the undead. Well, you always said you wished this would happen, and I hope it's everything you hoped it would be. Ha-ha, just kidding. This is a bad situation, and I'm glad you're still fighting for survival. I love you so much, and I'm scared without you.

My grandma and I are taking off. My grandfather was bitten. I really hope we can meet up soon. I'm so sorry I left you behind, but my grandma said she didn't want to go searching through town for you. After I dropped you off, I started seeing all sorts of chaos. When I got to the public square I was in danger. Cars were still smoldering, and trash was everywhere. I started seeing people walking toward my car, but somehow I realized they weren't people anymore. I wanted to turn back and pick you up right then, but something smacked my car, so I hauled ass to my grandmother's. The roads leading here were a fucking mess, and it took some careful planning. When I got here, two zombies were smashing on the door, and my grandfather kicked the door open when he heard my horn. I guess he thought I was a rescue squad, I don't know. When he recognized me, he ran to my car and told me to drive it around back and enter the house through the back door. I did as instructed, and when I was safely locked inside, my grandfather returned through the front door clutching his left shoulder. He explained how he killed the zombies but had been bitten.

Again, I'm so sorry I left without you, but I promise I'm going to do what I can to find you. We're leaving soon. I assume everyone and their brother is going to be cluttering the streets to the interstate, but we have to get out of here. I have no idea where grandma is planning on going, but when I get out of here I will tell the police, the army, and whoever else I can. I will do my best to send a search party. I hope we both make it out alright and are reunited soon. Grandma is putting supplies by the door and wants me to cut this short. Remember, I love you very much. I miss you, and I'm scared. I have to go; we locked Grandpa in the bathroom, and he is starting to pound on the door. I love you so much, and please, please come find me when you make it out. I love you! Megan.

"What's it say? Did she make it out of here alive?" Marston asked when I looked up from the letter.

"Dude, I don't know," I said after a long pause. "She said her granddad was bitten and turning, and she and her grandma were leaving town. Dammit!"

"She's a bright one. She's probably getting help as we speak."

"I hope she's safe."

I looked in the mirror to see two zombies coming up alongside the truck. One of them was trying to grab the driver's-side door.

"Look behind us," I said.

Marston glanced over his shoulder for only a second before shouting.

"Drive motherfucker! They're closing in, and one of them is sneaking up to your door!"

I hit the gas, but instead of moving, the truck started to sputter. I pushed the pedal to the floor, and we took off like a bat out of hell.

"Marston, we need some gas, or we're going to be walking."

"What the hell are you thinking? We can't do that on this side of town."

"We'll know if we can or can't soon enough," I replied.

I reached into my pocket and grabbed my smokes. I lit one up as I drove toward the end of Cooper Street, and there I took a right onto Mill Street. A half block up the street was a gas station.

I thought about the events of the day as I closed the gap between us and the gas station. I had accidentally killed some random guy, stolen a truck and a lot of guns, and driven all over hell only to find my girlfriend was gone. We were still not back to safety; dark was just around the corner, and a lot more zombies were coming soon.

I flicked my smoke out the window before pulling into the gas station, and parking next to the pumps. I put the truck in park and had a look around the area. I saw nothing that could ambush us, so I turned the engine off. All the pump's hoses were lying on the ground; I figured people had come here and tried to fill up before shit hit the fan. With the hoses on the ground I knew the last purchase on the pump would still be active. I told him to get out with me and give me some cover while I filled the tank.

I walked to the gas hatch as Marston watched for anything that might try to kill us. I grabbed my knife from its sheath and tossed it into the bed of the truck toward Marston.

"I don't want you to shoot anything," I said.

"Why?"

"Well, we are, in fact, at a gas station, and guns eject flames when shot. Therefore, I don't want to be blown to shit, and those goddamn things are attracted to loud booms like moths to a bug light."

I unscrewed the gas cap, picked up the handle, inserted it into the tank, and squeezed the trigger. To my surprise, the price meter started to go up.

After a couple of uneventful minutes, the handle of the gas pump clicked telling me the tank was full. I, placed the nozzle back into its rightful spot, screwed the truck's gas cap into place, and walked back to the door of the truck.

As I got in, I looked over at Marston in the seat next to me.

"You ready?"

"Can we hurry this up?"

I pulled onto Mill Street, hung a wide left turn, and headed down toward the square. As we went over the crest of the hill, I stopped the truck to plan a route. Ahead, the Mill

Street Bridge we needed to cross was cluttered with abandoned vehicles. As I looked out over the street, I saw there was enough room for us to squeeze the truck through the mess, so I started driving again.

The path was narrow, but the truck scraped through as we crossed the bridge toward the square. One of the vehicles we squeezed past contained a zombie, but it just slapped at the windshield of the car it was stuck in. When crossing the bridge, I thought one of the trucks we had seen earlier had plowed its way through some time previously. Whatever it was that made the path, I was grateful.

As we got to the end of the bridge, the small hill at the end of Mill Street led into the square. Factory Street was a sharp left from there.

As we passed Factory Street, I noticed the public square was unnaturally clean. During normal times, I'd have to enter the square and drive to the right and around to get to State Street, but now I just shot into the oncoming lane to the left.

"I hope we don't see one of those dump trucks," Marston said.

I turned left onto State Street and started up the small hill. As far up the road as I could see, everything was clear.

"Seamus, do you think Burto's drunk as hell, passed out?"

"He fucking better not be!"

"What are we going to do with the truck?"

"Park it across the street in the hardware store parking lot like I already said."

I stopped paying attention to him. I was tired of being out of the apartment, and I desperately wanted a beer. We only had to go four blocks, so I gave it some gas. It only took ten seconds before we pulled up under the apartment window. I pulled up on the sidewalk so Marston's door was flush with the building and couldn't be opened. He shot me a look, and all I did was chuckle. The glass shards under the tires crunched and snapped as I put the truck in park.

Marston crawled through the back window and started putting his guns back into the bag while waiting for the rope to come down.

I stepped out, looked up to the window and gave Burto a yell. He popped his head out.

"Thank god you guys are back!" Burto answered.

"Toss down the rope and the ladder," I yelled back.

Burto tossed the rope down, and it landed in the back of the truck. Marston tied the rope through the handles of the duffle bags. He made sure they were secure before going up the ladder.

As I waited in the hot sun for any word from upstairs, I heard a can pop open, and I couldn't believe it. I stood there waiting for Marston to come back to the window. Finally, he showed back up.

"You really do like fucking around, don't you?"

"Dude, I needed a beer."

"Can you and Burto lug those bags up the same way you did the carts?" I asked, annoyed.

I watched as Marston pulled Burto to the standing position and the two started heaving the bags up the wall.

"How's that leg holding up?" I shouted to Burto.

"I'm not putting much pressure on it, so it seems okay."

As the guys worked, I returned to the driver's seat and pulled the truck into the parking lot of the ACE hardware. I parked the truck, got out and then jogged to the ladder. I got to the ladder and I went up it pretty quickly. As soon as I stepped foot inside, I headed for the kitchen to grab a frosty beverage.

CHAPTER 17

We hadn't been back in the apartment for thirty seconds before Burto started playing twenty questions.

"Holy shit, I was getting scared! What did you guys see?"

"Basically everything we came across was destroyed, and we ran into a decent amount of zombies," I said.

"Did you find anyone alive?"

"We found some guy named Rob-o, but I accidentally killed him. Apparently, he'd resorted to cannibalism to stay alive. It seemed strange he didn't try and hit a store like we did," I explained.

"What took you so long?"

"The roads were blocked by abandoned cars and trash, so we had to drive way out of our way through Felts Mills."

"Damn, I can't believe you guys are back."

"Did I leave anything out, Marston?"

"That sums it up."

"Christ, I'm happy to be back in this shithole apartment! Unfortunately though, when it gets dark, I'm going to head right back out. Lucky me," I mumbled.

"What's that, Seamus?" Burto asked.

Marston tossed his empty on the floor and left the room, heading to the kitchen. I sipped my beer and began going over what I was thinking happened in Watertown to Burto.

"I'm going to head out on foot; I want to scout the area a bit to plan an escape route. I am thinking we might be able to take Washington Street out of town and then over to Sackets Harbor, but I want to see if the path is clear."

"That sounds like a good idea, but why do it right now when you just got back?"

"I want to get a rough idea of what it looks like before we try leaving in that direction. I figure if we all pile into the truck...say tomorrow, and get stuck trying to go down a blocked road we could be in trouble."

"Yeah, that makes sense. So, what do you think happened?"

"Throughout the day I've been piecing together an idea."

"Yeah that's great, I'm all ears," Burto yipped.

"The majority of the zombies we saw didn't have holes around their wrists. I'm thinking the ones with holes come out at night and the ones without come out during the day," I explained.

"What?" Burt asked.

"Remember the other night when those guys were walking the zombies with the bullhorns?"

"Yes."

"Well, halfway up State Street, we had to hide from a truck hauling dead bodies," I said.

"Yeah, those fuckers drove by here."

"Remember when you told me about the army guys during the evacuation?"

"Yeah."

"I think those guys somehow created the zombies. I also think they've figured out how to control them. I'm not a hundred-percent sure, but I think that's what's going on."

"You might be onto something with this, Seamus."

"At this point, nothing would surprise me. I'm going to sit in here and watch from the window while I have a few drinks."

I headed past him toward the kitchen. I grabbed the Jameson out of the cupboard, turned, and headed back to the living room.

"Hey, Seamus...did you find Megan?" Burto asked.

"We stopped by her grandma's place, but they were gone. She did leave me a note, but it didn't say where she was going. I have no idea if she's even alive at this point."

"Jesus, man, I'm sorry. At least we are well armed now, thanks to you guys."

"The guns are a big plus...how's your leg by the way?"

"I really haven't felt much from it today, so I think that's a good thing."

Yeah or it's severely infected and about to kill you.

"Hopefully we'll be leaving soon, and you can have an actual doctor look at that thing."

"I'd really like if that happened sooner rather than later."

I simply shrugged, then grabbed the only chair in the room, pulled it in front of the window, and had a seat as I unscrewed the bottle.

The first slug burned all the way down to my belly. I almost made the bitter beer face but stopped as the burning ceased. As I watched dusk turn into night, I realized it was quieter than usual outside.

I had a moment of solace to review what I had done that day. I picked up my bottle and took another swig--I was trying to drink the memory of Rob-o away. I knew it would take a lot more booze and time before I forgot about the day's events, so I stood up and headed for the kitchen to grab some Pabst.

Candlelight flickered on the walls. I didn't have to be in the kitchen to know Marston was telling exaggerated stories of the day's events.

"Oh man, you should have seen me escaping those zombies. One tried grabbing me from behind, but I shoved the thing and sidestepped out of the way, and Seamus slammed it with the club."

"It didn't exactly happen like that, Burto," I said as I entered the kitchen.

Burto looked up at me, visibly eager to stop talking to Marston. The two were talking over drinks.

"What's it like out there?"

"There's still nothing within eyeshot of the window," I said.

Burto raised an eyebrow and made a sound like he was pondering an idea.

"Anyway, if we hadn't kept our cool out there, the things we saw would have sent us spiraling into madness," Marston continued, sucking Burto unwillingly back into their conversation.

"Marston, why don't you tell him about you sitting on the ground rocking back and forth?" I said.

"Yeah, Marston, tell me about that."

"Oh, that was nothing, my stomach was acting up, and I needed to tie my shoe." Marston continued. "So, like I was saying the things we saw out there would crush humbler men."

I turned and opened the refrigerator door to find a half-empty twelve-pack. I pulled out a beer, popped the tab, and raised it to my lips. I didn't stop drinking until more than half was emptied. I placed the can on top of the fridge and grabbed a smoke out of my pocket.

Picking up my beer as I lit the smoke, I heard Marston blab on. I wanted to say something, but figured I would let him have his moment, even if he was full of shit.

"Those assholes in the truck were lucky Seamus grabbed me when he did. I was going to beat the ever-living piss out of them for this shit! The nerve they have to destroy my fucking town!"

Burto had obviously sensed the story was a load of crap and turned to me again.

"What are we going to do?" he asked.

"We have a truck and a lot of guns, so we need to get the fuck out of this city as soon as possible."

An awkward silence fell after I spoke. Marston stopped telling his lies and sat quietly. I realized I had to calm my mind from the day's events before having any decent conversation, so I turned to leave.

I figured I could sip on what was left in the can and then hit the bottle. I had to catch a buzz if I wanted my nerves to be at ease about my solo on-foot mission. The other two picked up their conversation in the kitchen, and it was more of Marston talking out of his ass. I figured they would come over to bother me as soon as the bottle of Bacardi they were working on had met its demise.

I sat in my chair and pulled another smoke from my pocket. I lit up and set the pack on the windowsill, sipping beer, and watching for anything out of the ordinary.

The smoke lasted a few minutes, and then I flicked it out the window to the street below. As I sat waiting for something to happen, my mind started to drift. Although I was wide awake, my brain began to act as it did when I was dreaming.

The men with the bullhorns, the dump trucks, the bar, and the bracelets were all connected. Who were they? Why did they pick Watertown?

As much as I wanted to be the hero and save the day, I just as badly wanted to say fuck it, and run away with my tail tucked snugly between my legs. Agitation grew from the pit of my stomach, snapping me back to reality. I chugged the rest of my Pabst Blue

Ribbon and chucked the can into the corner of the room. I can't remember how long I sat and stewed in the chair that night.

The sun was long gone; the night sky was full of stars, and there was no moon to be seen. I stood up and poked my head out the window, checking for anything to the right and left of the apartment. I saw and heard nothing--no moans, no groans, nothing.

As I was about to pull myself back in, I turned to the left again to see a big burst of bright orange light radiating from the square. It looked like the burst had come from the center of the square, but I couldn't see the origin because there were two massive buildings directly between the apartment and the square. I stared at the glow in confusion. It looked like someone was having a bonfire.

"Hey, you two, come check this out: something is going on in the square," I said as I pulled myself back into the window.

Marston came pushing Burto into the living room. The two were laughing and being clowns until Marston let go of the chair, and Burto slammed into the wall.

"What the fuck! I could have fucked my leg up again," Burto slurred.

"I'm sorry, man, my hands slipped," Marston said, winking at me.

"Would you both shut the fuck up, for the love of God. Look out the damn window."

Marston placed his hands on the sill and carefully looked out.

"What do you think is going on?" he asked.

"I have no idea, but I sure would like to find out," I responded.

Burto started hopping on his good leg toward the window. Given he was so intoxicated, he was doing a considerable job on one leg.

"Out of my way," Burto demanded.

He looked out for only a few seconds and then came back in, slurring. "That's definitely a fire," he said before flopping back into his wheelchair.

"You know those things are slow and stupid," I said to Marston.

"I know where you're going with this, and I want no part of it!"

"I wasn't going to ask you for help. If I keep to the shadows with a low profile, I should be fine and undetectable."

Burto suddenly punched me in the back, lurching me forward.

"Why the fuck did you punch me?" I asked angrily.

"Because you put me in a wheelchair, I can't do a damn thing, and my leg could rot off thanks to you!"

"I didn't do it on purpose."

"Yeah, maybe not, but it is still your fault and sucks pretty fucking bad!"

"You know what sucks even more? I could have left your bitch ass to be eaten, so I don't want to hear any of your shit! Dude, if you can't handle your alcohol, don't fucking drink it!"

Burto wheeled himself back to the kitchen for the comforts of another liquor bottle.

"Christ, Seamus," Marston exclaimed.

"I did fuck his leg up, but who was the dick that wrapped it so tight?"

"That's neither here nor there, so why don't we drop the topic altogether?"

"Keep it together up here while I'm out. I don't want to get back to some shit show with the two of you completely trashed."

"Don't worry about me, but before you leave, you might want to butter Burto up. He's our way in and out of this place," Marston said, walking to the kitchen.

I started thinking he was somehow going to foil my re-entry. I pushed the thoughts of betrayal aside and looked out the window. The glowing was already growing bigger, and more intense. I figured they were burning a building or a mountain of tires, so I pulled my head back in and walked to the kitchen.

Marston had grabbed a beer and struck up another conversation with poor Burto, talking plans for the coming days, and they both had a hint of panic in their tones. Then Marston started shouting.

"We're going to die up here! It's only a matter of time before those things get in! They're going to eat us, and no amount of gunfire is going to stop them!"

Before the situation could escalate out of control, I spoke up to calm the drunkards' nerves.

"Look, you two...we're getting out of here soon. We have enough supplies to last us for weeks if we ration them properly. Before we hit the road, I want to try scouting a little so we get an idea of what direction we should head in when we leave. I'd also like to get some information about what's happening here. I'd like to find out so I can tell the news or whoever else wants the story of the century. That's what this mission tonight is for. I'm not asking for help, because I want to do this, and I've already got a plan."

Marston and Burto just sat there staring at me. Their expressions told me two things: they thought I was an idiot, but they were also intrigued.

"We have guns, a truck with gas, and the will to get out of this hellhole. I want to find out who is running this and send the army after them," I continued. All we need to do is stick together, and we'll be ghosts in Watertown soon enough. Leaving right now during the night is a bad idea, especially with some massive fire down the street."

"Seamus, I don't like the term ghost...could you please say something else?" Marston said nervously.

"Sure, I'll use different words for the baby. Besides, Burto, your leg might need another few days before you can put pressure on it."

"I had a look at it when you two were out. It still throbs sometimes, but it doesn't hurt," Burto said quietly.

"We have it a lot better now with all our supplies, so why should we panic? Our barricade is stronger than a brick shithouse. The only thing we need to worry about is being spotted from outside by anything alive or dead," I explained.

"Burto, it's fucking scary out there! You're lucky this maniac hasn't tried to pull you along on one of his death missions," Marston said.

"I'd rather go on a death mission then sit up here drinking, smoking, and jerking off. I'm so bored. I want to do something," Burto returned.

"Just think, Burto, you can be bored to death now and still be alive in a week, or you could go out there and risk being killed right now," I said.

"I guess you have a point, Seamus,"Burto admitted.

I walked out of the kitchen and headed for the living room, where the bags of guns were stored. With the help of a little candlelight, I went to the bag Marston had loaded and pulled out a long gun with a hunting scope.

I held the gun to my shoulder and looked through the scope. There wasn't enough light to see anything, so I moved back toward the kitchen door. I pointed the rifle, and in the candlelight, lined the crosshairs on Marston's forehead. Confident it worked, I set the rifle up against the wall and returned to dig through the bag of ammo. I grabbed six random boxes of shells, picked up the gun, and returned to the kitchen.

I placed the shells on the counter, then handed Burto the gun. Marston looked at me and rolled his eyes. He picked up one of the candles and headed for the living room to look out the window. His antics were unnerving, but I was getting good at brushing them off.

"Load this bugger up," I said to Burto.

"I don't feel like it right now. I can't really shoot anything from here, now can I?" Burto said sarcastically.

"That's a great point," I said. "Alright, I'm going to go now. Are you going to be okay?"

"Well... how long are you going to be out?" Burto asked.

"Not long. I plan on getting into the retirement building across the street, getting to the roof, and looking toward the square to see if I can see something useful."

"Whatever you say, you crazy son of a bitch! Try to make it as quick as you can. I hate being up here alone."

"Well, you've got Marston."

"I'd rather be alone," Burto laughed.

"I don't like being out there at all, so trust me when I say I'll be back as quickly as possible. I just want to see what is happening so I can make an escape route for the three of us in the truck. Besides, if I don't come back, you two will have enough supplies to last until your leg is healed, and then you guys can use the truck and escape."

Reaching into my pocket, I grabbed the truck keys and handed them to Burto. I had no idea if I was going to be killed or even make it back, so I wanted them to have a chance to escape if I didn't make it.

"Don't tell Marston you have the keys, and make sure you wait at least a few days before you take off without me. There's no telling what I'll run into out there, so I could be a while."

"Seamus, my leg probably won't be strong enough to walk on for a while. If you're not back in a few days, we'll probably still be here."

Then, out of nowhere, Marston shouted something from the living room I never thought I'd hear.

"Come on, you drama queens, hurry your asses up! Seamus, are you ready to do this?"

Burto looked at me in surprise and opened his mouth to speak, but I cut him off before he had the chance.

"What the hell got up his ass...? He wants to leave?" I muttered.

I heard Marston shout again, this time directing curses and hatred out the window.

"The crazy fucker is screaming into the street!" Burto murmured.

I bolted to the living room. I snatched a handful of Marston's hair and pulled him into the dining room, then threw him on the floor. I got up close to him so I wouldn't have to shout.

"What in the *fuck* are you doing, you god-dammed fool?" I grunted into his ear.

The bastard was breathing like he had just gotten into a fight, and from the smell of his warm breath, I discovered the problem. I glanced at the floor where I had set my Jameson to see a half-empty bottle of Bacardi 151 next to it. As Marston sat on the floor, a puddle started forming under his ass as he pissed himself.

"Why would you tell me you're going with me knowing damn well you're too drunk to walk?" I asked.

I got no answer; instead, the bastard simply passed out. Burto had wheeled himself into the room to see what all the commotion was.

"I'll be a lot better off with him sleeping," he said, laughing.

"It's better for both of us he passed out."

"Honestly, the only thing that matters is that you hurry. I want to ride out of this town as soon as possible," Burto said.

"You got it. I'll do my best to stay alive and be back soon. Leave Marston in his own piss. That should make him happy when he wakes up. And don't drink anymore; I don't want you passed out when I need to get back in."

"Yeah, yeah, don't you worry, Seamus. I'll make sure you get back in."

Chapter 18

I lowered the ladder to the ground, thinking about my stealth mission to the square. This fire intrigued me, and I was really hoping I could see what I needed about Washington Street at the opposite end of the square. There were four different directions we could take, but Washington was the closest.

I placed my shotgun on the windowsill, and when I was firmly on the ladder, I grabbed it and slowly climbed down. I had all my guns holstered, and when I got to the ground, I carried my shotgun in front of me with the safety off.

Burto yanked the ladder up and out of sight as soon as my feet hit the ground.

Being out of the apartment felt different now; creeping around staying in the shadows felt eerie, and the chill of the night was strange. My skin crawled every time a slight breeze blew, but with my shotgun pointing toward the square, I started to walk.

The streetlights, now that they were working again, made the journey worse, as I was constantly avoiding the light. With trash everywhere and lights all over, I realized how dumb this trip was. I hoped nothing was in the area to catch a glimpse of me while I was in the open. If I had to fire a shot or two, I'd be spotted and swarmed within seconds.

The apartment was five blocks from the square, and I had already walked two. I darted across the street and into the Wendy's parking lot when I remembered an old unused road hidden behind the building. I walked toward where I remembered the road was hidden, and it took a few minutes, but I finally located it. It was overgrown with underbrush, vines, and tree branches. It was perfect; the road was hidden with the cover of trees, so nothing would find me.

I started pushing my way into the undergrowth, and after a second, I took notice of how the fire had gotten bigger since leaving the apartment.

After getting through the underbrush at the entrance the rest of the road opened up. The roadway was cracked and had chunks missing in the asphalt, causing me to trip and stumble as I walked.

I shouldn't have drunk so much before embarking on this trip.

I moved slowly, knowing the woods keeping me hidden would end soon and expose me to any onlookers in the area. I tried listening for noises around me, but only the sounds and chants from the square were in the air.

The hidden road came out behind a local bar called Thunder Dome. I knew if I walked straight out of the hidden area I would be under the streetlights behind the bar. I walked to the edge of the wooded perimeter and peeked through the remaining branches. The streetlight didn't reveal me, so I stood and looked through the parking lots across the street. Now that I was paying attention, I saw a cross on the top of one of the buildings, and the other looked like an apartment building. These were the two big buildings that blocked my view from the apartment. In between these structures was an alleyway, and that was where I was heading. This alley cut from the backsides of the buildings right to the center of the square, and that was where I believed the fire to be.

I had no choice but to walk through the illuminated area behind the bar and cross the street. I took a look out and studied the lot before making a move. The parking lot across the street was covered in darkness; the idea of running through the light made me nervous, but it had to be done.

As I stood at the tree line, I started to get an uneasy feeling about what I was going to do. Wasting no more time I darted out of the woods and across the street to find the cover of the first enormous building that was the church.

As I stood safely in the darkness of the parking lot, I let my eyes adjust. The light from behind the bar had messed with my vision enough for me to worry I might miss something. As I waited, I listened carefully for anything that might be trying to make a meal out of me, but still heard nothing.

After my eyes had adjusted to the darkness, I started walking toward the end of the first building where the alleyway was located. The shadows of the lot provided me with more than enough darkness to remain hidden, but the fire in the square was so huge it lit up the small alleyway. I got to the walkway and stayed next to the wall out of the light. I pressed my face against the wall and slid to the right, not exposing more than an eyeball. I figured this was the safest way to stay out of anyone's line of vision.

Right away, I realized I had been right about the fire's location. It was directly in the center. I watched as people carried bodies from a nearby pile and tossed them into the roaring flames.

I could hear people talking, so I knew some were alive. From where I was standing, I could see twenty to thirty people--alive or dead, I wasn't sure. As I stood with half my face exposed to the light, something caught my eye.

There were three men sitting together in bleachers. I hadn't noticed any bleachers when I had driven through there earlier that day, so I figured the men had brought them in sometime after that. They wore blood-red cloaks that hung to their ankles, had pointed hats and protective face masks. I assumed the masks protected them from toxins caused by the burning bodies. I stood there and watched the men from the bleachers yell through bullhorns.

"Add more to the fire!"

From where I stood, I could see the zombies being controlled were tossing bodies into the flames. I was willing to put money on it the bodies they were tossing into the fire came from the bar earlier that day. Every time a body hit the fire, clouds of black smoke billowed upward, and fireworks of embers shot into the atmosphere. As I stared at the fire, I suddenly remembered I was outside and very vulnerable. I glanced behind me to make sure nothing was sneaking up. After seeing nothing of danger nearby I returned my gaze to the men in the bleachers.

One of the robed figures stood up and turned around. The guy was taking a piss, but even from this distance, I noticed the son of a bitch had a Freemason logo on the back of his robe.Staring at the fire, the creatures waited for the men's instructions to toss more bodies on. Watching from afar, I found it strange the creatures did what they were told.

Just then, one creature started moving similar to a spooked horse, and started heading toward the men. Before it got too close, one of the Masons pulled an object from his pocket and stabbed at the creature. A second later, a barrage of blue beams erupted all over the creature's body. The light show went on for about twenty seconds. Then, the lights went off, and the monster dropped to the ground, smoldering like a leftover campfire. It twitched a few times before it stopped moving completely. I pulled my head into the shadows and leaned my back against the wall.

I realized it all started with the bar Marston told me about when I arrived at his place. This bracelet somehow injected some solution into the person wearing it, and when they stumbled off, they were abducted. I was thinking after the abduction the victim was taken to a lab where they had some sort of operation done on them. After seeing the events at the fire and remembering the horde that walked past the apartment the other night, what else could it be? If the zombies with the holes had some kind of mind control device implanted, this plan went haywire somehow, or somewhere along the way. The Masons couldn't control the monsters that hadn't been part of the original plan, so to decrease the numbers; they had to get rid of the ones of no use to them. To clean up after themselves, they sent the controlled zombies to kill whatever monsters they couldn't use in their experiment. To be completely honest I had no real idea what the hell happened. The things I had seen with my own two eyes, and the way my paranoid brain works this was all I could come up with.

I was making assumptions at this point, but they seemed believable to me. There were things I didn't understand, and for all I knew, my theory was completely wrong. Fort Drum was an army base, minutes outside of town, and I wondered if the military might be involved. After all, they did have the technology and capital to fund such an experiment. Maybe the army had set this whole thing up, and the Freemasons were running the operation. I figured if the army had been experimenting with mind control and biological weapons, someone would have uncovered them.

My mind was racing a mile a minute, and I decided sneaking any farther to check out Washington Street was a bad idea. I stood in the shadows and then finally got fed up with the hundreds of thoughts rushing through my brain and decided to head back to the apartment.

Before I left, I took one last look. The three men were laughing and having a good time while their monsters waited for commands. There were bodies still being tossed into the fire, causing a cloud of smoke I knew would be visible in the morning.

I wasted no time getting back to the apartment, jogging the same way I had come. I wasn't the best athlete, and I smoked a lot, so within fifteen feet, I was winded. I had my shotgun across my chest, and the guns in their holsters bounced as I ran. I was nervous about jogging, but figured if I ran across something, I could smash it with the butt of my shotgun.

It had taken thirty minutes to get to the square, but at my pace, it took only ten to get back. There was no caution in my return. I figured if I crossed paths with anyone on the way I would make short work of them. I thought it was strange I had only seen three men at the fire and wondered if many more sat around in the shadows out of sight. I really only had to worry about two blocks of light, so I just hauled ass home. I was under the front window before I realized it.

"Burto, I'm back, throw down the ladder."

A second later the ladder came crashing down. I was exhausted, and eager to head into the apartment for the night.

After climbing into the window, I turned and pulled the ladder up behind me. Only then did I feel safe.

CHAPTER 19

After I caught my breath, I sat with Burto in the kitchen. He had already asked me a dozen times, but I'd refused to explain until Marston was there to hear it too.

"I'm going to wait for Marston. I don't want to repeat this more than I have to."

"Well, something must have scared the shit out of you...you look sickly," Burto said.

"To be honest, I still have no idea what I saw. There was definitely some weird shit going on, but in reality, I have only assumptions and speculations at the moment. No real proof of anything."

I walked back to the living room where Marston was still passed out on the floor. I smacked him in the face a few times and started to shake him. I knew it would take a while for him to wake up, so I walked back to the kitchen for a smoke and a beer while I waited. I sat drinking in the kitchen for a few minutes before I heard Marston stirring to life. When I heard him bitching and moaning, I yelled to him from the kitchen.

"Get yourself together and come out to the kitchen."

"What the hell do you want?" Marston shouted back.

I finished my beer and grabbed another one from the fridge.

I pulled the last smoke from my pack and lit it, then tossed the empty box on the floor. I headed toward the counter, which was cluttered with empty beer cans that had been turned into makeshift ashtrays. There were so many cans I couldn't set mine down, so I swept them all off with the back of my hand. Cans flew everywhere and clattered loudly to the ground. Burto gave me a stare of disgust while the cans came to a rest.

"Dude, you want to try keeping it down? That's the only rule you made, and you're breaking it," Burto said.

"I'm sure you can see my concern," I snapped.

"So now you're going to be a dick for no reason?"

"Sorry. I'm still freaked out by everything, and my nerves are fried."

"Well, how about you keep the noise down and relax. You already have a beer and smoke, so try thinking about something positive," Burto said.

The candlelight flickered as Marston came walking through the door, mumbling about still being drunk.

"I am so glad you felt the need to wake me up for this. Which one of you thought it would be funny to dump water on my pants?" Marston asked.

"You pissed yourself, you moron! I'm not repeating myself, so pull up a chair and shut your mouth."

My tone told him I wasn't going to tolerate his bullshit, so he sat down.

"Alright, this is going to sound crazy. Let me rephrase that: it is going to sound un-fucking real!"

Burto's eyes widened as big as golf balls, but Marston rolled his eyes and fired up a cigarette.

I started by explaining what I had seen from the shadows of the square, the colossal bonfire, and the zombies throwing bodies into the flames. I went on to explain the guys in the robes with the Masonic logo on their backs. I glanced at both of them, wondering if they were following, and when I realized they were, I went ahead and mentioned my theory about some sort of mind-control device. Marston was the first to jump up in his chair and shout.

"What do you mean mind control?"

"Can your feeble fucking brain comprehend the idea? I think the people behind this operation have implanted chips into the brains of the undead. How else would they be able to control them?"

"So, Seamus, are you just going on some strange hunch you had, or do you have some actual proof?"

"Marston, I am so sick of you running your goddamned mouth, so shut the fuck up before I punch you in the teeth... do you understand?"

There was no response, just an eye roll and a sigh. Burto seemed ready to lunge out of his wheelchair and hit him because of his shitty attitude but didn't. Burto re-fixed his gaze on me, gesturing with his eyes to continue my story.

As the story progressed to the point of the electrocuted zombie, the room got awkwardly quiet. I thought it was strange that Burto was intrigued by the entire story, but Marston hadn't seemed to pay much attention to any of it. I thought he was checked out because of the booze, but even then, I wasn't sure what his issue was. It was only when I mentioned the strange device one of the men had used when he zeroed all his attention on me.

"If they're doing this kind of shit, they must have a few higher-ups in their pockets. Fort Drum is right outside of town; how the hell is the army not involved?" Burto asked.

"The same idea crossed my mind as I watched the fire. I was thinking the army might have paid the Masons to do their dirty work. Everything is strange about this whole situation, I mean we're in the middle of a zombie apocalypse, but I don't want to jump to any more conclusions than I already have," I said.

I peered at Marston who was now asleep and snoring and gestured for Burto to head to the living room. He maneuvered himself around Marston, and I grabbed my beer and the candle and followed him into the living room.

"Alright, Burto, let's keep this down. I think I might have a good idea, and I don't want ole Marston to find out."

"What are you thinking?"

"Well, to be quite honest, I got no plan."

"What the hell do you mean, got no plan?" Burto asked.

"Just as I said...I really don't know what to do about anything at the moment."

"Well sitting here talking about doing something isn't going to solve a goddamn thing. Let's make up a plan while Marston is passed out."

"There's no harm in that. He'd just bitch and moan about it anyway."

The two of us sat in silence, pondering our next step, and when I looked up at Burto, I could tell he was really thinking about something. I had plenty of ideas running through my head about what to do, but I couldn't speak for Burto. All he was doing was looking at the floor and shaking his head back and forth. He looked up and mumbled to me.

"The only plan I can come up with is getting the hell out of this place."

"Well, Burto...that's obviously the best move. How about we get out tomorrow?"

"You know, I have no disrespect for you, but that is the best idea you have had thus far. Besides, I'm sick of sitting up here listening to the moans and groans of the dead. Those bastards make it hard for me to sleep at night. I definitely want out!"

The thought of Burto's feelings when Marston and I were out had never crossed my mind. He was sitting up here alone, listening to the zombies on the streets below. He had no way of knowing if we were alive, dead, or coming back. This notion must have fucked with his head on levels I can't imagine.

The two of us sat there not speaking. I was pondering our next move while Burto thought of who knows what. The room wasn't completely silent though because we could still hear the dull roars of Marston snoring. Burto started to wheel out of the room toward the kitchen.

"Grab me one while you are going that way."

He came back a minute later and handed me a semi-chilled can of beer. I didn't bother looking at the label, opened it, and started to chug.

"Is Marston still passed out?" I asked.

"Hell yeah! He's facedown on the floor because he fell out of his chair."

"You know... something has been bothering me since I got here."

"What's that?"

"Do you remember when we got to the door, and he wouldn't let us in?" I whispered.

"Hell yes, I remember; we were being chased by fifty zombies, and I was about to die of blood loss. How could I forget?"

"Well, do you think that spineless piece of shit would have let us in if I had been weaker than him?"

"To be honest, I don't understand what his deal was or why he was acting like such a dick. I know he thought I had been bitten."

"I told him you hadn't, and the prick still wouldn't let us in. I don't think he planned on letting us in at all."

"I don't see how that matters now. We got in, and you smashed his face. All the beatings he has gotten since you got here can't be good for his self-esteem," Burto said, laughing.

"No, it matters a lot; it's bothered me the whole time. Marston is a selfish dick who only cares about himself, and I've been thinking about something I want to run by you."

"Well, let's hear it?" Burto replied.

"It's dark and twisted."

"Even better...lay it on me."

"I think we should give Marston a taste of his own medicine. I figure since he has fucked over too many people to count, I say we ditch him without looking back. How does that float your fancy?"

"Whoa, whoa, whoa, what the hell are you talking about? What did he do to make you want to leave his ass here?"

"Well, he fucked everyone and their brother over. That shit he pulled in North Carolina is still bothering me, and he never takes responsibility for his actions. I haven't liked him since North Carolina, but I was biding my time."

"What did he pull when he was with you down there?"

"The prick was too lazy to get a job, screwed us out of rent and groceries, and then took off for New York leaving us high and dry. Before he left though he blamed my brother for having a couple ounces of mushrooms that got my brother locked up. Marston was supposed to help pay for a lawyer, but when the time came for money, he took off, and I haven't seen him until I got here the other day. Hell, look at the way he acts up here, the things he says and does, and the fact he never wants to help with anything. What about the shit he pulled with you, man? I mean, that alone is worth ditching him. How are you ok with that? The way I figure, he seems content up here, so let's leave him. "

"Yeah, that guy has fucked over everyone who's come into his path, so I know what you mean, but I don't understand one thing."

"What's that?"

"Why haven't you beaten the hell out of him, and why are you dealing with his bullshit?"

"Well, I did fuck him up pretty bad with the door. Hell, he has gotten hurt the whole time I've been here. The things that needed to be done were two-man jobs, and you weren't helping, so I *used* Marston. Just like he has *used* everyone he ever knew."

I started to laugh at the thought of fucking Marston over. As I laughed and shook my head, I drank more of the beer Burto had brought me.

"So, Seamus, we bail and leave Marston behind to fend for himself. Is that what you are suggesting?" Burto asked.

"Yes, I just said that. You really should lay off the drink. I starting to think you've drank yourself retarded. I know it is fucked up, but what can I say, he's an ungrateful piece of shit and doesn't deserve to leave. All he's done up here is talk shit and go out of his way to piss us off. I don't think he's worth the trouble."

"You make a valid point I'm not disagreeing with you, but say we are to take off without him, how are we going to do that?"

"I say we get him nice and sloppy drunk, and when he passes out, we take off. Go out the window, grab the truck, and head for the outskirts of town."

"How about right now that he already is sloppy drunk and passed out?"

"Great idea, but we're not ready. We need to get the gear ready to go, and somehow hide it from him."

"Man, that's fucked up! I'm not sure I'd want to do that to anyone. I understand he is pure shit, but what you are saying is you basically want to execute him."

"I'm not going to kill anyone. We'll leave supplies, and that's more than he would do for us," I said.

"When my gimp ass tries to climb down the ladder, what if he wakes up? I can put some pressure on it, but I still only have one good leg. It will take me a few minutes to climb down."

"I've known Marston for a long time, and when he passes out, he normally doesn't wake up. How long has it been since you tried to walk on it?" I asked.

"I've tried a few times each day, mainly when I have to piss. I'll stand up and hop around on my good leg long enough to unzip my pants. At first, I stand there putting a little pressure on my foot to see what it feels like. Have you ever sat on the toilet so long your leg fell asleep? You know that tickling sensation you get when you try standing? Well, my leg felt like that times a thousand the first day. It has either healed a decent bit, or my leg is seriously messed up and on the verge of being amputated. Sometimes it still throbs and gets hot to the touch if I use it for too long."

"Let me have a look."

Unwrapping the wound and exposing the gash didn't take too long.

"When I pull this tape off, it's going to rip the hair out of your leg," I said.

"I'm not worried about the hair. My leg was split down the back and its muscle popped out, so I think a little hair pulling will be fine."

I got behind Burto and set the candle on the floor. The light was enough for me to have a good look at the wound.

"Has it hurt up until now?" I asked.

"Like I said, it has when I try using it too much, but I fought through the pain mostly. I figure if I somehow get used to the pain it won't hurt as much when I need to use the leg more."

I began to peel off the top bandage first. This bandage covered the top of the wound and had a little ointment smeared on it. There was no blood. After the top bandage came off I started to pull the tape off the middle covering. This one had covered most of the wound, and when the dressing came off, I noticed the smell. It stunk like it was decomposing. I saw expanding redness around the wound, and greenish-colored pus seeping through. There was increased swelling, and the wound felt warm. Underneath the skin I could still see the clump of muscle.

"You said this doesn't really hurt at all," I asked.

"Not really at all. Sometimes in the morning before I start moving, it's tender and hurts a little, but that's pretty much the only time."

"How long after you wake up do you start drinking?"

"I normally grab something pretty quick."

It's the drinking that's keeping the pain away. He really needs a doctor at this point.

"I think the booze has been fooling you, buddy. This leg is in rough shape. We need to get you to a doctor as soon as we can."

"Is it that bad?"

"I think so, but I'm not a doctor, so let's get that last bandage off."

I yanked the third bandage and its tape off quickly. Burto didn't like this, and jumped in his chair, giving me a look of agitation. This bandage covered the last bit of the wound, and there was ointment and dried pus all over it.

"Alright, now that the bandages are off, I need you to go lean over the couch."

Burto wheeled himself over and parked his chair in front of the sofa. He put the brakes on and pushed himself out of the chair. He quickly turned and sat down with his bad leg stretched out.

"Dude, you're going to have to turn around and bend your knee. I want to see if the wound bleeds or the stitches pop."

He looked nervous but did what I asked. At this point, I was assured the wound was in serious shit. The stitches didn't pop, but pus spewed from the wound like a popped pimple.

I quickly grabbed a bandage and wiped the pus from the area.

"How's it look?" Burto asked.

Not wanting to scare him to the point of a freak out I answered.

"Well, like I said, we're going to have to get you to a doctor. Once you see one that should clear this whole mess up."

"Is it healing?" Burto asked.

"It hasn't healed completely, and could probably use another week, but it looks okay considering.

I'm sorry, Burto, you're in bad shape.

I could tell it was still rotting, and of course the wound was still red and bruised.

"Alright, are you ready for the moment of truth? Let's see if you can walk on it."

CHAPTER 20

After Burto got off the couch, I laughed as I watched him try to re-teach his leg how to function. He fell back onto the sofa two or three times before he stood for more than ten seconds. On the fourth try, he started to limp around like a guy whose foot had fallen asleep. He didn't apply too much pressure; just enough to keep his balance and hobble around the living room.

I acted as a spotter because Burto was worried about crashing to the ground and splitting his leg open again. After a couple minutes, I realized Burto was fine, and I wandered over to the window to see if anything was outside. Thankfully for us, I didn't see anything.

When I glanced out the window again toward the fire, it looked like the party was over. The brightness of the blaze had turned to a soft glow instead of a vibrant orange, and when a slight breeze kicked up the stench of burning bodies filled the living room.

For a while Burto kept trying to walk around the apartment. I watched as he went from vibrant and motivated to exhausted in a matter of minutes. As Burto finally took a seat and shifted in his wheelchair, the candle flickered out.

"Well, Burto, I'm fucking beat. I need some sleep."

"Yeah, man, me too. So you think we're going to try and head out tomorrow?"

"That's what I'm shooting for. It's going to be tough, especially when I break the news to Marston," I said with a sick laugh.

"I bet he flips out, and who wouldn't? It seems to me though that he pretty much deserves it at this point. I know he has helped, but if you hadn't beaten him and threatened him with further violence, do you think he would have lifted a finger?"

"Honestly, buddy, it's highly unlikely. The dude is fucking useless, selfish, and inconsiderate," I replied.

Just then, a noise came from beneath us. I crept over to the window and looked down at the street. Below us, a lone zombie stumbled its way toward the park. The zombie was a fresh kill; its skin, still intact, looked milky, and there were blood stains on its clothes. As I watched the monster, I realized how sick I was of seeing these things.

With a disgruntled sigh I walked back into the dining room to talk to Burto, who was sitting uncomfortably in his wheelchair.

"Hey, I think we should try to grab some shuteye. We have a long day ahead of us, and I don't want to be tired."

Burto didn't say anything. He just sat there with a shit-eating grin on his face. Then, as fast as the smile formed, it turned into a scowl.

"What's the matter? You should look ecstatic."

"I was just thinking about Marston and how we're ditching him."

"Try to keep your voice down; there's one of those things outside, and Marston is asleep in the next room. I don't want either of them to hear us," I said.

"Don't change the subject. This is a fucked-up stunt we're going to pull."

"I'm surprised he hasn't already tried to take off without us. Hell, he could be planning on doing it while we slept. Look what he did to you before this even started. How could you even let that go? The way I figure it, there are plenty of cars out there, and one of them has to run. Let him fend for himself. He's grown accustomed to doing that."

"No matter how you justify it, it's still fucked up for us to leave him behind."

"Well, what do you think we should do with him? Do you want to take him with us?" I asked.

"Well, he has helped a lot... you said so yourself you couldn't have gotten these supplies alone. This is his place, and he let us in."

"Yeah, but maybe if he wasn't such a liar, thief, cheat, and a disrespectful asshole, I would have some compassion for him. Remember we would be dead right now if I wasn't stronger than him. "

"Yes, but it is still fucked up to leave your friend in a town full of the walking dead, and crazy people controlling them," Burto continued.

"First off, he destroyed that friendship when he fucked me over, so fuck him. If I knew anyone else would have been held up in any part of this town, I would have found them. I have put up with too much of his shit to care about him any longer. That shit he pulled in North Carolina was the final straw. Besides, why do you care so much? It's not like he's ever done anything for you besides given you a hard time, stolen your shit, and kicked you out of your own apartment. What's up with your bleeding heart all of a sudden?"

"Just remember, Seamus, what goes around comes around."

"Look, I know what you're saying, and I'm sure I will go to hell for it, but at this point, I really don't care. Let me tell you this, it's not the best thing to say, but it needs to be said. If you tell Marston about this and the two of you try to ditch me, I promise I will hunt you guys down and make you wish you had died right here in the apartment. Don't get any ideas that will get you killed."

"Calm down. I'm not planning anything like that. It was you who saved my life and thought enough about me to get the supplies I needed. Marston was here with us but didn't try to help me in any way, shape, or form. It would be best for you to put that idea right out of your head. On a lighter topic of discussion, you know what I wish I had right now? A nice big bong of some good pot."

I laughed, realizing how beautiful a bong would be at that particular moment. I hadn't smoked in years, but I would have loved to that night. I figured it would have helped me sleep better than I had in weeks.

"That's a good idea, but there's no weed around here. I'm going to sleep, and If you are leaving with me, you should probably do the same," I said.

I grabbed a pillow, a nasty sheet, and started heading to the front window in the living room. I figured I'd set up in front of the window in case those idiots tried to ditch me. As soon as I got close to the window, I was hit in the face with a gust of wind that might as well have been a baseball bat, because the stink that came with it hit me hard. I thought about closing the window, but I didn't want to miss anything if something came by in the morning. I lay down, shut my eyes, and the only sounds I heard was the humming from the streetlights outside.

Lying there as the minutes passed, I was getting anxious and decided to take a peek out the window. I hoisted myself up on my elbows to see Burto had passed out in his wheelchair where I left him. I pushed myself up and got on my knees, turned, and looked out the window.

There was nothing down below, so I decided to lie back down and think about the next day. I knew Marston would sleep until at least noon. I decided to gather supplies while the two guys slept and put them next to the window for a quick and soundless escape.

I grabbed both of the duffel bags and dragged them into the light from the streetlamp outside. The firearms I had were enough for the rest of the trip. As that stench punched me again, I piled my weapons to the right of the window where my head would be when I slept. Not needing any more weapons for myself I pulled out a 9-millimeter and a twelve-gauge for Burto. After I decided on the weapons we would take, I grabbed a few boxes of shells for each of them.

The rest of the supplies in the bags would be extra weight neither of us needed to carry. The bags still held a rifle, shotgun, and a few handguns. I figured Marston wouldn't be as mad with that many weapons.

After the guns were situated, I consolidated the bags and snuck into the kitchen with one pack to fill with food.

Entering the kitchen, I began grabbing canned foods from the counter. Unfortunately, it was too dark to read the labels. I grabbed ten bottles of water and a bottle of what I thought was vodka. I left Marston with the rest of the water and a lot of alcohol. I figured I had enough canned goods and water to last the two of us at least three days.

They both slept as I rummaged through the stuff we would need to survive outside the apartment. I figured we didn't need anything but food, water, guns, and booze. I zipped the bag and returned to the living room, setting the bag next to my pillow. I then grabbed the bag I intended to leave for Marston and put it out in the dining room. While

I stood in the dining room there was a brief moment I highly considered leaving both of the guys behind. I shook the idea fairly quickly because Burto had done nothing wrong and didn't deserve to be left for dead. As I was leaving the room, I bumped into Burto's wheelchair, but luckily for me, it didn't bother him.

The open window now carried smoke from the fire in the along with the putrid breeze. Strangely, it didn't bother me as much now. I lay down on the floor in front of the window, my holstered weapons and bag of supplies next to me. I felt better knowing I was packed and leaving in the morning. I fluffed my pillow and tried to make myself comfortable.

As I tried to relax, my brain kept reminding me of what I was about to do. I realized I didn't care enough to keep searching for a reason not to. This was going to be the last night I stayed in the apartment.

I think I lost part of my mind and soul that night. I truly didn't care if I died trying, but I needed to leave Watertown forever. I licked my lips and closed my eyes, hoping for sleep.

I passed out without moving another muscle.

CHAPTER 21

Sunlight crept into my eyes, and I sat up as soon as my brain recognized I was coming out of unconsciousness. Before I stood up, the aroma of fresh-brewed coffee hit my nose.

"Good mooorniiing, man, I feel great today," Marston said from the kitchen.

I stood up and poked my head out of the window. Instead of a summer breeze, I was greeted by the terrible stench of burnt meat. I pushed the stink aside and continued to look around.

There was a cloud of black smoke rising above the square. I shook my head and rolled my eyes before turning to my right. The only thing up that way was a street full of the same trash and destruction. No dead or living people to be seen anywhere.

I pulled back in and walked to the dining room where Burto still slept soundly in his wheelchair. I began to shake him and whisper into his ear.

"Wake up. It's time to move out; we've been evicted!"

"Where ya going, friend?" Marston's voice asked.

I looked up toward the kitchen. Marston stood there sipping coffee. He took a long drink and wiped his lips with his free hand, his blue eyes looking at me like they were trying to cut glass.

Marston gave me a raised eyebrow and sucked his teeth. The smug look on his face made me see red. The memories of the things he had done over the years instantly came rushing in: all of the lies, his stealing, his manipulating, every terrible little demerit he'd casually scribbled in his own ledger of bullshit and idiocy for the past twenty years. Not only did he basically kick Burto out of his own apartment, he'd also stolen Burto's guitar and left it in a snowbank. Instead of fessing up, he blamed my brother for it. He did shit like that all the time; commit a crime and then let someone else take the fall, so he could avoid an ass beating.

Another time he got busted with an ounce of pot and let the guy he was staying with go to jail for a few days. The guy was kind enough to let the asshole stay with him. At the time, Marston thought he was some hot-shot drug dealer, so he walked around with an attitude. That night he was twisting up a blunt in the living room when the cops came to the door for a noise complaint. The Dead was playing too loud, and the neighbors had called the law. Marston had set the blunt on the table next to a large sack of weed, and when the roommate opened the door, the police saw the table. When the cops saw the table, they let themselves in to inquire further. The cop nicely asked the guys who owned the grass, and instead of being a man, Marston pointed at the roommate. Marston wouldn't fess up to owning it, and since it was the other guy's house, the roommate was hauled off to jail.

Getting my brother busted for things Marston himself had done certainly didn't make me like him anymore. There were so many people he had either fucked over or rolled on over the years. Everyone he'd ever met. The cherry on the cake was him stealing Megan's entire music collection, selling it for twenty dollars and hopping a bus to New York.

I admit we had done some cool stuff, but he had done too many bad things to be let off with just a busted face. I hadn't seen Marston until the day I came knocking on the door of this apartment. He was great at running away from his problems, but this time he wouldn't get another chance to leech off someone.

I decided right then I wasn't going to leave him any weapons at all. Not a gun, a club or even a single bullet for him to end his miserable existence with. I would leave enough food and water for a day, and then he would either starve or go find more supplies on his own.

Fuck "humanity." I had none of it left to spare this morning.

Burto awoke and tried to get out of his chair and walk. He stood there for a second, made an awful noise, and fell back into his chair. Normally I might have laughed at him, but in my state of mind there would be no laughter.

Marston strolled into the dining room and started talking to Burto.

"How did you sleep sunshine?"

Burto was groggy and didn't reply. As Marston stood waiting for a reply, I realized he didn't notice the bag of supplies by the window, nor did he notice the bag behind the wheelchair. At this point I didn't even care if he did.

I didn't want to be around Marston because I might kill him, so I did one better. I walked into the kitchen, started crushing bags of ramen and dumping them on the floor. When I turned around, Marston was watching me dump bottles of water onto the crumbled mess.

"What in the fuck are you doing?" Marston shouted.

I walked over to the cupboard and found a large can of beef stew as thoughts rushed through my head. I gripped it tight enough to turn my hands white from the pressure, then turned back to face Marston.

"What in the fuck do you--"

I fast-pitched the can of stew at Marston's head. He grabbed his face and dropped like a leaf in a fall breeze as his coffee spilled on the floor. Blood ran down his chin, spurting from between his fingers.

I walked closer and stared down at him.

"Show me your face, you useless coward motherfucker!"

His hands trembled as he complied. His nose appeared broken, and his eye had already swollen up and was turning black. For a couple seconds he rolled around on the floor screaming before trying to climb to his feet. He was on his knees and mumbling through a mouthful of blood. That was when he opened his eyes, and I grabbed the back of his head and slammed my knee into his eye socket as hard as the Lord allowed.

Marston flew through the dining room doorway and into Burto's wheelchair, bouncing off it. Burto screamed in pain from the encounter, and I started snickering as I rubbed my kneecap. My knee hurt like a bitch, and I felt as if I had busted it open.

In the doorway Marston rolled onto his back with his eyes closed. I figured he was knocked out, so I stepped over him and walked to the living room grabbing a .45 out of my holster. I turned to find Marston on the ground, bleeding from the eyes and nose.

I walked over and rolled him onto his stomach, not wanting him to choke on his blood while he was passed out. His body was dead weight. I checked to see if he was breathing. The scumbag wasn't dead, but he wouldn't be moving for a while. I tucked the gun into my belt and started talking to Burto.

"I need you to grab that bag and put it next to the window; we're taking it with us."

"Seamus, Jesus, man. You really fucked him up."

"You think that's bad? I haven't even started," I said to Burto.

Burto seemed to know it was pointless trying to talk sense into me, and I think he feared for his life at this point. I had a strange temper. You'd never knew until I was lashing out that I meant to kill you. He gave me a look and wheeled himself off to do what I had asked. Marston was now making noise, so I walked over and turned him on his side.

When I moved him from his stomach to his side, blood poured out of his mouth. Satisfied he would live for a while I stood up and headed for the bedroom across from the bathroom. This room was full of random garbage you would find in any crack house.

The sunlight of the morning shone through the windows of this pigsty enough for me to find what I'd come for: an iron in a mound of soggy sheetrock and clothes with mushrooms growing on them.

It looked like one of the first electric irons ever made, the cord severely frayed, with wires sticking out, the face rusted. I climbed out of the room and returned to Marston lying in the doorway to the kitchen.

I knelt beside him and set the iron on his shoulder, holding the cord out as I stepped over him. In a last effort to stop me, Marston grabbed my ankle and gurgled some words I couldn't understand.

His efforts were worthless, and I decided to kick him in the already-busted bridge of his nose. I stared at the outlet a foot or so away from Marston's head. I had seen enough movies to know how to cauterize a wound. I didn't want him to die; I just wanted to make sure he never ran his mouth again.

Burto had finished his assigned task and come out of hiding. Parked between the living and dining rooms, he stared at me for a moment.

"Moment of truth," I said to him. He looked down at whimpering Marston.

"Ya know, Seamus, at first, I thought you were out of control. Now I'm thinking about all the shit he said and did to me, Megan, and Scotty, all the bad things he did to you and to all of us. Fuck this guy."

"Thanks, Burto. I'm glad you came around."

I plugged the iron into the wall, the ancient cord heating up and sparking a little. Marston reached for my ankle and screamed out a desperate plea, his bright blue eyes pleading for this not to happen. I startled when I felt his touch, the iron tipping face-down into the pool of blood from his mouth.

A tiny trail of smoke rose from the slick red hardwood around the iron's edges. I reached for its grip and felt a shock.

"Little fucker got me," I said. I bore down on the handle as I straddled Marston's back and leaned in to whisper into his ear.

"I should've done this a long time ago, you cunt."

He shook his head back and forth, saying, "NO." I just laughed at his pathetic struggles. The iron sizzled, the burning bloody bubbles on its surface now boiling rancidly sweet. Grabbing a handful of hair, I pulled his head back until his Adam's apple was the size of a golf ball.

I slammed the iron into his face, all while being shocked and zapped. The iron started to boil the skin, steam rolling off in little clouds.

He was trying to scream, "STOP," but couldn't manage the word.

"Seamus, this is taking it too far!" Burto pleaded.

"Don't worry, he won't die."

Placing the iron on the floor I got off Marston's back. I got around in front of him and knelt down to get a good look at his face. The iron had sealed the wound and seared his eyelids shut.

"God damn, buddy, that looks brutal," I said, laughing at his misfortune.

I walked back around Marston, who was now lying motionless, not moving a muscle. His body would tremble every couple seconds, but nothing so much as a thumbs up. I put a foot on each side of his body and bent down, lifting his hips off the ground. I rolled him to his right side, and with my left hand, I undid his pants. I pulled his pants and boxers down to his ankles, exposing his ass cheeks.

"I know why you're doing this," Marston gurgled.

"Oh, do you now?"

"Yeah, it's because I fucked you good down in North Carolina."

"Among other things sure."

"It was worth it...you've always been a mark; you just never knew it. You're to self-centered to realize there are people smarter than you," Marston said, spitting blood.

"Hey, Burto, you might want to go ahead and leave the room. You're not going to want to see this."

Burto turned himself around and went back into the living room, out of view. I looked back at Marston's tiny pecker lying underneath his nut sack. He started trying to squirm away from me, so I brought the heel of my foot down on the small of his back. I was barefooted and felt a bone move or snap.

I went into the living room to put my shoes on, wanting to be able to leave right after I was done with Marston. Burto looked at me, speechless, as I tied my sneakers. I shot him an uncontrolled smile and returned to the dining room, where Marston whimpered. The stomp had made sure his voice box was the only thing he could move at this point. I stepped over him to go into the kitchen for the hammer and a nail. The nails were on the counter next to the barricade where I had left them. I turned and walked back into the doorway, where Marston lay in the blood he had already lost from his body.

I knelt down, spreading Marston's legs as I took a knee. I grabbed his small penis and pulled it as far as it would go, placing the tip of the nail directly in the center of his dick and applying some pressure. He began to flail again when the pointed object pushed into his spongy flesh.

"You like ripping people off! You like fucking people over! That shit is all over now, buddy!"

After a bit more pressure, the nail held the dick to the floor when I let it go. I grabbed the hammer and gave the head of the nail a small tap. Blood erupted from his throat when he screamed to unknown gods. It was time to finish the job. I brought the hammer down like I was shingling a roof. Unfortunately, I missed the nail and slammed the hammer down on the tip of his pecker. When the skin pinched between the floor and the hammer he bucked like a bronco. I had to jump up and sit on his back just so the fucker wouldn't get away.

"That must have hurt like a bastard. Stop moving, or I'm going to make you feel more pain than you have ever caused anyone in your life!" I whispered into his ear.

He didn't listen, so I slammed the hammer as hard as I could at the base of his spine. That broke some bones, and he didn't move again.

"Let's try this again," I said as I placed the nail on his outstretched cock.

I brought the hammer down directly on the head of the nail. This time I hit it hard enough to drive it through the spongy flesh and into the wood floor. I wasted no time pounding it deeper into the wood as he screamed bloody murder.

After placing the nail, I went into the living room to the windowsill and grabbed my smokes. I lit one up and walked over to Burto who was in the corner out of sight from the dining room.

"Seamus, what the hell did you do? I heard some hammering?"

"Yes, I was hammering."

"Do I dare ask what?"

"Well, if you really want to know, I nailed his dick to the floor."

Burto blew up.

"Holy shit! Man, that's the sickest shit I've ever heard! Why would you take it that far? Last night you said we were going to sneak out, not hammer the guy's dick to the goddamn floor!"

"Well, he's lied, stolen, and just been an all-around shitty person for most of his life. Now ask yourself this, what can he never do again?"

"Reproduce, or steal, but what about the lying part?"

"I'm still thinking about that. What I've done already should be enough, and I'm sure he's gotten the point."

"I don't want to ask questions I don't want to hear the answers to," Burto said.

"I want to get you out of here before I finish with him. I think that will be better than what I have planned. You don't need to be up here when I finish what I started."

"I am more than okay with not being around for whatever you plan on doing."

That was the last conversation we had inside the apartment. Burto and I sat in the living room until I finished my smoke. Then I walked over to the window to see if the screaming had brought unwanted attention. I didn't see anything, except clouds of black smoke rising from the square. I flicked my smoke out the window and walked to my holstered weapons.

CHAPTER 22

I strapped on my shoulder and waist holsters while the moans and groans of our old chum came from the dining room. I returned my gaze out the window and looked at the truck. It hadn't been touched.

"Alright, Burto, are you ready to climb down this ladder?" I asked.

"You have no fucking idea how ready I am to climb the hell out of here."

"I'm going to toss the bags, the ladder, and your chair out first. When you're down, wait for me. We'll go to the truck together, and then it's out of town we go."

"You make it sound easy. I'll do my best, but I don't think this will be done too fast," Burto said.

Burto wheeled himself over to the window and propped himself against the wall. He now witnessed the bloody mess in the other room.

I tossed the ladder out, then folded the chair, and threw it to the street.

"I hope that chair survived enough for you to use it to get to the truck," I said.

I grabbed the two shotguns we were taking, stuffed them into the bags, and tossed each bag out the window separately. I'm sure the two-story fall fucked up some of the goods, but at this point, I didn't care because I had all the weapons I needed strapped to my body.

"Now, move as fast as you can, Burto. I'll be right behind you! If you feel pain you have to suppress it!"

He had placed a gun in his beltline and was thrilled we were heading out the window.

"I'm a little scared, but I can't wait to get the fuck out of here," Burto said.

"Trust me man, I agree a hundred percent."

He turned and tried to go out the window ass first, but when he bent his leg, the pain stopped him in his tracks.

"Jesus Christ, my fucking leg hurts!"

"Alright, let's try something different," I said.

I lifted him out the window feet first. He grabbed onto the window sill and clutched it with both arms. As both his legs dangled, he put his foot on the step of the ladder. It took him a moment to steady himself, but within seconds he was climbing down, gripping the handles for dear life. I held the ladder as steady as I could and watched him descend. I could tell he was in tremendous pain, but the fear pushed him through. I waited for Burto to get to the ground, and then turned to go finish what I had started.

Marston was walking the line of conscious and unconscious. His head moved a little and his fingers twitched, but that was all.

I walked over and placed a foot on either side of him, reached my hand into his hair, and pulled his head off the ground. This woke him up and made him open his one good eye to look me in the face. Blood was drying on his face while fresh blood trickled from the wound near his eye, and I was careful to not step in it. At this point, he was terrified of me.

He tried to close his eye, but I slapped his burned face to snap him back to attention. A single tear rolled out of his good eye, down his cheek, and then dropped into the pool of blood. Looking into his eye, I knew his soul had left his body, and was now waiting for Charon to cross the river Styx.

"Well, Marston, old boy, this is it for you. You have hurt enough people over the years. This is me helping them pay you back."

He tried to close his eye, but I slapped the burn on his face.

"You worthless piece of shit! I'm not going to kill you. I'm going to let you suffer with your dick nailed to the floor. I'm leaving with Burto in thirty seconds, and when I'm out that window, I'm leaving the ladder down, hell, I don't have a choice. With your cock nailed to the ground, good luck fending off anything. I want to leave you with these words--you are the biggest piece of shit I've ever known in my life. People like you are protected from people like me, but now those days are over. I want you to lay up here and think about all the horrid shit you've done over the years."

I reached for my holster and grabbed the .45. With his hair held in my left hand, I put the barrel of the gun under Marston's lower jaw. He thrashed so much I don't think he felt the pain from his dick. I let him shake around for a minute with the gun on his jaw before I had a change of heart.

"I was going to blow your lower jaw off, but I think I've done enough. Fuck you, scumbag!" I said as I slammed his face back to the floor.

I stood over him for a second and decided I would leave him with a few things to help his agony. I went to the kitchen and grabbed a bottle of gin and a butter knife before returning to his side.

"I'm leaving you this bottle for the pain. This butter knife is for you to use to pry the nail out of your dick. I doubt the knife will help much; you might just want to pull the nail through. If you do somehow survive this ordeal...don't look me up. We're through, buddy."

I stood up and tossed the iron out of reach so Marston couldn't strangle himself with the cord. I placed the gun back into my holster and spit in Marston's face. He tried moving as I left the room, but I kept on walking.

I had wasted too much time torturing Marston and started to move to the window. I looked before I went out and Burto had already gotten the bags into the truck bed. He realized I was looking out the window and shouted to me.

"Dude, hurry up, I think one of those things is coming."

"How the hell did you get that stuff in the truck in your condition?"

"It doesn't fucking matter! Let's go!"

That was it for me, and out the window I went. Just before my head went under the sill, I looked at Marston, who was still moving slightly. I made it a point not to look for too long, because I might have felt bad. I was down the ladder in seconds, and then I sprinted to the truck. Burto was on the passenger side, lifting his ass into the front seat. When Burto was in the truck, I tossed his chair into the bed, and ran around the front to the driver's side.

Once the door was closed, I frantically patted my pockets, searching for the keys. Burto helpfully jingled them next to my face, so I snatched them and started the truck. I was overjoyed to hear the truck start up without making any strange noises. I backed up and cranked the wheel to the right so the truck was facing the square. I dropped the shifter and started to drive.

As we rolled up State Street, I glanced up at the apartment. The ladder still hung from the window. I gave the truck some gas and picked up speed. I looked ahead and saw Burto was right: a zombie was lumbering down the street toward us. I had the truck going twenty when I hit the zombie. The thing's face smashed off the hood before disappearing underneath the truck.

We headed down State Street toward the square where the gigantic fire had been. I pulled one of my .45s from my waist holster and set it on the seat between us, already feeling scared.

"Seamus, do I even want to know what you did up there?"

"I told him some things and gave him a bottle of gin," I replied.

That conversation ended as fast as it had started.

"We're about to be in the square. I was going to try taking Washington Street out of town. What do you think?" I asked Burto.

"I don't care, take any direction you can that's not blocked by cars and garbage. There's no way I can make it out of here without a vehicle."

"Let's hope the street has been cleared like State Street," I finished.

Entering the square, I saw smoke still rolling off mounds of charred ashes, and while we had seen only one zombie up to this point, now we saw at least fifty.

I kept the truck at about twenty miles an hour until I saw all the zombies. My brain started running through the possibilities of all of them surrounding the truck at this speed. There were enough of them to completely stop the truck if they all came at us at once. I accelerated to forty, locked my door, and told Burto to do the same.

The night before, I hadn't been able to see much of the square; anything out of the fire's light had been in total darkness. So I was surprised to see nothing was blocking us from driving. I turned left instead of the normal right and headed the wrong direction in the roundabout.

I was almost at the turn before I realized I was still doing forty, so I stomped on the brakes to avoid rolling the truck. A single zombie started to hobble his way out of the center circle, which wasn't a problem, but when I looked into the rearview, I saw we were being chased by a lot more.

As I turned left onto Washington Street, I found myself staring at the statue that sat in front of the town's Masonic lodge. I had been past this statue more than a thousand times in my life, but I had never seen what I saw now: a doorway between the statue's legs seemed to lead down into its base.

"Holy shit, Seamus, where do you think that came from?"

"I don't know, but I'll put money on it that it has been there for years."

"I've lived here my whole life and never seen that doorway before."

"Do you want to check it out before we leave?" I asked.

"Hell, no man, I don't give a shit what's down there. After all the things you told me about that fire last night, I'm sure we would be killed pretty quickly. Whatever's down there can stay there for eternity for all I care. Let's get the fuck out of here."

"You took the words right out of my mouth."

I kept the truck cruising at forty because the streets were still surprisingly clear. There were cars on both sides of the road, but none in our way. I knew things were going too smoothly to stay that way. Sure enough, as we drove by the vast marble library on Washington Street, I saw the truck with the plow mounted on it parked in front.

"Must be too early for them," I said, glancing down at the radio clock. The time read 8:59."Damn, it's early as hell."

"Not really, Seamus. It's mid-morning. I wish we could have left earlier."

"Well, it doesn't matter now; we're going to be gone soon."

The farther away from the lodge we got, the worse the streets seemed. After the first mile on Washington, the roads got as bad as they had been when I first met up with Burto, but now the cars littering the streets had been shoved out of the way and were no longer blocking the road. I still sideswiped a few, but the scratches weren't going to be enough to stop the old Ford.

As we pushed past the hospital, the cars began to thin and weren't clustered together on the sides of the street. I was thankful the direction we were going wasn't completely impassable like State or Factory Streets. I figured this was another one of the back streets out of town that not everyone knew about. The locals knew but the transplants to the area really weren't aware of this route out of town.

Every couple minutes, I would check the rearview to make sure nothing was following us. I saw a few random zombies stumbling from behind a few cars, but there were no big trucks barreling down on us. Things were going as planned, which I thought was strange, because nothing ever went the way I expected it. Burto was getting fidgety in the passenger seat; soon, he tossed his shotgun out the back window into the bed, then tried to crawl after it. He moaned and complained, but after a few minutes, he'd made it outside the cab. He propped up near the tailgate, aiming for the zombies emerging from behind the cars.

Every so often he would yell, "Slow down, I want to shoot this one."

I would comply, knowing I could easily pick up speed again if I needed to. I knew Burto had been cooped up for a few days and needed some excitement, so I crawled the truck along at a snail's pace. The shotgun going off made me nervous at first, but then brushed it off. If anything was going to get us, I would go down fighting. I threw all caution to the wind, and I was paying more attention to what was happening in the rearview mirror than the road ahead of me.

A few times, Burto let a monster move close enough to shoot out its kneecaps, and then watched as they twitched and crawled on the ground. After a minute of this, I finally said, "Just kill the bastards!"

We were on outer Washington Street when I looked into the mirror again, and this time I saw Burto staring to the truck's left, looking confused. I followed his gaze just in time to see one of the creatures smash itself into the driver's door. The monster's fingers came into the window I had opened a few inches, its face pressed against the glass, and I was immediately overwhelmed by its odor. I freaked out and stomped the accelerator to the floorboard. With the sudden acceleration I heard Burto slam into the tailgate.

"Take it easy up there, would ya?"

"That's enough fucking around. I almost had a zombie in my lap," I shouted back.

The monster lost its grip as we picked up speed, nearly tearing out the window when it fell. Up ahead, an SUV surrounded by cars blocked the road, so I shouted back.

"Shoot that fucking thing! I'm not putting my window down to do it."

I reached down and rolled my window up, and as the window sealed back into the door, I heard the shot that put the zombie down forever.

"Dude, that was a little too close for comfort. You might want to sit in the middle with your back on the cab," I yelled back to Burto.

"Fuck that, I'll just pay better attention."

"That's a good idea! Next time you see a zombie sneaking up on my window, say something, don't just sit there sucking your goddamn thumb! Fuck, man, this driving slow shit is your fucking idea. Give me a fucking heads up next time!"

We got to the SUV, and I didn't feel like trying to push through, so I hopped the curb and went around it on the sidewalk. As we climbed the hill, the street seemed to clear out entirely. It almost looked like nobody had gotten stuck on this side of town. I didn't put much thought into it, because at that point, I didn't care. We were getting out.

Pushing the truck to sixty I put my window back down. The wind blowing and the roads clear enough to speed, I felt overjoyed. The fact we were close to getting out of this place made me happy, but I stopped myself before I could get too excited. We still had many miles to go before we were out of the fire.

"Hey, stop the truck for a second. I want to get back in," Burto yelled from the back.

"Are you kidding me right now? We're about out of this place and you want me to stop the truck?"

"Come on, man, you owe me that much for what you did to my leg."

I was pissed, but I stopped the truck in the middle of the street. Burto winced and fought his way back into the truck's cab, and I pulled off again.

Soon we began to drive past car dealerships, and ahead I needed to veer to the right onto another road. I looked at Burto and asked, "Where are you planning on going when we're out of here?"

"Honestly I hadn't thought about it. The longer I stayed in town the more it felt like I was never going to leave. Do you think Marston made it to the ladder in time to pull it up?"

"I don't know, and I don't care. For the record, there are, and always have been, two of us!" I said to Burto.

"Agreed."

Once I veered off Washington Street, I saw the road we were now driving had seen some destruction. The houses we drove by had been burned out; some were still smoldering. Eventually we passed the old power station that supplied electricity to Watertown. It appeared to have been heavily barricaded with razor wire and what looked like electric fencing. Random bits of trash and furniture were scattered all over the place, but there were hardly any cars, which made this better than what we had left back in the city.

The farther I drove, the stranger things got. There was a point where someone had set up an entire display of lawn chairs and tables in the road. I didn't bother slowing down; I just plowed through the white plastic junk. Burto jumped when he saw the explosion of plastic burst across the windshield.

We were now descending a hill, and at the bottom to the right was the on ramp for Interstate 81. As we got closer, I saw to my dismay at least a hundred cars lined up and down the ramps. Now I knew I wasn't going that way, so I paid more attention to the road ahead. I did, however, slow down enough to ease my way through the mess of cars underneath the overpass. Once I got us through the chaos of cars, I drove around a corner, and the vehicles disappeared.

We were now in the surrounding countryside of Watertown heading out toward Sackets Harbor. Even this far from town, destruction was still all around us. Instead of burning houses, this area was completely littered with trash, strewn across lawns, roads, and even a nearby stream had garbage in it. The houses themselves were rundown, their windows smashed with tree branches on some of the roofs.

Some of the houses had their windows boarded up from the inside, leading me to believe some people out this way might have survived. The primary infestation was at least twenty miles behind us, so if there were survivors out here, they probably didn't have to deal with too much madness.

As we drove down a long straightaway, Burto flipped on the truck's old AM/FM radio. I sighed through my nose and laughed quietly.

"You do know it takes people to run the radio station, right?" I asked jokingly.

"Yeah, and it also takes people to run a power plant. We had power, and now we might have a radio."

I let him twist the dial until he found nothing on either frequency and switched the thing off in frustration. I shook my head and lit a smoke as we tooled along the trash-covered road.

I glanced from the road to the rearview a few times and saw nothing in either direction. There were some zombies around, but with us going forty-five, nothing was going to sneak up on us. I didn't want to push the truck any faster, and I didn't know what would be in the road ahead.

At this point the two of us planned on hitting Route 3, and at the intersection hang a left. That would take us way out through Henderson, and other small towns. Initially our plan was thrown together so fast we didn't think about where we were going, but with the success of Washington Street this was now our new journey. We were almost out of this hellhole. We were coming to the final bend in the road, and after the curve, a long straightaway would run us into Route 3. This intersection had three different directions we could take. If we turned right, it would run us right back into Watertown. If we went straight through that would take us into Sackets Harbor, and the left would take us far away from this awful place. Knowing we were heading far away I decided to let myself be happy.

I looked over to Burto, who was staring out the window.

"Hey, man, what are you looking at?" I asked.

"I saw something in the mirror. I thought we were being followed. I've been watching to see if my mind is playing tricks on me. It must have been, because I haven't seen anything outside for miles."

I bet you have a fever setting in from the wound.

"Don't tell me things like that. I finally feel good about this vacation and you almost gave me a heart attack!"

"Sorry, must be the wound messing with my mind."

We continued on, and then, seconds after ascending a small hill, we saw the caution light that illuminated Route 3 at night. But when the light came into view, so did something else I didn't expect.

"Seamus, do you see something up ahead too, or is my mind playing tricks on me again?"

"Yes, I see something."

I couldn't believe what was standing in front of us. I brought the truck to a creaking halt a hundred yards away from what was unmistakably an army roadblock.

"Seamus, should that be there?" Burto asked with a quiver in his voice and look of surprise.

I was too busy staring to answer. I could see the army had built a small square community in the intersection. This was a four-way intersection and all four of the roads were heavily fortified. There were fences, razor wire, and trucks with .50 caliber machine guns mounted on top of them. I saw what appeared to be barb wire fence running a half a mile in either direction on all sides of the roadblock. As I examined what was waiting for us ahead, I saw a lot of troops running around behind the main barricade we would be approaching.

"Burto, we've come a long way, and now look at this shit!"

"What should we do? Approach the fence waving a white flag?" Burto asked.

"We could try, but I've got a feeling they will blow us away before we get within ten feet."

"Dude, we're driving a truck! Why the hell would they do that?" Burto continued.

"I imagine they would have orders to shoot anything that comes close to the fence."

From the corner of my eye, I could see Burto glancing back and forth from my face to the barricade. I couldn't take my eyes off the barricade. I watched every move each of those bastards was making. From where we were parked it looked like they were getting in formation behind the barricade, readying weapons.

"We need to let them know we're alive and not bitten. If you can think of a way to do that, fill me in," I said.

We were so distracted by the blockade ahead we weren't paying attention to our surroundings. Before I knew it, another zombie was right at the driver's door, sticking its fingers in between the gap in the window I'd left open.

"Goddammit! I really need to start paying closer attention," I shouted.

With a tug from the zombie the window shattered. I had my gun in hand when I turned to face it, but it was grabbing for me, and it had taken me by such surprise I did something I had done maybe twice in my lifetime: I froze.

The hesitation only lasted a second, but it was enough to let the zombie get close enough to almost end me in a second. Instead of shooting, I instinctively punched the gas pedal to the floor, but since it was in park, the truck didn't move; the engine only revved.

"Seamus, what in the fuck are you doing? Shoot that fucker!"

As the zombie reached for my throat, I placed the barrel of my .45 to the side of its face and squeezed the trigger. I stared into its dead eyes as the bullet blew them out the side of its head. Its eyes were gray where they should have been white, and their pupils were pen-sized and black.

There was now gray matter and bone fragments all over the inside and outside of the truck. The monster fell, lying in a pile of broken glass. My door and seat were covered in brain juice, and I wasn't happy about it. But I figured we wouldn't have to deal with the smell for long, because this was the end of the line for us.

"Christ, Seamus, are you okay?" Burto asked.

My ears were still ringing from the gunshot, so I was only barely able to hear what he said, and when I tried to respond, I couldn't hear myself speak.

"Yeah, I'm fine... Shit, was that close or what?"

"Hell yes, I thought that thing was going to grab you for sure. Then I thought the army was going to open fire on us."

Just then, I realized the truck was still revving because I hadn't taken my foot off the gas pedal. I had forgotten the truck was in park, but this ended up being a good thing; if I had started to drive toward the barricade, they would have killed us.

I took my foot off the gas pedal, then remained in my seat, pondering our next move.

"You know, those guys in front of us might be hired protection for those wacko fucks back in town," I said.

"Yeah, I was just thinking about that. What do you think we should do?"

I looked around for any more zombies. I didn't have a window anymore, so any other zombies could just climb in and kill me if I wasn't careful.

"You know what? I don't care if they shoot us on sight! I've done enough crazy shit, and we've come too far to be stopped now."

I slowly put the truck into drive and eased the gas pedal toward the floor.

"I hope you know what you're doing," Burto said warily.

"Look at it this way: I haven't had any idea about what I've been doing up to this point, and we're still alive. I go with what I feel in my gut, and so far, so good."

I kept the truck moving slowly so the army wouldn't think I was a crazed maniac. I stopped the truck about twenty feet away from the barricade and started to honk the horn. I tried honking out a song or rhythm. If the guys ahead of us knew anything about zombies, they would know they didn't try to honk out songs with beat-up Ford trucks.

After I honked for a few seconds, I placed my right hand on the horn and held it down. I then put my left hand out the broken window and started to wave at the men behind the barrier. The army men stayed in formation with their weapons pointed right at us.

We sat still, not moving for fear one of the thirty or so men with machine guns would get trigger-happy. I knew who joined the army and why, so I wasn't going to push my luck with some dumbass infantry douche bag. The truck sat idling while we waited to see what would happen next.

It didn't take long for some guy in a uniform to step up behind the troops, holding a bullhorn.

"How many are in your party?" asked the man.

I didn't yell or hold my hand out the window. I just honked the horn twice. Burto looked from the soldier back to me, and then back to the soldier.

"Have either one of you been infected with the virus? Honk once for yes and twice for no."

I honked twice, then watched as some of the men started talking to one another.

"Were either of you injured by the dead?"

Again, I honked twice. The words that came through the bullhorn next were a little more comforting.

"Get out of your vehicle and slowly approach the barricade. If you do otherwise, we are authorized to use deadly force."

"I don't know about this, Seamus... what if they try to take us back to town?"

"If they try some shit like that, they will have to kill me. There is no way in hell I am going back."

"Step out of the truck, unarmed, with your hands up," the soldier repeated. "If you do otherwise, we will shoot to kill."

I had already set my .45 on the dash for all to see. Burto set his shotgun on the floor and his pistol on the dash next to mine. Before I got out of the truck, I yelled through the window.

"One thing you should know. My friend has a laceration on his calf. That was because of me, not the dead."

"Step out of your vehicle!"

"He's not going to be able to stand for long is what I am saying!" I yelled back.

"Is that true? Do you have a cut on your leg?"

"Yes, sir. I can stand on it for a minute or so, but I'll collapse after that."

"Just get out of the truck, NOW!"

"I am stepping out now. I have holstered weapons I will remove when I am standing next to the truck," I said.

I stepped out and removed my holsters. After they fell to the ground, I put my hands above my head. Burto got out next and leaned against the truck.

"Now, before we let you through our gate, I'm going to ask you boys a few questions. Is that clear?"

"Yes, sir," we responded simultaneously.

"Help your friend walk to the barricade so we can hear your answers more clearly."

I walked around to Burto and threw his arm over my shoulder and began approaching the barricade. The men stood as still as hunters, no doubt ready to blow us to hell. All the men behind the man with the bullhorn were wearing their fatigues, but the man with the horn was in a different uniform.

"I am Captain Clemson. What are your names?"

"Seamus and Burto," I said, heading closer to the barricade.

"Seamus? Huh. A lady came through here a few days ago with her grandmother. She was begging us to go into town and find her boyfriend, Seamus."

"Holy shit, are you serious? Where is she? Is she alright?"

"Seamus, relax, she's fine. We have an established safe zone down the street at the country store, and she's there right now. I can't say the same for her grandmother; she had been bitten by her husband, and we had to... put her down. Sorry, kid."

"I don't care about her grandmother. Shit happens; it must have been her time to go. You are positive the girl is okay?"

"Yes. That's enough about her for now. I need to know more about the two of you. How long would you say you have been in town?"

"Four days," I said.

"I've been here my whole life," Burto shouted in anger.

"How exactly did you arrive in the city?"

"I got drunk on the drive up from North Carolina and got lost on the back roads. I know I drove in through Lowville and passed out after that. My girl was upset about me driving drunk. She made me pull over so she could drive, and I fell asleep. When I woke up, I was at my stepfather's house on Franklin Street. She dropped me off and headed toward her grandmother's. I haven't seen her since."

I stood there holding Burto up, waiting for more questions.

Captain Clemson watched us, then said something I couldn't hear to the soldier standing next to him. The second man ran off to a tent a few feet away. I instinctively looked around to make sure nothing was sneaking up on us, and then Clemson spoke again.

"It's odd you and your lady got into town without driving through a barricade."

"Why is that?" I asked.

"The town has been locked down for over a month now. We have barricades set up at the four entrances coming into town. Nothing comes in or out without the brass knowing about it."

"Sir I don't mean to speak out of line, but I believe there are five main entrances to Watertown, and possibly more with all the back roads. Your people couldn't possibly have covered them all."

"We'll sit down and discuss that later. For now, we have a few more questions, and then we can get you two out of the area. How did the two of you stay alive?"

I looked to Burto, who only stared back at me and blinked a few times as if to tell me our secret was safe.

"We made a stronghold in a second-story apartment. We barricaded the door, made some weapons, got supplies, guns, and this truck, and then we left. We didn't feel the need to hang around any longer than we had to."

"You said you've only been in there a few days. Why did you gather all those supplies if you were just going to leave?"

"The supplies were a necessity. We weren't sure how long we would have been stuck in the stronghold, so we wanted to make sure we could survive as long as needed.

Are we in some sort of trouble? This seems to be an interrogation, and not a couple of questions," I replied.

"You said the boy there was injured; how did that happen?"

"I was driving down a side street, and he came running out of an alley to get my attention. Before he could get his leg into the car, I pushed the gas pedal and jolted the car. Unfortunately, his calf was stuck between the door and the frame as I scrapped our car past a busted down Geo Tracker. The crushing door caused enough pressure to blow his muscle through his skin."

"Wow. That must have hurt like a son of a bitch."

"Yes, sir, it hurts real fucking bad!" Burto snapped. "If we could hurry this along, I could have someone look at it!"

"Damn, Burto, quiet down, they have bigger guns than us."

"Okay, here's the thing. Besides the two ladies, we haven't seen anyone alive come out of town for over a month. We ran an evacuation two months ago, but there were hold outs. The holdouts then realized the city had serious dangers, so they made their way out of town the best they could. The last survivors we've seen at any barricade were over a month ago. We didn't think anyone could survive more than a day or two. With that said, you have to think how crazy it is for us to hear you telling us you lasted damn near a week. One last thing: you are one hundred-percent sure neither of you have been in any contact with the creatures? Remember, if you're lying, my boys will put fifty holes through your bodies."

"The only injury either one of us has is his leg, which was caused by me. Can we please come through? I'm sure you have a person here who could examine my friend's leg. If he needs to, he can examine me to make sure I'm not infected."

Captain Clemson once again spoke to the solider next to him, and then nodded.

"Okay, let's go. Follow me."

Burto and I started walking toward a section of the barricade that looked like a door. As we walked along the perimeter, I could hear the hum of electricity going through it. I looked at Burto, who stared back with terror behind his eyes. I figured it would be a good idea to take a few steps away, just in case.

We eventually reached the door the Captain was standing behind. Clemson then motioned to a soldier in a nearby tent, and the humming of electricity stopped.

A few GIs joined Clemson as he unlocked and opened the door. As soon as it was open, two soldiers grabbed Burto and rushed him away from me somewhere inside the compound and out of sight. The officer motioned for me to enter, so I walked through the doors, and waited as he locked it behind us.

CHAPTER 23

I was told Burto was going to go through surgery, and I wasn't allowed to watch, or be there for support. Instead, I was taken to a tent and drilled with questions for over an hour. Some of the questions didn't even have anything to do with the actual events we had witnessed.

A man who could hardly string sentences together, whom I thought might be a lower-ranking officer by the way he talked, began his barrage of questions: where in town we had holed up, what we had done for supplies, how did we got the guns, what happened to my friend's leg, where I was going to go after this, what did I do for a living, how much I made a year, and a few other questions regarding my life outside of Watertown. He also made me sign a confidential agreement promising I wouldn't talk to anybody about the nature of this whole dilemma. This made me uncomfortable, but I decided not to raise any hell.

After an hour and a half of the bullshit Q&;;A, I was agitated, and demanded I be released so I could find Megan.

To my surprise, the soldier released me. I didn't like that I had to leave my weapons behind, but for the first time in a while, I felt safe.

As I walked out of the tent, I was greeted by another solider who escorted me through the camp toward the tent Burto was now resting in. While we were walking, I took notice of the camp and was surprised how big it was. There were three rows of tents and none of them had names on them. I didn't know how any of the soldiers knew where they were going. I received many looks and stares from the soldiers walking around the camp as we walked.

Finally, we reached the tent Burto was in and the escort said, "This is your stop. Congratulations on making it out of there alive."

"Thank you, have a good day," I said as I poked my head into the tent.

Looking in, the doctor at Burto's bedside quickly asked me to wait outside while he finished what he was doing. I stepped out and saw a solider walking by, so I asked, "Do you know what time it is?"

"It's about noon," the man replied as he continued walking.

As I sat outside the medic tent waiting for news about my friend's condition it dawned on me, I needed to take a piss. I decided I would wander off and find a bathroom while the doctor finished up with Burto. There were troops scattered throughout the camp, but none paid attention to me as I walked around. I walked up to one of the men and asked about the bathroom, and he pointed me in the direction I needed. After walking in the direction the man told me to go I saw a porta potty tucked in the corner of the barricaded camp. I walked into it and shut the door behind me. While I was peeing, I realized I could probably shit too and decided I'd rather do it now rather than when I met with Megan.

As I sat there relieving myself, I began hearing men chatting outside the shitter.

"Clemson has lost his mind. What are we going to do with these guys?"

"Calm down, He knows what he's doing."

"The Masons were very specific about how to handle any survivors. This needs to be handled now. We've already pushed our luck with the girl."

"The girl was only kept alive to see if her story was true. Clearly now we know she was telling the truth. Don't worry this will be taken care of tonight."

"If you're wrong and it's not, we're fucked."

The voices faded as they walked past the outhouse, and I sat there unnerved.

What the hell are they talking about? The Masons? Jesus, we have to get out of here now.

I sat on the toilet until the voices could no longer be heard. I wanted to make sure they were completely gone before I left the bathroom. After I was convinced the coast was clear I finished and left the bathroom. I walked back to the tent Burto was in trying to act as normal as I could. There were troops standing outside other tents talking, but I focused on getting back to Burto. I would casually wave or nod my head at the men, but that was all.

Waiting outside the door of the medic tent my hand trembled as I pulled my smokes from my pocket. I opened it, there was one left, so I pulled it out and put it to my lips. As I tried lighting it my hand shook so bad the flame on the lighter went out twice. I was now engulfed in fear as to what my next move would be. There was a plastic garbage can outside the door of the tent, so I tossed the empty pack into it as I devised yet another plan.

I can't leave Burto here, I have no idea what to do. How are we going to get out of this mess? This situation is worse than the zombies.

Puffing the cigarette like a chain smoker I decided to play it cool. I figured my chances at escaping these men would be better if I didn't act like an idiot.

What do these men have to do with the zombies or the Masons?

The doctor came out just as I heeled the butt of my cigarette into the ground.

"Well, son, whoever sewed that poor fellow's leg up did a decent job. Unfortunately, that's the only thing that was done semi right. That leg is in real bad shape. I had to reopen the wound and remove the clump of muscle. I cleaned out as much of the infection as I could, and even had to remove some of the skin around the wound. I stitched his leg back up and gave him some antibiotics. He's still not out of the woods. If that infection doesn't clear up, I might have to take the leg off below the knee. Honestly, I have no idea how that boy survived with that wound."

"Why did you have to take the muscle out?"

"It had started to rot inside his leg. If you hadn't gotten here, your buddy would have died of infection within a few days."

"How did the operation go? Was he kicking and screaming?"

"We put him under for a short time so there was no screaming. After the operation I gave him enough morphine to slow a horse. He's feeling no pain."

"Is he alright to leave?"

"I would say yes, but certainly in a wheelchair. Listen, the two of you have gone through some traumatic events over the past week, so I think it would be best if both of you stayed the afternoon, and maybe even the night."

Nice try. Neither of us are going to be staying here.

"That's fine with me. I really want to see my girlfriend. Honestly, after what we went through, I'm sure Burto would like to see her as well. He's heard a lot about her. We can come back after. I was told she is a few miles down the road at some store."

"I've been told to give you a mental evaluation, but I think it's alright for you to go visit your girlfriend. When you return, I would like to do some blood work. Now, one last thing before you go."

"What's that?"

"I need to check for bite marks. Captain Clemson wanted to get the questions out of the way before we checked."

"That seems like something that should have been done right away."

"Yes, that's true, but we have seen what a bite does to people, and you both had no signs of being infected, so we went with the questions first."

"So you guys know what's actually happening in there and have done nothing to stop it?"

"Son, it's better for you to just go visit your girlfriend and not ask too many questions. Just go and enjoy yourself."

What the fuck is going on here?

"Are we in some sort of danger?"

"If Captain Clemson said its okay for you to check on your girlfriend, you should. Your friend has a serious wound, but I think you should be able to keep an eye on him."

The doctor had a look on his face like he wanted to tell me something else but couldn't. I took this as a sign maybe Burto and I should get away from this checkpoint as soon as we could. I had to take what the doctor said at face value because there was no way I could do anything to these people. If they did have some sinister plan, I wanted no part of it. I hoped I was just being paranoid, but I wasn't going to risk it. I would take the doctor's advice and go see Megan.

Instead of asking any further questions I stripped all my clothes off.

"Do you see anything worth worrying about?"

My actions had attracted the attention of a few soldiers who were standing nearby, and it must have looked suspicious, because they had their guns ready to fire.

"No, I do not, and for future reference, if you plan on stripping naked at least go into the tent first."

"Duly noted, and yes, I will for sure do that next time. Is Burto okay to move now?"

"Yes, but he will be a little loopy for a few hours. He might not be much for conversation."

"That's okay. He'll be happy just to see her face."

The doctor and I went inside the tent and helped Burto off the cot and into the wheelchair. After about five minutes of getting Burto situated we wheeled him out the tent's door.

The doctor pointed me toward the camp's entrance and told me a shuttle van would be coming back from the store in a little while. I quickly pushed Burto over to the entrance. A solider standing guard opened the door, and I pushed the wheelchair through back onto Route 3 heading in the direction Burto and I had planned on taking.

"So, you guys have a shuttle running here?" I nervously asked the solider.

I figured the soldier would have been a little more talkative than he was, but instead he stood around ignoring me like I was nonexistent.

"I can see why you pricks catch a bad rap," I said after he didn't reply.

"You do know I could shoot you and not get reprimanded in any way, right?" the man asked.

"Good point. I'll just be quiet now."

Jesus Christ, I need to get out of here right now!

As we waited for the bus the guard had a call come through his shoulder radio. I tried to listen to what was being said, but the man muffled the speaker and spoke softly. I was getting very nervous at this point. With the way the doctor was acting and now a secretive conversation between the guard and someone else. I very much wanted this damn shuttle to show up. I continued to look up the road for the bus to show up. While we waited, I noticed Burto was barely conscious. His head was slumped, and he hardly moved a muscle.

"Don't worry, buddy, we'll see Megan soon."

Burto's reply was a slew of mumbled words I couldn't understand. I was sweating like I had been on a treadmill, and I wasn't sure if it was from the July sun or the fact that I was more nervous now than earlier in the week.

Finally, I saw the sun reflecting off a windshield down the road.

"Thank God," I said with relief.

The asshole guard didn't acknowledge me; he just continued staring at the road. I waited and watched as the bus got closer and closer. Finally, it pulled up to the gate. The asshole walked to the left of the gateway and pushed a button. The bus driver must not have seen me, because he began to drive in almost immediately, and only stopped when the asshole held out his hand.

The guard walked out to the door of the bus and exchanged words with the driver. The words were short, because within seconds, he waved me over to the bus. As I pushed Burto toward the bus the dickhead solider stood off to the side of the door with his M16. I helped Burto who was barely able to stand on his own. I helped him onto the shuttle and placed him in the first seat. I stepped back off the bus and folded up the wheelchair and lugged it on the shuttle. The driver shut the door and put the bus in reverse, then backed into the driveway on the left side of the road and had us turned around in seconds. When the bus was moving away from the metal gates of the compound, he started talking.

"So, what was it like in the city?" the driver asked, looking in the mirror.

"It sucked and was scary as hell."

"I admire the fact you survived. It looks like your buddy there had a little issue."

"Yeah, he had it the worst. I don't mean to sound rude, but I would rather not talk about it."

"So where are you guys heading after this place?"

"I'm heading to North Carolina. I can't speak for him though."

"Wow. I'm from North Carolina, Rocky Mount. Ever been there?"

"I've been past a few times, but never in the actual city."

"Check it out some time; it's a pretty chill place."

"I'll keep that in mind."

The driver didn't waste time driving slow like I had. He had the shuttle van going as fast as it could. As he drove, I admired the vast landscapes that were all cornfields and cow pastures. There were no abandoned cars lining the streets, and I didn't see any trash scattered anywhere.

"What's up with this store? Why is my girlfriend here, and not at the roadblock?

"The store is the only one for miles and the only place for any kind of supplies. Your girlfriend was brought there because there's a small strip motel on the side, and Clemson thought she would be more comfortable there."

"What have you heard about this whole fiasco?" I asked nervously.

"If I were you, I wouldn't ask too many questions."

"Sounds good to me. Thanks for the heads up."

I need to get the fuck out of this place now. What are these army dicks doing here?

We rounded the last corner on the road that led to the store where Megan was. The bus began to slow, and in seconds, we were pulling into the parking lot.

"Is Megan in the store?"

"I doubt it. She's probably in her room. Man, she sure is a spitfire. She refused to leave, saying you would come to get her. We all laughed and thought she was full of shit. You must be one tough motherfucker to make it out of a place like that."

"I just did what I had to. I don't think I'll have a problem finding her. Are there clothes in the store? I would really like a nice hot shower and some fresh clothes."

"Yeah, beachwear mostly."

"That will be fine. Hey, thanks for the lift; have a good day."

"I've been told to come pick you up a little later this afternoon."

"Just give me a few hours to make good with the lady."

"Have a great time, and I will see you soon."

I was standing before the driver opened the door. When he finally did, I put the wheelchair outside and helped Burto off the bus. As I pushed Burto toward the entrance of the store the driver closed the door and began driving away back toward the camp we had just left. As I wheeled Burto toward the shop's entrance I looked around at our current location. The store was right next to an old strip motel. Both establishments were old wooden structures that had been rundown from lack of upkeep. There were miles of corn fields and cow pastures for as far as I could see. This was a place I had seen since I was a child, but today it caused me to fear what was going to be coming. I knew this was our only chance to make a get away, but I didn't know what I was going to do. I parked Burto's wheelchair under the awning in the shade and knelt down to speak to him.

"We're not out of the wood yet. I need to come up with a plan soon, or I think we're doomed. You sit out here, and I'll be right back."

I walked into the store and instantly smelled coffee. This caused a minor flashback of Marston and his torment. I pushed that sight out of my head just in time for the shop keeper to start chatting me up.

"Haven't seen you here before," the old grizzled shopkeeper said as I entered.

"Yeah, I'm new in town. Do you have new clothes for sale?"

"Where you from, partner?"

"Look, buddy, I have had a really long couple of days. Can you please tell me where the clothes are?"

"Alright, take it easy, no need for attitude. They're back in the corner on the wall, "the man said, pointing to the back left of the store.

I walked past the racks of chips, muffins, magazines, and all the other random items until I found the clothes. I didn't care about the designs on the shorts; I simply grabbed a pair that fit and a package of white tees. I returned to the front and placed the items on the counter.

"How much for this stuff?"

"Don't you want a pair of flops?"

"I think the shoes I have now will be just fine."

"Well, normally, that stuff would be fifteen bucks."

"Really? That's cheap."

"Yeah, prices dropped when the whole thing in town went down. Anyway, like I said, that would normally be fifteen bucks, but in this case, I'm going to make an exception and just give it to you."

"Why is that?"

"Because you smell worse than anything I have ever smelled. What the hell have you been rolling around in?"

"I just came out of Watertown. I know you know what's happening there, so stop fucking with me. Fifteen miles down the road is infested with zombies! Sorry to disappoint you, but I didn't have time to take a fucking shower."

I didn't wait around; I grabbed my things and walked out of the store.

"Sorry! Didn't mean to offend you," the shopkeeper yelled after me.

"Asshole," I mumbled under my breath as the screen door shut behind me.

I walked to Burto and began pushing him to the left toward the shady motel rooms. I knew Megan was here somewhere, but where I wasn't sure. The black shirt I was wearing attracted all the sun's rays, and I was already burning up in the heat. I paused briefly and stripped the shirt off. When I pulled it over my head, I got a whiff of what the store clerk had been talking about.

I tossed the shirt into the parking lot, continuing to push Burto toward the hotel office. When I got to the door, however, there was a note that read: "If you want a room, speak to the clerk at the store."

Damnit!

I was about to turn around with Burto when I heard a voice that made me jump.

"Seamus?"

I turned to see the face of the woman I loved staring back at me. *Megan.*

"My god, you made it! I knew you would...I'm so happy to see you!"

She ran at me while I stood there in surprise, then slowed down just enough to avoid knocking me over. She clutched me tighter than ever before, practically squeezing the air out of my lungs.

"I can't breathe!" I grunted.

"Sorry, sweetie. I'm so happy you made it out! I told the army guys you would, and they just laughed at me."

"Fuck those government goons!"

"You smell terrible; let's go back to the room. There are some things I want to show you!"

"I can't wait to see what you have to show me. What should I do with Burto though?"

Burto was passed out from whatever drugs the doctors gave him. His chin rested on his chest as he sat in the blazing sun.

"There's an awning down the whole property, just put him outside one of the doors in the shade. He doesn't look like he would mind. What happened to him anyway?"

"It's a long story that I will tell you--later."

I pushed Burto back to where Megan's room was and put him in the shade of the porch. He was in front of the room next to Megan's. I knelt down and put the wheelchairs break's on and stood back up. I hugged Megan one more time before we went into her room.

"I'm so happy I found you babe. Holy shit am I glad I found you," I said from our loving embrace.

Before entering her room, she began asking me questions.

"How did you survive in there?" she asked.

"You're never going to believe it, but I actually ended up staying with Marston."

"Are you fucking kidding...after all the shit that guy pulled you shacked up with him?"

"I didn't exactly have many choices in the matter."

"He's not going to be showing up, is he?"

"No, he didn't make it."

"Are you and Burto the only ones who made it?"

"Unfortunately, yes. We didn't have many encounters with actual people."

We stood in the sun gazing into each other's eyes like love at first sight.

"Why is Burto in a wheelchair?"

"His leg's pretty messed up; the doctor back at the camp said he would have been dead in a few days without proper medical treatment."

"How the hell did you guys survive in there?

"Sweetie, I don't want to sound like a dick, but can we not talk about those things right now? I need to take a cold shower; this sun is frying my back," I replied.

"Of course, baby. We can do whatever you want."

"There's about a hundred things I want to do right now, but I have to clean all this nasty shit off before I do any one of them."

"That sounds a little dirty."

"You have no idea what's in store for you, sexy lady."

"I'm up for anything once you clean that horrendous stench off your body. Did you sleep in an Indian restaurant's dumpster...? Jesus," Megan said with a laugh.

We turned and walked for her room's door. I opened the door and was immediately blasted with the refreshing cold of the air conditioner.

"Is this place condemned? It's a bit rundown, don't you think?" I said, looking around inside.

"It's similar to any sleazy motel that rents by the hour. Don't worry, I cleaned the rats out the first day. I didn't check for bed bugs though, but I haven't been bitten by any, so we should be alright."

"Are you paying for this shithole?"

"Fuck no. I guess the army guys took care of it."

"I hope so. The wood-paneled walls on the outside look like a strong breeze could blow them off."

"Enough with the demographics; get your ass in the shower, you stinking bastard, I have plans for you."

"Will Burto be alright there passed out like that?" I asked.

"He should be fine. Now hurry up."

I went to the bathroom, turned the water on, then walked back to the front door of the room. There, I stripped off what was left of my disgusting clothes, opened the door, and threw them outside in front of our room. I glanced around uneasy about the situation. Burto was snoring a little, and there was nothing else to be seen anywhere. Feeling satisfied about my surroundings I turned to walk back to the bathroom. To my wonderful surprise I saw Megan lying on the bed, naked as I pulled the door shut.

"If you hurry, this can all be yours for as long as you want," Megan said smoothly.

"Yeah? I think you're in store for about six minutes of eye-rolling fun," I said as I passed.

I walked into the bathroom and hopped into the shower. The water was cold, but I didn't care. I let it run off my head and down my body for at least five minutes before finally turning the heat up and reaching for a bar of soap.

In the process, I got a look at the water going down the drain. There were chunks of meat falling out of my hair, and the water going down the drain was grossly brown. The whole thing was disgusting, but surprisingly, I didn't feel the urge to throw up. I lathered my entire body up with an inch-thick layer of suds, then rinsed. I repeated until the water going down the drain was clear. It was the longest shower I had ever taken, and so satisfying I momentarily forgot about Megan.

The water was hot enough by now to fill the room with steam, so I turned it off and stepped out, only to be greeted by my wonderful girlfriend, who was still very naked and clearly ready to make up for lost time. I didn't even get the chance to grab a towel; she tore me from the bathroom and threw me onto the bed.

Her warm embrace was the best feeling I had experienced in many days. I closed my eyes, but I suddenly had a flash back of the last time I saw Marston. I snapped them open and focused on the situation. It took me a couple seconds to shake the eerie feeling, but when I did, boy oh boy, was it amazing. Being back with the woman I thought had long since perished felt very comforting. The memories of the week vanished, and for the first time I was overcome with joy. As much as I would like to go into detail about the things that happened, I will instead leave it to your imagination. We rolled around that tiny room for what seemed like hours, and it was the best sex I'd ever had. After we finished our sexual Olympics, we lay on the bed, just enjoying each other's company.

"I'm so glad you made it out alright. I went to your grandma's to get you, but you were gone, and there were zombies all around."

"Yeah, I know... my grandfather turned, and when we were locking him in the laundry room and clawed the shit out of my grandmother."

"That sucks. I'm sorry that happened."

"I am too. I loved her dearly. They shot the hell out of her while she was still in the car."

"What the fuck! Was she thrashing around in there or something?"

"No not at all. We left her place and found a path through suburbia to outer Arsenal Street. She had become ghostly white and began frothing at the mouth. I knew right then I was fucked, so I hammered the gas."

"Why didn't you get her out of the car right then?"

"At that point she wasn't that bad, and I didn't want to waste the time. I had a clear path out Arsenal Street to Sackets, and I wanted to put as much distance between us and Watertown as I could. Anyway, I was racing out down the road and she started mumbling at first then screaming like a crazed person. She yelled that her brain was being squeezed in a vice, and that her eyes felt like they were swelling and going to explode."

"What the fuck!"

"Baby, it was horrible. She was screaming and thrashing, and then all of a sudden, she stopped and slumped forward in her seat passed out. If it wasn't for her seatbelt, she could have knocked her teeth out on the dashboard."

"What did you do then?"

"I shouted her name, but she never regained consciousness. I drove down outer Arsenal past all the trailers and farms that lined the streets and dodged as much of the garbage blowing into the street as I could. After driving another ten minutes the roadblock came into view. I pulled up to it and a man with a bullhorn screamed at me to get out of the car. I did what he asked and then he asked why the old lady wasn't moving. I explained to him she had been scratched by my grandfather who had been bitten. He told me to approach the door and come into the camp. I asked about my grandmother, and he said she was going to be taken care of. No sooner than the gate door closed behind me the troops opened fire on the minivan. I turned and screamed for them to stop, but they fired until the front end was on fire. The officer had to hold me back as I screamed and kicked at him."

"Holy fucking shit, lady, that's intense. I still can't believe you made it out."

"Driving with a crazy old lady who's turning into a zombie is something no one should ever have to experience. I ran things over with a minivan I didn't think a minivan would go over. I hit so many zombies I lost count."

"I don't want to talk about those things right now. Burto and I have to go back to the camp and take some mental examinations. Then all of us can get out of here once and for all."

"Baby, I've been at this hotel for a week. Do you know why?"

"Because you were waiting for me, right?"

"Not to be a bitch, but no. I am stuck here; the army guys said we're not going anywhere. They said we wouldn't get a chance to get out and tell anyone else what's happening here. This thing is going to be a huge cover-up, and we're stuck in the middle."

"There's no fucking way I will be sticking around, and that's a goddamn fact!"

"We can't exactly go anywhere. That man in the store is one of them. He looks and acts sweet enough, but he watches my every move."

"Maybe he's just an old pervert."

"Nope, he works from 6a.m. to 6p.m., and then another guy is dropped off to take over. I was informed by a different solider if I tried to escape, I would be hunted and killed."

"Now why would some random stranger be so forthcoming with such an evil plot?"

"Don't be mad, babe, but I kind of seduced him."

"And he told you this stuff after that?"

"Not exactly after the seduction, but yeah."

"Jesus, bitch, it's only been a couple days, for fuck's sake!"

"I thought you were dead, what was I supposed to do? I needed information about my situation so I got it anyway I could."

"I hope you wore a condom, Jesus Christ."

My eyes widened at the thought of Megan cheating on me. At first, I was devastated, but that feeling quickly passed. I realized I had seen things that only happen in movies, so her cheating on me didn't really faze me. In her defense she did think I was dead.

"Don't worry we did. Stop being so negative. I only did it to get information and hopefully escape."

"I'm not even mad about it. I can't blame you, and that's pretty smart thinking on your part. We can talk about that later, right now we're sneaking out of here, so get dressed."

I was mentally and physically exhausted from the stress and drama I'd gone through, but there was no way those army dicks were keeping me around. They were going to have to send out the bloodhounds because we were leaving.

I got dressed in my clean, fresh shorts and a new T-shirt. I didn't have clean socks and regretted not grabbing a bag when I was in the store. The fact my shoes were outside and covered in shit bothered me as well.

"How are we going to get out of here?" Megan asked.

"I told them I was heading back to North Carolina after this. That makes me think when they see we've left, they're going to go south. I plan on going north."

"How do you plan on doing that? Like I said, that man's in there watching. Why do you think this room is so close to the store? Plus, there could be other men in these rooms keeping an eye out," Megan continued.

"I don't care about the goons watching the place. We're in Sackets Harbor, and there are boats down the road in any one of the three marinas. I don't think they'll look for us in a boat."

"That's a good idea, but there's one problem with that."

"What's that?" I asked.

"We'd have to walk right past the store on our way there. The clerk would see us, and then he would tell the army where we went," Megan explained.

"That would be a problem, but lucky for us, I've already figured that out."

"You are not going to kill the store clerk," Megan insisted.

"Now why would you just assume I was going to kill someone? What the hell is wrong with you? Anyway, there are no doors or windows in the back of this room. If we walk out the front we will be spotted for sure, so I'm going to kick a hole in the wall of the shower. Then I'm going to bust a hole in the exterior wall. After, we climb through the wall and take cover in the woods behind the hotel, and then make our way to one of the marinas. The lake is directly behind us and I think that's our only option."

"Well, that's a plan...but what about the noise you make when you smash the wall."

"That's something we are going to have to risk."

"What are we going to do with Burto?" Megan asked.

"I have no idea. There's no way we can carry him that far, he would slow us down and get us caught for sure. Do you think we could just leave him out front?"

"Jesus, Seamus that's heartless! You fought to get him here and now you want to leave him?"

"I was just thinking out loud. This is a survival situation and sometimes hard decisions have to be made."

"You need to figure this out. I would never sleep right again knowing we deserted him."

"I will, babe, don't worry. For now though let me at least get started on our escape plan."

I kissed Megan on the forehead and then picked up the room's sturdy desk chair and carried it to the bathroom, then moved the shower curtain and pointed the chair's legs at the tile wall of the tub. I smashed the chair into the wall with great force, dislocating every tile the legs touched. The sound wasn't too loud, so I repeated the process until several tiles had fallen into the tub. I hit the wall a few more times until holes were behind where the tiles once were. Before I continued, I yelled to Megan.

"What time is it?"

"It's about 1:45."

"We've got about an hour to get ahead of these pricks."

"Why do you say that?" Megan asked.

"I think my escort will be coming back at around 3:00 to pick me up. He said he'd give me a few hours."

"That doesn't really leave us with much time..."

"That's more than enough time, and I'm not too worried."

I looked at the plywood behind the tiles. It was rotten and moldy. I grabbed a towel off the rack and laid it over the tiles in the tub so I could stand in the tub without slicing my feet. I grabbed the chair, ripped one of its legs off, and went to work on the wall.

The wall broke apart like stale bread, crumbling into the tub and onto my feet.

"Hey, babe, this wall is fucking rotten. I guess it's been here so long the health department didn't care," I shouted from the tub.

I hit pipes behind the hole, so I had to widen it. Eventually, the whole back wall of the shower was torn out, covering my feet.

Next was some pink insulation I had to pull out, and beyond that was the outer wooden wall. This was a problem, because the exterior wall wasn't as old and weathered as the shower wood. I started pounding with the leg of the chair, and the thuds were so loud I thought the lookout shopkeeper might be able to hear them. I decided I would try throwing my body against it instead. I thumped into it with my left shoulder, and though I didn't break through, I did see one thing I could use to my advantage.

When I rammed into the wood, I had seen sunlight through the right side of the wall. My common sense told me with enough effort, the nails holding the wood in place would pop out, and we could push the rest of the panel out and make our escape. Thankfully the place hadn't been remodeled since it opened and there was no siding or bricks to push through.

I made a second attempt, and by now my feet were bleeding in a few spots. After the third slam, the sunlight stayed exposed.

Megan had come in a few times to see how the process was going, expressing her amazement at the speed at which I was stripping the wall.

"I have renovated a few houses in my time, and I like smashing stuff, so why wouldn't it go quickly," I joked.

"Good for you. Hurry up!"

I kept throwing myself into the wall until the wood on the right came off the building completely. We were ready.

"Alright, this should be ready to go through. Let's get going. Are you ready?" I asked.

"Yes, I'm ready, what about Burto?"

"I'll go check on him and see how he's doing."

CHAPTER 24

I walked through the room and to the front door. I opened it just enough to peer outside and see Burto was still passed out in his chair. After seeing him I opened it farther and looked around the area for anyone watching me. All I saw in any direction were corn fields and pastures. There were no men or women anywhere to be seen and this made me happy.

I slowly stepped out of the room and grabbed the disgusting shoes I had left outside. I slipped them on my cut feet and then turned to talk with Burto. I approached him and he was hardly moving. I shook his shoulder and started trying to wake him up.

"Burto, buddy, wake up. I want to talk to you."

I repeated this for a minute until Burto started to come out of his drug-induced coma.

"What do you want?" Burto asked faintly.

"I'm going to push you into our room. There are a few things I want to talk to you about."

"Seamus, I need some rest; can't this wait?"

"I wish it could, buddy."

I released the wheelchair's brakes and then grabbed the handles of the chair and started pushing Burto into the motel room. I got him over the threshold and shut the door behind me when I did.

"Is he alright?" Megan asked.

"He's had a rough week and is on enough meds to knock out a horse," I said as I tried getting Burto to pay attention.

"Hey, man, I need you to pay attention for a minute," I said, shaking his shoulder.

"Goddamn it, man, what do you want?" Burto asked, clearly agitated.

"I think those army pricks are coming back to pick us up soon. I don't want to be here when they do."

"What are you worried about?"

"I don't trust them and want to get out of here now."

"It's the American government, Seamus; I think you're being paranoid again."

"You can think what you want, but she and I are leaving."

As I had my conversation with Burto, Megan was sitting on the edge of the bed with her legs crossed, bouncing her foot. She looked like she was becoming more and more annoyed that the process was taking as long as it was. I looked at her and mouthed the words "I'm sorry" while lifting my eyebrows.

"Burto--I need to know what you want to do. I don't think you'll be able to run, and I can't carry you."

"I don't really care at this point. I'm so damn high I feel great," Burto replied softly.

"So--are you okay staying here for now?"

"I'm okay, Seamus; I just want to sleep and rest. I'm sure you're overreacting like always," Burto said, with his chin against his chest.

"You must be high as hell to think I'm overreacting," I said before continuing. "Look, buddy, I don't have a lot of options here. She and I want to leave, but you are incapable of going anywhere. Are you sure you're okay to stay behind?"

"Yes, I am. I'll stay right here and sleep for a while. Don't worry about me. I'm sure I'll be alright."

"If you say so,Burto. Look man, I'm sorry about the leg and hope you don't hate me because of it. I want you to know you've been a good friend and I will be sending someone back here to pick you up. Don't worry, this whole thing will be over soon."

Burto had once again fallen asleep in his chair, so I looked at Megan and said, "That doctor told me he gave Burto a heavy dose of drugs; he wasn't kidding."

"Leaving him here--is that the best idea?" Megan asked, clearly distraught.

"I don't see another option. Look at him, he can't even keep his eyes open," I said, pointing to Burto.

"Jesus, I feel bad. Who knows what those psychos are going to do to him."

"This is our only option, so that's what we'll have to do. I'm going to push him against the door and put the brakes on his chair. This will at least slow them down when they come for us."

I pushed Burto's wheelchair flush with the door to the room and put the brakes on. As I did this Burto didn't move or make a sound. Megan stood up and walked over to us. She patted Burto on the head and said, "Goodbye, Burto. It was nice seeing you even for a minute. We have to catch up the next time we see each other. Stop by if you ever come through North Carolina."

I looked at her and rolled my eyes a little. She hushed me with a stern look and a shoulder shrug.

"Alright, babe, we have to get going," I said.

She nodded and we prepared to head out. I wasn't sure what time the shuttle was coming back, and I didn't want to wait around to see if my prediction was right.

"You do know these guys are going to come gunning after us pretty hard, right? I mean they are going to kill us on sight, if what you said has any merit," I whispered to Megan.

"I feel really bad leaving Burto behind--are you sure?"

"Yes, there are no other options, or I would be taking them. Even if we steal a car and risk running, I think they would chase us down and machine gun the car. This is our only option."

"Bye, Burto," I said as she and I walked into the bathroom.

Megan was wearing a pair of shorts, a tank top, and a pair of Birkenstocks. I told her to go first, and I would push on the wall as she did, making it easier. She climbed into the bathtub, and I pushed the wall out far enough for her to squeeze through. She hopped out and started to pull on the wood so I could climb through after her.

"Hey, let go for a second. I have an idea."

The wood snapped back in place, and I went to the room and yanked the mattress off the bed. I had it on its side, and I pulled it in front of the bathroom door. I shut the bathroom door and climbed back into the tub.

"Alright, I'm heading out."

She pulled the wood back and before I went through, I pulled the shower curtain closed behind me so, at a glance, no one would see the massive hole from inside. I was out of the hotel seconds after.

The timbers weren't as dense as I had hoped, but they were thick enough to provided cover from anyone driving the streets looking for us. We started trucking through the woods, bee-lining for the marina. As we went, I hoped desperately there would be boats stored at one of the docks. I had no plan B, so this had to work. We walked through thorn bushes, then the bushes went away, and we were in a forest of pines. The needles had fallen and blanketed the forest floor, so walking was a little quieter. Megan kept stopping to remove twigs from her sandals, so eventually I told her to stop lollygagging. After I said that, we moved fast and rarely stopped for anything.

The woods covered us for about a half mile before we emerged in someone's back yard. I looked around and saw we were now emerging in the town of Sackets Harbor. The lawns of the places I could see were overgrown and everything seemed quiet. I wasn't a hundred-percent certain, but it didn't seem like people were staying in the area. We had stopped in the wood line to catch our breath and listen for oncoming vehicles. The only sound we heard was the occasional chirping of birds nearby.

"You ready, sweetheart?" I asked.

"More than you know, baby."

We both started sprinting through the overgrown yard, and I nearly left her in the dust before I slowed down so she could catch up. We quickly made it to the backside of the house, but because I had smoked so much in the past few days, I couldn't breathe.

"This hasn't taken as long as I thought it would, so they might not be looking for us," I said through winded gasps of air.

"Yeah...or they are hunting us like wild animals. There's no way to tell. I don't hear any helicopters, vehicles, or even dogs, so I have no idea."

"Either way, let's keep moving."

Even though we were both hot we pressed on. Every time I thought I was going to collapse from lack of oxygen, I had flashbacks of the zombie-infested Watertown and kept running. I had severe cottonmouth and desperately needed a drink.

We ran from house to house, across streets and through backyards until we passed through a schoolyard. I hadn't been in Sackets for a while and couldn't remember how far the water was from the school, but it didn't slow us down. We kept moving through the yards until eventually there weren't any more to run through. At that point, we needed to cross the road, and I saw one of the marinas waiting for us on the other side. I could see boats bobbing up and down ;the lake wasn't as still as it usually was. I needed to catch my breath, and Megan didn't mind standing around catching hers.

"I'm sure they found Burto and figured out we're not in the room anymore," I said.

"Do you think they will come this way?"

"I don't know, babe. I hope not. I don't see any boats out there in the lake, do you?"

"Not a one," Megan replied after staring at the water.

"That's pretty fucking weird there's no one patrolling the waters."

"They probably haven't had to in a while, but we should try getting through here before they do."

My heart was beating so hard I figured it would beat right out of my chest, and my legs burned and ached from running. We sat behind the last house on the street for about five minutes. I wanted to dive into the water when I reached it but knew it would be a waste of valuable time. I was sweating like a whore in church. The humidity that day must have been seventy-five percent, and the temperature was in the high nineties. For the last minute we stood behind the house, I listened for any oncoming traffic again, but I heard nothing. I decided it was time to make our move.

"Ready for this, baby?" I asked.

"Yes... can we get going? I want out of this place. It scares me to death, hearing no signs of life, or seeing any traffic. Those army scumbags are the evilest bastards I've ever seen. Let's go!"

Just before I started running to this marina, an idea suddenly popped into my head.

"Babe, remember those guys at the roadblock?"

"Yes. They shot my grandmother. Why?" she asked irritably.

"Those buildings across the street are the old barracks of Sackets. A lot of GIs were at the roadblock, and I'm sure a lot more stay right in those buildings."

"So what are you saying?"

"I think running to this marina is a bad idea. If some dick-nose army guy is in there and spots us, we're fucked. I suggest we stay on this side of the street behind the houses. Let's do that while we head to the main marina in Sackets, and then cross the road to the lake."

"Whatever, let's just go."

I grabbed her hand and darted for the house to the right. The homes here were all in great shape, and I didn't see any trash or abandoned cars. It was like the shit happening ten miles down the road hadn't affected these people.

We ran behind seven more houses, and then had another street to cross in front of us to get to the public marina of Sackets. I saw four boats tied off, and my heart skipped a beat. The smells of water and seaweed were in the air; it was much better than smelling death.

We stopped one last time to catch our breath.

"Seamus, do you think any of those boats have keys in them? I don't know how to hotwire anything, and I'm pretty sure you don't either," Megan stated.

"I hope so, because you're right; I don't know how to hot wire anything."

As we sat there, I thought about our plan. We had to make it across the street, then split up and start investigating the boats to see if any had keys. The marina was a decent size, but not big enough to lose sight of each other. Then, all we had to do was start it up and take off. We both knew how to drive boats, so once we were in and moving, our escape would be effortless.

Just as we were about to make a break for it there was a series of shots fired off in the distance of where we had came from.

"Did you hear that?" I asked Megan.

"Yeah... they were gunshots."

"I hope they didn't just blow Burto to hell."

"Why do you have to say things like that?" Megan asked.

"It was either them shooting Burto, or the monsters got through their stupid barricade."

"Babe, don't say that, they had no reason to shoot him. If the zombies get through the barricade, they're going to be all over the place."

"Good! Those bastards deserve it. We better get a move on."

Megan started running for the boat launches, and I was right behind her. We ran from the house across the street and up to the docks where the boats were tied. When we got to the edge of the water, I saw a rowboat with a pull-start motor tied off nearby.

"If none of them have keys, we can take this little rowboat," I yelled to Megan.

She didn't answer; she was already in the first boat. It was a twenty-foot Mercury with an inboard engine. I ran down to the last boat on that side, a fifteen-foot pontoon. I started searching for the ignition immediately, but before I could find it, heard an engine fire up.

I looked up to see Megan at the wheel of the Mercury she had gotten into. I was out of the party boat in an instant, running down the dock as fast as I could. I reached the boat Megan had commandeered and started to untie it from the dock.

"This is convenient," I said as I worked.

"Just hurry up and get in."

"Are you going to be alright driving this?" I asked.

"Hell yeah! My dad had this same boat. I may be a bit rusty, but I'm sure it's like riding a bike."

Standard rules stated you could do no more than five knots in a marina, but the rules were washed away in this case. In seconds, Megan had the boat moving full bore with its bow pointing at the sun.

Even though she was rusty, she had the boat trimmed down and planed in a few seconds as we headed out into Lake Ontario. I took a seat, kicked my shoes off, and watched as the land grew smaller and smaller behind us. Water splashed into the boat every time we hit a wave. Megan had cut the wheel left toward the direction of Henderson Harbor.

"Just go straight out into the lake until we get to the backside of the islands in the middle."

"Why?" Megan asked.

"If they questioned Burto and he mentioned anything about my cottage, they'll go there and see us out front. Hell, its only ten minutes down the road from them now anyway. Regardless, I'm sure they have access to boats, but I'm more worried about helicopters. If they do see us out here in a boat, they will send an attack chopper and blow us out of the water. I don't want that to happen, so just haul ass to the middle of the lake."

"Fine with me," Megan said.

"What do you want to do?" Megan asked after a few minutes.

I thought momentarily and then said, "I think our only option is to drive across the lake into Canada."

"I've never driven a boat that far."

"I don't want to risk heading to another spot in New York just to be overrun with zombies again."

"Whatever you say... how do we get there?" Megan continued.

"Is there a compass over there anywhere?"

"Yes, of course."

"Just keep it pointing west, and we should get there eventually. I think once we're on the back of the islands we should be safe from anyone on shore looking out."

"Ten-four, Captain," Megan said with a smile.

I stood up and placed a kiss on her cheek as she drove on.

Megan kept the boat at full throttle, and by now, we were so far out all land had disappeared, except for the three islands to the south.

"Cut back on the throttle," I said.

"Why?"

"To save gas. I think we should be alright. I can't see the shoreline anymore, so I doubt they can see us."

She brought the boat to about rowing speed and guided us slightly left.

"What's the gas situation?" I asked.

"We don't have much babe, just at a half tank."

"Shit, were going to have to keep it slow. We can't be marooned out here."

"This is pretty terrifying."

"Don't worry; we've made it this long I think we can handle this."

I kicked off my shoes and then took my white tee off. The damn thing reeked like body odor. Then I sat back, trying to catch some rays as we passed around the back of the first island.

"Hey, babe, remember that island in front of my cottage I took you to that time?"

"Of course I remember. That cinderblock cabin was weirdly out of place."

"That one is called Gull Island, and the other two we are going to pass are called Horse, and Bass Island. I was thinking to use Gull Island as a point of reference. I think heading south to Gull Island and then directly west from there would be our best bet. I remember someone telling me from Gull Island to the first big land mass in Canada is roughly 36 miles in a straight line across the lake."

"Do you think the gas might be a problem?"

"You said we have a half tank? I think we should be fine. These islands are only a mile and a half apart. Our longest stretch will be west of Gull Island. We might be running on fumes, but we should be able to make it."

"I remember the water being shallow at Gull Island."

"The water on the front side of the island facing my cottage is shallow. We're on the back and heading the opposite direction. We should be fine. From where we're going to be, we won't even be able to see the cottage."

"Do you think the army dicks will find us?" Megan asked worriedly.

"I damn sure hope not, baby."

I stood up and walked to the front of the boat where I sat and splashed myself with water. I wanted to jump in to cool off but decided to deal with the heat a while longer.

Horse Island began to shrink behind us as Bass Island became larger before us. It was about the same size as the first, probably not much bigger than a single building in an apartment complex. Bass Island came and went, and soon we were coming up on Gull Island, but something caught Megan's eye, and she cut the throttle.

"Babe, is that a boat up ahead?"

I was lying back in my chair, and my eyes snapped open and I sat straight up.

"What?" I asked.

"Look," Megan said, pointing past the bow.

I looked straight ahead. Directly behind Gull Island a boat, bobbed up and down in the waves.

"Who do you think that belongs to?" Megan asked quietly.

"I don't know. It could be abandoned."

"Come on, really, abandoned?"

"With all the crazy shit going on you never know. It's strange but that boat looks familiar."

"What do you mean?"

"I mean, I've seen that boat somewhere before."

Then it hit me. The boat belonged to an old family friend, Mr. Sampson. I had known the Sampson's my entire life, and they lived in Dexter, New York. They literally lived a half mile from the Dexter Marina, so it was very possible it was my buddy. Megan and I had actually been on the boat that now bobbed before us.

"Slowly creep up to the boat. I'm not sure if the Sampson's even still own the thing."

"Are you sure?"

"Yes, positive. You do remember that you've ridden on it before?"

"Oh! Yeah, I have, haven't I? It's been a long time."

"It hasn't been that long, are you feeling alright?

"Yes, I'm fine, what do you want me to do?"

"Creep up alongside the boat. I want to see if it has more gas than we do."

CHAPTER 25

Megan slowly started moving toward the boat, and within minutes, we were tying off to the second craft. I jumped from our boat into the other and took a look around.

Almost immediately I spotted a few shotguns poking out from under a tarp on the back seat. That's when a loud *boom* frightened me half to death. There were several small splashes as the gunshot hit the water near the boats.

"Get the fuck away from my boat!" a man yelled from shore.

"Hey, man, we thought this was abandoned! We're trying to get the hell out of the area but thought we might be able to get some gas out of this. What's your name?"

"Who the fuck wants to know?"

"I'm Seamus, and this is Megan. We recognized this boat because one of my old friends used to own it."

"The son of a bitch still does. How the hell are you, Seamus?"

"Sweetheart, kill the engine and throw the anchor; we're going inland," I said to Megan.

"Are you sure it's safe?"

"Yes, of course it is."

That was all I said before I dived off the side of Sampson's boat into the cold refreshing lake. It felt good to dive into crystal clear water. I surfaced a few feet from the boat and commenced to swim until I could stand up in the water. When I reached the shoreline, I found walking on mussel shells barefoot was very tricky. Walking out of the water I turned to see if Megan had followed me into the drink, and she had, but she was wearing a life jacket and was slowly floating in.

I gave him a hug, then stepped back and had a long look at the shaggy dog.

"Holy shit, how are you?" I laughed.

"Well, I've had better days, but who hasn't?"

"Damn, dude, your hair is a lot longer, and you've lost a ton of weight. Those shorts look like they went through a meat grinder, and where's your shirt?"

"It's nice to see you too." Laughing, Sampson continued, "I've been living on an island for a couple of months, and I didn't exactly bring a sewing kit and extra fabric to repair my shorts. My shirt's inside the shack with the rest of what I have left."

"I can't believe you're out here. Are you alone?" I asked.

"Yup, I realized shit was happening and acted fast. I wasn't going to get caught up inland in the middle of whatever the hell was happening, so I got out of there as quick as I could."

"You don't know what's going on back there?" I asked.

"Hell no, but I assume it's bad. I've seen fewer and fewer headlights at night, and a while ago I saw black smoke daily for over a month. I didn't think it was safe to leave so I stayed right here. What happened?" Sampson asked.

"It was the zombie apocalypse, bro."

"Get the fuck out of here...really?"

"Yeah, man. We can talk about that later. Are you losing your mind yet?"

"Seriously, you're going to brush that news off like its nothing?"

"Not exactly, I just don't want to talk about it right now," I said.

"Alright, but I'm going to want details at some point. What the hell are you doing here? Last I knew you were in North Carolina."

"Megan and I came up for a vacation. We had no idea what we were driving into."

"How the hell did you make it all the way out here?" Sampson asked, looking astonished.

"It's a long story. I'll tell you sometime. So, I assume it's pretty safe out here?" I continued.

"I haven't had a problem yet. I figure it's about 3 miles from here to Route 3 in front of your cottage. Each night I see headlights driving by your cottage, but I know they haven't seen me."

"How can you be so sure?"

"Mainly because I'm still here," Sampson laughed.

"I sure could go for some food; do you have anything to eat inside?"

"Yeah. I'm running short on packaged items, so I've been fishing and eating what I catch."

"You cook it, right?"

"Oh yeah, almost every time," Sampson chuckled.

"What do you mean?"

"Well, it depends on how hungry I am when I catch it."

"How are the living arrangements?"

"I've got a small cot I found inside, but I wasn't expecting company. Hey, Megan, how are you?" Sampson asked, directing his attention to her. "I'm sorry about my greeting. I had no idea it was you two. I just thought it was a couple of assholes trying to steal my boat."

"I'm as good as one can be in a situation like this. You scared the hell out of me, but I guess I would have done the same thing if I were you," Megan said as she climbed ashore.

"Come on, let's go inside. We have a lot of catching up to do."

The two of us followed Sampson on a path he had bushwhacked to the old cinderblock shack. We walked around to the front and entered through the door. The structure had no windows whatsoever, and a small wood-burning stove in the corner of the room.

"Home sweet home, guys," Sampson laughed.

With the door open the sunlight lit the room. We could see he had a nice little setup. I saw the cot he had mentioned off to the right of the stove, with old newspapers and magazines lying next to it. There was a small kitchen area to our left. I saw a propane camping stove on the makeshift countertop. Twenty or so empty cans of random different soups and vegetables sat on top of the counter. Then I saw something that caught my eye: a bottle of Mr. Boston vodka.

"You mind? I've had a long day," I said, pointing to the bottle.

"Not at all. Take it easy, though, that's the only booze I have. There was wine, but I've already drank that. Figured I'd save the best for last."

"Beggars can't be choosers, old friend," I said as I unscrewed the cap.

The liquid burned down my throat and into my stomach. As I slugged the bottle, Sampson walked outside and came back holding two five-gallon buckets.

"Here you go, have a seat. I have three of these I use as shitters, and these two are the ones I'm not using at the moment. Don't worry I wash them out in the lake."

"Why don't you just shit in the corner of the island?" Megan asked.

"Because it takes me a long time to shit, and I can't squat that long," Sampson said, laughing.

Megan sat down on a bucket, and I walked over and took a seat on the other.

"I'm so happy to see you guys. I've been so lonely out here thinking about what happened to everyone I know. Sometimes I think about ending it. Matter of fact, I was seriously thinking about that just before I heard the boat pull up."

"Shit, man, I'm glad you didn't pull the trigger. Our plan was to use this island as a guidance point. We were cruising here when Megan spotted your boat. I thought for some reason I recognized the boat, so we took a chance. I actually thought the boat may have been abandoned and planned on trying to siphon whatever gas I could. Anyway, how did you get out of town?"

"My parents were both in Watertown when shit hit the fan. I had just stopped by their house to grab some things. I turned on the television, and a reporter was live, standing in the square, yelling into the camera about the army forcing people onto buses and detaining others. I had no idea what was happening as I watched. I stood there for a few minutes watching all the pandemonium and chaos behind her when I saw a solider come up from behind and club her in the head. The screen went fuzzy, and then the emergency broadcast bars came on. I was fucking terrified. After a while of pure bewilderment, I remembered the conversations we had about what to do when shit hit the fan."

"I'm glad you did."

"Remember when you told me you had packed a bug-out bag in case something huge ever happened?"

"Yeah, of course, it's what any good prepper would need at any given notice. I have one at home, one in the trunk of my car back in North Carolina, and one in Megan's trunk. Speaking of which, did you ever pull it out?" I said, looking at Megan.

"I didn't have time. Grandma's place was crawling with zombies, so I ran inside instead. Everything was so hectic in there after grandpa was bitten, I forgot, and we left in the minivan."

"It doesn't matter now," I finished.

"Anyway," Sampson continued, "that went through my head, and I remembered I had actually packed one a few months ago. When I saw the panic on TV, I remembered it was in my old bedroom closet buried under all the shit I didn't move out."

"You're a smart man."

"I ran into my old room and dug through the closet until I pulled the bag out. With pack in hand I ran toward the front door. I dropped the bag next to it and went into the kitchen, grabbing a few garbage bags from under the sink. I began loading everything I could find into each bag. I emptied out my parents' entire kitchen and set those bags next to the door along with my bug-out."

Right then Sampson looked and me and motioned for the bottle I was still holding. I handed it off to him, and he took a long-drawn swig of the remaining vodka. Sampson coughed and gagged a little after taking the swig. It took him a minute to regain himself as Megan and I sat there listening intently.

"Anyway--while I'm doing this the TV is still showing the emergency bars, so I knew something was definitely going down. I ran into my parents' room to the gun cabinet and saw they had shotguns and a rifle. I figured if my parents did somehow make it back, they would want at least a shotgun, so I left them a shotgun and some ammo. When I went back to the door for my supplies, I stood there with no clue about where I was going to go. Then I saw my dad's boat key hanging on the wall and remembered the island in the middle of the lake with the stone shack built on it. I grabbed the key off the hook, and the bags of food, and took them to my car. I went back in for the rest of my stuff and left. I didn't even turn the TV off; I just left, door open and everything. I headed toward the marina down the road from my house, and at least fifty cars were flying by me going the other way. People honked and flashed their lights at me, but I didn't care. I got to the marina and pulled up as close to Dad's boat as I could. I gathered my things and tossed them into the boat."

"The boat was already in the water?"

"Yeah, Dad had put it in a few days before. Anyway, I guess a few people had seen me loading up the boat and wanted to join. There were only three or four, but I pointed my gun at them and told them to get the hell away."

"Wow, that doesn't surprise me. I'd a tried to do the same thing if I were them."

"I did tell them my car keys were still inside the car, and that there was half a tank of gas left."

"Did they take it?"

"Hell yeah, they took it. They were in it before I told them about the keys. Then I started the boat and drove straight here, and I've been here ever since."

"What are you going to do? Sit here until you're an old man?" I asked.

"I don't know. I've been trying to figure that out since I arrived."

"Jesus, you sound just like Marston. He didn't do shit either. You can't wait around for someone to save you; you got to get that shit done on your own."

"Who is Marston?" Sampson asked.

"Some useless piece of shit; it doesn't matter. Megan and I are going to be heading to Canada. You're more than welcome to join."

"Are you developmentally disabled? Did you think once I saw you, I hadn't already planned on leaving with you guys?"

"I don't know, man, you might like living here. Hell, who wouldn't want to stay on a deserted island and live for a summer?" I asked.

"So, Sampson, how have you been catching your own food?" Megan asked.

"Lucky for me, a fishing pole was in the boat. Not much else of any use, though."

"Cool. You mind if I fish a little? I'm getting hungry," Megan asked.

"Sure. Hold on, let me grab the pole."

Sampson stood up and went up the stairs again.

"Do you know how to cook a fish over a fire?" Megan asked me.

"Sorta, kinda, but not really. I'm sure he can gut, fillet, and cook it for you," I chuckled.

Sampson returned a minute later, holding out a bright pink Barbie fishing pole.

"Here you go," he said as he handed Megan the Barbie fishing pole.

"Sampson, it fits your personality."

"That's not funny."

"Yes, it is," Megan said teasingly.

"It's not mine. Besides, it works. Just go off the backside of the island; that's where I've had the most luck fishing."

"Are you guys going to come out with me?" Megan asked.

"I don't see why not," I said.

The three of us went outside and around to the back of the stone house. The walk was short since the island was small, half trees and half rocky shoreline.

"This is Gull Island, right?" I asked Sampson.

"As far as I know it is."

"Where are the fucking birds? I'd eat one right now if I could. I haven't had any meat in what seems like forever."

"That's gross, man. Those things are rats with wings," Sampson replied.

"I don't care. The meat would be a nice addition to the fish."

Sampson scoffed as he led the way through the brush and small saplings to the right of the boats. We emerged from the underbrush at a clearing. Sampson walked to the tree line and pulled a can of corn and a loaf of bread out of the bushes.

"The corn works the best. I haven't got any worms because I haven't felt like digging them up. Besides, it hasn't rained in I don't know how long."

Sampson handed Megan the can of corn and the bread, and I took a seat in the clearing. He soon joined me, and we relaxed as we watched Megan start fishing.

"What the fuck happened in there, brotha?" Sampson asked.

The two of us sat on the beach, and I filled Sampson in on the whole thing up until this point. His facial expressions were priceless, and he clung to every word. I chose to leave the brutality of Marston's demise out by saying he just took off on us one night. I explained all my theories and everything I had come up with. He was completely caught off guard.

"I figured we had been invaded by another country or something," Sampson claimed.

"Honestly, that would have been better, I think."

"What do you plan on doing when you get to Canada?" Sampson asked.

"I don't know. There's really not much to do. Tell the authorities about this bullshit, I guess," I replied.

"I hope they take us seriously."

"They will. Why would we make up shit like this?" I continued.

"Good point. But what if they try to bring you back?"

"They'll be bringing a dead body, because there's no way in hell I will be coming back here. Do you know how much shit I had to go through to get out of there?"

"Only what you've told me."

"Man, I hope Burto's alright," I said quietly.

"The two of you fought your way out of town, didn't you?" Sampson asked.

"Yeah. The army stopped us at the intersection of Route 3 and the road that ran into Sackets. Then they drove us to the hotel by the ice cream shop where Megan was waiting."

"Wow. You two are lucky you got away."

"Honestly, I have no idea how Burto is doing right now. We heard gunshots shortly after our escape," I said.

As Megan sat nearby, the rod between her legs as she waited for a fish to snap at her bait, Sampson and I began planning our adventure into Canada.

"I've never taken a boat that far across the lake before," Sampson said.

"Neither have we, so we'll learn together. How much gas do you have?"

"A little under a quarter a tank. Does your boat have more?"

"The tank is just under half, and our boat's bigger, so I say we take it."

"You talked me into it," Sampson said.

"It's still pretty early; do you guys want to leave now?" I asked.

"I was thinking the same thing, but since none of has ever driven that far across should we wait until morning? I figure if something does happen at least we will have the whole day to deal with any issues we may encounter," Sampson said.

"I'm fine with leaving tomorrow," Megan chimed in.

"I've been on this island for too long, and I need to leave before I go crazy."

"Alright then, we'll leave in the morning," I finished.

"Just a heads-up, guys, I still block the front door every night," Sampson said.

"Why the hell do you do that?" I asked.

"It's the only entrance. I figure if someone shows up to investigate, I won't be caught off guard."

"Whatever works for you, pal. I don't care what you do; I'm just glad to be the fuck out of Watertown," I said.

Just then, Megan yelled, "Got one!" She started to reel, and the drag started going nuts as the fish tried to escape.

"I set the drag to reel in some whoppers. Be careful; the line's only an eight-pound test."

She reeled madly as the line kept screaming. Finally, the drag started to slow; the fish was getting tired. She slowly reeled the line back, and every few seconds, the fish would try to take off again. Each time it lasted only seconds.

Megan finally got the fish close enough to the shore for us to get a look at it. It was a large white fish with a pointed nose: a Great Northern pike. She reeled and reeled, and soon enough, the massive fish was on shore, fighting to breathe.

"Wow, baby, great job! That's a hell of a catch," I exclaimed.

"Thank you, sweetie. He's a big one!"

"I would say twenty inches, at least," Sampson added.

"Well, hun, let's get this thing ready to cook," I suggested.

"I think I want to put him back."

"Really? Why?"

"Well, he got this big...that means he has escaped fishermen for years. Why should I be the one to take him?"

"Because you said you were hungry for one. I would love some fresh fish right now," I said.

"Yeah... but I think I want to let it go,"

With that, she bent over, picked the fishing line off the ground, bit through it, and tossed the fish back into the lake with the hook still in its mouth.

"What was the point of even fishing?" I asked, annoyed.

"I thought I wanted to eat fish; I changed my mind, I'm sorry."

"Honestly, I'm not surprised you did that. Seems like we're going to be eating whatever Sampson has left for dinner," I said.

She looked at me and then came jogging over.

"I caught a fishy! Hooray for Megan. "She hugged and kissed me like this was the happiest moment in her life. The way she was acting made me think the things she went through were messing with her head.

After the fishing episode, the three of us explored the rest of the island. It wasn't very large, so it didn't take too long to walk around the whole thing. While exploring we found an old wooden toilet seat and driftwood, which Sampson picked up to take with him. After a while we decided to return to the windowless shack. When we went inside, Sampson tossed the driftwood and the toilet seat next to the woodstove for later. The three of us then sat outside the entrance chatting while the afternoon turned into dusk, and then dusk quickly turned into night.

The three of us went inside, and Sampson started a fire in the stove for light. Without fish, our dinner was canned food, and Megan got first pick. She picked some beefaroni, and then I pulled pork and beans. Sampson went last and picked a bag of ramen noodles. He didn't bother cooking them; he just poured the seasoning into the bag and started to eat. The selection of grub was pathetic, but at least it was food.

"Man, can you imagine how good fish would have tasted?" I asked Sampson.

"I'm sure it would have been delicious. Too bad the hippy had to release it. You're lucky we're leaving in the morning or I'd make you find that hook you just lost," Sampson said, smiling.

Megan shot us a look but didn't reply.

After we ate dinner, Sampson went into the kitchen and pulled a huge quilt from under the counter.

"This is your guys' bed tonight; sorry, this is the best I can do."

I grabbed the blanket enthusiastically.

"This will be fine, and it will be warm enough in here if we keep the fire going and close the door."

"I normally douse the fire with a bucket of water before I sleep. If I don't it gets stifling in here."

"This is your party, brotha; do whatever you want. I'm beat, so I'm going to lie down and try to get some rest."

I stood up and spread the blanket out on the floor opposite the counter. If there were any rats and roaches, they wouldn't bother me, but I wasn't sure about Megan. She had been in a strange mood all day, acting distant and not talking much.

I lay on the hard floor and felt comfortable right away. Sampson left the shack with the bucket to get some water to put the fire out, and Megan came over and lay down next to me.

"Are you sure you're feeling alright, babe?" I asked.

"I don't know how I feel. This whole thing has been such a nightmare my brain seems scattered. It's like it doesn't comprehend everything that's happened."

"Oh, trust me, I know the feeling. Some of the things I did over the last few days are going to stick with me for the rest of my life. Hell, this whole damn thing is going to stay with me forever. If you want to talk about anything just let me know. We'll make it through this together."

"I know baby, you're the best," she said, kissing my cheek and snuggling up beside me.

Sampson came back in closing the door behind him a minute later.

"Do you guys need anything before I put this fire out?"

"I'm all set, man. I'm looking forward to a night of rest without the dead lumbering around outside."

"Yeah, Sampson, I'm all set too."

"Alright then, I'll see you two in the morning, goodnight."

"Goodnight," we said simultaneously.

Sampson opened the glass door of the wood stove and poured the water in dousing the flames and light. The fire sizzled and popped, but eventually was fully out. After five minutes the room was awkwardly quiet. I lay there, my mind racing over the events of the week. I started wondering if I should have brought Marston with us when we left. I felt tears forming in my eyes as I drifted off to sleep.

CHAPTER 26

Intense nightmares ran nonstop through my head, and I suddenly snapped awake and sat up, disoriented. The room was darker, pitch black, and sweat ran cold down my spine and soaked my body from the neck down. I was breathing like I had run a mile, and my heart thumped so loudly I thought everyone in the room could hear it.

I reached my left arm down to see if Megan was next to me. She was snoring, and I could hear Sampson breathing heavily from across the room. I lay back down, hoping I could fall asleep again. I soon realized that wasn't going to happen because, for the first time since childhood, I was afraid of my dreams and didn't want to sleep. I stared up into the blackness of the room for an hour before I decided to move.

I stood up and made my way to the door, where I felt around for the board wedged under the door handle. I moved the board and leaned it against the wall, then pulled the door open, stepped through, and quietly shut it behind me as I walked out.

I walked to the front of the island where an old cement dock sat in the calm waters. The moon was out in full tonight and was halfway through the sky, telling me it was probably around three-thirty or four in the morning. I sat on the cold concrete and dipped my legs into the water.

Memories from the past few days again flooded my brain, and I was annoyed I couldn't stop them. I covered my eyes with my hands, then applied enough pressure for little colorful dots to burst behind my eyelids. I decided to lay back with my legs in the water and try to relax for a minute, and before I knew it, I was out.

I woke up to the harsh heat of the sun. It stung my eyes when I opened them. My dreams had stopped long enough for me to sleep for a few hours. I sat up and realized I couldn't feel my legs; they had fallen asleep and were still submerged in the water. I couldn't stand, so I began to pull myself backward along the dock, and then damn near shit myself when someone suddenly grabbed me under the arms and pulled me back. My legs came out of the water, and I lay there, not moving.

"Ha! Take it easy, dumbass. It's me," Sampson said.

"Don't you know sneaking up on people is rude?" I shouted.

"Sorry, dick. If you want to play that card, then you can't be leaving the only door open at night."

Sampson stopped talking and started to laugh as soon as he saw my legs. When I saw what he was laughing at, I stared at them in shock. My legs had turned white, looked like they were a hundred and fifty years old.

"Anyway, although I want to do nothing more than sit here and laugh at you, we have to get going."

"Where's Megan?" I asked.

"She's already on the boat. She saw you out here sleeping and didn't want to wake you up. She figured you needed the rest. Try standing up."

He helped me stand, and both my legs started to tingle right away. I had to shake each one around until the feeling went away. The wrinkles and whiteness slowly started to fade once I got moving again.

"What time is it?" I asked as I rubbed my eyes.

"The sun came up about an hour ago. Megan and I sat and watched it rise."

"Why didn't you wake me up?"

"You looked peaceful. Besides, we were having a heavy conversation."

"Whatever, let me get my legs back in working order and get the hell out of here. Take one last look, because more than likely you won't ever see it again," I said.

"You're right, it sucks. I've lost everything, but at least I don't have anything tying me here anymore."

"Do we have everything we need in the boat?" I asked.

"The only things we're taking are the fishing pole and the shotguns."

"Let's get moving. I don't want the morning to go by as fast as it did yesterday. Hopefully, come noon, we'll be in Canada," I said.

We made our way to the back of the island. Megan was lying out in the front of the boat while she waited for us. I eased my way into the water until I was waist-deep and dived under. I came up with the initial shock of coldness, but a second later, it was gone, and the water felt warm to me. The boat wasn't too far out, so the swim was short.

Sampson was carrying a gun, so he could not submerge himself like I had. He got up to his waist in water and turned over onto his back and started kicking his feet. Sampson held the gun up over his chest with one hand and steered his body with the other. The kicking worked out for him, and he was at the boat a few seconds after me.

"Here, take this; my legs are burning," Sampson said, clearly exhausted.

He handed me the shotgun, then turned over onto his stomach. The boats were tied to each other, and I noticed Megan hadn't grabbed the leftover guns from Sampson's boat.

"Good morning, lady," I said.

"Good morning, baby. How did you sleep?"

"Not good at first; the dreams were bad last night."

"We saw you sleeping on the dock. Was that comfortable?"

"I slept like a stone, but when I woke up, I was far from comfortable."

"Sampson woke me up a while ago and asked if I wanted to watch the sunrise."

"He told me about the sunrise, and the conversations."

"Last night you told me if I needed to talk about anything you'd be there. That same thing goes for you," Megan said assuredly.

"Are you two ready?"

"Yes!" Megan and I said as I climbed back into our boat.

"Off we go then."

Sampson started the engine and let it idle for a few minutes. While the boat was warming up, I untied our line from Sampson's boat.

After a minute Sampson lowered the prop into the water, throttled up, and we started to move. The day was perfect, and the lake was as smooth as glass.

"Let's open this baby up," I called to Sampson.

"I thought you'd never ask," Sampson said has he pushed the throttle forward.

The boat sped up to about to about 50 knots, and we were really moving now.

"What's the speedometer say," I yelled to Sampson.

"Right around fifty-five, buddy."

Thankfully the waves were about a foot high, and we were able to handle them easily. I sat there enjoying the wind blowing through my hair. I turned in my seat and had a look back at Gull Island. It was getting smaller and smaller as we hauled ass across the lake. Just as I was about to face forward again something caught my eye. I saw a helicopter to my left. It looked like it was flying toward the islands from Sackets.

"Sampson, push this fucking thing as fast as it will go. We need to get the fuck out of here now!" I shouted.

Megan looked at me and put her hands out asking what the issue was. Pointing back toward the islands I yelled, "Helicopter."

Sampson pushed the throttle to the max, and I felt a burst of speed.

"Do you think they see us?" Sampson yelled from the driving chair.

"I can't tell yet; it's still pretty far back there, but it could catch us pretty easily if it spots us," I replied.

As the chopper became smaller like the island had, I happened to notice it was flying directly south toward Gull Island.

"Sampson, I think they spotted your boat," I yelled through the wind.

"That should buy us some time," he returned.

I turned to face the island again when I saw a fire ball erupt into the sky.

"Sampson, they just blew your boat up! How fast are we going?"

"It's redlined at sixty-eight."

"Are we going to make it?" Megan yelled from the front.

"At this speed we should be crossing into Canada pretty soon. I don't think the American government has any authority in Canadian airspace," I shouted.

I wasn't sure about this, but I didn't want Megan to freak out. I kept watching the back of the boat, and eventually I couldn't see anything back there. I was thinking if the chopper had seen us, they would have been on us by now, but they weren't.

"Don't let up on that throttle until you know were in Canada," I yelled.

"Wasn't planning on it!"

The boat was moving so fast I thought standing up would be a bad move, so I stayed where I was and continued looking back. I still didn't see anything coming our way, and a sense of relief came over me.

"The lake's getting a little choppy, and we're burning through gas," Sampson shouted.

"It doesn't matter, keep pushing this thing. We have to be close to crossing the border. I had no real idea where the border was. All I knew at that very moment was that we were way out in the middle of a lake and none of us could see any land anywhere.

"Megan, how are you up there?" I shouted from the back.

"I'm scared, baby, are we going to make it?"

"Yes, we'll be fine," I said.

By now we had been traveling for thirty minutes at over sixty miles an hour. We had to be in Canadian waters, so I shouted to Sampson, "How's the gas?"

"We're in bad shape."

"How bad?"

"Bad enough that I feel very uncomfortable."

"Goddamn it, how much!?"

"We're barley above *E*."

"Pull back the throttle. We should be okay. I haven't seen the chopper for a while."

Sampson pulled the throttle back and the boat began to slow down. I went to the front and started talking to Megan.

"Jesus, it's a good thing you guys woke up early."

"I know, right? This has been a bumpy ride, my ass hurts," Megan claimed.

"I know what......"

"Babe, what is it?"

"Sampson punch the fucking gas...the chopper is coming!"

I grabbed Megan's shoulders and held her tightly as Sampson slammed the throttle wide open. We were flying over the waves and slamming into the water every time.

"It's okay, babe, we'll be fine," I whispered in Megan's ear.

I looked back to see the chopper was gaining on us. I turned to face the bow and saw land was actually coming into view.

"Holy shit, Sampson do you see that up ahead?"

"Fuck yes, I do. Let's hope we make it."

At this point it was a race against the clock. The chopper was gaining on us at a tremendous rate, and for the first time I thought we were fucked.

"How fast are helicopters?" Megan asked.

"A hell of a lot faster than we are," I said, shaken.

"How fast are we going?" Megan asked.

"Sixty-five," Sampson shouted.

"Feels like a hundred," Megan said.

"I wish it was a hundred," I said

I looked ahead and saw the land was getting bigger by the second. I decided to grab the shotgun off the seat and have it ready just in case. I knew the gun was absolutely useless, but it was mildly comforting nonetheless.

"That chopper is going to be on us before we get to the land," I said.

"I'm pushing this thing as hard as it will go."

We ran the engine at top speed for what seemed like forever, and suddenly the boat started spitting and sputtering.

"We're running on fumes!" Sampson shouted.

Looking ahead I realized there were two land masses on either side of the boat. We couldn't have been more than a mile from a shoreline when I had an idea.

"Hey, Sampson, is there a radio over there?"

"Yes, of course," he replied.

"Turn it on and send an S.O.S to the Canadian coast guard."

"What channel is that?"

"I have no idea, just try every channel, and hurry."

As Sampson tried the radio the chopper flew overhead, passing us. It went a way up and turned around, facing us.

"They're going to fucking kill us!" Megan shrieked.

"Hold on," Sampson yelled as he cut the wheel hard to the right.

The boat ripped to the right, and we were heading straight for the shoreline at maximum speed.

"Slow the fuck down or were going to crash," I yelled.

Sampson pulled the throttle back so fast the engine cut off. It didn't matter though because our momentum was enough to keep up skipping across the water toward the shore.

"Reverse, reverse," Megan began shouting.

Sampson turned the key and the engine fired up. He put it in reverse and the screaming sound we all heard scared us. I wasn't sure but I thought he had fried the transmission. His move had slowed us down considerably, so I wasn't as terrified of a crash as I had been moments before. I turned to see the chopper had again changed course and was now to our left facing us.

"I think they're going to shoot," I yelled.

I looked ahead and saw there was a beach area directly in front of us with a handful of people on it.

"Hold on everyone; we're going to crash!" Sampson shouted.

As soon as Sampson said that, I heaved the shotgun over the side of the boat and braced for impact. Seconds later I heard and felt as rocks began smashing the underside of the boat. We skimmed across them at first, but then we plowed into a shallow rocky shoreline. We were all slammed forward and almost thrown over the bow. On the sandy shore of the beach the boat came to a stop. I checked to see if we were about to be fired on, but saw the helicopter heading back in the direction it had come from.

I let out the biggest sigh of relief I have ever had and gave Megan a hug. I jumped up and hugged Sampson as the beachgoers ran to the side of the boat.

"Is everyone okay?" a stranger in swimming trunks asked.

"Holy shit, I think we are now, buddy," I replied.

"What the hell was that all about? Are you terrorists?" the man asked.

"Sir, I think you and all these other people just saved our lives."

"What was that helicopter doing chasing you?" asked an older beach lady in a one-piece swimsuit.

"It's a long story," I replied.

"I want out of this boat right now," Megan said, standing up.

"I'm right behind you, sister," Sampson said.

The three of us began climbing out of the boat one at a time. A friendly middle-aged man with children standing behind him started helping each of us out of the boat.

"You have no idea how happy we are to see you," Megan said to the group forming on the beach.

"I'm glad this place isn't packed, we could have killed someone," Sampson said.

"This place isn't exactly a huge destination spot for many people. It's more of a small community of people who have been coming here for years," the helpful gentlemen said as I jumped down onto the shoreline.

"Where are we?" I asked the man.

"This here is Back Beach Park."

"This is Canada, right?"

"Oh, absolutely. Did you come from stateside?"

"Yes, we sure did," Sampson turned and said.

Megan had taken a seat to regain herself as Sampson and I talked with the people on the beach.

"Is there a payphone somewhere near here? I need to call the police," I asked the man.

"There's no phone here, but there is a farm about three miles up the road on the right," the man replied.

I walked over to Megan and had a seat next to her as people crowded around us, whispering to each other.

"How you feeling, babe?" I asked.

"I don't exactly know. I've never felt like this before. I am overcome with joy, fear, and excitement. It feels really weird."

"I think that's probably a heavy dose of adrenaline you have there," I replied.

She turned to me and grabbed me with a monster bear hug.

"Thank you so much, baby. I would have died back there if it weren't for you," she said, tearing up.

Sampson walked to us in the middle of our embrace and started talking.

"That guy over there in the neon orange shorts said he would take us to the police department. I told him some of the stuff we went through, and he thought I was bullshitting him," Sampson laughed.

"That's awesome. I didn't know what to do," I said.

As the three of us waited for the man to get ready to give us a ride, we got bombarded with questions from everyone standing around.

"Why was the helicopter chasing you, who are you, do you need a drink, is this your boat?"

The three of us just looked at each other and lifted our eyebrows.

"Do you want to take this one?" I asked Sampson.

"Why not?" he replied.

"Alright everyone, can I get your attention for a moment."

As Sampson answered the people's questions Megan and I sat there hugging and smiling. This was the exact moment I had been waiting for the last few days, and it was worth the wait. The feelings of happiness shot through my veins like a drug, and it was incredible.

Chapter 27

The drive from the beach to the police department took about twenty minutes. The man drove an SUV, and I stuck Sampson in the front seat.

"My name's Mike everyone," he announced as he drove.

"Thanks for the ride, Mike," Megan said.

"Oh, it's no problem at all. That entrance you made was one I'll never forget."

"We didn't think we were going to make it to land. If you people hadn't been on the beach that chopper would have blown us away," Megan said.

"Why where they chasing you?" Mike asked.

"They were trying to stop us from escaping Upstate New York and exposing what they're doing there," Megan continued.

"Someone mentioned zombies on the beach. Was that metaphorical for something else?"

"Nope, that meant zombies, as in the ones that eat you," I said.

"Wow, that's the craziest thing I have ever heard. What was it like there?"

"It was total chaos, and honestly I would rather wait to discuss this with law enforcement. I'm still shaky from the whole thing."

"I bet so, damn. I'm glad you three are alright."

"Thank you," we all said.

When we entered the police station Mike wished us luck and left. The three of us walked into the department and spoke with the lady at the front desk.

"We are seeking asylum in Canada. I'm not sure if we're in the right place, but here we are."

The lady looked at the three of us with a confused look on her face before speaking.

"Do you have documentation or any paperwork?"

"Lady, look at me. My shorts are falling off, and I don't have a shirt. Do we look like we have paperwork?" Sampson stated.

"Wait here a moment," the lady said before walking off.

She returned a moment later with a younger man in a Canadian police uniform. The man looked as confused as the lady at the counter was.

"You three can come with me. We're going to have some questions for you," the officer said.

The three of us were taken to a room in the headquarters and told to sit tight. After a few minutes a middle-aged female officer came in and had Megan leave with her. A little while later Sampson was escorted out of the room, and I sat there all alone. I was finally taken to another room where I began my story but was stopped because the man claimed it wasn't his department. I was taken to a different room, and this is where I waited for the man who was going to ask me about my statements.

'�'�'�'

"I told you that story was a winner. Do you believe me now?" I asked the agent across the table.

The bald man sat in complete disbelief. He had watched me tell the story like he had been watching a thriller at the movie theater. He had been on the edge of his seat the whole time, and it had been amusing to watch.

"Well, Mr. Seamus... you have outright confessed to several crimes, one as severe as attempted murder. I'm going to have to talk with my superiors to see what our next move will be."

"Oh, that's fine with me. You go and do whatever it is you need to do. I'll stay right here and put my feet up. Take all the time you need. I'm in no hurry to do anything."

The man stood up, walking for the door.

"Oh, one more thing...could you grab me a six pack and some smokes?"

The man looked back at me like I was out of my mind, but I didn't care. I kicked my feet up on the table, laid my head back, and finally felt safe.

Made in the USA
Las Vegas, NV
24 November 2024